Trust Me Once

Books by Jan Coffey

ROAD KILL

MERCY

AQUARIAN

BLIND EYE

PUPPET MASTER

THE JANUS EFFECT

CROSS WIRED

SILENT WATERS

FIVE IN A ROW

TROPICAL KISS

FOURTH VICTIM

TRIPLE THREAT

TWICE BURNED

TRUST ME ONCE

TRUST ME ONCE

What she needs to stay alive— is someone she can trust.

INTERNATIONAL BESTSELLING AUTHOR

JAN COFFEY

Trust Me Once by Jan Coffey

Copyright © 2014 by Nikoo K. and James A. McGoldrick

First U.S. Edition Published by Mira Books, 2001

This is a work of fiction. Names, characters, places, and incidents either are the product of the author's imagination or are used factiously, and any resemblance to actual persons, living or dead, business establishments, events, or locales is entirely coincidental.

Printed in the United States of America

Prologue

The black Mercedes rolled to a stop in front of the gray stone building. The driver of the car lowered the tinted passenger window and stared across thirty feet of concrete at the armed guard, who was frowning with scarcely veiled disgust from behind bullet-proof glass. Sweating profusely, the driver flipped the air conditioner to high and turned his head toward the line of concrete barriers leading from the prison's gate to where he sat waiting.

Moments later, a heavy door swung open, and a tall, athletic man in jeans and a black polo shirt emerged. The driver, grunting as he leaned his ponderous body across the center console, pushed open the passenger door, and the inmate climbed nimbly inside.

In a few minutes, the Mercedes had passed beyond the outer gate. Frankie O'Neal, his sausage-like fingers wrapped around the wheel in a death grip, kept glancing into the rearview mirror as he picked up speed. They passed the sign pointing toward the Interstate and made the turn.

Letting out a half-sigh of relief, the driver wiped away the beads of perspiration from beneath his lower lip before lighting a cigarette. He looked over at his passenger. "How much time, Jake?"

Jake Gantley's eyes flicked toward his cousin. In a single motion, one hand went to the power window button while the other snatched the cigarette from between Frankie's lips. Jake crushed the cigarette in his fist as he tossed it out of the car.

"This stuff will kill you, Frankie. Don't you watch TV...or read?" His mouth turned up in a half smile. "And secondhand smoke is even worse, you know."

"Stop screwing around, Jake!" Frankie's eyebrows, already a straight line connecting above the bridge of his nose, bunched up in agitation. From the driver's side control panel, he rolled up Jake's window and glanced nervously again at the mirrors. "I asked how much time!"

Jake Gantley glanced into the back seat and smiled. "You brought my suit." He reached over and pulled the plastic-wrapped garment onto his lap. "And you had it cleaned."

The driver banged a heavy hand against the steering wheel. "Come on, Jake! Of course I brought your suit. You never do a fucking job without wearing your suit." He put another cigarette to his lips, then immediately raised a hand protectively. "And you mind your own goddamn business about my health! Now, are you gonna tell me how much time we have or not?"

"Look at you, Frankie. You're a fat pig. You smoke. And you worry too much, besides. Last month's *New England Journal of Medicine* had an article about stress. I'll send it to you."

The driver rolled his eyes and gnawed at a sore on his lip while his passenger changed his clothes. A few moments later, Frankie watched his cousin knot his tie in the mirror.

"Listen, Jake. This is important. I need to know—"

"Have you collected?"

"What? Yeah, of course. Half the full amount." Frankie glanced over and found himself begin to relax. All dressed up—his thinning hair combed back, his tie in place, the gray eyes in that cold squint—Jake Gantley had finally joined him. Frankie ran his fingers along the side of the center console until he felt the button beneath the carpeting. As he pressed it, a panel behind the gearshift popped open, revealing a hidden compartment. He pulled out a leather case and handed it to Jake. "How much time?"

"Five hours." Jake unzipped the case, slipped the chrome-plated 9mm handgun from its holster and ran a hand over the gleaming metal. Laying the weapon on the floor, he attached the holster to his belt. Then, with movements that were slow—almost reverent—he picked up the pistol, slid in a cartridge clip, and placed it in the holster.

Chapter 1

Rhode Island
August 16

Out of nowhere, the headlights appeared behind her, blinding Sarah with their intensity. Blinking her eyes against the glare, she tilted the mirror and hit the rear defrost button again.

"A lovely night for tailgating," she murmured, cracking the driver's window.

Sarah fished into her bag on the floor of the passenger side and pulled out her friend Tori's wallet. Flipping it open, she held it up into the light from the car behind her as she glanced again at the contents. The money, the credit cards, the California driver's license were all there. A pang of guilt settled in her stomach. She could just imagine all the trouble the young woman must have been through over the past two weeks. Sarah knew first-hand what a pain it could be, replacing all this stuff.

Wind-driven rain continued to slash at the windshield, and Sarah peered through the darkness, trying to ignore the vehicle on her tail.

It was easy to see when it had happened. Earlier on the same day Sarah had left for Ireland, she'd picked up Tori at the airport. She remembered watching her friend sling the purse into the trunk.

Sarah dropped the wallet on the passenger seat and tightened her grip on the wheel as her car hydroplaned around a bend in the road. A truck passed in the opposite lane, buffeting the sports car with wind and spray.

Letting out a nervous breath, she turned up the volume on the radio to hear the weather report of the storm that was punishing the coast. The heavy rains were likely to continue through the night. She turned off the radio and focused on the road ahead.

This weather was not part of the cheerful welcome she'd been envisioning for the past two weeks. Well, at least she was home. The worst was behind her.

She tightened one fist on the steering wheel and tried to make herself believe that.

Fighting back the sudden pooling of tears, she tried to erase the image of her father as the dark-suited corpse she'd seen in the open casket. John Rand was no longer the tall man with dancing green eyes and the powerful laugh.

It was the laugh she would make herself remember, and not the arguing before the separation. She would force out the memories of those nights as a child when she had prayed aloud and buried her head in a pillow. No, she would remember his laugh, and his eyes, and his warmth as he cuddled her on his lap and held her close to his heart.

The rain was coming down even harder now, and she flipped the wiper blades on to full speed. The high beams reflecting in her mirrors were as unrelenting as the sheets of rain.

She had no clear memory of the day he left. She knew she didn't want to remember it. And maybe someday she would forget the bitterness that had lived in her mother's eyes and put the edge in her voice to the day she died.

Sarah shook her head. As for herself, she would just remember him as John Rand. Maybe even as the father he never was. Just green dancing eyes and a laugh.

The car behind her edged closer. The high beams glared threateningly in the side mirror.

"And can I help it if there's no passing zone?" Sarah sped up a bit.

She glanced at the clock on the dash. Ten thirty eight. Not too late to call Hal again when she got home. Sarah had left him a message, but she knew better than anyone his penchant for checking them about once a week.

She was bone tired. The flight from Shannon had been long. And the wait at JFK for the connecting flight to Providence had seemed even longer. But there was too much on her mind, and she needed to talk to someone. Someone who would listen. Someone who had recently gone through what she had just gone through. Someone like Hal.

Sarah glanced again in the mirror and frowned at the headlights of the car behind her. There wasn't another car on the road. She pressed her foot on the accelerator, and her sports car gained some ground. The gain was only momentary, and the headlights closed the distance.

"Ass." Sarah pressed her foot to the floor. Her effort was in vain as the lights again slithered up behind her.

The shoulder widened, and Sarah pulled the car off the travel lane. Slowing down, she glanced back for the driver behind her to make his move past her.

The other car pulled onto the shoulder, as well, staying on her tail.

Sarah tried to swallow the sudden knot of fear that rose in her throat, and reached for the lock button. She pressed it hard and tried to get a look at the driver beyond the blinding high beams. But there was nothing she could see—nothing but the lights' fierce glare piercing the driving rain. Pulling back into the travel lane, she looked at a passing speed limit sign. Forty-five.

"You're in no danger," she murmured, trying to ignore the cold pool of liquid in her belly. With the exception of that truck, the road was deserted because of the weather and the hour, but she was only about three miles from Wickford, if she needed to get to a town.

The sudden dimming of the headlights behind her and the appearance of flashing lights on the dash of her pursuer elicited a gasp of relief from Sarah. She immediately eased up on the gas. Again there was no shoulder, but she pulled to the right side of the road to allow the unmarked police car to go by. The large sedan stayed behind her, though, lights flashing.

"You scared me into speeding!"

She slowed and stopped.

As the police car halted behind her, a dark figure emerged from the passenger side. Then, to her surprise, the vehicle pulled around and angled in front of her, effectively blocking the car.

"Oh, brilliant. Just what I need. Officer Overkill makes the collar!" She reached for her license and registration, keeping an eye on the driver of the unmarked car. He was just stepping out. His flat-brimmed hat was covered with plastic, and he shrugged into a raincoat before coming around his sedan.

Before she got a good look at his face a flashlight was shining in her window, drawing her attention. The officer kept the light directly in her eyes, and Sarah lifted a hand to block the glare.

He was standing close to the car, and she glanced away from the light. Dark gray pants flapped in the wind, and large black shoes reflected the red flashing light of the police car. The two policemen didn't appear to be concerned with the driving rain, and the driver of the unmarked vehicle was now flashing his light into the car from the passenger side, covering every inch of the interior.

Before the officer could say anything, Sarah had her driver's license and car registration sticking out of the small opening of her window.

"Lovely night, isn't it?" she asked, watching him flash his light on her license. The brim of the hat obstructed her view of his face.

"So what have I done wrong, officer?" Suddenly, it struck her as odd that at least one of them wasn't returning to their car to run a check on her license. The wind pushed at the raincoat. She hadn't even seen a badge.

A small noise to her right brought her head around. The passenger door was locked, but she was certain the second man had tested the door.

"I'd like to see some identification, officer." She could hear the hint of a quiver in her voice. He ignored her request. "Excuse me..."

"Switch off the car, Ms. Rand, and step out, please." The flashlight was blinding.

"I...I am an attorney in Newport." She forced herself to stay calm. "I'll be glad to follow you to the station, but I believe you are required to identify yourself."

Sarah tried to see the license plate on the police car, but the angle of the vehicle prevented her getting a clear look.

"Step out of the car. *Now!*"

Squinting her eyes, she turned her head into the glare of the light. "Officer, you know that I am within my rights to ask to see—"

The shattering glass of the windows on either side of her showered Sarah with glittering pebbles.

She barely had time to let out a scream before the man's hand clamped around her throat.

It was adrenaline. It was panic. It was the sudden terror of knowing she may have just taken her last breath. Rather than clawing at the man's brutal fingers, Sarah's hand reached for the center console of the car, and she blindly yanked the gearshift into Reverse. Slamming her foot on the gas, her body jerked forward as the car leapt into motion. Sarah found her throat still caught in the man's grip for an endless moment, before he finally let go and stumbled into the middle of the road.

Fifty feet away, she came to a screeching stop and, still gasping for breath, stared in terror at the two men advancing toward her, their drawn weapons pointed at her windshield.

There was only one thing to do.

Putting the car in drive, she jammed the accelerator to the floor. One of the men jumped directly in the path of her car, and Sarah jerked the steering wheel in an attempt to miss him. She felt the body of the other man bounce off the side of the car, and a split second later the sports car wiped out the tail light of the unmarked police car as she sped past.

Glass splintered around her as the windshield became a lacy mass of crystalline webs.

They were shooting at her.

She quickly left them behind. But as she tried to peer through the shattered windshield, a cold fear flooded her with the realization that at any moment her assailants would be coming after her.

Sarah's body began to shake uncontrollably.

Acting on impulse, she suddenly yanked the wheel to the right. The car responded and plowed through a gully of water onto a gravel road. In an instant she was out of sight of the main road, following a narrow track of gravel and mud and flooding rains.

The rain lashed at her face, but she continued on until the low-slung automobile suddenly dove into a water-filled gully. The vehicle lurched out of control and entered the woods. Sarah felt the car bouncing through the undergrowth as she frantically jerked the wheel right and left in an effort to dodge larger trees. In seconds that felt more like hours, she managed to bring the car to a shuddering halt between a pair of scrub pines.

Wet branches jutted in through the open spaces that had once been windows. Her breath was still coming in gasps, her body shaking as the adrenaline continued to pump through her. Sarah shut off the headlights and listened to the rain falling in waves on the car's roof. Protected as she was by the surrounding trees, the sound of the wind and the storm seemed so distant. Then, the vaguely ominous scent of pine and wet earth enclosed her, and real fear began to steal into her bones, cold and numbing.

She had to get out. Grabbing her bag off the floor, she pushed the door open against the weight of the trees and shouldered her way out. Branches and needles scratched at her face, soaking her clothing, and a shard of broken window glass, jutting up from the door, cut the palm of one hand, but in a moment she was standing in the semi-darkness behind her car.

Lightning lit the forest floor with a ghostly flash, and a thunderous crack rocketed through the woods. She didn't know where she was. She had no idea where she was going. But she knew she had to run.

That is, if she wanted to stay alive.

The room had all the warmth of an empty art gallery.

Owen Dean placed his wine flute on an angular glass shelf and excused himself from the pair of chatty socialites who had cornered him there. Ambling past a bored-looking string quartet, he climbed a wide set of stairs to a loft-like area and paused at the top. He looked out over the rail, letting his eyes wander over the room.

Frank Lloyd Wright had to be the coldest, most academic stiff ever to sit at a drawing board, Owen thought, eyeing the sharp, sterile lines of wood and stone and glass.

"Quite a place, isn't it?"

"Yeah, I was just thinking that." Owen turned and looked at the speaker. Tall, middle-aged, tanned, with the build of a former linebacker. He'd been introduced to Senator Gordon Rutherford earlier in the evening.

"This house of Warner's is quite a showpiece. Though, to be honest, my taste runs more to Middle Georgian architecture."

"Actually, I'm more an Early Ski Lodge type, myself."

"Are you?" Rutherford flashed a mouthful of square, well-cared-for teeth and waved off his minions hovering in the background. "May I call you Owen, Mr. Dean?"

"Of course, Senator."

"I have to tell you, that show of yours, *Internal Affairs*, is one of my guilty pleasures."

Owen cocked an eyebrow. "Well, I'm glad to hear that you're a satisfied viewer. But why guilty, if you don't mind me asking?"

Rutherford looked down at the glittering crowd of guests below. "I've built my political career on being a law-and-order man. If it got out that my favorite TV series portrayed the police every week as a bunch of corrupt self-seekers, with moral standards that often sink beneath those of criminals on the street, how would it look?"

Owen mulled that over for a moment. "Hmm. I see what you mean. But I like to believe we simply tell it like it is, Senator. After all—regardless of profession—none of us is perfect. And, in the case of this show, our premise is that police have human failings, just like everybody else."

The senator smiled again and accepted a drink from a passing waitress. "Right you are, Owen. And who knows about human failings better than a politician these days?"

Owen let the comment hang in the air as his attention drifted down over the railing. His gaze immediately lit on Andrew Warner, distinguished-looking beneath a shock of white hair. Andrew was lighting a pipe and speaking to two deans from the college. Outside the large windows, lightning briefly illuminated a rain-drenched scene of fenced fields bordered by woods.

"This is your fifth season, isn't it?"

Owen accepted a glass of champagne from a passing waitress as distant thunder rumbled. He turned again to the senator. "Yes, it's the show's fifth season."

"Ratings good?"

"Damn good."

"And if I remember correctly, you left a successful acting career in film to get into starring in and producing this TV show."

"Success is a relative term, Senator. I was ready for something different."

The politician laughed and shook his head. "You movie stars are hard to understand. I would have thought somebody with your screen appeal would have stayed in the fast lane—bigger movie roles, more money—instead of stepping back into television work."

"Stepping back?"

"Well, perhaps that's the wrong term. But here you are in Rhode Island, at Rosecliff College, doing God knows what for Andrew."

"It's called 'teaching,' Senator." Owen straightened up at the rail.

"Don't take me wrong, Owen. It's just that the way Andrew brags about you, a person would think Steven Spielberg sweeps out your offices. Just a little odd having such a big fish in our little pond." The senator leaned forward with a conspiratorial smirk on his face. "What does he have on you, anyway?"

Owen replaced his untasted champagne on a passing tray and looked the politician in the eye. "Extortion isn't the only way of getting a friend to help out, Senator. But maybe you need to get out of Washington more often."

Rutherford's perfect tan turned a darker shade. "No doubt about that, Mr. Dean. But an honest legislator's work is never d—"

A woman's voice floated in over the party noise as she climbed the steps. "Well, there you are. I'm glad you two got an opportunity to talk."

A flash outside the large, plate-glass windows was accompanied by a loud crack of thunder, punctuating the sentence of the small, gray-haired woman who joined them at the railing.

The sound of a man coughing cut through the guests' surprised laughter in response to the thunder. Owen looked over the railing and saw Andrew retreating to a corner, his shoulders hunched as he fought to control the hacking fit.

"Wonderful party, Tracy," Rutherford declared.

"Thank you, Gordon. It is a nice way for the college benefactors to get to know one another before the school year starts, don't you think?" She took Owen by the arm, pulling his attention back to her. "And this year they also get to meet our very own Hollywood celebrity."

"I'll only be teaching a course."

"Yes! And Andrew tells me you were at the college today, checking out the campus."

"I was."

"Dull place compared to what you're accustomed to, I'd wager. It will probably be a relief to get back to your very own exciting life."

"Not before the semester is over."

"But you must find the whole lot of us extremely boring." She winked at the senator and waved a hand over the guests. "Not a supermodel or a rock star among us."

From the first moment Owen had met Andrew's wife nearly thirty years ago, he had known that her resentment for him ran deep. He'd been too young then to attempt to understand her reasons. Later, he'd become too detached to care. He glanced at the fake smile Tracy had plastered on her face for Rutherford's benefit. Her eyes, though, were bullets.

"Well, Tracy, I'm glad to hear that I'm not the only one so thoroughly impressed with the presence of Owen Dean at Rosecliff College. We were just—"

"Senator." Owen cut him off, extending a hand toward the politician. "It was an experience meeting you."

"You're not leaving, Owen."

"Sorry to be a disappointment, but I have to run."

Owen put out a hand. Tracy took it and pulled him down to where she could brush a kiss across his cheek.

"Of course."

Turning his back on the two of them, Owen took his time heading down the steps. Andrew Warner, his face back to its usual color, his snow white hair back in place, had returned to playing host by the far windows, joking with another group of the college's benefactors.

When Owen was a couple of steps from the bottom, Andrew glanced up, caught sight of him, and motioned for Owen to join him. Owen shook his head and pointed at his watch before waving and heading for the entrance hall.

He had only come out to the party as another favor to Andrew. But being a good ally didn't mean he had to put up with Tracy's subtle barbs.

The rain was falling in sheets when he stepped onto the porch. Even in the darkness, he could see that the gusts of wind were scattering leaves across the yard and the gravel drive. Owen watched the storm for a moment as another bolt of lightning lit the sky, giving the scene a surreal look. The broad creek flowing into the pond at the far end of the field was a raging torrent. The crack of thunder that immediately followed was sharp and loud.

Taking out his keys, Owen turned toward the steps and the long line of luxury cars choking the circular drive.

"Last in...first out," he whispered into the wind, turning the collar of his sports coat up and running across the rain-softened drive to his Range Rover. The rain, changing directions with every gust of wind, had him nearly soaked by the time he climbed behind the wheel.

Putting the key into the ignition, he glanced at the brightly lit windows of the house. Through the large plate glass windows, the well-dressed crowd could be seen milling in small groups. Separating himself from one of them, a rather frail-looking, white haired man stared out into the storm for a moment before turning brusquely on his heel and moving away from the glass.

Owen turned the key. "What a waste. So little time."

Chapter 2

The lightning was all around him. Owen headed down the long and winding drive that separated the Warner's house from the main road.

He was out of his element. He knew that. But teaching had nothing to do with it.

Before coming to Newport, Owen had considered the fact that in taking this one semester position at the college, he would once again be allowing his life and Andrew's to become enmeshed. He would be poking at old wounds. But when the older man had dropped the bomb on him about his illness earlier this summer, Owen's common sense had dropped out of the equation.

Owen had to be there for him, just as Andrew had been there for him so many years ago.

And Tracy's resentment of him was something he'd just have to endure.

A flooded section of the road slowed the Range Rover to a crawl. The rushing waters of the creek had spilled over its banks, washing over the gravel surface.

Owen flipped on the high beams and answered the cell phone on its first ring. It was Andrew.

"What did she say to you?"

"Nothing." Owen frowned at the wheezing he could hear clearly through the phone.

"I warned her."

"You're jumping at shadows, Andrew. I was tired, that's all. Just not the party animal I used to be."

"You don't have to protect her, Owen. I'm not blind...or deaf. Last Sunday at the brunch, I know she sent those damned reporters to our table. And then yesterday...that flu business...canceling our lunch at the last—" The cough cut off the words.

Owen heard the sound of a drink being gulped down. "Andrew,

it's not worth getting riled about."

"I won't let her do this. You're a son to me."

"Tracy's your wife. She's trying to protect you."

There was another fit of coughing. "Don't! Don't let her get to you. I'm telling you I want you here."

"I'm here." His head was beginning to pound. "I'll call you tomorrow night after that Save the Bay thing I got hooked into. Maybe we could meet for a drink."

"Good." Another pause. "We need to talk."

"Sure." Owen ended the call. "And it's about time we did."

Though Owen didn't like getting patted on the head, Rutherford hadn't really been too far off the mark. Owen had put his life on hold to come to Newport for these four months or so. But he had no regrets, so long as he and Andrew could finally resolve what was past. He was tired of playing the game.

A brilliant stab of lightning hit the ground somewhere to his right, illuminating a small river where half of the road had been just a couple of hours earlier. Jerking the wheel, he suddenly saw the woman appear in his headlights. Owen slammed on the brakes.

"Dammit!"

His reflexes were quick, but he couldn't be certain if he'd hit her or if she'd just fallen against the front of the car. She lay sprawled across the hood, her face resting on the metal, and he was out of the vehicle and at her side in an instant.

"Lady, you okay?"

She lifted her head slowly off the hood and tried to straighten up. Owen reached for her quickly as she wobbled a step.

"You stay right here. I'll call for an ambulance."

"No!" Her response was sharp as she looked up, clutching at his hand.

In spite of the dripping jacket and pants that at one time must have been tailor-made for her, the woman was a muddy mess. She was soaked to the skin, her hair plastered against her head. All in all, Owen thought, she didn't look like someone who should be wandering in the rain in the middle of the night.

"No," she repeated more softly, letting go of his hand and standing up straight. "I'm fine. It just...took my breath away...running into the car. I'm okay."

The rain was streaming down her face, and lightning continued to flash above them. Unconvinced, Owen held his ground and studied her in the glare of the car's headlights. Clearly distraught, she nonetheless turned her face away from him. Pretending to adjust the shoulder strap of the case she was carrying, she peered into the darkness of the woods she'd just left.

"Your car break down?"

"No...yes."

"Well, which is it?"

"I...I ran out of gas." With a scowl, she stepped around him, out of the headlight's beam, and pushed a lock of short wet hair out of her face. Again, she shot a glance into the woods. "I thought it would be safer passing through the woods than walking on the shoulder of the state road."

Owen stared at her in the darkness. She looked so familiar to him. A bit worse for wear, but she was well-dressed and well-spoken. But it was her face that was nagging at him. Oval-shaped eyes—he couldn't tell the color in the darkness. The high cheekbones, streaked with mud. Or were those scratches? He tried to imagine how she would look cleaned up.

"Have we met before?" he asked.

"I don't...believe so."

She shivered and transferred the long strap of her briefcase from one shoulder to the other. He spotted the dark stain by one sleeve. He looked down at his own hand where she'd touched him. There was blood on his hand.

"Did you cut yourself?"

She looked down at her palm and then pulled a folded wad of wet tissue out of her pocket. "I just fell back there. It's just a scratch. Must have done it on a rock or something."

A bolt of lightning struck close by, and she jumped back a step. Owen suddenly realized that they were now both soaked through.

"I'll give you a ride. Climb in."

She hesitated a moment and looked about at the storm-tossed woods.

"I would appreciate a ride to the closest gas station. I think there's one about a mile up the road."

He gave her another once-over look. "Okay. Get in."

Without another word, she moved to the passenger side, but then paused before getting in.

"I'm muddy and wet. I'll make a mess of your car."

"If it makes you feel better, I'll send you the cleaning bill."

Frowning, she hopped in and shut the door. Without thinking, he locked the doors. She immediately reached over her shoulder and unlocked hers.

He didn't blame her for being nervous. Running out of gas at this hour of the night, in this storm, and now getting into a car with a total stranger. Not a particularly comfortable situation. He turned to her. "Where's your car?"

"Just...just up the road."

"There's the phone. You're welcome to use it."

She shook her head. "No, I'll be fine when we get to the gas station."

"It'll probably be closed. It's late."

"It doesn't matter. I can call for a cab there."

He shrugged. "Okay. Where are you heading?"

"Newport."

Owen reached the end of the private lane and turned onto the main road. There wasn't a car in sight that he could see. Once he'd made the turn, he noticed she was glancing nervously in the passenger side mirror.

"I'm going to Newport. I can take you there."

Her eyes, dark in the dim light of the car, studied his face for a moment. He looked over at her and she looked away. "If...if you don't mind. I wouldn't want to put you to any trouble."

"No trouble."

He watched her attention turn to the outside mirror again.

"Owen Dean." He stretched a hand in her direction. She tucked her injured hand out of the way and reached over with her other.

"Sarah Rand."

He repeated the name in his head. Sarah Rand. Even her name sounded familiar, but he couldn't quite place it.

"Are you certain we haven't met before?"

She shook her head.

"What is it you do?"

"I'm an attorney," she whispered, pulling her briefcase tighter into her chest.

Owen swerved into the other lane to avoid a good-sized tree limb that had fallen into the road.

"What kind of law do you practice?" he asked, glancing back at the blackness of the road behind them.

She continued to stare out the window, obviously pretending she'd never heard the question. He let her be. Owen concentrated on his driving, but as the silence descended, he could feel the weight of her gaze occasionally on his face.

Owen found it curious that this woman hadn't once pushed down the visor to check her own reflection in the mirror. She didn't seem to care at all about how her short blonde hair looked, plastered around her pale face. Or how the rain might have messed up her make-up. He glanced at her. Those *were* scratches running down her face, but she didn't seem to even notice.

He frowned and looked back at the road. Something was gnawing at the edges of his memory.

For the next ten minutes, they drove on without talking, with only the wipers and the wind-driven sheets of rain to break the silence. She appeared totally content to be left to herself. Glancing in her direction now and then, Owen found her face turned toward the passenger window, her hands tightly fisted around the handle of her briefcase. Only once did she move at all, bending down to fiddle with the heel of her shoe as a car passed, going in the other direction.

"You'd be better off calling tonight and having your car towed someplace safe."

"I'll take care of it." Her voice was distant, dismissive. She was looking ahead at the Newport Bridge, the top of which was enshrouded with rain.

But Owen was not ready to be dismissed. "Are you from around here?"

"You can drop me off by the Visitor's Center in Newport. I can get a cab there."

She was definitely dismissing him, working at a front of arrogance and coldness. This, however, only piqued his curiosity more.

"I'm an actor...and a producer," he said, shooting her a half glance. He knew he sounded like an arrogant bastard. "I've already told you my name is Ow—"

"Nice to meet you again, Mr. Dean. But I would still appreciate it if you'd drop me in front of the Visitor's Center."

"And I suppose you're one of those people who doesn't watch TV." Owen glanced at her and then looked back at the road. Her face would probably crack if she smiled. "What kind of cases do you handle?"

"Corrupt law enforcement," she said after a pause, this time meeting his eyes. "Racketeering. Murder. Substance abuse. Very realistic and often quite scary."

"Tough way to make a living."

That couldn't have been a smile, he thought. But her furrowed brow did open up for a fraction of a second before she answered.

"No, not me! *You*. That's what you do for a living. I know who you are, and I've seen your show, Mr. Dean."

"That's great. But you still don't think we've met?"

She shook her head more decidedly this time. "I'm positive, though we did come close once."

Owen watched her attention turn to a police car, sirens and flashers going, traveling in the opposite direction on the bridge. Here was something different, Owen thought. A woman not trying to hit on him.

"Please take the first exit after the bridge," she said. "If it's out of your way to take me to the Visitor's Center, I can get off at the gas station at the end of the ramp."

"It's not out of my way," he said gruffly, flipping on his turn signal.

When they stopped at the first light, he watched her for the first time running her fingers through her wet hair and pushing it behind her ear. A couple of pine needles dropped onto her shoulder.

She had a long, beautiful neck and a firm, well-shaped chin. Owen's eyes were drawn to her earrings. Very striking. Antique-looking. A large diamond, set in the starlike setting of smaller stones. Even her earrings looked familiar to him. He studied her profile once again. She was a classic beauty. Kind of a Garbo look to her. Lost in thought, she was looking straight ahead. Her eyes suddenly focused.

"It's green." She pointed at the light.

He put his foot on the gas and started down the road. Making the next turn, he frowned as they rounded the corner and headed downtown. The tent-like architecture of the Visitor's Center loomed just ahead.

Letting her just disappear seemed like the wrong thing to do. Of course, he couldn't force her to do otherwise. He pulled up to the curb.

"It looks closed to me."

Her look of disappointment was all too apparent. "I can wait here. I'm sure there'll be a cab coming soon."

He used her hesitation to his advantage. "It's raining. I can drop you off where you're going."

He pulled away from the curb before she had a chance to protest. After a short pause, she gave him an address on Bellevue Avenue.

"High rent district," he commented, continuing on America's Cup Avenue.

"It's not my place."

Then it must the boyfriend's, he decided, suddenly annoyed. He hadn't seen any wedding band on that fist clutching the briefcase.

He brought the car to a stop at a red light and turned to her again, almost in spite of himself. "I'm fairly new in town. Any suggestions on things to do for excitement?"

"The Visitor's Center has lots of flyers." A police car pulled up in the right lane, and the officer behind the wheel stared over at them. Sarah turned her face to Owen. "I...I'm sorry. That was rude."

"Okay."

"It's been a tough night."

For the first time, she looked unguarded. Even scared. Her eyes were riveted to his own. They were incredibly large. Beautiful. When her gaze flitted away, he looked again at the scratches on her face.

"Are you sure running out of gas was the only thing that happened to you tonight?"

The light turned green, and the police car beside them moved on. She turned her attention back to the road and nodded. "I'm sure."

The small gate where she had Owen drop her was on a side street off Bellevue Avenue. The granite walls that protected the mansion rose a good twelve feet above the street. He saw no plaques by the iron-gated side entrance.

"Thanks for the ride, Mr. Dean." She reached for the car door and opened it.

His hand shot out and took hold of her elbow. He fumbled in the pocket of his sport jacket and withdrew a card. "Here's my number. Call me sometime."

She hesitated, then took the card, staring down at it for a moment in the dim light of the car. "A local number. I thought you were new in town."

He shrugged. "A couple of weeks hardly makes you a native."

She gave him a polite smile and tucked the card in the pocket of her muddy jacket. "Thanks again."

She swung the briefcase over her shoulder and stepped through the puddles to the gate. Owen sat there and watched her search in the case for keys. The rain continued to pound his car, and he waited until she opened the gate. Turning, she gave him a final wave and disappeared inside the walls. He looked up at the darkened building.

"There resides a lucky man."

The irritation he could hear echoing in the empty Range Rover struck Owen as odd. As attractive as the woman was, Hollywood was full of beautiful women. They were always around...and always very willing. How many years had it been since he'd made an effort to pursue a woman?

In a few minutes, the mansion was far behind him. Out on Ocean Drive, a sports car raced by, going too fast for the wet roads. The wind was steadier here, howling in off the Atlantic, and he could feel it pushing his own vehicle. Involuntarily, Owen's mind again returned to Sarah and where he might have met her.

Considering the way she was dressed and the expensive earrings she wore, she could be any one of the 'trust babies' that spent so much time in this town. He might have seen her picture in the local paper, attending one of the society events.

He turned his car into the long drive of the converted mansion. Waves were crashing onto the rocky sea wall, and throwing up buckets of spray over the car. At the end of the spit of land, the stone, French-style chateau stood solidly against the battering winds of the storm.

Parking in the spot assigned to his apartment, Owen pushed up the collar of his wet jacket and took off for the main door. The place he was renting was on the first floor in one wing of the mansion and had a separate entrance off the stone terrace, but the large central hallway held the panel of chrome-faced mailboxes. Hauling out the assortment of mail, he headed down the hallway to the apartment.

A copy of the Newport Daily News lay on the floor. Owen picked it up, stuffed it under his arm, and unlocked the door. The apartment was silent, except for the sound of the rain beating at the windows.

Dropping his keys on the counter, he dumped everything else on the kitchen table. Opening the fridge door, he reached in for a beer...and froze in his tracks.

Whirling, he turned back to the kitchen table and studied the picture of the woman staring back at him from the right-hand column of the newspaper.

Of course he knew her. After all, Sarah Rand had only been dead for the past two weeks.

Chapter 3

"My own men confirmed it, sir. She *is* alive."

There was a slight pause on the other end of the phone line.

"I told you before not to leave it to amateurs." The sound of a stifled yawn came through the receiver, but the authority in the voice came through when he spoke again. "I'm not happy, but the arrangements still work, and your instructions still stand."

The rain hammered like bullets against the windows of the car. "I do, sir. And I'll take care of it."

If this were a nightmare, why couldn't she wake up?

Her eyes took in the burnished gold of the oak paneling on the walls in the outer office. The smell of old leather and parchment hung in the air from the shelves of antique law books. The secretary's desk, the door to the Judge's private office, the open door into her own office—they were all the same. This wing of the Van Horn mansion, converted into a home office when the Judge had decided to retire was as familiar to her as her own apartment.

And yet, everything had changed in just two short weeks. She looked again at the newspaper in her hand.

"In a second bail hearing, held in Providence today, District Court Judge Elizabeth Wilson denied a request made by the attorney of former colleague Charles Hamlin Arnold in..."

Sarah scanned the page for the fifth time. Her gaze rested once again on the picture of Judge Arnold, leaving the courthouse. She threw the paper aside and worked her way through the pile. Headline after headline proclaimed the alleged guilt of her friend and mentor. She pulled another paper onto her lap.

"*Jealousy Possible Murder Motive.*" She stared at the full-length picture of herself. It was a photograph taken at the Heart Ball last year. The Judge stood on one side of her, and Hal on the other.

Leaving that issue spread on the floor, she went through the piles of newspapers stacked neatly in the bin beside the bookcase, working her way back in time. Last Sunday's issue ran a front page article listing Sarah's accomplishments. Two issues before, a piece with Hal's picture. She skimmed the article, which quoted the wealthy developer speaking of his mother, Avery Van Horn, and her lengthy battle and final defeat by cancer only a month ago. And a line about the alleged murder of his closest friend by his own step father, Judge Arnold.

"But I'm alive, Hal!" She wiped at the tears on her cheeks.

She found it. The August 4 headline read, "Attorney Missing -- Assumed Murdered." Sarah sat back. "Judge Arnold Held."

Prominent Newport attorney Sarah Rand is believed dead. Homicide detectives, acting on a tip from unnamed sources, today found blood in the luxury condominium home of Attorney Rand, who has been missing since August 2. Judge Charles Hamlin Arnold was later arrested at his home and will be charged, according to the district attorney, for the murder of his colleague.

Rand has been connected with the Arnold and the Van Horn family for a number of years. Attorney Rand was a close confidante of the Judge's late wife, Avery Van Horn Arnold, and has been linked romantically to Mrs. Arnold's son, Newport developer Henry "Hal" Van Horn...

Sarah leaned back against the bookcase, reading through the article again. Murdered. Assumed dead. But *how* could she be assumed dead?

"Oh, God. Tori!" Sarah whispered as she dashed for the phone at the closest desk and dialed her number at the condo. Steady rings. No answering machine. Just the same as when she'd tried to call her from Ireland. The same as when she'd tried to call from the airport.

She hung up and looked around her. The piles of mail on Linda's desk. The missing computer. The closed door of the Judge's private office. They thought she was missing. No, dead. She reached for the phone again to call Hal. The answering machine picked up on the second ring again. She waited impatiently for his message.

"Hal! Listen…this is Sarah again. There is something wrong…I am at the office on Bellevue…"

The sound was faint but distinct, and Sarah froze. She was almost certain the noise had come from the small kitchenette off the hallway. She peered into the darkness and quietly placed the phone back in its cradle. She was sure she was alone. When she came in, she had unlocked the door and disarmed the security system, locking the door behind her.

Reaching for the closest thing at hand, she picked up a heavy pineapple-shaped paperweight. Clutching the weight in one hand, she listened. There was the noise again. She switched on the light in the hallway. The door into the kitchen was slightly ajar.

She was a step from the door when the smell of gas registered.

Acting on reflex, Sarah took a deep breath, pulled open the kitchen door, and moved to the small stove, searching for the knobs in front of the unlit burners. Solid stumps of greasy metal were the only thing that met her fingers. The knobs were gone.

Panic immobilized her for a moment as the low sound of escaping gas continued. She whirled and started for the door. It was her only route of escape.

The door slammed in her face.

"No! Wait!" she screamed.

Owen stared at the newspaper, his eyes going from the picture to the article text and back to the picture again. He laid the paper on the kitchen counter and walked into the living room. The accumulating pile of last week's papers on the coffee table supplied everything else about the case.

He could hear her voice deep in his mind. It was the same woman. It had to be. Why would anyone in her right mind want to take a dead attorney's name? But it wasn't just the name, it was also the way she looked and dressed. She was Sarah Rand, no doubt about it. The inside of the Range Rover had been dark, but there was no mistaking her.

He glanced at another picture of her in the paper. Even the earrings were the same. They must be her favorites, Owen thought. In every head shot of her he'd seen, she appeared to be wearing the same earrings. Star-shaped, with a diamond in the center. Her trademark.

Last Sunday's magazine section had a big spread about her. Including exterior shots of the condominium apartment she owned.

On the surface, she seemed to be all money and easy living. But the article portrayed a different kind of woman—hard-working, independent, and smart.

Owen scanned the article for the information about the murder. Her apartment was on the ground floor of a converted mansion, with a terrace looking south over the Atlantic Ocean. From what the paper reported, the police were assuming that she'd been shot, probably in the face, just inside her front door on the afternoon of August 2. The detectives in charge were speculating that her body might have been wrapped up and carried out onto the terrace and then down to a waiting car. Sarah Rand's body, they assumed, was at the bottom of the Atlantic.

Owen leafed through the pages and stared at the picture of Sarah standing between Henry Van Horn and Judge Arnold. An unexpected knot twisted in his gut. From the newspaper account, their relationship had all the earmarks of a love triangle in which the Judge had ended up as odd man out. And it appeared that the police were looking at that as the motive for murder.

He carried the paper into the kitchen. Something didn't jive. It just didn't seem possible that the woman looking back at him from the photo could be playing a part in this twisted script.

"You should stop going out to parties entirely," he muttered, reaching for the phone. "Or at least stop picking up strays."

But then again, he thought, you meet such interesting people.

☙ ❧

No matter what she tried, the metal stumps on the stove would not turn.

Going back to the door, Sarah put her shoulder to it once again. The gas was horrible, and a fit of coughing racked her body as she threw herself against the door. It was no use, she thought, sinking to the floor. Helplessness flooded through her, and she lay her cheek against the cool tile.

As she lay there, waiting for the gas to finish her, visions collected in her head, memories pooling in her consciousness before sliding off, only to be replaced by others. The funeral of her father. The open grave with John Rand's casket at the bottom. The cheerful face of her friend Tori when she'd last seen her standing in the doorway of the apartment. The glare of flashlights.

They were after her. On the road and now here. But why?

There was no longer any reason to fight. She waited for the end to come and the face of Owen Dean flitted into her mind. Those youthful dreams. The silly crush she'd had on him...a movie star. She'd been barely seventeen when she and Tori had hitched a ride from Boston to New York. They stood for hours in the pouring rain just to catch a glimpse of him at the premier of *Restless*. To think that tonight she hadn't even recognized him, at first.

Her thoughts darkened. And now someone wanted her dead, and for no reason that she could think of.

The seconds ticked into minutes, and Sarah wondered why she was still alive.

A phone rang somewhere out in the office.

The gas was burning her eyes, but as she glanced at the glass-block window above the sink, she realized that she couldn't hear the hiss of escaping gas. There was the sound of movement outside the door.

She found the brass pineapple lying on its side on the floor.

The door beside her head opened slightly. Sarah remained still and clenched the paperweight in her hand.

A few more moments of silence, and Sarah held her breath.

When he kicked her in the shoulder, she rolled onto her back and lay still. A moment later she heard him step past her into the kitchen.

She opened her eyes. A short, heavyset man was bending over the knobs, a white handkerchief over his mouth and nose.

He didn't have a chance when the pineapple paperweight came down like a hammer on his head.

Sarah watched him go down and, clutching her weapon in one hand, she backed out of the kitchen. Once in the hallway, she staggered for the door.

As she passed the telephone in the outer office, she paused...then picked it up and dialed.

Nothing was said openly, but Owen knew. He was the enemy.

Most of the scripts of his show—in which he played John McKee, an internal affairs investigator for the FBI—dealt with the workings of local law enforcement. So he knew that police departments were close-knit. Protective of their own. Suspicious of everyone. No surprise he'd been on hold for close to ten minutes.

After introducing himself, he'd told the dispatcher that he might have come upon some information regarding the Sarah Rand case. The cop had been polite, asking him to hold and telling him that Detective Captain Daniel Archer would probably want to talk to him. He'd been on hold ever since.

If it weren't for the fact that the papers had all kept mentioning this specific detective by name, Owen would have hung up long ago and left a message for the guy's superior. For a change, he was determined to be agreeable. But Archer had roughly thirty seconds.

Owen started water for coffee. Another voice came over the wire.

"Mr. Dean. Are you still there?"

"Barely."

"Captain Archer had to leave on a call. But he said if you'd come down to the station, he should be back in an hour or so."

Owen glanced at his watch. One twenty. "No chance."

"Then maybe I could take down your information over the phone."

"No. Just tell him it's very important and have him call me in the morning."

He left his number and hung up. What Owen had learned tonight was too important to leave on a note in a pile of pink notes on the desk of an overworked detective. Nope, he had liked Sarah, somehow, in spite of the lie she'd fed him about running out of gas. Something wasn't right, but Owen didn't think she needed the entire Newport Police Department coming down on her tonight.

The phone rang and Owen, certain it was Archer, reached for it. He couldn't have been more wrong.

"Mr. Dean. This is Sarah Rand. You told me I could call you."

"I did."

"I...I need your help, Mr. Dean. Please...there's been another attempt on my life."

"Another?"

"I don't know what is happening. I need help."

"I'll call the police."

"Don't," she begged. "They're here already...but I can't let them find me. Please, I'm frightened. I need your help."

She made no sense. And yet the fear and desperation in her voice were very real. "Where are you?"

"The Ju...the same place you dropped me earlier. But I...you'll have to wait...until they leave."

"The police?"

"Yes. Please wait for me outside. I'll explain everything. I haven't done anything wrong. But don't let them see you. Please!"

Owen knew at that moment he had totally lost his mind. "I'll be waiting outside."

The piercing headlights of the two police cars cut sharply through darkness. The rain continued to pelt the ground, the gusting wind twisting the raincoats around the men's legs.

Dan Archer flipped the fan switch to high and watched the fog retreat across the windshield. He stared at the police officer sweeping the broken glass on the deserted road. A second officer, shining a flashlight around the perimeter of the accident scene was inspecting the gravel shoulder. There was a pronounced limp in the man's step.

Archer lowered his window as an unmarked police car pulled up beside his own car.

"Anything?" he barked.

"Too dark to see. But she must have turned off on one of the side roads along the way."

Archer banged his hand on the wheel. "Goddamn it. I thought we fucking had her this time."

Chapter 4

The wind had eased up, and it was not long before the rain stopped completely. Drumming his fingers on the steering wheel, Owen filled his lungs with the fresh air. It was salty and carried a hint of briskness.

He must be insane to be here. He was a fool not to have called back the police station and reported the call.

From where he'd parked on the road off of Bellevue, the side entrance to the Van Horn mansion was only fifty feet away, an old fashioned gas street lamp throwing light on it. Not far from the high gate that opened along the wall, he could see a smaller gate for pedestrian traffic. That was the one she'd used before.

Owen took another deep breath and frowned, remembering Sarah's brief but desperate-sounding plea.

This wasn't TV police drama, Owen reminded himself. This was real life. He ran over what he'd be telling the detective, once Archer finally got back to him.

He'd given a stranger a ride. Later, he'd come to suspect she was the murdered attorney. He'd called the police. It was just Archer's tough luck that he'd been too busy to take the call the first time. And right now he was just making sure he wasn't way off base in thinking the woman was really Sarah Rand.

After all, he could hear himself saying, he didn't want the police thinking he was just some Hollywood crackpot.

Five minutes after arriving at the Van Horn Mansion, Owen had seen two men in a silver van with "Steele Security Company" on the side, putting a chain on the barred main entrance gate. He just hoped that she was still inside. If she'd already left the estate, he would have no clue where to go after her.

Circling the mansion before parking on the side street, Owen had realized that the estate took up the entire block. Other than these two gates, he'd found another two chained gates facing

Bellevue and an old delivery gate on the back street that looked like it hadn't been opened since the Crash of '29. If she was going to come out, then she was coming out here.

The same silver security van he'd seen before passed along Bellevue Avenue at the end of the road, and in a few minutes Owen saw its headlights in his rearview mirror. The van had circled the block and was rolling up the street, the two guys inside eyeing the perimeter of the estate wall. He tilted his seat back to a reclining position, and the van passed by and turned again on Bellevue.

As Owen returned his seat to an upright position, the hackles on his neck rose.

In the silence that was so peculiar to this time of the night, the click of the deadbolt came through the darkness. His eyes were riveted to the iron gate as it swung open. An instant later, a dark-coated figure emerged, casting a look up and down the side road.

He started the Range Rover's engine. She immediately spotted him and hurried across the street.

She'd pulled on a black raincoat that was about three sizes too large for her, and with the collar of the coat turned up, there was little of her that could be seen by any pursuer. But Owen knew it was Sarah. From the bulge at her hip, he could tell that the briefcase she'd been carrying was still slung over her shoulder.

She was beside the car when a police car appeared on Bellevue, and she came to a dead stop. Panic was apparent in her stance, and Owen thought for a moment that she was going to run. He lowered the passenger window and turned on the headlights.

"Get in."

Regaining her wits, she quickly went around, pulled open the door, and hopped in.

"Let's go."

"Not yet, Ms. Rand. Not until..."

"Please, Mr. Dean." The panic was audible in her whisper as she reached over and took hold of his arm. The cruiser came down the street. As it reached them, she leaned over the center console and buried her face into the crook of his neck. The brush of her breath against his skin was too warm and too difficult to ignore.

The police car passed without stopping. Watching in the mirror as the cruiser crept to the end of the block, Owen frowned when the same security van appeared again, its driver waving the policemen to a stop. A conversation ensued, but he could hear nothing at this distance.

Owen looked down into the face inches away from his. It was pale, and he could feel her shivering.

"What kind of trouble are you in, Ms. Rand?"

She looked down the street where the two cars were still idling. "I don't know. But I haven't done anything wrong."

"Why are you running away from the police?"

"I'll tell you everything...but later. Please get me out of here...this street."

"Everybody believes you're dead. There is an innocent man in jail. A man who—"

"Please help me," she interrupted, pulling at his arm as the two drivers finished their conversation at the end of the block. The security van came by at a faster clip this time, turning in the direction of the town center when it reached Bellevue.

Owen could feel her fingers clutching his arm. He grabbed her by the chin and lifted her face to his. "Ms. Rand, I don't trust you."

"Please, I just got back tonight. I've been away. In Ireland. And...and they're trying to kill me...and I don't know why." Owen heard her let out a ragged breath. "I only ask you to take me away from this street. That police car will be back, and I need a few minutes...just to...just to think what I should do."

Owen frowned, watching her as she looked beseechingly into his face. She was trembling from head to toe. From the cold or from fear? His money was on the latter.

"And just what would *you* advise a client to do here, Ms. Rand?"

"Wait! I can prove that I've been away." Quickly, she let go of his arm and fumbled beneath the raincoat. Hauling up her bag, she unzipped the top of the brief case and reached inside. A vision flashed through Owen's mind of Sarah pulling a gun out of that case.

"Here's my passport. The ticket stubs from my flight. They're tucked inside of it. Could we please be on our way? They'll be turning the block any second."

"Why not go to the police?"

"*They* are the ones who are after me, trying to kill me, and I don't know why. Please, Mr. Dean." She practically shoved the passport into his hand. "This proves where I've been. Please, just give me a chance!"

Owen stared at her for a long moment, knowing better than to trust anything she was trying to feed him. But at the same time, she'd called *him* for help. Of all the people she must know and work with, she'd called him, a stranger.

She, indeed, had to be desperate.

"I'll help you, but only to get away from this street. After that, we talk."

She nodded and pressed down the door lock herself.

The two detectives' silent exchange went unnoticed by Frankie O'Neal as he sat at one end of a steel table, his head buried in his hands. At the far end, a muscle-bound rookie in uniform sat operating a tape-recorder.

"Let's see if we got this right." Disbelief evident in his voice, Bob McHugh lifted a shiny, black wingtip onto a chair and leaned two hairy forearms on his knee. Dan Archer straddled another chair and looked at Frankie. The heavyset man never raised his head. "You left your brand new Mercedes just off Bellevue and decided to take a stroll down to the Cliff Walk at midnight, in the rain, where somebody assaulted you?"

Frankie groaned and dug his fingers deeper into his hair. "My head is exploding. If this ain't a concussion...?"

Archer took a pack of cigarettes out of his pocket and slid it in front of the suspect.

Frankie peered through puffy eyes at the pack. He didn't reach.

"And whoever it was that clocked you, carried you all the way back from the Cliff Walk, crossed Bellevue, hauled you another half a block to the Van Horn's side entrance, dragged you into the Judge's office wing, and dumped you in that little kitchen off the library." The red faced detective rolled his eyes. "Jeez, Frankie. Can't you come up with a better fucking story?"

"I want my lawyer."

Bob moved in, looming over the ailing suspect. "We want to know what the fuck you were doing in the Judge's house, Frankie."

"I told you before that I didn't go in there of my own free will." His eyes lifted only as high as the coffee cup on the table. "I was knocked unconscious. I was dragged there."

"Dragged by who? And why? Oh, and have I mentioned that your goddamn fingerprints were all over the place?"

"You're full of shit, but I told you I want my lawyer."

"What the fuck for?"

Frankie lifted his head for the first time and squinted into the officer's red-rimmed eyes. "I'm the victim here, and you're treating me like shit."

"Victim, my ass. We could be talking breaking and entering. Theft. Resisting arrest."

"I know my rights. I'm not saying another word until my lawyer is sitting right there."

Archer dropped a thick folder with Frankie's name on the tab onto the table, then moved over to the coffee pot, pouring out two fresh cups. "Let him be, Bob."

The short detective turned his sights on his superior. "What do you mean, let him be? This scumbag—"

"Let him be!" Archer commanded harshly. "Hand him that phone. Better yet, take a hike and cool your jets."

There was a moment of silence as the two glared at each other. Muttering, Bob kicked the legs from under a chair and huffed out of the room, slamming the door behind him.

Frankie's surprised gaze traveled from the door to the casual shrug of the remaining detective.

"Just sugar, right?"

Frankie nodded, staring at the steaming cup Archer placed in front of him.

Archer pulled an economy-size bottle of Tylenol out of his jacket pocket and put it on the table next to the cup of coffee.

"Help yourself. I got a concussion myself last year. It was a pretty nasty thing. What with puking all night, I just wanted to crawl into a hole and go to sleep."

Again there was only silence for a moment. Frankie reached for the pills.

Archer picked up the chair that had been overturned and sat in it, positioning himself about half way down the table from the suspect—and in a direct line with the only door out.

"Hey, sorry about all the grief Bob was giving you. He watches too much TV."

Frankie snorted as he dumped a half dozen pills into his hand.

"Take too many of those at one time, and your liver'll shut down." Archer sipped his coffee as Frankie dropped all but two back into the bottle.

"I still want a lawyer."

Archer paused, patting the thick file on the table as if considering something, and then moved his chair closer to Frankie. Taking a cigarette out of the pack on the table, he lit one for himself and slid the pack back down the table. "We don't really have anything we can book you on."

"I didn't think so."

"That was all standard bullshit Bob was pulling on you...that stuff about resisting arrest." Archer inhaled deeply. "I mean, I'd be going nuts, too, if I were knocked out and then woke up to a bunch of uniforms pawing me."

Frankie took a swallow of coffee and shook a cigarette out of the pack. Archer slid his chair a little closer and held a lighter for him.

"And we both know there are no fingerprints of yours in that house."

"So I guess you're letting me go then." Frankie took a long drag before crushing the newly lit cigarette on the edge of the table.

"Sure. But before you go, there are just a couple of things." Archer paused, searching in his jacket pockets for a moment. Having no success, he stood up, finally locating a crumpled piece of paper in his back pocket. Sitting down again, he flattened it out on the table. "Just answer a couple of questions for me, and I'll get one of the guys to take you out to your car." Archer looked at the man apologetically. "They towed your Mercedes to the pound."

Frankie eyed him warily as Archer reached inside his jacket pocket for a pair of reading glasses. Putting them on, the detective looked the crumpled page up and down.

"Here we go. First...there were these...these knobs from the stove in your hand when you were found lying on the kitchen floor. Well, never mind that. They could have popped off on their own." He lowered the glasses on his nose. "Okay. Here we go. I definitely need help with this one. The uniforms arriving on the scene found a key to the Judge's house in your possession. We'll hold off on that one for a sec, too. What's this next one? Oh yeah...when we towed your car, the uniform helping the tow truck operator finds these dark spots in the trunk of that nice clean Mercedes of yours. He says blood...I say no. Now, we still could do some testing and stuff like that to find out what it is."

Archer looked at him over the rims of his glasses. Frankie closed his mouth and fixed his gaze on his coffee.

"Unless you want to tell us about it and save us some time. But what's worse, Frankie, we found this bag in a little compartment in the front seat and...and there was a..." The captain looked at his paper again. "A silver-plated 9mm handgun in there. But, of course, I'm sure you have a permit for that, and can explain where in Newport you might have fired off a round or two?"

Archer looked up at Frankie's pale face and turned again to his list. "There are still some other questions that I have. Like this phone call that you got tonight at O'Malley's Pub."

Dan Archer paused and watched Frankie's eyes move from the coffee cup in his hand to the bottle of Tylenol to the wrinkled piece of paper on the table.

He slid his chair closer and spoke in a low, confidential voice.

"I could have all of these checked out myself, Frankie. But I thought, since I know you're a decent guy and...Look, I understand how things happen, and you know the person who was with you in the Judge's house—the person who called us—is bound to turn up sooner or later." Archer leaned forward and touched the man lightly on the knee. "Listen, Frankie, I can help you out if you'd just—"

"I'll talk."

Chapter 5

The Range Rover sped past dripping trees and dead-end streets, past mansions, sullen and dark behind the gilded gates and iron fences. Gas-fed street lamps too flitted by, no more than dim and dying stars in Sarah's blurred vision. She tried to blink back the tears, but more and more she found them working their way down her cheek. She was losing control, and suddenly she was so tired. She tried unsuccessfully to swallow the thick knot that seemed to have lodged itself permanently in her throat.

Mansions gave way to a blur of shops, restaurants, a museum, a synagogue. They were winding through the remains of colonial Newport when a gas station came into her view, awkward and out of place.

"You should call your lawyer."

His voice was muffled, and Sarah pushed herself against the heavy blanket that seemed to have descended over her. She pressed her head against the window. The glass lacked the ability to cool her fevered skin. She concentrated on his words.

"You *do* have someone to call, don't you?"

The car stopped at a traffic light, and Sarah barely managed to focus enough to see him turn and stare into her face.

"Maybe the emergency room should be our first stop."

She shook her head as adamantly as she could muster and tightened her hold on the leather bag in her lap. "I...I'm fine."

She turned away as more tears slid down her face.

"Right there. That brick building just past the next light is the police station, if I'm not mistaken. And in a minute that's where I'm dropping you off."

Her head snapped around. "Please don't! Not yet...I need a bit of time to think this through."

"You'll have plenty of it in the police station."

"No." her voice cracked. "They're trying to kill me."

"The police? That's ridiculous."

"I know." Sarah nodded, burying her face in her hands. She tried to fight off the numbing chill, willing her body to stop the persistent shivering, to control the tears that kept coming.

"You seriously expect me to believe that the police are trying to kill you."

Even in her frame of mind, she could hear the skepticism in his voice.

"They stopped me on my way back from the airport. One of them tried to choke me." She touched her neck where she could still feel the bruising grip of the man's hand. "When I tried to get away, they shot at my car. I was barely able to get on a dirt road and escape on foot. That's where you found me."

"So you're a fugitive from the law."

"How could I be? I'm already dead, remember?" She took a deep breath before continuing. "Look, Mr. Dean, I went away two weeks ago and came back to a nightmare. And since my plane landed, I don't know how many hours ago, I've had two attempts made on my life. *Two* attempts!"

"But you don't really think the police can be involved."

"I do." She stabbed at her wet face with a heel of her hand. "I can trust no one. They've put Judge Arnold in jail for murdering me. I think they're trying to finish the job...destroy the loose ends. I think they mean to—"

"You've been watching too many movies, and we have a visitor."

Sarah's spine froze at the sight of the police car pulling up on their right. She turned quickly to him. "I need a..."

Owen shoved a tissue into her hand.

The policeman's sharp nose angled in their direction. "Everything okay?"

"Yep."

"It's been green for a while."

"Sorry, officer. Lost in conversation, here."

"You all right, miss?"

"She's fine!" Owen responded as Sarah nodded, keeping her nose in the tissue. "Just a little...uh, domestic discussion. You know how these things go."

Sarah stopped breathing as silence linked the two cars. She didn't dare look at the officer for fear of being recognized, so instead she turned toward Owen, speaking loud enough for the policeman to hear. "I...I feel much better now."

"Well, have a good one, officer."

Owen didn't wait for a response as he closed the window and drove through the intersection. At the next light, he didn't turn into the parking lot of the police station, instead continued along Broad Way.

"Thank you."

"Don't thank me yet. Our friend has decided you need a knight in shining armor."

Sarah glanced in the side mirror and watched the police car follow them past the hospital. Cold dread again took hold of her body.

"They knew my car. They know where I work, where I live, when I was coming back. I can't get away." She couldn't keep the tremor out of her voice. "And I don't understand any of this, why all of a sudden..." She fought for her next breath. It was another long moment before Sarah again found her voice. "Please let me out...anywhere. I shouldn't drag you into the middle of this."

The words died on her lips as he signaled and pulled into the semi-brightness of a convenience store parking lot. Inside the plate-glass window of the store, a lone cashier sat with his back to the parking lot.

He had done as she'd asked. This was the end of the line. Sarah reached for the door. "I appreciate the..."

"Come here."

His mouth stifled her questioning gasp as he grabbed her arm and drew her face to his. For an insane moment, the shock of his lips on hers immobilized her. Before she could articulate the sensation, she felt the heat of him penetrating the layers of chilling fear. Then reality kicked in, and she tore her mouth away.

"What are you doing?"

"Trying to convince your persistent hero that you're okay." His mouth continued to linger right above hers. His arm slipped around her. "Don't turn around. But he's parked right by the entrance to the lot."

It was difficult not to turn and look.

"And he's going to stay there until he knows everything he needs to know about me...and then some."

"What do you mean?" she asked.

He reached over to wipe the wetness on her face. "I have a woman who is disheveled and clearly upset in my car. I used the wrong word. Domestic. He is going to hang around and make sure that I won't beat you some more. He doesn't want me dropping your body somewhere off the Cliff Walk before dawn."

"Everybody else is trying to do just that."

"Yeah, well, it doesn't look to me like he's in on your conspiracy theory." He stole a look over her shoulder at the police car. "If you get out of this car, then you get to talk with him. Or you can stay with me—for a short time, anyway—and try to make some sense."

"I'll stay with you."

He gave her a half smile. The same killer smile, she thought, that she'd been seeing in the tabloids for years.

"Then it's show time, Sarah. We'll have to send him the message that our domestic squabbling is over, and you just can't wait to get me back home with you."

She stared up into his handsome face. The dark hair was starting to gray at the temples, and the lines around the eyes were deepening, but the piercing blue eyes were as clear as ever, and she knew he was right.

"Look, I'm a professional," he said. "All you have to do is..."

Letting go of the leather case, she raised herself and took Owen's head in her hands, bringing his mouth to her lips and kissing him as she had long ago dreamed of doing—as if nothing that had happened this night truly existed and this was yet another part of a dream.

His eyes reflected his surprise when he pulled back.

"A Garbo kiss," he murmured vaguely.

In a split second his mouth was crushing down on hers, and suddenly she was filled with the taste of him. His mouth was rough and hot, and for an instant her mind emptied of everything else but the need to take what he gave.

Though blinded momentarily by this unexpected burst of desire, Owen still knew that he was treading on extremely dangerous ground. This woman spelled trouble any way you looked at it. And yet, having her in his arms, her mouth so soft and willing, his concern for real life dissipated into thin air.

At that instant, only the two of them existed. No police. No cameras. Nothing beyond the heat of a man and a woman. He pushed aside the oversized raincoat and let his hand run over her breast through the wet fabric of her jacket. Her soft moan in the base of her throat was just one more step toward his undoing. He wanted her. It was as simple as that.

A pickup truck pulled into a space not far from the Range Rover, and Sarah practically leapt out of his arms, pressing her back against the passenger door with a look of shock on her face. He watched her struggle to catch her breath.

"Well...where did *that* come from, I wonder?" He glanced at the entrance of the lot before looking back at her.

She quickly looked away, but even in the light from the convenience store window, he could see the blush spreading across her face.

Beautiful, he thought. Too beautiful for comfort. Too soft and too vulnerable. And he was clearly too aroused to be thinking straight.

He lowered the driver's window to let in some fresh air.

"I guess we put on enough of a show for our friend to send him on his way."

She turned around and stared at the empty curb.

"Why did you call *me*?"

His gruff tone snapped her head around. "I...I'm sorry! I shouldn't have."

"I'm not asking you what you should or should not have done. I asked why you called *me*."

Those incredible eyes were again tearing up, but Owen fought off the urge to pull her to him. She was messing with his head.

"There was no one else I could think of. No one that they

wouldn't know about."

"They? Who are 'they' exactly?"

Two bruisers dressed in jeans and work boots came out of the store carrying coffees and got into the pickup truck. She watched them back out and threw another nervous glance at the empty street.

"I've told you. The police! And a heavyset man who tried to gas me in Judge Arnold's house. They must be the ones who killed my friend the day I went away."

"Killed what friend?"

"My friend who was house-sitting for me. They must have killed her by mistake, trying to murder me to frame the Judge."

Owen looked at her doubtfully.

"Well, I can't think of anything else. Judge Arnold has always been after the Newport Police for different things…excessive use of force…failure to follow established procedures." She shrugged and shook her head. "That's all I can think of. This must have been a setup."

"But I found you in Wickford. That's a different township."

"I know, but they could have been Newport police. Between the night and the rain and their flashlights, I couldn't tell the difference."

He shook his head. "Think about it for a minute. Even if it were some group of rogue cops setting all this up, do you really believe they could…or would…hire a thug to gas you at that mansion within an hour of trying to bump you off on the road? A bit of a stretch, don't you think?"

She leaned back against the head rest and looked at him with weariness in her eyes. "I know none of this makes sense. But I didn't imagine those attacks. Someone is trying to kill me. You saw it in the papers. But they killed an innocent woman in my apartment and…and got rid of her body." She closed her eyes and he saw another tear trail out of the corners. "She was my friend."

She was a mess. A beautiful, rumpled mess. And she was upset. But Sarah Rand didn't look like someone out of her mind. Neurotics, psychotics…he'd run into a lot of them in his business. But she wasn't one of them, from what he could tell.

He picked up the passport she'd shoved in his hand before. Turning on the overhead light, he leafed through the pages, glancing from the picture of a sophisticated professional woman to the real woman across from him. The one made of flesh and blood. The one with the soft mouth and the heat just beneath the surface. There was no mistaking that they were one and the same.

Owen leafed through the passport some more, checking the stamped departure and arrival dates. The ticket stubs matched the dates on the passport.

"Tell me everything."

"My friend Tori arrived from California the morning of August 2nd. That same evening I left for Ireland." She rubbed her forehead. "No one knew I was going away. The whole thing was a last minute family emergency. But I also hadn't told anyone that Tori was coming to visit me, either."

A slew of questions ran through Owen's mind, but he decided to wait.

"When I arrived at the airport, I tried to call her. She'd left a message for me. I know why, now. She'd left her wallet in my car. There was no answer. No answering machine, either, which was strange. I tried to call her again from Shannon when I got to Ireland. Same thing yesterday, from JFK. No answer."

"Didn't that worry you a little?"

"Not really. I've known her for too many years."

She clutched the briefcase tighter to her chest. "But last night, after I read what had happened in the papers, the blood in my apartment...the matching traces of it on the Judge's boat...I tried to call her again." She stabbed at another tear. "That was when I realized that she must have been killed, instead of me."

He closed the passport. "What do you think you're going to accomplish by *not* going to the police?"

"I will go to them. Not local police, or the state police. Someone at the federal level. But first, before I do that, I have to sort out a few things." Her eyes met his. In the light of the car he could see them now. They were dark green, almost the color of jade. "I have to figure why these people want me dead. Also, I have to figure what the connection is between all of these attempts on my life and the framing of Judge Arnold."

"And you think you'll be able to figure all that out in a few hours on your own?"

"I'm so tired now, I don't know if I can think clearly at all. But I have to try, Mr. Dean. I can't just go to the FBI and tell them, 'Here I am! I'm alive.'"

"Why not? That would free your Judge Arnold."

"True. But it doesn't get us any closer to the reason behind the attacks. They're still out there. We don't know who they are. What's going to stop them from making another attempt on my life, or hurting somebody else?"

"Police protection."

She shook her head. "I would have been killed if I had trusted those two officers earlier."

"If your friend really was killed, then you're withholding evidence and obstructing an ongoing police investigation."

"And what if the FBI doesn't believe me? What if they turn me over to the very men who tried to kill me while they check out my story?" She shook her head again. "No, I can't risk that."

"'*I* can't risk'? You use that word pretty loosely, it seems to me."

She pulled the belt of the raincoat around her and knotted it, reaching for the door handle. "I apologize again for dragging you into this. As far as I'm concerned, we've never met."

His hand shot out and took hold of her elbow. "And where are you planning on going right now?"

Uncertainty etched the features of her frowning face. "My own apartment is out of the question since these people know where I live. They probably know who my friends are, too. I can check into a Bed & Breakfast, I suppose, or a motel."

"Ms. Rand, your face has been on the front page of every local newspaper for the past two weeks."

"But for what I need to do, I have to be in Newport. There are files in our law offices downtown that I can check. The last few cases I worked on. Judge Arnold's appointment files and books, if the police don't have them."

"Why is that important?"

"Now that I think of it, there was something the matter with him. I noticed it before I left. He wouldn't explain, either. I can't put my finger on it, but the answer must be here. Something, maybe a case that involved both of us. I have to stay in Newport." She glanced down at the hand on her elbow. "But none of this needs to be your concern. Thank you for the ride."

Damn, the woman knew how to reel him in. "How much time?"

"You shouldn't involve yourself any more than you have. An innocent person is already dead."

"How much time?"

The green eyes showed a flicker of hope. "One day. Just enough time to gather some information to take to the FBI."

One day. He could do that. He stared ahead at the lights of the convenience store, knowing in his gut that he was lying to himself.

"Christ," he said, starting the car.

They had nothing on him. Absolutely nothing.

Frankie O'Neal felt the relief flood through his aching body. Trying to keep his hand from shaking, he stretched it out toward the pack of cigarettes still sitting on the table. He took one out and stuck it between his lips, and every remnant of nervousness drained away. As Archer reached over and held a match for him, he could see the gloat hovering in the cop's washed-out eyes. The asshole would break out in a tap dance in a minute.

Frankie took a couple of deep drags and mulled the whole thing over. His head, where the bitch had bopped him, still hurt like a motherfucker. She'd pay for that. He was going to drag her out to that warehouse in Portsmouth and she was going to fucking pay...in spades. He closed his eyes and rolled his head to one side and then to the other, stretching his thick neck muscles.

But that was for another day. Right now, finding out this asshole had nothing on him was making Frankie feel better by the minute.

"You're one smart man, Frankie. You should have applied to the Police Academy when you were younger. We sure could use stand-up guys like you. Stand-up guys with brains, I mean."

The asshole was actually pretty funny, Frankie thought, taking another deep drag. Too bad it was so late. He had no patience left for dicking around. He blew smoke above Archer's balding head and looked at the uniformed toad sitting at the other end of the table working the tape recorder.

Archer flicked ashes into his paper cup. "Why don't you start from the beginning, buddy."

Frankie took one last drag and looked his opponent straight in the eye. "I'll make you a deal, Captain. I answer all the questions you asked, if you'll let me call my lawyer right now. I want him here when we're done talking."

"Frankie, I don't think you are in the position to make deals."

He crushed the cigarette on the edge of steel table and threw the butt on the floor. "Then I guess I'll just sit back and catch some shut-eye."

Brushing some ash off the front of his fitted black shirt, Frankie sucked in his stomach at the sight of the buttons pulling across his middle. Jake was right. He should take better care of himself.

"Come on, Frankie. You aren't going to pull this shit now? I thought we were ready to talk. Man to man." Archer glanced at the tape recorder. "You said you didn't want a lawyer. Listen, if you're trying to pull a fast one on me..."

"I wouldn't dream of it, Captain." Frankie gave an innocent shake of his head, winced a little, and made a cross over his heart. "On the grave of my mother."

The scrape of Archer's chair almost brought a smile to Frankie's lips. Archer reached back impatiently and banged the phone on the table in front of Frankie.

Otto Wessel was no stranger to getting calls from his clients at three twenty-five in the morning. Knowing Archer's eagle eyes were glued to his mouth, Frankie spelled out the basics, told Otto to get down to the station, and hung up on him before the lawyer got too chatty.

Archer was back in his face as soon as the receiver hit the cradle. "From the beginning, Frankie."

He touched the lump on the back of his scalp. "Refresh my memory."

"Come on, quit screwing around. Start with that key you had in your possession."

"Oh, yeah. The key. I remember now. The thing that fucks your 'breaking and entering' charge. You were wondering how I had a key to the Van Horn mansion." Noting with satisfaction the detective's stony silence, Frankie continued. "The key was sent to me by Judge Arnold's office. I've had it for over a month."

Archer's eyes were about as lively as a dead flounder's. The rest of him didn't look much healthier, either, sitting there. He'd suddenly developed a funny twitch in his fingers.

"Yeah, you see, Captain, I'm in the business these days...antiquing."

"Antiquing?" Archer spat out.

"Just a little something to do with my free time. On the side, you know? With the Judge's wife dead, the furniture in the mansion had to be appraised."

"You...Frankie O'Neal...an antique dealer?" The look of disgust on Archer's face was truly comical.

Frankie shrugged. His head was really pounding, but he didn't care. He was rolling now. "Don't you think antiquing is a respectable job, Captain?"

"Okay, Mister Antique Dealer...appraiser...whatever the hell you are. So you decide to pay a house call at midnight?"

"What's the difference? The place is empty all the time, now that the Judge is locked up for snuffing that babe, the one the whole family was banging." Frankie thought for a moment about the banging *he* was going to give her. He frowned. "How did I know some fucking teenager, or whoever it was, was going to clock me when I decided to make myself a cup of tea."

"A cup of tea?"

"I'm trying to cut back on coffee."

Archer came to his feet, and Frankie threw his weight on the back of the chair.

"They told me that antique dealers always drink tea."

"Why all that cockamamie bullshit before?" the detective snapped back at him.

Frankie started to touch the lump on his head again, but decided against it. He folded his fingers over his belly. "You mean about the Cliff Walk? Well, I think I was still a tad hazy after the...after the severe blow to the head. That tape still running, toad boy?"

The young uniformed policeman looked up at him blankly, and then glanced at Archer.

"The truth is," Frankie paused. "Well, you know all the talk about the old lady's will. Now with the Judge in stir and all that talk about him being guilty of God knows what, I didn't wanna waltz in there in broad daylight. It'd make it look like...well, you know...I don't want nobody tagging the guy with more stuff than he's dealing with already." He shrugged. "I was just looking after my client's interests. That's all."

Archer didn't look anywhere near convinced, but Frankie didn't care. It was a good story, and he could make it work once he got in touch with his contact.

The detective rubbed his hands over his face and then poured himself yet another cup of coffee. Frankie watched him.

"And what fairy tale are you gonna hand me about the gun and the blood in the car?"

"Come on, Captain. You think I don't know what guns I have permits for, and what guns I don't?" He grinned. "Not that I have any guns that I *don't* have permits for."

"We're running a ballistics check on that gun right now, Frankie. We're going to get a match on the bullets we found in the Rand apartment. Then I'm going to run a DNA check on that blood, and after that I'm going to mount your fat head on my wall!"

Frankie looked up at a cobweb in the corner of the ceiling above the door. He dropped his gaze to the scratched metal tabletop. He let his eyes wander back up the pale green cinder block to the cobweb again. Then he turned his eyes on the detective's ashen face.

"Fish."

Archer's eyes turned murderous. The cup of steaming coffee hung forgotten halfway to his lips.

Frankie rocked back on two legs of the chair. "Yeah, fish. Me and a buddy of mine were out in his boat off King's Point and this big motherfucker of a fish tried jumping into that boat. I'm telling you, Archer, it was either a Great White shark or toad boy's grandmother."

He nodded at the policeman sitting at the far end. The cop's knuckles were white on the edge of the table.

"Why, we had to shoot that sucker at least once or twice to discourage the son of a bitch. And good thing you told me about my trunk, Detective, because if there's a drop of blood in there, then it probably came from that fucking bait bucket. I can't believe I missed it when I was cleaning it last week."

"And you think I'm going to swallow that shit?"

You can choke on it as far as I care, Frankie thought, leaning forward and straightening the creases in his pants as he rose to his feet.

"Swallow anything you want, Archer," he said nonchalantly. "But I've answered your questions, and I'll be waiting downstairs until my lawyer gets here."

"Frankie..."

"Fish," Frankie whispered, brushing past the detective and heading toward the door.

Once this lump on his head got better, he thought, maybe he'd really give the fucking sport a try.

Chapter 6

Leaning in the doorway to his bedroom, Owen watched her place the phone back where she had found it.

"Who were you trying to call?"

Surprised, Sarah practically jumped off the edge of the bed. She quickly recovered.

"A friend in town. But the answering machine picked up, and I didn't think it would be too wise to leave a message."

As she stared at the phone for a moment, he let his eyes wander over her from head to toe. Fresh out of the shower, her wet hair was neatly combed behind her ears, while the rest of her was wrapped in his oversized terry-cloth robe. Her legs, crossed at the ankles, were strong and well-shaped. From sitting, the robe had fallen open a little, and his gaze lingered on the gentle curve between her breasts. The skin was smooth and cream-colored, triggering a stir in his loins that he had to work hard at ignoring.

Sarah drew the lapels of the robe together at the neck. Owen looked up and met her eyes. A blush had spread across her cheeks, but she held his gaze with those jade colored eyes of hers. Cleaned up, with no makeup, she was even more beautiful than he'd thought.

He had to get out of the bedroom.

"Want some breakfast?"

She nodded, but Owen didn't wait for her as he headed toward the kitchen.

After arriving at his apartment, he'd shown her to the bathroom, given her towels and the robe, and in a moment he'd heard the shower running.

Using the time to his advantage, he'd rummaged through the briefcase she left with the raincoat on the chair in the bedroom. The case was open—he'd watched her take a toiletry-and cosmetics bag out of it—and the materials he found in the bag matched the information that she'd already given him.

Round-trip airline tickets from Providence to JFK to Shannon and back, and the passport that he'd already looked at. Her wallet with a few credit cards, the license missing. A notebook with scribbled records pertaining to connecting flights, finances and what he assumed to be the place that she'd parked her car at the airport. A couple of case files that she must have been working on during her trip.

In the sturdy leather case Owen also found some newspaper clippings containing the death notices. "John Rand, deeply regretted by his sorrowing brother and two sisters, and his daughter..." Owen scanned the other for her name. "Very sadly missed by his loving daughter Sarah..."

As Owen had put the articles back in her case, his sympathy for the woman grew. "May I help?"

"Pour the coffee," he said, dropping bread in the toaster. "You like your eggs fried or scrambled?"

"Either way, thanks."

"Scrambled, then."

He glanced at her back as she reached for the coffee pot and filled the two cups he'd put out. Her hand shook a little as she poured, and a wave of guilt hit him broadside.

"After you eat something, you should lie down."

She shook her head and took the cups to the table. "The clock is already ticking. I have too much to do."

Owen dumped the eggs into the skillet and reached for a wooden spoon. "Where are you going to start?"

"I wish there was a way I could get in touch with the Judge. I know it would, at least, be a relief for him to know that I'm alive." She came back to the counter and picked up some paper napkins, folding them and smoothing the crease as she considered her words. "I can't believe how these people have arranged for all the evidence to point to him. He would be the last person in this world who would ever hurt me."

Owen remembered the tone of some of the articles. The insinuations that jealousy was the motive for the murder. He glanced at the woman's features, at the line of her neck, at the shadows of skin were the robe had opened up again. He didn't want to think about the nature of Sarah Rand's and Judge Arnold's relationship right now.

"He knows he's innocent," she continued. "But I can't even imagine what he's feeling right now, thinking I'm dead...and that he is being held for my murder."

Owen scraped the eggs onto two plates. "Going to see him would be as good as handing yourself over to the police."

"I know." Without asking, she pulled open a couple of drawers until she found the silverware. Carrying them to the table, she laid them down, arranging them neatly.

Owen put the plates on the table. "Look, I've allowed myself to dive neck-deep into this business. I'm not going to just sit back now while you take your time and do whatever you're planning to do to get out of this jam. And I'm not going to apologize for prying into your private life, either. You owe me that." Dropping toast on the plates, he met her gaze, daring her to stop him right there. But she said nothing and instead sat down and wrapped her hands around the cup of coffee. "It would help if we went over the facts. Everything we know from the papers about the murder. And whatever else you can add to it about the events preceding your trip."

"This is starting to sound like one of your shows."

"I wish it was. Then I'd know how it was going to come out." Owen took a seat across from her.

"I'm sorry," she said. "Sorry to have involved you like this."

"You're forgiven. At least for now, anyway." He stabbed at his eggs. "But let's talk straight about the facts, okay?"

"I only skimmed the papers in the Judge's office."

"The police believe a crime was committed in your apartment. There was definite evidence of foul play. Blood and bullets."

"But they didn't find a body."

"That's right. But the matching tissue and blood samples from your apartment and the Judge's boat makes them believe that your old partner has gotten rid of it." He took a sip of his coffee. "There is no doubt that someone was killed. The only confusion is that it was someone else and not you."

He looked up at her. Once again, her face had turned pale. "Tell me about your friend."

"She arrived from California the day I left. She lived there."

"Why was she coming east?"

Sarah placed her elbows on the table and buried her fingers into her scalp. "Just to visit me."

"But you were going away."

"She didn't know that. I didn't know it, until the day before she arrived. My father passed away suddenly. There was no advance warning."

"Why didn't you call her and tell her not to come?"

"I did. I called her from my office downtown. But she said she wanted to come anyway."

"Why?"

"Mr. Dean, I don't believe you need to know *everything*."

"But I do! And call me Owen. Considering the way you've already dragged me into a life of crime, I think you could at least call me Owen." He pushed her plate of eggs closer to her until it bumped her elbows. She snatched up a fork. "So why was this friend so intent on coming?"

She poked at her eggs. "I don't know. That's the way she was. Once Tori made up her mind, there was no changing it."

"Other than you, who else knew that she was coming?"

She continued to push the eggs around on her plate. "No one, I think."

"Why not?"

"Because it was nobody else's business."

"You know, your openness is truly flattering."

"Look, I know you're trying to help, but I really don't think you need to—"

"Come on, Sarah. Think of what the FBI will be asking you. Do you expect them to believe that you have a friend coming all the way from California, and you hadn't mentioned it to anyone? That you had done no planning, whatsoever, to introduce her around to your million other pals in Newport?"

"Despite what you might think from the newspaper reports, before this disaster I led a quiet life here in Newport."

He pushed his plate away and considered her answer. "Okay, so you didn't tell any friends. How about your co-workers? Office staff?"

She shook her head. "It's August. We always shut down the office for the month. And there was no reason to say anything to anybody."

He rose to his feet and refilled their coffee cups.

"What about your trip? Who else knew about you going to Ireland?"

Her fingers tightened around the cup. "No one other than Tori."

"You know, if you try to sell them a story this lame, they're going to lock *you* up for her murder."

"What do you mean?" A look of horror spread across her face.

"You had the opportunity to do it, Sarah. And believe me, they'll dig into your past until they find a motive. You're a lawyer, you know how it works. The fact that you left the country for two weeks, and the fact that you can't even come up with reasonable answers to the simplest questions will cook your goose, for sure."

"I told you, the news about my father came out of the blue. I thought the only person that had to know was Tori. She was the one I was leaving high and dry. And then I was busy. Busy making airline reservations and packing and everything else a person does when they get a call telling them that their father is dead. I wasn't thinking about developing a solid alibi."

Silence fell between them. Owen watched her as she gazed into the blackness of the coffee. Her face didn't show any grief. Only concentration.

"Who made your airline reservation?"

"I did," she answered after a moment's pause. "And as for the rest of your questions, originally I planned to be away for a week at the most. I thought Tori could tell whoever asked..."

"But you stayed away longer."

She shrugged. "Things happened. The funeral got delayed. And then there was the family. My father's family and property issues with the will. I just couldn't walk away so soon. I tried to call Tori."

"How about getting in touch with your co-workers...your boyfriend...when you were away?"

Owen didn't know why he'd added that last part of it, but it was already out and that was that. Her green eyes lifted and searched his own.

"Being away for two weeks is not too long." She pushed the cup and the plate away. She was all business when their gazes locked again. "As I mentioned before, the office was closed. Tori was supposed to let the Judge and whoever else might call know where I was. And to answer your next question about why didn't I worry when I couldn't get a hold of her? The answer is that my friend is...was...a free spirit. I knew she would use the house as her base, but she'd come and go as she pleased. She had a lot of charisma. She attracted men."

"Had the Judge and your friend ever met?"

His question threw her for a moment, and she paused before answering. "Yes, they met about two years ago. She came to visit me around the holidays. I took her to the Christmas party Avery, the Judge's late wife, threw every year. It was the last party she threw because of her illness."

"Is it possible that something might have developed between your friend Tori and Judge Arnold?"

"No!" Temper brought a flush to her cheeks. "Absolutely not. Judge Arnold was devoted to his wife."

"From what the papers say, she was increasingly ill. Now, don't you think it's at least possible for a wealthy, middle-aged man to have a fling or..."

"Not this one."

"How can you be so sure?" Owen cleared the area before him. "Think of it the way the police might look at it. Suppose, just suppose they did have something going before, dating from that party. Suppose Tori called him about your departure for Ireland, so he came over and things got started again. The Judge is no longer married, so your friend sees him as fair game."

"I don't care for your insinuations in any way, Mr. Dean."

"I don't either. I'm just playing devil's advocate here. Suppose something happened, an accident, and Tori is killed."

"No! This is real life, not one of the episodes from your show."

Anger blazed in her eyes. "Judge Arnold didn't have anything going with Tori. Not now, and not two years ago."

"And how can you be sure?"

"Because he is not one for a frivolous fling."

"You don't know much about men, do you, Ms. Rand?"

"I know that the Judge would not have cheated on his wife."

He leaned toward her. "Why?"

"He is an honest man. He is a loyal man. A truly upright and good man." Owen watched her trying to keep her emotions in check. "I was there. I saw the way he suffered during Avery's long and painful illness. I saw the way he stayed with her to the end, never giving up hope. Never letting her spirits flag. Always showing his love to her." She shook her head. "No. I'll never believe that he acted improperly with Tori or anyone else."

He waited a moment, giving her a chance to get her emotional legs under her. In that second's pause, he decided not to ask the question that was burning his tongue. The question about her own relationship with the Judge. He changed tack. "What about you?"

"What about me?"

"Would the Judge have a reason for wanting *you* dead?"

"We were friends."

"That's not what the papers said!"

"What did they say?"

"That you and the Judge had been having some heated arguments in the days preceding your supposed murder. That there are witnesses who are coming forward and talking to the police about the extent of the quarrels. There is talk of you storming out of his office two days before the shooting, threatening to leave him."

"Not leave *him*, but the office. And I didn't 'storm' out." She rose to her feet and took both of their dishes to the sink. "None of this is new. Judge Arnold and I always argued. And as far as ending our association, I'd been considering that for a while."

She didn't want to talk about her relationship with the Judge either. He drained half of the cup of coffee and studied the square cut of her shoulders, the silky blonde hair that was starting to curl at the ends as it dried. His gaze moved down over the graceful arch of her back. And she said this Tori attracted men.

As Sarah bent to put the dishes in the dishwasher, Owen's eyes riveted to the gentle swing of her breasts beneath the robe. Frowning, he forced himself to look at her profile before speaking. "Are you and your friend very much alike?"

She straightened up and tugged at the belt of the robe as she faced him. "We...we were roommates in college."

"And?"

"I finished, and she...well, she dropped out. We stayed friends." Sarah crossed her arms over her chest as she leaned back against the counter. "She hated order of any sort. I was always fairly organized. When I decided to go on to law school, she was totally disgusted with me. Later on, we grew apart to some extent. But every now and then, out of the blue she would call."

"Actually, I was wondering about your looks. Did the two of you look very much alike?"

"Not so much when we were younger, but this trip, she had cut her hair, and she was a blonde. She's always gone with the color of the month, but I was surprised to see that her hair was about my color. Actually, it looked good on her." Sarah glanced down at her bare feet on the white tile. "We were both about the same height, but she was much better endowed in certain places, if you know what I mean."

Owen kept his eyes on her face. "So, then, is it safe to assume no psychotic boyfriend chased her all the way from California?"

Sarah considered for a moment. "I believe it's safe to assume that."

"And I think we can assume that this was not just a simple robbery gone bad because they never would have gone to the trouble of getting rid of the body."

"Okay."

"Then your comment that someone might have murdered your friend, thinking it was you, is not inconceivable. Certainly the police think it was you."

"Someone who had only been given a description, perhaps. But I don't know why anyone would *want* to have me killed."

She was the picture of concentration, but his mind clicked over, registering more provocative images. He shifted in his chair a little before drinking down the last of his coffee. "So what's next?"

"I have to get to the information inside our offices."

"You were just there."

"No, the law offices downtown. That's where most of the law firm's current files and schedules are kept." She pushed away from the counter and padded back and forth across the kitchen floor. "I think I mentioned to you before about something, some case, that the Judge was all stirred up about in the weeks before I left."

"You think there's a connection?"

"I don't know. But whether or not I was the intended victim, or the Judge is being used as a scapegoat, the answer might be found at the office. That's the only place I know to start."

"All right."

She hesitated by the table. "I can call a cab and have them take me downtown, but there's a slight problem."

He was already getting to know that 'I'm brave and grateful but I need a favor' look. It was a powerful tool.

"What's the problem?"

"My keys to our downtown offices are on the same key chain as my car keys. They're in the ignition of my car, I think. Also, I need to have my laptop for some files. I left that in the car, too."

"You want me to take you to where you ditched your car?"

She gave a small nod. "You've already done so much, and I can't thank you enough."

Owen came to his feet. "Save it. You'll be able to return the favor by giving me the name of a good lawyer. I know I'm going to be needing one."

She nodded guiltily and then hesitated before turning to go. "Oh, I need another favor."

It would be too much to ask, he thought, for her to want to have sex with him right there on the kitchen table.

"My clothes are wet. Could I borrow something, anything, until I can get my suitcase from the car, as well?"

"Absolutely not. You want a ride, you'll have to come as you are."

As he walked toward her, Owen saw her eyes widen, her lips parting. Sarah only took a half step back when he stopped right in front of her. Her breath caught in her throat as he ran his finger from the hollow of her throat downward into the valley between her breasts and beyond, stopping only when he reached the belt at her waist. He looked from her stunned face down to the inside curve of her breasts. She wasn't breathing. Then again, neither was he.

Looking away from her, he crossed the room as her hands quickly drew the front of the robe together and tightened the belt.

"Go through the drawers and the closet and get what you want. I'll be taking a cold shower before we leave."

Chapter 7

"*Allahu Akbar!*"

Amir bowed to the east, straightened, and cupped his hands before him.

"*Allahu Akbar!*"

Jake stared at the knit cap covering the shaved head of the black man, and started to whistle, "When You're a Jet," from *West Side Story*. His cellmate ignored him, continuing to pray loudly. It was a kind of tradition they'd established.

Because Amir woke him up two hours before he had to, Jake would normally curse out the son of a bitch when he started, then move on to whistling. Today, however, he decided to wait until Amir was finished before hurling some select and particularly vile epithets at the Muslim and his *Allahu Akbar*.

After all, he thought generously, today he'd already been awake when his cellmate had rolled off his bunk.

"*Allahu Akbar!*"

Jake, lying on the top bunk with his hands tucked behind his head, continued to whistle as he glanced over at Amir's scarred hands stretched to the ceiling.

"*Allahu Akbar!*"

"Yeah, yeah, yeah." A devious smile broke across Jake's lips. He rolled onto his side and reached under his pillow, dragging out the bootlegged printout of the photo he'd taken off the Internet the day before. Starting to whistle his tune again, Jake stared at the picture of the couple on the page and felt himself go hard.

Amir's face appeared over the printout.

"You filthy mick. How you think Allah is gonna hear me, when you're whistling up the devil and jerkin' off while I pray?" He pulled his small knitted cap off his head and threw it disgustedly into the bunk below.

"That's one ugly buzz, Amir." Jake looked past the picture at his cellmate's shaved head. It was nicked in half a dozen places. "What did you do? You didn't let that faggot Jerome take a blade to your head again, did you?"

"Not your damn business." Amir pulled the picture out of Jake's hand and stared down at it. Jake sat up in the bunk and hung his legs over the side, watching his cellmate's face.

Amir hit the paper with one hand. "Hey, that McKee guy from *Internal Affairs*."

"And you're a frigging genius." Jake jumped down from the bunk and, stepping in front of the toilet, started to relieve himself. "Owen Dean. His real name is Owen Dean."

"Whatever, man. More important, who's the bitch with tits?"

Jake walked over and snapped the page out of Amir's hand. He looked down again at the picture of the movie star having sex with the woman.

"As a matter of fact, my friend, her name is Tori Douglas. And it just so happens that I know this bitch."

Riding up and down the state road, Sarah found it impossible to identify the place where she'd left her car after the shooting. They did a U-turn and slowed again at the place where Sarah remembered the police car initially pulling her over. Even here, it was difficult to find anything to support her story.

No glass on the road. No skid marks. Nothing.

Sarah could feel the skepticism growing by the moment in the Range Rover.

"It has to be one of the first two or three gravel roads," she said.

"Okay, but do we want to get arrested for trespassing on a dismal Thursday morning?" Owen frowned. "I don't think so."

In spite of his words, Owen abruptly turned onto one of the side roads, and she glanced over at him in surprise.

"This is the drive I was coming out of when I saw you last night."

Sarah tucked a loose strand of hair behind an ear and pulled a baseball cap on her head as Owen brought the car to a stop.

"Here we are. This was exactly where you came out of the woods."

Sarah looked uncertainly into the woods, dark and forbidding beneath a shroud of morning mist. Try as she might, she could see no break in the thick undergrowth. No place where her car had entered the woods. No gap were she'd come out.

An icy chill had formed a permanent pool in her belly. She glanced at the man sitting silently behind the wheel and found herself momentarily distracted by the memory of his touch in the kitchen.

Owen's short black hair was still wet from his shower. The muscles in his jaw continued to flex as his eyes probed the scene before them. She felt a shiver run through her, and this time it had nothing to do with fear.

"Ready?"

She looked at him and again felt her treacherous pulse leap at the way he glanced at her. The gym shorts she'd borrowed were way too big, but with a draw string, she'd been able to gather the waist enough to keep them up. The T-shirt with the logo for his television show on the back was hanging a little limply over her breasts, but tucking it loosely into the shorts had helped. She should have opted for a sweatshirt, but she hadn't seen one in the drawers and didn't want to ask. Her shoes—black suede, muddy, and still wet—made for a perfect match to the ensemble.

"As ready as I'll ever be."

They both stepped out of the car, and Sarah jumped at the bleep of the car alarm. She pushed into the heavy underbrush.

As soon as the branches closed behind them, she had a sense of being in another world. Damp and dripping in the early morning gloom, the trunks of the trees looked black and ominous. She slipped on a wet rock and recoiled at the feel of some fungus growing on the side of a tree.

"Real nature girl, eh?" Owen stood beside her.

"It's these shoes, and this place. How do we know the men who attacked me aren't still around?"

Owen looked around and frowned. "No way we can know for sure. But we saw no sign of them out on the main road."

"I realize I probably should have asked this before, but you don't have a gun, do you?"

He fought back a smile. "Do you want me to shoot somebody

now?"

"No, I just thought, if they're waiting for us at my car..."

"Then they'll be pretty wet sons of bitches." He peered ahead. "Probably with the storm and all, there is no way you remember which direction you ran from."

"This way, I think." She led him through the tangles of vines and suckers that cluttered the forest floor. "I remember trying to keep my distance from the main road."

In a few minutes, they reached a small clearing. She stopped and looked around her.

"I think I came through here." She lowered her voice to a whisper. "We're not far from the car." She turned around and looked again at the tall trees, at the denseness of the woods. "Even with the storm howling as it was, I could have sworn I could see..."

She hesitated, gauged where the main road was, and then pointed in the direction that she remembered seeing the lights from a house. "Yes. In fact, it was from right here...I could see lights coming through the trees as the wind blew them. A house, I remember thinking. I didn't know whether I should go toward it, or stay clear of it. I just couldn't think straight."

"Warner's house."

His words brought her head around. She was surprised by the sudden seriousness in his voice. He reached for her hand and pulled her toward a gap in the brush.

"There are two separate roads that go up onto their property. The one you took may have been the old logging road that circles up around the house. Andrew hasn't done anything to keep it up."

She freed her hand and moved ahead of him. "You said that the house is Warner's. Is this Warner as in Andrew Warner, the president of Rosecliff College?"

"Do you know him?"

"Somewhat." She looked ahead through the woods for something recognizable. "I believe he is a friend of the Van Horn family. I remember meeting Warner's wife at Avery's funeral. Mrs. Warner is...hmm, a hard woman to figure out."

"You don't have to mince words on my account."

"I didn't." As she turned to glance at him, she tripped over a log protruding from the leaves and undergrowth. Just beyond, the ground dropped off into a gully slick with mud. Before she plunged into the muck, he grabbed her wrist. He reeled her in and she slipped against him.

His scent was intoxicating. Soap and spice. She was appalled at the reaction that the contact wrought in her body.

"Okay?"

She nodded and tried to push back onto her own feet, but he had one arm around her and appeared to have no interest in letting her go. She glanced up and saw the look. The tabloid look. The eyes that spoke of desire. Of sex. His eyes were focused on her mouth. She swallowed hard.

A sudden breeze in the tree tops brought a shower of last night's rain down on them, breaking the moment.

"This is a very slippery slope," she murmured.

The rustle of undergrowth behind Owen jerked them apart. Turning, he held her behind him. Sarah fought back the sudden rise of bile in her throat. She'd been so foolish to think that she would be safe. How quickly she'd forgotten how close she'd come to death just a few hours before.

"Stay here," he whispered.

He picked up a good-sized stick off the ground and walked along the gully. Sarah was not about to let him walk into some danger alone, and she followed, glancing about for another stick. Abruptly, a cock pheasant erupted from the forest floor in front of them, disappearing in an instant into the treetops in a flurry of feathers and falling leaves.

Owen gave her a half-grin.

Sarah's eyes were caught by something beyond him. There, the sun that was beginning to filter through the trees was reflecting off the hood of her sports car.

There was no one around it, and there was no sign Sarah could see that anyone had been near it since last night. As Owen busied himself checking the damage to the hood and the windows, Sarah pushed past the pine branches, took her keys out of the ignition, and popped open the trunk. She pulled out her two suitcases and her laptop.

"Are you going to leave the car here?"

"I don't have much option, do I?"

"I wonder if it'll start." He reached out for the keys.

The ignition clicked, but the engine was not about to turn over. She watched him as he studied the bullet-shattered windows from the inside. "There is certainly enough proof of an attack here. No casual run through the woods would have produced this kind of damage to your windshield."

She closed the trunk and stood with her arms full, watching him. Despite the hell she'd gone through, it was a relief to know that someone else could see that none of this was the product of her imagination. As she watched him through the broken rear window, he leaned over and picked up something off the passenger floor.

She knew what it was.

Tori's wallet.

A pang of grief stabbed at her chest. After today, after she'd gotten her own mess straightened out, she'd have to call California. Someone had to break the sad news to Tori's mother, and she knew she would have to be the one to do it.

Mrs. Douglas...Tori is dead.

Mrs. Douglas...your daughter was murdered...instead of me.

There was that choking feeling in her throat again. Dead. An innocent woman, who had her whole life in front of her, was dead because she was in the wrong place at the wrong time.

The rustling of leaves accompanied the sound of footfalls not far from where they were. The muffled rumble of a man's voice came through the trees.

Sarah dropped her things and pushed to Owen's side.

"That way." she whispered. "Someone's coming."

As agile as a cat, he was out of the car and motioning for her to get down. Without protest, she moved back, keeping the vehicle between her and the approaching intruders.

The two hunting dogs burst into sight, their noses to the ground as they wove around the trees toward the car.

"Slow down, boys. Slow down." It was the voice of an elderly man, from the sound of him, and quite out of breath.

One of the dogs caught sight of Owen and barked threateningly. He dropped to one knee. "Chip! Skip! Come on, good boys."

The animals bounced toward him.

"Owen, is that you?"

"Yeah, Andrew," he called out. "Over here. Watch out for the gully."

Relief flooded through Sarah, and she stood up, stretching palms out toward the excited, friendly beasts. Having greeted her, the two turned their attention back to Owen, racing back and jumping at him with muddy paws and quick licks at his hands and face.

In a moment Sarah saw a white-haired man appear through the woods. As he gave an enthused wave to Owen, the man she immediately recognized as Andrew Warner was seized by coughing that would not quit. He reached out for a tree trunk, gasping for air.

Owen went to him. "Where's your inhaler?"

Continuing to cough, the older man couldn't catch his breath long enough to answer.

"You *do* have it, don't you?"

Andrew Warner gasped for breath, his face turning an ugly shade of purple. He patted the leather pouch at his waist. Owen's hands were quick, unclipping the pouch and pulling out an inhaler.

It was a few moments and a couple of puffs on the medicine before Warner's coughing subsided enough so that he could lean his head back against the tree.

Sarah's eyes turned on Owen's face and what she saw in his expression surprised her. He was clearly worried about the elderly man. And it was not just worry that one would see in the face of someone helping a casual acquaintance. This was deeper.

She knew the look. It was the visual reflection of the helplessness that you feel when you're losing someone you really care about. She'd seen it in her own mirror while her mother had been slowly wasting away. This was close to the same grief she'd seen in the Judge's face while Avery had fought so valiantly against death.

"Owen, I was hoping you'd come." There was more coughing, but not nearly so violent as the medicine took effect.

"Didn't your doctors discourage you from going out in this kind of dampness?" His voice was irritated, snappish.

"The hell with doctors. I had to get out of the house."

"Christ, Andrew! These attacks could kill you."

"I've had it with that house, Owen. And with her."

"Don't do this. You asked me to come. I'm here. We made a bargain. I've met my end. Now it's your turn, dammit! You've got to hold up your end of the deal."

Apparently forgotten by Owen, Sarah felt like a trespasser. She knew she was listening to a private conversation—one that she had no right to know anything about.

"I made another appointment with my doctor for next Friday."

"That's a start."

"I want you to come with me."

"I don't think that's such a good idea."

"Why? Because of Tracy?"

"She is your wife, Andrew. It's her place to go with you."

"The hell with Tracy!" The old man's face turned red again as he started wheezing. "The hell with her selfishness. The hell with her blaming you for everything that *I* did."

Owen's impatience was too apparent as he jammed the inhaler inside the bag again. "Andrew, if you think this is helping anything..."

"And stop defending her. She has never in her life said a single kind word about you. Even knowing my feelings for you, in all these years she's barely been able to muster a shred of civility toward you. So stop taking her side."

"I don't take her side." He shoved the bag at him. "But you've been married to her for fifty years, for chrissake. She's put up with all your screwing up for a long time, and if you ask me, she has every right to be bitter. And if she wants to hate me along with you, then let her. I am not a ten-year-old anymore. What do I care if she slams a door or two in my face? Christ, Andrew, you said yourself that she's treated you better than you ever deserved. That's all that matters now. You've got to keep on getting what you need."

One of the dogs barked, and the college president's blue eyes fell for the first time on Sarah. There was a momentary pause, but his gaze narrowed with immediate recognition, in spite of her baseball cap and baggy clothes.

"I'll be damned." Andrew's eyes took in the abandoned car. Gray eyebrows arched as he surveyed the shattered glass and the scrub pines hedging in the vehicle.

"What the hell is this all about?"

Owen was standing next to her before Sarah could find her voice. "Who said real life is not as exciting as the movies? Andrew, I want you to meet Sarah Rand."

"You know her?"

Sarah extended a hand toward the elderly man. He clasped it in his own. "Actually, we...we only met last night."

"Aren't you supposed to be...dead or something?"

"News of her death has been exaggerated. Sarah only returned from Ireland last night."

"I was away for the past two weeks."

"Well, that'll make at least a few people we know quite happy," Andrew remarked.

"Yes," she agreed. "Judge Arnold is innocent."

"May be innocent. A little early to tell, if you ask me," Owen continued. "At any rate, Sarah flew into Providence last night, totally unaware of the circus going on here, and immediately ran into some trouble." He nodded toward the car. "Some people, it appears, tried to finish what they'd thought was a done deal before."

Andrew threw a questioning look from one to the other before turning his attention to the car. He looked back at her. "Shouldn't you be going to the police, young woman?"

"She is."

"I am."

"I'm glad you at least agree on that."

"But she needs a day, Andrew. A day to try to figure out what's going on. Why the frame-up of the Judge. If it was a frame. And maybe figure out how a couple of guys who were posing as cops knew she was coming back. They were waiting for her."

"As it stands, I can't trust the local or state police, Dr. Warner." She motioned toward her car. "That's what they did to me last night. They were ready to kill me."

"Wait a minute! Wait a minute! Let's start from the beginning."

"Let's not." To Sarah's surprise, Owen put an arm around her shoulder and pulled her to his side. She didn't understand what he was doing, but decided to go along for the moment. "Considering everything that's happening, the less you know, the better."

"But—"

"She'll be contacting the authorities by the end of the day. All will be made clear to everybody, then. With any luck you can see it on the news tomorrow night."

"Owen, if her life is in danger, then so is yours, now."

His arm released her. "You don't have to worry about me. I've been able to take care of myself for a long time, as you know better than anyone."

"Owen—"

"Do this for me, Andrew. Keep a lid on it for today. For a couple of days, at most."

The older man fell silent. "You be careful."

"We will."

Sarah felt Andrew's eyes on her back as they walked back to the car for her laptop and luggage. As she reached for one of the bags, Owen picked up Tori's wallet, open on the ground where he'd dropped it, and handed it to her, taking the luggage himself.

Andrew Warner and his dogs were still watching them as they moved into the woods toward the Range Rover. Glancing at Owen's face as they pushed through the underbrush, Sarah saw a different man than the one she'd walked into these woods with such a short while earlier. The man who walked with her now had a past. He had feelings. He displayed emotions. Instead of a movie star, Sarah now saw a man.

"So I've got a couple of days, you say?"

Gray must have been the color of choice when the visiting room of the prison had been redone ten years earlier. Light gray for the top half of the wall, dark gray below, and a medium gray furniture and tables to complete the look. The flooring was white—with gray flecks, naturally.

By the gray steel door, a guard wearing charcoal slacks and a white shirt with epaulets watched the only occupants of the huge visiting room—two men conversing by way of telephones through the glass divider at one of the rows of tables.

Wearily putting a check on the list he'd compiled, Judge Arnold looked at the legal pad on the table in front of him, scribbled a few more notes, and then glanced up at the man on the other side of the divider. "Anything else?"

Evan Steele, the head of Steele Security, flipped through a few pages of his own small notebook. "We are still unable to find anyone who can pinpoint the getaway car on the day of her murder. There were a couple dozen cars—tourists and year-rounders—lining the dead-end street. We're continuing to check, but nobody is coming in with any useful information."

"How about the police? Do they have anything on it?"

"No hard evidence. I think they've decided that Sarah's own car was used to move the body, since the vehicle is still missing." Steele, an unsmiling, studious-looking man with salt-and-pepper hair, flipped through his book a few seconds more and then closed it, tucking it into his inside jacket pocket. "Senator Rutherford's office called again. They want you to know that the senator himself is planning to call Judge Wilson next week to request another bail hearing."

"Right. Well, fat chance of him getting anywhere with that bitch before the preliminary hearing." A small muscle started to twitch in the older man's neck. "What's my stepson up to these days?"

"The papers are still hounding him at work and at home. But Hal is laying low."

"All right, Evan. That's the official report. Now why don't you give me the report I'm paying you for."

"He took off sailing on Monday for Block Island."

"So, the bastard is already flaunting the control of his inheritance at me."

"Actually, it was your lawyer's suggestion. Scott thought that Hal's image of all work and no play could prove detrimental to your case," Steele explained. "Also, by convincing Hal to go away, he thinks we might manage to take some heat off of you. The media loves him, and as long as he is around, and suffering from all his recent loss…"

"Bullshit!"

"Well, sir, with him gone I had a better chance of digging into his books as you wanted me to."

"Now you are getting someplace." The Judge rubbed the jumping muscle in his neck. "What did you find?"

"He made a large withdrawal from his trust account this month."

"How large?"

"Fifty thousand."

Judge Arnold sat forward. "That could be something, Evan. That money could be a payoff for any kind of job…even murder. Did you tell Scott about it?"

"Yes, sir. But he already had an idea what the money was for."

"What?" the judge snapped.

"Your son was planning—"

"*Stepson!*"

"Stepson," Steele repeated with a frown. "Hal hinted to Scott that he was planning an elaborate marriage proposal. It's possible some of the money was used on a ring we know he picked out for Sarah."

"She wouldn't take him four years ago. She certainly wouldn't have a damn thing to do with him now." The tic in the judge's neck appeared to be worsening, but he gave up rubbing it. "And I don't believe any of this bullshit. There was no way Sarah would have kept it from me if she was getting involved with him again. No way in hell she would do such a thing to me."

Steele sat back, his gaze intent on the judge's face.

"Keep a close watch on him, Evan. He can pull all the wool he wants over everyone else's eyes, but I know what he is all about." Judge Arnold lowered his voice. "I want to know every step he takes. Everyone he speaks to. I am not going to let that son of a bitch take me down. No way in hell is he going to come out on top on this. Do you hear me?"

"Perfectly, sir."

Archer reached for the single-page report Bob McHugh dropped on the desk.

"There were three outgoing calls made from that mausoleum last night." He sat heavily on the metal chair. "Number one went to Henry Van Horn's home number, who by the way is still out of town. The second one was the 911 call. And the third phone call was made to our new celebrity in town, Owen Dean."

Archer shuffled through a stack of pink messages on his desk and dragged up the one he was looking for. He stared at it, comparing the phone numbers.

McHugh peered at the message, reading it upside down. "Hey, check out the times."

The detective nodded. "He leaves me a message at 1:07a.m., and then gets a call from the Van Horn Mansion at 1:22. Now, who would be calling him at that time of the night?"

"Should I ring him up and drag his pretty face out of bed?"

Archer pushed the slip of paper into a thick file on his desk. "Nah. I think I'll just pay Mr. Dean a personal visit this morning."

Chapter 8

Andrew Warner was dying. Aside from Tracy, Owen knew that just a few others knew what was coming.

Owen had read everything he could find on lung cancer. He'd read about hospice. He'd read about death and dying. They all said essentially the same thing.

Everybody eventually died. It was part of the deal. Sadness for some final moment shouldn't dominate a person's life; rather, celebration for each passing day should be the driving force. What an incredible opportunity to wake up in the morning and be able to challenge the world again and again. Living every moment.

What a crock of shit, Owen thought as he sped across the Jamestown Bridge. All bullshit. But it was the same bullshit that he had used to convince himself to come to Newport. To try to recreate something he and Andrew had never had. Something they would never have.

"You mean a lot to him."

"I don't know what you're talking about."

Her silence drew his glance. She was staring out the window. The morning sun had completely burned through the mists and was sparkling off the raindrops on the bridge. Christ. He had no reason to snap at her.

"We're old friends," he said, his tone gentler.

Her face turned, and her eyes met his. "It shows."

He shifted his gaze back to the road. She didn't ask any more questions, so he let it go. It wasn't something he wanted to talk about.

Old friends. For years, that had always been his answer to anyone who asked about Owen's relationship with the older man. But that hadn't always been his answer.

He's just a friend of my mother's.
He's the guy who takes care of us.

He's the one who checked my mother into this...this hospital.
Yeah, he's the guy who pulled some strings to get me out of that mess.
Him? He just keeps track of me. He knows the headmaster.

Owen had given a number of answers over the years. But he'd been a kid at first, living in the slums of West Philly with his substance-abusing mother, and not understanding what exactly Andrew Warner was to them. And to this day, after all the half-assed explanations the older man had given him over the years, he still didn't know. Not really. Not *really*.

Well, maybe now was the time.

"Would it be too much to ask if we were to stop at your place first?"

Sarah's question broke into Owen's brooding thoughts, and he threw a quick look at her.

"I'd like to change into my own clothes. Also, I'd hate to drop in at the office in broad daylight and run into someone I know."

"I thought you said the office was shut down for the month."

"It is. But with Judge Arnold being held at ACI, and me supposedly dead, I have no idea what the schedule is. Linda could easily be there today."

"Linda?"

"Our office manager. She pretty much runs the office, the schedules, the business side of things." She adjusted the laptop by her feet. "I can call the office, and if there is no answer, I can access a lot of the files remotely."

"Don't you trust this Linda?"

"Of course I do. But I don't want to get any more people involved than I have. I am supposed to be dead, and it's just not that easy explaining to people in twenty-five words or less what I'm trying to do." He sensed her gaze on his face. "And not everybody will be as trusting and as accepting as Dr. Warner."

It was his cue, but he was done discussing Andrew. He was done even thinking about him for today. There was a big mess in Owen's lap right now. A big mess named Sarah Rand.

Owen made a quick stop at a convenience store and picked up some necessities while she waited in the car. There was nothing that resembled food in that refrigerator.

It was still just a little after seven in the morning when they turned off of Ocean Drive onto the long driveway leading to his building. He pulled into his usual parking space.

She took her laptop, her leather case, and one of the grocery bags.

"I'll make a second trip for the other bags," he said, picking up her suitcases.

"Could we use your entrance off the terrace?"

"Of course." In fact, it was probably a good idea. Being a working actor had its rewards, but privacy wasn't one of them, and bringing home a woman was sure to attract the attention of...well, at least a few of his neighbors.

He led the way along the stone wall to the flagstone terrace and his own sliding glass door and unlocked it.

Once inside, Owen paused a moment by the door and watched with amusement as Sarah moved comfortably about the place, dropping her case on the sofa, putting the laptop on the coffee table, taking the groceries into the kitchen. All traces of vulnerability were gone and this suited him just fine. He couldn't afford to let himself forget who she was and why she was staying with him. He remembered the suitcases that he still held in each hand.

"You can leave those anywhere."

He met the friendly green eyes. "I only have one bedroom."

A blush crept up into her cheeks, but she didn't look away. "I...I should only be here...until tonight."

"That's good."

He could feel her eyes following him as he took the suitcases into his bedroom. He deposited them on the bed and went back to the living room. She was still standing where he'd left her. There was no mistaking it. There was a sexual pull between them. But somehow, running to Andrew had sobered Owen to his responsibilities. "I'll get the rest of the groceries out of the car."

"Do you want help?"

"No. I can handle it."

There was a smile and an expression of gratitude.

He was shutting the back door of the Range Rover when he

heard the car coming down the drive. The sixth sense he'd culti-vated as a certified juvenile delinquent told him who it was before he even looked. The car pulled up beside him.

"Mr. Dean?"

Owen looked blankly at the man behind the wheel. At the wrin-kled, white, short sleeved shirt. At a shiny tie so shapeless and worn that Owen figured it must have been handed down father-to-son since some time around the Crusades. The driver's arm was draped over the mirror on the outside of the unmarked car.

"Aren't you Owen Dean?"

"Captain Archer, I presume."

"That's right. Dan Archer." A set of uneven teeth flashed in the man's pallid face. He ran a hand through his thinning hair. "How did you know?"

"Just a lucky guess." Owen moved the bag of groceries from one arm to the other. "What can I do for you, Captain?"

"Hold on." Archer pulled into the parking space next to Owen's and quickly got out of the car. "Actually, I'm here to ask you the same thing."

Owen leaned against the back of his car and faced the man. "A return phone call would have done just as well. No reason to drive all the way out here."

"Hey, it's not every day I get a chance to visit a movie star in his little hideaway." The man surveyed the stone chateau. "Nice place to hang your hat."

"It's all condos, Captain. I only rent a little apartment. Not much to it, really." The way the man's eyes continued to scan the build-ing, Owen knew no matter what he said, Archer was still deter-mined to be impressed. "I really appreciate you coming all the way down here, but as far as my phone call last night..."

"Anything in the bag gonna melt?"

Owen glanced down at the bag of groceries in his arm. "No. I just got back. Now as far as the call..."

"I was just finishing up the nightshift. So, no problem swinging by. But yeah. Jeez, it was a long night. How about a cup of coffee for an overworked civil servant, while you tell me what you called about?"

"Sorry, Captain, but I'm expecting an important call."

"Hey, I understand. I won't stay long. You want a hand with that bag?"

Owen frowned at the detective. No longer distracted by the building or the fancy cars parked nearby, Archer was focusing on Owen himself. The detective's eyes had a hawkish look to them. Owen had not invited him in, and the policeman's instincts were obviously aroused. "I'm fine with the bag. Why don't you come in, then?"

He led the detective through the main door of the converted mansion. "Have you been inside the chateau before?"

"Nah! I don't often get to see the insides of any of these fancy places. Unless, of course, there's a drug bust or something. My wife and I got a little place in the Fifth Ward. A little noisier now with tourists than it used to be, but it's home."

Owen stopped in the great hall beyond the entry foyer. Archer's eyes assessed the giant crystal chandelier hanging overhead. The twin sets of marble stairs hugging the two walls. Owen pointed at a sofa near the dark, cavernous fireplace.

"If you wait here a minute, I'll just run this down to my apartment. There's a library at the south end of the building. It looks out on the terrace and the ocean. Worth the price of admission itself."

"I'll take a rain check on that one, Mr. Dean. It was a long night for me, and that cup of coffee would do me just fine."

"Sure. Another time."

As they walked down the hallway toward his own door, Owen's mind raced with explanations for Sarah's presence in his apartment. They reached his door, and he jingled the keys in his hand, pausing as Archer bent down to pick up the newspaper.

Owen turned the key in the lock and pushed the door open.

"Honey, I'm home."

"What are you worrying about? If she was going to go to the goddamn cops, she'd have done it last night, when she clocked me with that fifty pound dumbbell."

"You were already paid for the job, Frankie," the voice barked through the phone.

"Look, I tried to snuff the second broad for you. Gratis, as my lawyer would say. Now, if Jake was out, he never woulda agreed to doing a second hit for nothing like that."

"For nothing, you fat fuck? You never did it in the first place."

"I did. I mean, Jake did." Frankie weaseled. "Trust me, that was no hundred pound fish we dragged outta that condo. I mean, how else could those cops have made the blood match between the bitch's apartment and the Judge's boat, if there was no stiff?"

"That won't mean shit if she turns up, asshole." The voice turned low and menacing. "You know how I feel about being crossed, Frankie. In fact, just last night I met with a couple of your friends who were telling me they'd be more than willing to stuff your face down a john for free."

Frankie swiped at beads of sweat forming out on his brow with the back of a fleshy hand. "Look, what do you want me to do? I don't even know where the bitch is hiding right now."

"Read my lips, Frankie. Finish…the…fucking…job. If you don't, I'll get someone who will finish her and you both. Got it?"

Scott Rosen shut the telephone off and placed it on the arm of the oversized leather chair in his study. His fingers reached for the TV remote. The lawyer immediately turned the volume back up as the morning news flashed video clips of the news stories ahead.

A five car pile-up on the S-curve into Providence. A fourteen-year-old girl previously missing from Warwick found in Boston. A shot of Senator Gordon Rutherford commenting on a botched drug bust in Cranston. Sports. Weather.

"You didn't come to bed last night." Lucy's arms encircled his neck from behind and he trapped her two hands in one of his own. "Does my tossing and turning bother you?"

"No, of course not."

She stroked the morning whiskers on Scott's face before reaching up and removing the glasses from his nose. She cleaned them with the bottom of his own T-shirt before putting them back on his nose. "I've never seen you so consumed by a case as you are with this one."

"Hmm."

"Judge Arnold might be the one locked up, but you are the one who seems to be suffering the most. What is it, Scott? I've never known you to keep yourself away from me like you have over the past couple of weeks." She brushed a kiss across his temple. "You know I'm not a nosy wife. I never pry into your work or try to compete with it for your attention. I'm just starting to worry about you."

He placed a kiss absently on her arm, but his attention remained focused on the television set. "I have a lot on my mind right now, honey. I'm sorry."

The uncomfortable silence was filled by an obnoxious car commercial.

"I think this baby is coming sooner than we think." She placed a kiss on top of his mussed hair and pushed herself upright. She was a master at maintaining her dignity. "I wish you could have come with me last night to the birthing class. Everything seems so real now. So imminent."

Lucy continued to talk as she headed toward the kitchen, but Scott reached over and picked up the remote, turning the volume up higher as Senator Rutherford's tanned face flashed onto the screen.

"...should all be commending these dedicated police officers, rather than criticizing their actions. But in the end it all comes back to the bill I have been pushing in the Senate. A bill that will put more police on the street, and provide more resources for local and state law enforcement agencies across the country."

The caption Murder by the Sea showed in red letters behind the newscaster, who introduced the segment with a comment that new allegations were surfacing that Judge Arnold, being held for the murder of Sarah Rand, might have had a hand in the death of his wife, a month earlier.

Scott watched the senator again appear onscreen, responding to a question obviously posed at the same press conference.

"These rumors of Judge Arnold's possible involvement in the tragic death of his beloved wife Avery are despicable. Anyone who was fortunate enough to know Avery Van Horn Arnold, knows that her death was the result of a long and courageous battle against cancer. I know what it is like to lose a spouse, and Judge Arnold does not need the added pain of such unfounded innuendo."

"Clever. Very clever." Scott absently reached up and accepted the cup of coffee Lucy handed him.

"I didn't know he ever was married." She sat down on the arm of the oversized chair, both hands protectively wrapped around her bulging stomach.

"Twenty years ago."

"What happened to her?"

"She ran away with a traveling salesman."

Lucy took the remote out of his lap and muted the volume as another commercial came on. "Seriously. What happened to her?"

"She took off during his first Senate race."

"Why?"

"I don't know." He shrugged. "Probably because he is a workaholic. No doubt she couldn't accept playing second fiddle to anything in his life."

Lucy's fingers lifted his chin until he was looking into her large brown eyes. "Well, you can forget it, Scott Rosen. I am not running away."

"Good!" he said, his hand resting hesitantly on her firm belly.

"But you, on the other hand, had better get going before I have to kick your butt all the way from here to the office."

Scott Rosen made his way up the stairs. As he stepped into the shower, he could not know that his wife was picking up the phone and dialing the code to check the last incoming call.

Wordlessly, Lucy scratched the number on a piece of paper and tucked it safely away before heading upstairs herself.

Chapter 9

She was nowhere in sight. The laptop sat open on the coffee table. Her leather case sat on the floor, tucked halfway under an oversized pillow that had fallen to the ground. The bedroom door was nearly shut.

"You married?" Archer asked, surprise in his voice.

"No, why do you ask?"

"Well, that 'Honey, I'm home' thing sounded pretty domestic."

"No. Just a private joke. It goes with the territory, you know? Talking to yourself? Writing at all hours of the day?" He closed the laptop on his way to the kitchen. "High test or decaf?"

"Nothing but the real stuff for me."

Owen, dropping the bag on the counter, was relieved to find no sign of Sarah in the kitchen, either. The coffee was already started.

"Very trusting, leaving your doors and windows open like this."

"They tell me it's a safe neighborhood." He watched as the detective walked toward the terrace door. He slid open the screen door and stepped outside. Following him, Owen picked up some old newspapers from a side table and dropped them on the floor, effectively hiding Sarah's leather case.

"Nice view." Archer came back inside. His trained eyes surveyed the spacious living room. "It must cost a few bucks to live in a place like this."

"Not too bad." Owen returned to the kitchen and put the groceries away.

"How about a twenty-five cent tour?"

"What you see is what you get." Owen thought his tone was a little short, but he suddenly didn't give a damn. "All that you haven't seen is the bedroom, and if you don't mind..."

"Hell, no!"

"It might be the end of the shift for you, Captain, but I'm just starting my work day. Sugar or cream?"

"Black for me."

Two mugs were sitting next to the already percolating pot. Owen filled the cups and plunked them down on the counter separating the kitchen from the living room. After studying the pictures on the walls, Archer finally came by the counter and sat on the high chair facing the kitchen. "You live alone?"

Owen bristled at the question. But he took a sip of his coffee and nodded curtly. "Most of the time. Now about my message last night—"

"I guess, being as popular as you people are—"

"Did I mention that I'm waiting for an important phone call?"

"Yeah, as a matter of fact, you did."

"Good." Owen frowned as Archer openly eyed a stack of unopened mail sitting near his elbow.

"So, they've found you already. Prison letters."

"Just part of the job."

"Do you ever use them?" Archer picked some up, checking the return addresses on each of them. "I mean, in your shows and everything. Do you use them for material?"

"No. That's what I have script writers for. I don't do it all, Captain." Owen took the envelopes out of the detective's hand, tossing them onto the kitchen table. He glanced down at his watch. "My free time is running out, Captain."

Red patches appeared in the detective's pale face. "Okay. Why don't you start from the beginning?"

"Sometime before midnight last night, I was coming home from a dinner party out past Wickford. I gave a ride to a woman who was stranded on the side of Route 1A. She said her car had run out of gas. I brought her back to Newport and dropped her off at the Visitor's Center."

Archer's face had regained its customary ashen hue. He took a pack of cigarettes out of his shirt pocket, but seeing Owen's frown, he put it away. "Sorry. Go on."

"When I got back to my apartment, I was just glancing at yesterday's newspaper, and I just thought the woman I picked up and dropped off looked a little like this Sarah Rand. So that's when I called and left a message."

"What was her name?"

Owen took a long sip of the coffee. "Mary or Marie or Marla...I don't really remember. She didn't give me a last name."

"What did she look like?"

"Light brown hair. Little bit rounded, especially around the hips. And she was soaking wet." He shrugged his shoulders. "I thought she kind of looked plain."

"Mr. Dean, you ever met Sarah Rand?"

"No. Just pictures in the newspapers."

Archer looked around him and spotted the newspapers on the floor. He got off the stool and crossed the room. Leaning over, he picked up yesterday's paper. Owen looked at the leather case, now exposed to view. The detective folded the paper and put it on the counter in front of Owen.

"Did she look anything like this?"

Owen glanced down at Sarah's classic face. "Is this a new picture? You never know with photographs. I mean, this could have been taken during her college years."

Archer frowned at him and then studied the picture. "No. This was taken less than a year ago. She was making a presentation at some Bar Association thing. Now, the woman you picked up last night—did she look anything like this one?"

Owen looked at her again. "The nose. Or the mouth. Something struck me. She was pretty well dressed, despite being completely soaked by the rain."

Archer reached into his back pocket and took out a small note pad. "So you believe this woman, this Mary or Maria or Marla, was Sarah Rand."

"I can't say that. What I said was that she looked a little like the dead woman."

Archer scratched his balding head. "So you called to tell us that?"

"I didn't remember reading in the papers anything about close kin. Family, that sort of thing. So I thought, maybe she could be a sister or something. I don't know...just trying to be of some help. Hey, it was late."

Archer took a pen out of his pocket and leafed through the small notebook until he got to a blank page. "Did you get a license plate number on her car?"

"Nope. I didn't see the car."

"But you said she ran out of gas."

"That's what she said, but she'd been walking in the rain looking for a gas station. She wasn't next to her car."

Archer tapped the pen on the counter and looked up at Owen. "Did you pass a car on the side of the road before you saw her?"

"Don't remember any. I was talking on my cell phone, so I wasn't paying any attention."

"Who were you talking to?"

"It was business." Owen looked down at his watch again.

"Did she tell you where she lives?"

"No."

"Did you wait at the Visitors Center until she got into a cab?"

"No."

"Why not?"

"No reason to. The place was well lit, and she said she was all set."

"Did she ask to use your cell phone when she was in your car?"

"No."

"If her car was out of gas, wouldn't you think she'd want to call AAA or the police or..."

Owen straightened from where he was leaning against the counter. "Captain, I'm a busy man and now you know what I know."

"To be honest, Mr. Dean, that's not much."

Owen picked up the detective's coffee and put it in the sink with his own cup. "If you'll excuse me."

Archer climbed down from the stool and put the notebook and pen back in his pocket. "Mr. Dean, have you ever been acquainted with the Van Horn family?"

"No, I've never had the pleasure."

"How about Judge Arnold?"

He shook his head. "I can't help you there either, Captain. This is my first visit to Newport."

The detective cast a cursory glance around the room. "Last night, after you left a message at the station, what did you do next?"

"I went to bed, of course." His answer was immediate, but the quick recollection of the cop following Sarah and him to the convenience store parking lot flashed into his mind.

"Did you receive any calls after calling the station?"

"I am working both the East Coast and West Coast hours, Captain. Of course there were more calls," Owen responded, defensiveness evident in his voice. He stalked around the counter, ready to usher the man out. "I know my call to you might have been a nuisance, and I apologize for the unnecessary trip you had to take this morning."

"No, not at all." Archer responded breezily. "I don't get a chance to chit-chat with the rich and famous too often." The hawk eyes scanned the apartment again, this time focusing on the half-closed bedroom door. "You mind if I use your bathroom before I go?"

Owen hesitated for a moment remembering Sarah's wet clothes in there. "Sure. Just give me a second." He marched straight to the bathroom door and walked inside. To his annoyance, Archer was right behind him.

Glancing inside, Owen could see that Sarah's things were gone. On the far side of the bathroom, a second door that connected to his bedroom was wide open. Owen closed it firmly.

"All yours."

He walked out. As soon as Archer had closed the door, Owen took a quick look inside the bedroom. No sign of Sarah or her suitcases. He glanced in the direction of the walk-in closet before going back to the sofa and picking up her leather case. A makeup case and lipstick were visible in the open bag. He tucked it next to his desk on the far side of the room.

The toilet flushed in the bathroom, but when Archer didn't immediately appear, Owen realized with dismay that the detective had used the door into his bedroom.

Sarah's words flashed back to him. Two cops had made an attempt on her life. After seeing the condition of her car, he believed her. But the true identity of those 'cops' was still a puzzle. Fake IDs, stolen police cars—Owen made movies, so he knew how easy it was to make things look believable and official. But that was television. Now, realizing the son of a bitch was in his bedroom, Owen bristled with alarm.

He picked up a couple of sealed letters and the letter opener off his desk and moved quietly toward the bedroom door.

Glancing in, he watched Archer paw through the junk Owen dumped on one of the dressers every night. Pocket change. Credit card receipts. Business cards. Then Owen saw Archer's gaze shift. The bedside table. The fancy appointment book open beside the phone.

It wasn't his. It had to be Sarah's. Archer took a step toward it.

"So you decided to give yourself the twenty-five cent tour anyway?" Owen slid the scale model of the Wallace's sword under the flap of the envelope and ripped it open with a snap.

Archer stiffened and turned to him slowly. He eyed the gleaming blade briefly, but then put on an embarrassed look.

"Couldn't help myself. Hope you don't mind."

"As a matter of fact, I do." Without taking the letter out of the first opened envelope, Owen used the model sword to rip open the second one.

Archer's eyes lit again on the ornate weapon in Owen's hand. "Impressive dagger you got there."

"Just a letter opener. A gift from Mel Gibson."

"No kidding?" The detective's eyebrows shot up, and Owen backed away, giving Archer room to pass in front of him and out of the bedroom.

"Oh, one more question," Archer said. "What time was it exactly that you picked up this woman?"

Owen drew a blank, trying to sort out the significance of the question. "I really don't remember the exact time."

"You called the station at 1:07."

Owen shrugged. "As I said before I didn't really pay much attention to the time."

"I can see how that could happen. But I might have to call on you again, Mr. Dean. In case it turns out that this Mary Maria Marla is important, after all."

Owen ushered him straight to the door. "You have my phone number, Captain. I'd much prefer a call over a visit."

Archer's eyes narrowed before stepping into the hall. "They all do, Mr. Dean. They all do."

She was already up, installed in a Mackintosh chair at the table by the bay window, a cup of tea in front of her, when Andrew came into the kitchen.

The dogs, happy to be free of their leads, ignored her completely and disappeared through the doorway into the house. Andrew stood by the mud room door and considered doing the same himself.

"Have a nice walk?"

He ignored the question and took his jacket off, hanging it on one of the hooks that lined the wainscoted mud room wall. He kicked off his heavy boots.

"You didn't come to bed at all last night."

Sparing her not even a single glance, he took off the pouch of medicine at his waist and threw it on the counter. Getting a glass out of a cabinet, he filled it with water and headed for the door. She left her empty tea cup on the table, following him as Andrew picked up the newspaper and left the kitchen.

"Don't you want some breakfast?"

"Not hungry."

Tracy followed Andrew into his study.

This was his domain. All dark wood and leather. All bookcases and clutter. She hated the room and that made Andrew all the more eager to love it and spend his time there.

"Did you take your pills this morning?"

"Of course." He sat in his favorite chair and buried his nose in the morning paper.

"The Johnsons invited us to go sailing with them out to Block Island next weekend. I told them I'd need to check with you first." She started tidying up the newspapers on the coffee table. "And Mildred called again. She is still being quite nosy about seeing us coming out of that...damn, what was his name, anyway? that oncologist's office last month. She's got great intuition, never mind all the people she knows at the hospital. She'll guess at it sooner or later."

Andrew said nothing. No grunt of acknowledgment. Nothing.

He tried to focus on the box scores. Red Sox were still making it interesting, and here it was almost September.

"Andrew, I still can't understand why you're making all this fuss about keeping everything private. I've been doing quite a bit of reading on the subject. To battle cancer, doctors and medicines are not enough. They all say it. You need the support of friends. People who care for you and will help you get through the difficult times."

Andrew lowered the newspaper onto his lap. "I need Owen."

A frown creased Tracy's face as she straightened up beside the table. "I wasn't talking about him."

The old man folded the paper methodically and dropped it next to his chair. His blue eyes were tired when they met his wife's. "I'm dying, Tracy."

"You're not dying, Andrew."

"Did you see anything about 'denial' in all that reading you're doing?"

"I'm saying this is not the time for exaggeration."

"You're right. Nor is it the time for guilt or lies or vindictiveness."

Thin arms folded across her chest. "I'm sure I don't know what you're talking about."

"Fine. It's your call, Tracy. Admit it, live through it, or let me be."

She avoided his stare and walked toward the window. "You are talking in riddles. And that's all his influence. He wants to ruin you, ruin our marriage. Right now, with the stress of your illness, I just can't deal with it. He has to leave. You have to send him away."

"No." The quiet severity of his tone snapped her head around. "I'll never make that mistake again. I want Owen in my life. That's my choice. And for the first time in my life, I'm going to have my way in this."

Tears pooled in her eyes. "So you're forcing me to leave. After all of our years together, you are choosing him over me."

"Only if you make it that kind of choice." He shook his head. "This is not some stranger. This is Owen. Tracy, I have to make up for the past somehow. There's no time left. I have only two months to live to do the—"

"That's a lie," she cried. "Those doctors. They said six months. The ones in Boston said maybe two years. Mildred's husband…"

"Look." Andrew's words were spoken slowly, matter-of-factly. "I'm not about to let anyone hook me up to a bunch of tubes. I'm not going to live like that, lose what dignity I have, just so I can keep breathing for a few extra weeks. What's the point of that?"

"But you can't just…"

He waved her off. "Two months. That's all I have left, and I can accept that. But this time that I have left, these last few weeks of my life, I'm not going to waste any of it. I'm going to mend the past."

"But with him. It always has to do with him. What about me? What about the wrong he's done to me? To us? To our marriage?"

A moment of silence fell between them. He could feel the cough coming on, but willed it back. Picking up the glass of water, he drank half of it down. Andrew leaned forward heavily on his elbows, his eyes tracing the patterns on the large Persian rug on the floor.

"Tracy, I know I don't deserve the loyalty you've given me, the love you've managed to sustain for me. God knows, I've been unworthy of the years you've put in with me."

A small sound escaped her throat as the woman glided to her husband's chair. Crouching on the floor, she reached for his hand. "I love you, Andrew. I've always loved you."

His face lifted, his blue eyes misty. "I know. And I think that's been the worst part. The guilt of having you stick by me no matter how much I tried to screw up our marriage."

"Andrew."

"No, Tracy." He clasped one of her hands tightly in his own and looked fiercely into her eyes. "Listen. Because, by God, if you don't listen now, I'll go right out that door. I'll walk away from our marriage and from our life."

"You can't do that to me. Not in these last days."

"I can and I will. It's up to you. Don't force me to choose."

The older woman's back straightened. Her lips formed a tight, thin line. But she remained silent. Her gaze did not waver as she looked into her husband's eyes.

"Owen's mother wasn't the first woman I had an affair with. There were many before her. Coworkers, students, friends. Remember the day you had that last miscarriage? I left the hospital that night with Angie, your cousin. We got drunk together and..."

She made a choking sound and wrenched her hand out of his grasp. She stood up and moved to the bookcase on the far side of the room.

"I know how horrible that sounds. So self-centered. Heartless, even. I was a man who was so confident of your love, and yet I still took such pleasure in screwing every woman who even looked twice at me." He paused until she turned around. "I wanted a son. I was the last of my line. I wanted a child then so badly I considered divorcing you a thousand times. Instead, I just went out and had sex with every woman I could find."

A sob escaped the older woman's throat as she stared down at the floor. Andrew watched tears roll down the drawn face, dropping onto the expensive silk house dress.

"As much as you loved me, Tracy, I was ready to leave you. An excuse. I know now that's what I was after. A woman...another woman carrying my child. The illicitness of it? An ugly divorce? None of that mattered to me. I didn't care about the consequences."

Andrew gazed steadily at his wife. Finally, she lifted her chin and looked across the room at him.

"And don't tell me you didn't know any of this," he continued. "I was not discreet. But you were the very picture of devotion, understanding. You never threatened to leave me. You never even confronted me about the rumors that I know went around every place we ever lived."

"I knew we've had problems, Andrew. But I loved you then as I love you now. I knew with time you'd change. You'd settle down."

"And I did change. I changed the day I found out about Owen. My son."

Anger flashed into Tracy's eyes. "She lied. The woman was a whore. That boy could have been the offspring of anyone."

Andrew slammed a fist into his other hand, temper quickly erupting in his blue eyes. "Becky was no whore. When I started that affair with her, she was my student. A simple, eighteen-year old girl. I was the first man she ever slept with."

"But you didn't see her for years after that first year. She left school. He could have been anyone's!"

"But he wasn't. I checked all of that. Hospital records. Talking to people she stayed with after she dropped out of school. For God's sake, she was already several months pregnant when she left school."

"If the baby was yours, she would have told you."

"No." Andrew shook his head. "Not Becky. She was too proud, and too guilt-ridden about having an affair with a married man. No, she took it all on herself."

"She wasn't too proud when she contacted you later, wanting money to take care of her brat."

"My son," he snapped. "She needed money to take care of my son. By the time she contacted me, she was desperate. And I had done all of this to her. I was the one who had ruined her life."

"You didn't pour liquor down her throat. You didn't put needles in her arm or make her pose for disgusting pictures. You didn't turn her into a whore."

"But I did, Tracy." Andrew ran his fingers through his hair. "Don't you see? You're doing it again. Blaming Becky, blaming everyone, refusing to admit that the true fault lay with your husband. If I hadn't seduced that young woman, she would have finished her education and gone back home. She would have had a chance for a decent life—a husband, children, a future. But I destroyed that chance. I destroyed her."

His voice was shaking, and he sat back in the chair.

"Even with the mess her life turned into, even with her addiction, the pornography, the prostitution, everything...I still would have divorced you and married her when I found out about Owen. But she wouldn't have any part of that. Any part of me. Even as screwed up as she was, she still wouldn't break up a home."

Tracy's voice was as still as a mountain pool. "After all these years, you still love her more than you ever loved me."

"I was infatuated with her when I first laid eyes on her. Her beauty, her innocence, her youth. But like it or not, in my own twisted way, I still loved you. I continued to love you until the day you turned Owen away." Her gaze avoided his as he looked across the room at her. "He had never done anything to you. He was only a child when I brought him home with me after Becky died. Do you remember that day?"

She was silent, but he knew she remembered.

"I told you everything that day. The truth about Becky, about Owen. I promised you I'd change. And you acted as if nothing had ever happened. As if I were some saint, and all my confessions were just made-up tales. Stories invented for effect."

"You wanted forgiveness, and I gave it to you."

"You didn't give me forgiveness. You gave me denial. But what I really wanted was acceptance. Acceptance of my son. A home for him. But you refused. You treated him with less compassion than you'd have given a stray dog." He rested his head on the back of the chair and stared blankly ahead. "Do you remember your threats? That if I were to claim him openly as my son, you would ruin him. You said you would tell everyone what a whore his mother was. That it was a lie that I was his father. Everyone would know, you said. You would torment him until he ran away."

"It was just money what he was after. And you gave him plenty of it over the years."

"For God's sake, Tracy, he was only ten when I brought him home. He needed a family. A home. A real home. And you refused to let him stay. Money!" Andrew snorted. "God, it's amazing that your bile hasn't choked you over the years. Do you know why Owen dropped out of college the first year? Do you know why he moved across the country and tried to put as much distance as he could between us?"

Her chin lifted and she stood rigidly.

"He went away because he didn't want my money. Because, like his mother, he was too proud to accept charity from a stranger." He ran a thin hand over his face. "A stranger. I was just somebody who'd paid for him to grow up in good boarding schools. That's what he thought of me all those years growing up. Not a father.

Just an old man who'd been kind to his mother in her last days. Tracy, you kept my son from knowing his father. You kept us from being a family. And I let you. I let you."

He turned in his chair and looked away from her. A knot rose in his throat that he thought would choke him. One small arm encircled his shoulders. She was sitting on the arm of the chair.

"He is a grown man, Andrew. He has everything he needs. There was nothing you could have done for him that could have been better than what he's done for himself."

He turned to her, shaking off her arm. Blue eyes, red-rimmed with anger, met hers.

"You still don't understand. This is not about him anymore. This is about me. About me dying without ever having had the chance to tell Owen that I'm his real father. This is about me begging forgiveness of my son."

Chapter 10

The deadbolt slid into place with a loud snap. Owen moved quickly across the room and closed the sliding glass door, locking that as well. Next, he pulled the cord for the shades, shutting out the light and the prying eyes of intruders—and policemen.

Standing in the protective darkness of his plush cocoon, he still had difficulty quelling the irritation Archer's visit.

He went to his bedroom in search of Sarah, and crossed to the far side of the room. When he opened the door of the large walk-in closet, he first saw her suitcases piled up under his own hanging clothes. She was sitting, knees drawn up, her hands clutching the crumpled material of the suit she'd worn last night. Her face was buried in her knees. But as he switched on the light, her head lifted, her anxious green eyes gazing searchingly into his face.

"He's gone."

That look of frustration, almost hopelessness, that he saw in her expression quickly gave way to a look of relief. He stepped into the closet and stretched out a hand. Sarah reached up, and Owen pulled her to her feet.

"Thank you. It would have been much easier for you to turn me in."

"I don't know, if the rest of his department is anything like him, I can see why you don't want to go to them."

"Archer's department doesn't have the best reputation." She followed him out of the closet. Stopping at the bedside table, she picked up her appointment book and closed it. "Too much temptation, I guess, with so much money floating around this town."

"Have you had any dealings with Archer in the past?" he asked as they went back into the living room.

"Not with him directly, but I made a couple of his officers sweat pretty badly over a case about six months ago. The city settled and the case never went to court, but in the process one of them took an early retirement, and the other was forced to resign." She sat down on the edge of the sofa and started her computer. "I somehow ended up with three traffic citations in the month following the trial. So you might say we are not the best of friends."

"What was the case about?"

"Scaring the hell out of a fifteen-year-old girl until she couldn't even remember her own name, never mind the name and description of the animal who raped her and the woman who set the whole thing up." She picked up the newspapers off the floor and stacked them into a neat pile. "Of course, it was absolutely unrelated to anything that the young man accused of the crime was the son of one of the richest New Yorkers that summers in Newport. A man with a very large checkbook when it came to civic donations."

"Did the cops intentionally scare her?"

"Absolutely." She saw her briefcase next to his desk and retrieved it. "I was able to prove that this wasn't a first for those two officers, either. They'd made a career out of taking that 'good cop, bad cop' routine a few steps over the line. That's bad enough to begin with under ordinary circumstances, but this girl was the victim."

"Did the guy who was responsible for the whole thing ever get caught?"

"No. We sued the department after the creep had gone free. The girl was a mess, having contradicted herself on a half-dozen points, so there was no case. I heard the creep is back in Newport this summer, again. After getting off so easy, he's probably gone right back to paying that woman—or someone like her—to set traps for other young girls."

Owen watched her drawn face as she tried to focus on the screen of the computer. She'd had no time to change into her own clothes, but guessing at her mood, how she looked was the last thing on her mind. "What happened to the girl?"

"She never went back to school, and then just took off for parts unknown this spring. Last time I checked with the family—which was just before my trip to Ireland—there was still no news of her."

The two fell silent for a few moments. Then, Owen reached for a pad of paper and a pen and started jotting down some notes.

"Could I run something by you?"

She glanced up from the laptop.

"I know you believe somebody killed your friend, thinking it was you, so they could set up Judge Arnold."

"So?"

"I have another possibility."

"What?"

"Murder, Sarah. A frame was not the goal. Someone is trying to murder you, not someone else, only you. The fact that Judge Arnold is the number one suspect might just be coincidental."

"What about the blood in his boat? That had to be planted there."

Owen nodded. "True! Still though, when it came down to the actual hit list, you were the target. You were the one they were gunning for. Maybe you know something incriminating. Maybe you've already done some damage. There are some vindictive people out there." He pushed the pad of paper across the counter. "Help me out with this."

She slowly got up from the sofa and walked over to the kitchen. He saw her rub her arms, as if suddenly cold.

"List them," he encouraged. "Cases like the one you just mentioned. Results that might have hurt someone. People whose lives were turned around because of something you've done. Most important, who might still think of you as a threat to them."

"This is no one-page list." She stared down at the pad.

Owen handed over the pen. "But I've already started the list for you—with the Newport Police Department at the top."

Between the Chinese antiques and the paintings hanging on every wall, the luxury condo could have been a museum. Not wanting to sound stupid, Archer fought back the urge to ask if all these pieces were originals. At the same time, he tried his damnedest not to bump into anything as he was led through the spacious rooms.

"Thank you for letting me stop by like this."

"No problem, Captain."

Hal Van Horn smoothed down the front of his white oxford dress shirt and opened the screen door. A light breeze carried the scent of expensive cologne back to the detective as the developer led him onto the balcony overlooking the busy harbor.

"It was lucky that you found me at home. I got in less than an hour ago."

"I know," Archer said politely, seating himself in a wicker chair that he was sure cost more than his own dining room set. "One of my men saw your boat dock at the pier and gave me a call."

"*Gracias, Maria. Desearemos el café, por favor,*" Hal said to his housekeeper. She placed a plate of fresh pastries on the small table between them. "I'm sorry, Captain. I had no idea you were anxious to speak with me again. If I'd known, I would have sailed back from Block Island sooner."

"I'm glad you didn't," Archer responded. "After all you've been through this past month, you needed to get away from Newport for a while. If there was anything urgent, we would have gotten hold of you out there."

Hal's expression was serious as he brushed off an invisible piece of lint from his tailored gray flannels. "There is no getting away from this for me. Sarah is still too much with me. Here...and here." He touched his heart and his temple. "Actually, Scott Rosen encouraged me to take the entire week off. But I couldn't."

Archer watched his host pick up a pair of sunglasses off the small glass table and put them on. The breeze off the harbor played with the perfectly cut strands of the man's wet hair. The reflection off the dark glasses now hid the sadness the detective had seen in the man's eyes. Archer recognized Van Horn's need to compose himself, so he refrained for a moment from asking the questions that had brought him to the luxury condominium.

"This trip to Block Island was supposed to be the one. I had it all planned. I'd picked out the perfect ring. Stocked the boat with her favorite wine. Had my secretary call the chef at the White Horse Tavern to plan just the right dinner for the occasion." Hal Van Horn smiled bitterly at the detective. "I had every intention of sweeping Sarah off her feet this time. Four years ago, when we broke off our engagement, we were too young. We weren't ready.

But this time, I was sure I would win her over."

Hal rose to his feet and walked to the railing. He stood for a few moments, looking out at the yachts lining the harbor.

"There is a rather large rock in a platinum setting sitting on the ocean floor about a mile northeast of Block Island's Sandy Point Light. I stood on the deck of my boat and threw that ring overboard. I couldn't stand looking at it, knowing that the woman I loved was out there in the murky depths of those cold waters. And here I was, just staring at this bauble...thinking if only..."

Archer fidgeted in his chair as the other man's voice cracked. Hal Van Horn leaned on the railing and stared straight ahead.

The detective cleared his throat. "Listen, Mr. Van Horn. I really do apologize for breaking in on you. But because of the incident last night at the mansion, we thought it was essential."

"What incident?" Hal turned his back to the rail. "Was there a break-in?"

"That's something we are trying to determine right now. Evan Steele, the owner of your security service, tells us that, as far as he can tell, nothing was either damaged or missing." Archer's fingers inched toward the pack of the cigarettes in his pocket, but he stopped himself. "Do you know a fellow named Frankie O'Neal?"

"O'Neal?" Hal paused for a long moment, mulling over the name. "It doesn't ring a bell. Why? Should I know him?"

"That's what we're trying to figure out." Archer took a notebook out of a pocket and flipped through it. "Mr. Van Horn, do you know if Judge Arnold or anyone from his office might have been in touch with any antique dealers regarding the appraisal of some pieces in the mansion?"

Hal removed his sunglasses as a dark patch of clouds blocked the sun. "Of course. But that's old news. After my mother's death, Sarah acted as executor to Avery's estate. I know she approached a large appraisal company about putting together estimates of everything that was left in the house. My mother was a collector of practically everything. Estimating the values for a final settlement looked like it was going to be pretty much a mess. I tried to stay out of it as much as I could."

"Do you recall the name of the company Attorney Rand hired?

Or perhaps a contact name? Of course, I can always try to get hold of—"

"Island Antiques. My understanding is that they are the largest outfit of this sort in Newport. They appraise, as well as buy and sell antiques." The housekeeper walked onto the balcony again carrying a silver tray with coffee. "I haven't had any direct dealings with them myself in the past, but I know my company has used them a number of times in furnishing the model homes in our new developments. The name you mentioned, Frankie O'Neal, does he have any connection with Island Antiques?"

"We're working on that." Archer declined the offer of coffee and, seeing his host's quick glance at his watch, rose to his feet. "Is it safe to assume that Attorney Rand's work on your late mother's estate was not anywhere near finished?"

"Considering everything, it is more than safe to assume that Sarah hadn't even been able to scratch the surface of my mother's affairs." Hal led the way back into the living room. "Because of the turn of events, we still haven't decided on an attorney who could finish what Sarah started. Just before I left for Block Island, I did have my assistant call Island Antiques and ask them to send me a status report. We also asked for the return of the keys to the house."

"Any response from them?"

"I haven't gone through my mail yet."

"There are a few messages waiting for you here." Archer looked down at the blinking light on the answering machine.

Hal looked down at it, as well. "So there are. If someone needs to get hold of me, they can call the office or call back when I'm here."

"If you don't like having answering machine, why have it?"

"Sarah bought this one for me. She was the only one who I'd check the messages for. Hell, hers were the only phone calls I always returned." Hal started toward the door of the apartment. "But don't worry, Captain. You can get hold of me at my office anytime. I have a live assistant there who takes my messages. She's a pain in the butt, but she makes sure that I return every call."

Archer accepted a firm handshake from the developer by the

open door. "One last thing, Mr. Van Horn."

Hal waited, a polite smile in place.

"Was anyone staying at your apartment last night?"

"Here? No. Maria is only here during the day and on evenings when I might be entertaining...which, by the way, are not too many. Why do you ask?"

"There was a call made last night from the Van Horn mansion to this number, your private residence. I was just wondering if you wouldn't mind checking those messages to see who made the call."

"Sure, if it would help." Hal glanced at the machine across the room. "But I'm sure the messages on it are only calls that have come in this morning."

"Why do you say that?"

"Anytime I'm away, my secretary calls here first thing in the morning. She goes through the messages and empties the mailbox. You see, she doesn't even trust me at home."

"Then maybe you don't mind me talking to her."

"Of course not. I don't mind at all. Her name is Gwen Turner. You can call her if you want, but I'd advise you to stay out of her path today. Between all the harassment from the media and me being away for most of this week, she'll be loaded for bear."

Archer stood where he was, looking at the answering machine. Hal shrugged.

"Okay, Captain. I can read your mind. Just in case Gwen didn't get to it yet today." He headed across the room, Archer on his heels.

"I don't mean to be a nuisance. You understand that we can't let any stone go unturned."

"No problem." Hal nodded and pressed the messages button. Two messages. One from Gwen at the office, and one from a news reporter who had somehow gotten his private number. Both had clearly been left this morning. "Sorry. I warned you."

Archer nodded with a frown and followed the other man again toward the door.

"One last thing, Mr. Van Horn."

"Actually, this'll make it two 'last' things...maybe even three." He ran a hand through his thick hair and gave Archer a pleasant smile. "But go ahead. Better to ask everything you have now, rather than to try to get hold of me later. Gwen's going to keep me running until I'm caught up with my work."

"I know this might sound sorta far-fetched. But last night…or was it this morning…" Archer scratched his balding head. "Anyway, I had this crazy notion that I wanted to run by you. What if Sarah Rand was really not dead?"

"Captain, I don't see the point in—"

"Hold on, Mr. Van Horn. I mean, we have yet to find a body. We haven't found her car. A lot of personal items were missing from her apartment—toilet articles, wallet, even her passport. And so far, the tests we've done have only matched up blood we found on Judge Arnold's boat and in Attorney Rand's apartment. But let's say…what if she wasn't the victim of a homicide at all? What if *she* killed someone else there?"

Archer watched Hal's already tanned face darken with anger. "This is the most ridiculous thing I've ever heard. Sarah could no more commit murder than I could. What in God's name would make you think something like that?" Before the Captain could voice an answer, the developer exploded. "This is too much! It really sickens me that everything in our lives has been turned into some disgusting headline for these tabloids I used to think were real newspapers. Well, let me make something very clear. I'm through sitting on my hands while this kind of crap gets printed about people I care about. A lot of this crap, by the way, sure has the look of information leaked from Newport Police files."

Archer shuffled his weight, gazing blankly at the wall beyond Van Horn. Unfortunately, the man had a point. Somebody in the department did seem to be leaking investigation information to the press. "Well, I can't say anything that."

"Under the advisement of my lawyers, I have continued to refrain from making public statements about the Judge and my own feelings regarding his guilt or innocence. But if Sarah's name gets dragged into the middle of this thing as anything but the victim that she was, then you and I are going to war." Van Horn's finger was in Archer's face. "I'm well aware of Sarah's battle with your department. I know all about the closed society of police, and the retribution that gets meted out to those who call you onto the carpet for your actions."

Archer opened his mouth to speak, but Hal Van Horn's quick words cut him off again.

"Sarah Rand was a flower in a jungle of weeds, Captain. You mess around with her good name, and I'll set the wolves on your ass so fast that you won't even know which one of them took the first bite. And now, if you'll excuse me, I'm expected at the office."

Archer stood frowning in the hallway for a long moment after the door shut behind him. Jeez, even the carpet out *here* was better than his brand new one at home.

Chapter 11

Owen folded up the newspaper and laid it down as Sarah walked out of his bedroom and into the living room. She had changed into a simple jade green running suit that was nearly the same color as her eyes. Wordlessly, she settled again on the edge of the sofa and focused on the screen of her laptop. The dark circles under her eyes spoke of her weariness, but determination showed in her face.

"Do you want something to eat?"

She shook her head.

"Something has been bothering me."

"Only one thing?" she replied wryly, without looking up.

"How did those people—the guys who stopped you on the way back from the airport—know that you'd be there that particular night and at that particular time?"

"I don't know."

Owen came to his feet and stretched. "Did you have a roundtrip ticket?"

"I did, initially." She looked up. "But I had to cancel my return flight after the first week. In fact, I came back on standby yesterday."

Owen shoved his hands in his pockets. "Even if we figure they somehow had access to the flight information, or passenger manifests, or customs info, it still doesn't add up. How about the guy who was waiting for you at the Van Horn mansion? I doubt he was camping there for the last two weeks, thinking that you'd be coming back sooner or later." Owen walked into the kitchen and looked out across the counter at her. "After all, why would he wait there and not at your condo?"

"My place must be secured by the police."

"That's true, but you didn't know that. You didn't know you were dead. So under normal circumstances, you would have gone there first. Did you call anyone from the airport?"

Her face colored, and she shot a quick glance at him before looking away.

"Are you trying to protect someone, Sarah?"

When she didn't answer, he walked back into the living room and stood before her, staring down. After a long moment, her face lifted.

"What's going on? Do you know who's behind all this? Are you just using me to kill time?"

"No!" She shook her head. "No! Trust me when I say I'm stunned by everything that's happening."

"Who did you call from the airport?"

"I—I tried my house first. But there was no answer. Then I tried the Judge's number, but I didn't leave a message."

"What time was that?"

"I was at JFK. The flights into Providence were delayed because of the storm. It was about four in the afternoon, I think."

"Anyone else?"

She paused a long moment before answering. "I called Hal. Hal Van Horn."

Owen felt the muscles in his jaw tighten. All the innuendo in the papers flashed back at him.

"But he wasn't home either. So I left a message."

"Then he's the one."

Sarah rose quickly to her feet. "It's not what you think. He probably hasn't even gotten my message yet. Hal's notorious for never checking his answering machine." She started pacing the room, her hands running up and down her arms. "Hal has no connection with those cops. He has nothing to gain by any of this, and I know he would never hurt me."

Owen glared at her, perplexed by the rawness of his own feelings. He'd known Sarah Rand for less than a day, but still it angered him to hear her defending this other man, a man who was very much a part of her past. Hell, a part of her present!

"I can drop you off at his place this morning, if you want. The two of you can continue on with whatever it is you're trying to do here."

"No!" She abruptly ceased her pacing. A hand darted out and rested on his arm. "Please don't!"

Flustered, she dropped her arm and her chin sank onto her chest for a long moment. Owen stared at her and waited.

"A number of people have access to Hal's answering machine. His secretary...his housekeeper...I even heard one of his friends once kidding Hal that practically everyone in town knew that machine's code. So you see, even though it's true my message might have clued somebody in about my return, it doesn't mean it was Hal. And it doesn't mean he is personally responsible for these attacks."

"Thank you, counsel for the defense." Owen cringed at his own sarcastic tone. "Listen, if you love him, why don't you want to be with him right now?"

"I don't love Hal," Sarah protested. "I know I'm asking a lot of you. Without knowing me at all, you've already given me much more help than I could reasonably expect. And I understand your curiosity about...well, my personal life."

Owen felt that pull again. Curiosity? Christ, the sexual pull between them was getting very tough to ignore. It was like that proverbial eight-hundred-pound gorilla sitting in the middle of the room. She looked up. His fingers itched to touch her face. His mouth was hungry to taste those lips again. But he turned toward the kitchen instead, giving himself some room.

"Sorry," he said over his shoulder. "You've got to remember my life has been an open book for years. In fact, I have to call the tabloids myself to find out where I'm going next week and who I'll be seeing."

He turned in time to see her smile.

"Well, being dead has put a bit of a cramp in my style. Not being alive makes it a little difficult to correct what the papers have been printing about *my* personal life."

"Does this mean you're planning to set the record straight?" He reached inside the fridge and took out the fixings for a sandwich.

She walked over and leaned over the counter, facing him. "I guess I owe you that. Would you like to hear the ten-cent version of the Van Horn-Arnold-Rand connection?"

"Ten cents sounds pretty brief."

"I'll sell you the million-dollar version when I know how it turns out."

"Good deal." He was tired of coffee, so he put the water on for tea.

"I'll skip the sob story of my childhood. Let's see. Well, Hal Van Horn and I met a little over four years ago through some college friends. I was already working as an attorney in Boston. We hit it off pretty quick, and in no time at all he was proposing marriage." She played with the corners of an envelope on the counter. "Meeting Hal's family and friends in Newport was an eye-opener for me. Here I was, a half-Irish Catholic girl from South Boston with enough college loans to choke a horse. And there he was, the sole heir to the Van Horn fortune, old money. You know the rest, rich boy, poor girl. Just one problem. I had never been looking for Prince Charming. I'd been very happy to go through college and then law school my way. I liked Hal—to be honest, I was confused enough to think I even loved him for a while—but not enough, I guess, to feel comfortable with such an enormous social jump."

"But you still gave up your job and moved to Newport."

"Yes, I did." She nodded. "I got along pretty well with both Hal's mother and her husband. And about the same time that I was feeling myself getting cold feet about marriage, Judge Arnold told me about his plans of retiring from the bench so that he could spend more time with Avery. It was then that he asked me if I'd be interested in forming an association with him in a law office in Newport."

She reached for the mug of tea Owen placed before her.

"I think they knew I was getting anxious and wanted me to be closer. They liked me—that was clear—and it was a great professional opportunity for me. So I made the move." The tea bag dipped again and again. "Despite what the Judge and Avery had hoped, my living and working in Newport further distanced me from Hal. Within six months, we called off the engagement. We were two different people, from different worlds, with different interests and views on almost everything in life."

Sarah placed the teabag on the little saucer on the table. In the silence, Owen could hear the sound of the tide rolling into the inlet that bordered the estate grounds. He said nothing, waiting.

"Interestingly enough, my split with Hal had no effect on my connection with the Arnolds. In fact, over the years, Avery and I became fond friends. And I really came to value Judge Arnold. I witnessed firsthand the love and devotion he had for his wife. That only added to the respect I already had for the man as a lawyer. The Judge became a mentor to me."

A dozen questions popped into Owen's head, but he only asked one. "How did Hal deal with all of this, after the break-up?"

"Very well. We stayed friends. And despite what the papers claim, we kept it platonic. Yes, we attended social and family events together, but the spark between us was dead. It wasn't passion that each of us sought in our relationship, but companionship...maybe even solace." She took a sip of her tea. "I believe the long period of Avery's suffering, and then her death, taught Hal a few things. I saw him changing. He became more emotionally...I don't know...connected, I guess. Anyway, it made our friendship stronger. I found myself more willing to talk to him. That was why he was the one that I tried to call from the airport. I was coming back from the funeral of my last surviving parent. Hal had lost his mother this summer. I knew he'd understand what I was feeling."

When she looked up at him, Owen saw the tears glistening in her eyes. He too knew how it felt to lose your only parent—to grow up alone—but he didn't think his own twisted past made him much of an expert in compassion.

"So, there. You have it all." She took a long sip of the tea. "Hal has suffered a lot this summer, and I don't know that he'd quite be ready to have me come back from the dead and land on his doorstep. On the other hand, you're doing a great job of protecting me and driving me around and feeding me." She eyed the counter. "By the way, is it too late to change my mind about the food?"

"Well, speaking as a mature and emotionally connected guy...that depends on how much you eat."

"Sorry to wake you up, Dan, but this is really important."

"Hmm."

The phone propped against one ear, Archer rubbed his hands over his face and squinted at his watch. 4:32. The late afternoon sun was coming through a crack where the draperies came together.

"Yeah. Okay, what's going on, Bob?"

"I just got the results of the dusting we did last night at the Judge's place."

Dan Archer pushed the sheet off and sat up groggily in the bed. "What have you got?"

"That scumbag Frankie was planning on going in and out clean. There is nothing on him. But we did pick up something else— somebody else's fingerprints—and you won't believe who." McHugh's voice was high-pitched, very excited. "Sarah Rand."

There was a long pause.

"Are you still there, Dan?"

"Aha. I'm here."

"Did you hear me all right? It was her, I'm telling ya. We have fresh prints, not two-week-old prints. New ones. They're everywhere. By the door, on the security box, her desk, the telephone. She was there last night. Can you believe it?"

"How many people know about it?"

"You, me, and the genius downstairs who thought to cross-check the prints before filing them. I could have kissed the son of a bitch."

"Talk to him. I want to keep a lid on this, Bob."

"What do you mean, keep a lid on it? If she's alive, then that means somebody else is a corpse right now."

"Just shut up, Bob. For now." Archer was already reaching for his clothes. "Not a word to anyone. I'll be there in half an hour."

He slammed the phone down and reached for a clean shirt.

Well, of course she was alive. Now, if he could just keep it quiet until he had a chance to take care of things.

All day, Owen had been conscientious to the max about conducting business. Just making it look like a usual day. He'd answered his phone calls from the West Coast. He'd held the conference call to New York that had been arranged two days ago. And he'd even gone to work out in the exercise room a little while ago. So unless someone broke into his apartment and discovered Sarah there, there was no way anyone could think anything was amiss in the life of Owen Dean.

Still, he felt like he was blundering around on an unfamiliar set. Archer's visit this morning had made him neurotic. Hell, he thought. He just had to be careful. It was Archer's job to be suspicious.

Owen went to the front lobby to get his mail and returned just in time to see Sarah toss a legal pad on the coffee table and rise stiffly to her feet. She had cast aside the top of the jumpsuit and was wearing a short sleeve shirt over the pants. As he watched her stretch, his eyes were momentarily drawn to the mold of the shirt to her body.

She looked too good to him, and this concerned him even more than Archer's interest. She turned and caught his eyes on her and smiled. He looked quickly at the brass clock on his desk. Five o'clock.

"Any progress?"

She nodded and picked up the yellow pad. "I've copied and downloaded all of Judge Arnold's appointments and calendar notes for the month of June and July."

Owen dropped the keys on the counter. "How does that help you?"

"If there is one flaw that Judge Arnold has, it's that he's too meticulous about documenting everything in his files. Kind of a control freak in some ways. He keeps all types of records. From the content of phone calls to the file record numbers of the follow-up letters, to the names of people he's met on a certain day and when, both in and out of court, and even whether there is a follow-up needed. It's like a religion to him. Linda, our office manager, told me once she thinks he's afraid of getting senile. But it isn't that. He's always been that way. The Judge just loves to be in control. And he loves the electronics. He is very much into keeping up with technology."

"I am surprised these files weren't already seized by the police as part of the investigation." He took all of the mail to his desk. "I would have thought they'd be the first thing the cops secured."

"I imagine they must have taken his computer, but the way our office computers are networked, every night all the files are backed up." She gave him a knowing nod. "So I just tapped into the network."

"You are a jack of all trades, aren't you?"

She ran her fingers through her short crop of hair. "I try to be."

"What did you find out?"

She leaned her hip on the side of the desk. Owen tried to focus on the paper in her hand.

"I think I am getting close. Look at these." She placed the pad on the desk so he could see. "As I was expecting, he has been meticulous about everything. I've categorized the information. Personal contacts, business contacts, legal ones, old and new cases. Of course, there are overlaps, but I just came across something that is a lot more important than all of these."

He could hear the excitement sparking her voice.

"Look at this."

He stared at where she was pointing. "July 10 through the 14?"

"There is nothing here that makes sense. All of a sudden, it seems that Judge Arnold decided to create a special code for his notes and appointments."

"Was he away during those days?"

"Nope. And it's not as if he left the days blank. See, it's just very different. No names, no phone numbers, just letters that make no sense. It looks as if he was afraid of someone knowing who these people were that he was in contact with."

"Do you remember anything about that week?"

"Absolutely. That was start of it all," she replied. "And interestingly enough, after the 14, he starts recording information again, but it's not the same. After that date, he is very cautious in his entries, as if he knows or thinks he is being watched."

The ringing of the phone on Owen's desk drew both of their eyes. For a moment he considered letting his answering machine take care of it, but the same impulse that had driven him all day to function with an air of seeming normalcy made him reach for it.

"Owen Dean here."

"Mr. Dean. Hello. This is Evelyn de Young." The woman's voice was loud and breathless. "I'm so glad you answered. We were getting so concerned when you hadn't shown up here yet. The TV crews are here. Most of the guests have already arrived, and all of us are eager, of course, for the arrival of our guest of honor."

Owen closed his eyes and cursed silently.

"Shall I send my driver, Mr. Dean? I know you aren't scheduled to make your speech until six o'clock, but the cocktail party is in full swing. You never know what kind of traffic jam you might run into. Of course, we have valets to park your car."

"I'm leaving in about fifteen minutes, Mrs. De Young. And no, you don't have to send your driver. I'll be there. Thanks for calling." Owen hung up the phone and saw the smile tugging on Sarah's lips. "I guess you heard everything."

She nodded. "I had a ticket to that event myself."

"Do you want to go, anyway? You could go as my date."

The prettiest of blushes crept into her cheeks. "I think I'll have to take a rain-check on that."

He rose to his feet. "I have to give a twenty-minute talk and then schmooze for a few minutes for the cameras. I'll only be gone an hour at the most."

She stood up, as well. "I'll be here."

He took a step toward his bedroom and then turned around again. "You aren't going to turn yourself in to the police while I'm gone, are you?"

She shook her head and tried to sound breezy. "Not until you get back."

A sudden feeling of anxiety gripped him. Owen found himself genuinely worrying about her. She was putting up a great show of valor, but after all she'd been through, he guessed she must be just about ready to crumble beneath it all.

"One hour." His hand reached for her fingers. They were icy. He could feel the slight tremble she was trying so desperately to hide. "Don't go anywhere."

Chapter 12

Hal Van Horn looked up from the paperwork on his desk as a willowy young woman tapped softly on his office door. "I was getting ready to leave for the day. Was there anything else?"

"Any more news of Gwen?"

"She called about a half hour ago from the hospital. You were on the phone, so I just took the info."

"How is her son doing?"

"He is out of surgery. I guess they had to insert a pin in his leg because of the break. Gwen said he might end up with a body cast from the chest down before he is done." She walked inside the office and picked up Hal's empty cup from his desk. "I can stay late if you want me to. I—"

"Did you send a basket to the hospital?"

"I sure did. Balloons and teddy bears and the whole nine yards." She leaned her hip against the desk. "Seriously, Hal. I have nothing to do tonight...so staying late would be no trouble at all."

The suggestion was unmistakable, but Hal was not interested. "I'll be okay. Plan on coming in early tomorrow, in case Gwen's late getting in. I'll see you then."

Hal paid no attention to the woman's pouty frown as she huffed out of his office. There were still piles of work left ahead of him before this day was done. He pushed aside the phone messages from the previous days and reached for the stacks of contracts requiring his signature. After five minutes of perusing paperwork, he heard the front door of the outer office open and shut. His clerk-turned-assistant-for-the-day had let herself out.

Twenty minutes later, when Hal saw his direct-line light up on the phone, he picked it up on the first ring.

"Hal Van Horn."

There was a long pause on the other end. "Just remember...you are too young to have a heart attack on me, Hal. This is Sarah."

"*Sarah!*" The pen slid through his fingers and dropped on the papers.

"In the flesh…well, sort of. Listen, I don't feel very comfortable talking because I think someone might be tapping your lines at home…or at least has been listening to your messages or something. They might be doing the same thing here, and I don't want this call traced."

"You are alive, Sarah! My God! Are you okay? Where are you?"

"Could you meet me somewhere, Hal? I have something I want you to take a look at. It has to do with Avery's safe-deposit box. I need your help."

"Where?"

There was another pause. "Do you remember where we had lunch three Saturdays ago? The last time we met."

"Yeah, at…"

"Don't say it. Just go there. And please make sure you're not followed. Someone…some people are after me, trying to kill me, so please be careful." There was another long pause. "It'll take me at least an hour to get there. I'll see you in front."

"I'll be there, Sarah. God, it's good to hear your voice!"

Hal stared blankly at the phone for a moment after hanging up. Suddenly, a noise in the outer office drew his attention. Picking up his keys, he walked through his partially open door and glanced around the spacious room. Two empty cubicles. Gwen's organized desk. The doors to the other three offices were tightly shut. The computer's quiet hum was the only noise that he could hear now. He turned to leave and saw the front door to the office was slightly ajar.

Keeping his eye on the door, Hal reached for the phone on Gwen's desk and dialed a number he was getting to know by heart.

Sarah frowned with disapproval at her reflection in the mirror. She removed her favorite earrings. Hurrying, she changed into a pair of well-worn jeans that were buried deep in her suitcase. Pulling on a pair of flats, she rummaged through Owen's closet until she found an oversize navy blue sweatshirt and a baseball cap of the same color.

Sarah needed no eyes in the back of her head to know she was being closely watched by the two. So she scuffed her sneakers on the walkway and snapped her gum until the cab pulled up in front of her.

"Bellevue. The Tennis Hall of Fame."

Sarah didn't release the breath she was holding until the cabbie had rounded the drive and was heading back out onto Ocean Drive.

And that, she thought, was probably the easiest part of what lay ahead of her.

Owen knew he may have set a new land-speed record for walking in, giving a speech, and walking out of a fundraiser. An annual event for Save the Bay, the affair was well publicized and very well attended. He knew the media had not been too happy with the minute and a half he gave them for questions. The socialites had obviously felt snubbed, too, because he had not come sooner or stayed longer. The average ticket holders in the crowd were clearly pleased when he did stop to talk for a few moments to those in the back rows.

All in all, the organizers, led by Mrs. de Young, appeared pleased, for in addition to the fact that Owen Dean had previously arranged for his speaker fee to be donated back to the organization, he had also written a very large check to the foundation before departing.

He'd even had the valet keep the car running by the front door.

Now the brilliantly golden rays of the sun were slowly losing their battle against the lengthening shadows of the late summer evening. It had been a very long time since Owen had had anyone but himself to worry about. Nearly thirty years, he recalled, speeding his car along Ocean Drive. He did worry about Andrew, he corrected himself. But that was different, for there wasn't a thing that he could do for the man other than just being here.

His own feelings toward Sarah were confusing the hell out of him. He'd never been one to bring home an injured animal. Hell, for most of his childhood, he'd been little more than a wounded animal himself.

Putting on his clothes, she studied her reflection
shoes had to go. She changed into her sneakers and
peak of the cap lower on her face. Searching in her brie
found a package of gum left over from her flight and stu
it into her mouth. No makeup, no jewelry, she struck an
in the mirror. She looked sixteen at the most.

Sarah dialed the number for Newport Cab Company a1
hurriedly pushed everything back into her suitcase. It took
few minutes to restore some semblance of order to Owen'
room. Before leaving the apartment, she wrote him a long
explaining where she was going and what she was about to do
left it on the counter.

She couldn't risk going out through the terrace. Without a l
she couldn't lock the glass door. Going out the front door throu
the building's entry foyer offered the only route of escape. Sara
tucked the list she was going to show Hal into the pocket of he
jeans.

As she opened the door and peered down the hallway, all kinds
of images flashed through her mind. Neighbors seeing someone
they didn't know leaving Owen's apartment, someone underage.
Great. Paparazzi hiding in the bushes outside, ready to take pictures of Owen Dean's new Lolita. Brilliant. Oh well, there was no
help for it.

Sarah moved briskly down the hallway. It wasn't until she was
passing through the great hall of the building that she saw anyone.

The couple was walking through the entry foyer, and in a moment of panic, Sarah paused by the door. The woman pursed her
lips suspiciously as they came face-to-face with her.

"Can we help you?"

Sarah dropped her chin, refusing to offer a better view of her
face. "No. My dad already called for a cab." She tried to look
around the man's shoulder while mumbling her answer.

"Your dad?" the woman repeated with some interest. "And in
which unit does he live?"

Catching sight of the taxi coming down the drive was all Sarah
needed. "Thanks for your help." She slipped by the two and was
out the door in an instant.

Putting on his clothes, she studied her reflection again. The shoes had to go. She changed into her sneakers and pulled the peak of the cap lower on her face. Searching in her briefcase, she found a package of gum left over from her flight and stuffed all of it into her mouth. No makeup, no jewelry, she struck an attitude in the mirror. She looked sixteen at the most.

Sarah dialed the number for Newport Cab Company and then hurriedly pushed everything back into her suitcase. It took only a few minutes to restore some semblance of order to Owen's bedroom. Before leaving the apartment, she wrote him a long note, explaining where she was going and what she was about to do. She left it on the counter.

She couldn't risk going out through the terrace. Without a key, she couldn't lock the glass door. Going out the front door through the building's entry foyer offered the only route of escape. Sarah tucked the list she was going to show Hal into the pocket of her jeans.

As she opened the door and peered down the hallway, all kinds of images flashed through her mind. Neighbors seeing someone they didn't know leaving Owen's apartment, someone underage. Great. Paparazzi hiding in the bushes outside, ready to take pictures of Owen Dean's new Lolita. Brilliant. Oh well, there was no help for it.

Sarah moved briskly down the hallway. It wasn't until she was passing through the great hall of the building that she saw anyone.

The couple was walking through the entry foyer, and in a moment of panic, Sarah paused by the door. The woman pursed her lips suspiciously as they came face-to-face with her.

"Can we help you?"

Sarah dropped her chin, refusing to offer a better view of her face. "No. My dad already called for a cab." She tried to look around the man's shoulder while mumbling her answer.

"Your dad?" the woman repeated with some interest. "And in which unit does he live?"

Catching sight of the taxi coming down the drive was all Sarah needed. "Thanks for your help." She slipped by the two and was out the door in an instant.

Sarah needed no eyes in the back of her head to know she was being closely watched by the two. So she scuffed her sneakers on the walkway and snapped her gum until the cab pulled up in front of her.

"Bellevue. The Tennis Hall of Fame."

Sarah didn't release the breath she was holding until the cabbie had rounded the drive and was heading back out onto Ocean Drive.

And that, she thought, was probably the easiest part of what lay ahead of her.

Owen knew he may have set a new land-speed record for walking in, giving a speech, and walking out of a fundraiser. An annual event for Save the Bay, the affair was well publicized and very well attended. He knew the media had not been too happy with the minute and a half he gave them for questions. The socialites had obviously felt snubbed, too, because he had not come sooner or stayed longer. The average ticket holders in the crowd were clearly pleased when he did stop to talk for a few moments to those in the back rows.

All in all, the organizers, led by Mrs. de Young, appeared pleased, for in addition to the fact that Owen Dean had previously arranged for his speaker fee to be donated back to the organization, he had also written a very large check to the foundation before departing.

He'd even had the valet keep the car running by the front door.

Now the brilliantly golden rays of the sun were slowly losing their battle against the lengthening shadows of the late summer evening. It had been a very long time since Owen had had anyone but himself to worry about. Nearly thirty years, he recalled, speeding his car along Ocean Drive. He did worry about Andrew, he corrected himself. But that was different, for there wasn't a thing that he could do for the man other than just being here.

His own feelings toward Sarah were confusing the hell out of him. He'd never been one to bring home an injured animal. Hell, for most of his childhood, he'd been little more than a wounded animal himself.

It had been difficult focusing on his speech. Even tougher talking to people before and after the brief talk. His thoughts constantly drifted back to that woman in his apartment. Sarah. Of course he was worried about her. Passing Brenton Point, he cursed himself for not having had a better security system installed in his apartment. He'd reached for his cell phone twice, but then had decided against calling her. She wouldn't answer his phone anyway.

Owen saw the taxi pulling out of the long driveway as he approached the chateau. The rays of the descending sun reflected off the windows of the cab, blocking his view of the passenger in the back. But for an insane moment, he thought that Sarah might be in the cab.

No, she wouldn't just go like that, he told himself. It was not yet the end of the day. And one day was what she'd asked for.

As the taxi sped off toward Bellevue, Owen fought down his anxiety, turned down the drive, and pressed the gas pedal to the floor. She said she wouldn't go anywhere until he got back. She would be there. Waiting.

Porsches, Mercedes, Lincolns, and Hondas sat at every intersection along the clogged thoroughfare that had been named Bellevue in a far more genteel era. Drivers waited with varying degrees of patience for halter-topped and polo-shirted pedestrians to crisscross between their standing vehicles. Traffic, as it always was at this time of the evening, was slow, but moving.

On the wide sidewalk in front of the restaurant, middle-aged preppies in green shirts and red-checked pants maneuvered around tattooed bikers in leather vests and black, sleeveless T-shirts. Teenage boys with hair the color of nothing found in nature skateboarded in figure eights around throngs of women wearing flowing flowered dresses and Italian shoes. Small groups of well-dressed diners, all waiting for tables inside, stood chatting and drinking, casually vigilant of the skateboarders and one another. The evening held all the promise of a great party night. A night no different than any other summer evening in the bustling tourist town of Newport.

"Stand by. Yes, I see him." The man spoke into his cell phone from a gray sedan parked in the lot across the street.

"What about her?"

"Not yet." He paused. The sounds of people and cars filled the interval. "He's crossing the street toward the restaurant. He is glancing at his watch. Looking up and down the street again. There are too many fucking people around."

"Focus! We cannot afford to screw up this assignment."

"You need to get here *now*."

"Just stand by. And don't let him out of your sight. I'll get there as soon as Lard Ass heads your way." He snorted as Frankie O'Neal stopped to light a fresh cigarette from the butt of his last one.

"Do we really need him to clean up after us again?"

"The boss wants it, so shut up and focus on your end of the assignment." Another pause. "This time, Lard Ass won't just clean up. This time, he takes the fall. Stand by. We're moving…"

Instead of getting out of the cab where she had originally planned, Sarah asked the driver to go past the intersection and turn into a narrow side street. Paying him, she stepped out and turned toward Bellevue.

The same streets that she had not so long ago considered absolutely safe, now struck her as threatening. Every tourist and summer resident looked strange, suspect, dangerous. She pulled the peak of the cap lower over her eyes and watched a group of teenagers go past her in the same direction that she was headed. Mimicking the bored attitude showing on their faces, she tucked her hands in the front pockets of her jeans and fell in behind the last of them.

At the light by the busy intersection of Memorial Boulevard and Bellevue, everyone stopped to cross. As she waited with the rest for the light, Sarah found herself standing beside a short, heavyset man with the butt of cigarette hanging out of his mouth. He was frowning and peering straight ahead between two people, at the milling groups on the opposite corner. There was something familiar about him—the clothes, his build, his hair. She held back a little, keeping him in front of her as he moved with the others across the street. It took only an instant for her stomach to twist into a painful knot of recognition.

She spotted Hal standing in front of the restaurant and glancing at his watch. The heavyset man went right by him without even giving him a glance, and stopped to look into the display window of the antique store just beyond the restaurant. She hesitated at the corner and looked around. Across the street, she spotted a police car in the large parking lot, facing the restaurant, a single officer inside talking on a phone.

They were everywhere. Panic washed through Sarah, cold and deadening. She buried her hand deeper into her pocket and clasped the piece of paper. She practically brushed against Hal, moving by him, but he never saw or recognized her.

The hostess standing in the open doorway of the restaurant looked curiously at Sarah as she approached.

"May I borrow your pen for a moment?"

"Well…sure."

Sarah took the paper out of her pocket and scribbled a note to Hal on the back. Returning the pen, she turned again to the street and found Hal standing by the curb.

She folded the paper and walked directly to him.

The red light created a mini traffic jam at the intersection, and this suited Owen just fine. He scanned the sidewalk for some sign of her.

"Christ," he muttered. "A needle in a goddam haystack."

He was mad as hell at himself. He was mad as hell at her. But what pissed him off the most was that he didn't know why in hell he was coming after her, anyway. He'd asked her to wait for him, but she'd decided to come and meet her boyfriend alone. For chrissakes, he'd offered to bring her to the son of a bitch. He'd never been a third party in any relationship, by God, and he wasn't going to start now.

In spite of that, a nagging feeling had forced him to come after her. He was worried about her, goddammit.

He recognized Hal Van Horn from the pictures he'd seen in the papers.

"Well, what do you know." he muttered under his breath, immediately irritated at the man's polished looks. Before he had any time to dwell on his animosity toward Van Horn, Owen spotted Sarah wearing his baseball cap and sweatshirt, and moving at a pretty good clip toward the guy.

He lowered the passenger window of his Range Rover as the light turned green up ahead.

Sarah bumped against the man, and Owen saw her drop a piece of folded paper on the ground. Obviously annoyed at being jostled, Van Horn nonetheless looked past her, not giving her a second glance and ignoring her muttered apology.

The fact that he hadn't recognized his own girlfriend gave Owen a twisted moment of satisfaction as he glanced ahead. In spite of the light change, the traffic still was not moving. He looked back in time to see Hal turn and walk closer to the curb.

"Hey, man," Sarah called after him. "You dropped this."

Owen saw Hal turn sharply in her direction at the same time as he saw the knife blade flash in the hand of a man who suddenly appeared between them.

He didn't know how he was able to crawl across the seat, but somehow he managed, shouldering open the passenger door.

"*Sarah!*"

It was as if everything were happening in slow motion. Like a dream in which you see a terrible event occurring but cannot move quickly enough to stop it.

Owen's shout yanked Sarah's head around as the man snatched the paper from her hand and thrust the knife toward her.

The cigarette fell from Frankie's lips, but he didn't notice it. His eyes were glued to the man wearing the cheap shades who slid the knife out smoothly and pocketed the blade as if nothing had happened. It was a fucking work of art.

Of course, when Van Horn's body hit the ground, the screaming started.

Frankie stepped forward and the man in the shades gave him a long look before moving brusquely past him and heading down the street.

Now, that's the way to do a job, Frankie thought, stepping closer to the tight circle of people forming around the victim. He was sure that nobody on that entire street could identify who did it. Nobody, of course, except him and maybe Sarah Rand.

He glanced over his shoulder and, as a cop came running from the lot across the street, Frankie saw the Range Rover disappear around the corner at the intersection.

"Fuck it," he muttered, reaching for a cigarette and looking at the fish on the sidewalk. In about a minute flat, the sirens were coming from every direction, so Frankie just edged away from the crowd.

Frankie O'Neal knew everyone in this town who had any connection with the business. And he sure as hell recognized the shark doing this job, in spite of his cheap shades.

One thing he didn't know was that making hits was the guy's new line of work.

Shit. This bozo was cutting into his business. Literally.

Chapter 13

Working his way through the narrow residential streets behind the Tennis Hall of Fame and then past the college, Owen had a hard time keeping his eye on the road. Although he was certain the blade of the knife hadn't touched Sarah, it was the psychological blow that seemed to have left its mark. Three attacks on her life in less than twenty-four hours gave her ample cause for distress. And then, add to that the fact that she'd just witnessed someone she deeply cared for step into the path of a knife obviously intended for her. Not a good day.

He didn't know how badly Hal Van Horn had been hurt, but Owen was not about to hang around to find out. His main concern after the attack had been Sarah, and getting her out of there. She'd felt like a rag doll in his arms when he'd grabbed her and pulled her into the car. And after curling over and burying her face between her knees, she hadn't seemed to improve much since. Improve? Christ, she hadn't moved.

Owen ran a yellow light that took him back onto Bellevue about eight blocks south of the scene of the attack. He could hear sirens in the distance and looked out the back window. No one was following them. He reminded himself that there was no reason why anyone should. The whole thing had happened too fast. There had been too many people on the street. All of them jumping away from what looked like a simple push and shove. And Owen and Sarah had been out of there just as the screaming really got started.

Her baseball cap had fallen to the floor, and Owen laid a consoling hand on Sarah's back. She was shivering violently.

"Sarah?"

He couldn't bring himself to comfort her about Van Horn's condition. Another string of lies wasn't what she needed right now. He continued to caress her back.

"We're almost home." He took the sharp right that led from

Bellevue to Ocean Drive. The wail of the sirens was becoming fainter. The streaks of clouds in the sky were slashed and blood-stained as the giant sun finally nose-dived beyond Point Judith.

At a sharp bend in the road, her head slid off her knees, and Owen touched her forehead. Her skin was cold and clammy. Frowning, he tried to remember the symptoms of someone in shock. He touched her neck and felt the racing pulse.

He knew the smarter move would be to take her to an emergency room. Better yet, he should drive them right out of town and head for Boston. He could call his lawyer in New York from there.

Instead, he turned down the drive to the chateau and pulled into his parking spot. There was no one outside, not that it really mattered at this point. He went around the car and opened her door. She didn't move.

"Sarah?" He touched her hair, pulling her toward him. "Let's go inside."

She continued to tremble. Owen lifted her, studying the pale face and the tightly closed eyes.

"Come on, hon."

As he pulled her out of the car and onto her feet, she clutched at the collar of his jacket. Owen felt her legs go rubbery beneath her and thought for a second that she might faint. Sweeping her up in his arms, he crossed the terrace to his apartment. Once inside, she stirred and pushed at him. He put her down, and she made her way unsteadily, but under her own steam, toward the bathroom.

Owen locked the door and shut the curtains and then strode to the closed door of the bathroom.

The retching sound from the other side was stunningly difficult to listen to.

Senator Rutherford left his small circle of guests and took the call by the window on the far side of the room.

"What can I do for you, Chief?"

"My apologies for calling you so late, sir, but I knew you'd want to be informed immediately."

"No apologies needed, Dave. What's the problem?"

"Well, sir..." The Newport police chief paused. "There's been an incident in town, and I'm figuring the press will probably be at your doorstep as soon as the news gets out."

"I appreciate the forewarning." Gordon Rutherford turned his back on the half-dozen people in the room and lowered his voice. "What's happened?"

"There was a stabbing on Bellevue this evening, sir. The victim was rushed to Newport Hospital, where he was pronounced dead on arrival." The phone went silent for a lengthy pause. "The victim has been identified as Henry Van Horn."

The senator's knuckles went white on the handset, his shoulders becoming rigid. His voice had a choking quality to it when he spoke again.

"Has...has the Judge been notified?"

"Yes, sir," Calvin assured him. "In fact, even though you were the next on my list, Judge Arnold himself suggested that we notify you immediately. In the absence of any next of kin available, he said he believed you could be counted on to make any arrangements that were necessary."

"Of course...of course. Hal was like a son to me." Gordon leaned a hand against the table to support his weary frame. "Do you have the killer in custody?"

"No, sir. But we have an extensive list of eye witnesses. Our detectives have already started the interviewing process."

"Who is handling the case?"

"Dan Archer, sir. But I'll be personally overseeing everything."

"That's fine. Archer's a good man," Rutherford replied solemnly. "Keep me posted on everything, David."

When Gordon Rutherford finally returned to his guests, everyone saw the grief that was etched on the senator's face.

"I've just received word from the chief of police in Newport." He took a handkerchief out of his pocket. "It's impossible to believe...but Hal Van Horn is dead."

She had blood on her hands. Hal's body lay at her feet. She stumbled toward the sink and turned on the faucet, but a brownish liquid sprayed out, spattering her before turning to a steady stream of blood. She tried to turn the knobs, but they turned to two stumps of metal in her hands. A loud hammering was coming from the door. Sirens were screeching in her head. She ran to the door. The doorknob came off in her hand. As she stumbled backward, the door crashed open. The man standing there, she knew him. It was Owen, standing on the other side of the threshold, staring at her hand. Sarah looked down and saw the doorknob was now a bloody knife.

Sarah sat up with a start. The room was dark. She was alone in a bed. For an insane moment, she didn't know the difference between the nightmare world and the physical one. The two had become interwoven with terrifying realness.

A sudden chill raised the flesh on her skin as the chain of events in front of the restaurant flashed through her mind. She remembered Hal's annoyance as the other man grabbed the paper out of Sarah's hand. She saw the look of death gripping Hal's face before Owen dragged her away.

Owen. He'd come for her.

Through the partially open bedroom door, Sarah saw the glow of a television set flicker in the darkness of the next room. She pushed the covers aside and placed her bare feet on the floor.

Sarah remembered heaving so hard that she'd thought her insides were coming apart. She also remembered Owen being in that bathroom with her—wiping her face with a wet towel, giving her something to rinse her mouth with. Later, when she couldn't stop her shivering, she'd found herself in a hot shower. That was the last thing she remembered.

She stood up. Her body felt weak, her legs wobbly. She was wearing one of her own sweat suits, but the thick cotton was no help at all in easing the chill that washed with shivering regularity through her body.

As Sarah entered the living room, her gaze was drawn to the television screen. A news banner across the top framed a video clip of Senator Rutherford waving the cameras away as he entered Newport Hospital. Beneath it, the closed-caption flashed words at her.

The face of a local news anchorwoman filled the screen. The

volume of the set was too low for Sarah to hear anything. She walked closer and tried to focus on the words.

Van Horn's stabbing death is the second homicide in a month to rock the city by the sea. Newport city officials...

A thick sheen of tears blurred Sarah's vision. The words seem to waver and run off the screen. She realized her teeth were chattering and she couldn't control it. Her shivering body seemed to belong to someone else.

"You should have stayed in bed."

Owen's soft whisper in her ear and the feel of his arms pulling her into the warmth of his embrace was a blessing. She buried her face against his chest and tried to stop the choking tears. She couldn't.

"Come here."

He sat down on the sofa and pulled her onto his lap. She felt a blanket being tucked around them, trapping for her the heat of his body.

"I shouldn't have called him. I killed him. I...so many people are dead...because of me...it should have been me."

"Don't say that." He rubbed her back. He held her so tightly against him that they were practically molded as one. "Listen to me. These are ruthless people. Killers. You are not responsible for their actions."

"I have to go to the police. I have to go to them before someone else gets hurt."

"Did you see the man who did it? Could you identify him?"

"No. I...I only saw the knife coming. And then Hal was in the way. He stepped between us." Her tears were soaking into his shirt. "I have to go to them tonight. You could be next."

"You are not doing anything tonight." He brushed his chin against her hair. "You are staying right here until we think this thing through."

Sarah drew her knees up to her chest. He tucked the blanket around her feet, but neither the tears nor the shakes racking her body would stop.

Owen gathered her even closer and pressed her wet face against his bare neck. She was feeling completely helpless—he knew that—but so was he in terms of knowing how to help her. But some strange bond was forming and he felt it. Somehow, they had connected with each other. She needed him and, in some inexplicable way, he needed her, too.

He leaned over for the remote and turned off the television. They were immersed in the darkness of the room. Only a sliver of moonlight cut across the carpeted floor.

After his mother's death, Owen had recoiled from personal attachments. Detested them. Spurned them. Even after so many years, even after so much water over the dam, he'd continued to live the same way. Nothing was permanent. Nothing lasted. He would not allow himself any involvement that could lead to any depth in a relationship. Hell, there was no need. The women in his life had always come in easy and walked out the same way. He was safe. He was protected. Last in, first out.

So what was going on here?

He didn't want to even think about it right now. Later, maybe. Not now.

They stayed like that for a long time. No words passed between them. Only the comfort of a touch, the warmth of two bodies, the soft darkness of the room.

The ragged sound of her breathing gradually eased, and then she simply stopped shivering.

Sometime later, she pushed away from him and sat up. "It *must* have something to do with the safe-deposit box. There *must* be something in there, something they want."

Owen held on to the blanket and stared at her face in the shadow. Her eyes were puffy from the crying, but he could see a major step had been taken.

"What safe-deposit box?"

"Avery's." She stabbed at her tears. "I am an executor of Avery's estate. After her death, I made a transfer of four safe-deposit boxes into one. There was a delay in disbursement of everything to the family because of some provisions in her will. We're talking a lot of money and a lot of personal possessions. It was complicated. The end result was that I put together a list of everything that was in these particular boxes. Judge Arnold and Hal each had a copy."

"Hold on a second," Owen said, sliding her off his lap onto the sofa. Getting up, he went to the kitchen, turned on a light, and returned with a box of tissues and a glass of juice for her.

"I don't deserve all of this." She gave him a broken smile, taking the tissues first.

"Hey, as king of this castle, I'll be the judge of what you do and don't deserve." He sat down next to her, surprised once again by the way she huddled against him, and even more so by the way he felt about it. He smoothed the blanket over her shoulders. "Now, tell me how you think the safe-deposit box ties into the attacks?"

"Yesterday, I told you about the discrepancies I noticed in Judge Arnold's calendars. Well, after you left, I did a cross-reference of my own schedule, and I realized that during those same days I went with the Judge twice to the bank so he could check something in that safe-deposit box."

She took a sip of the juice he pushed at her.

"Twice in one week. And now that I think about it, that was the week that he became impossible. If it weren't for me stepping in, he would have fired Linda over nothing. And then, there were several other fights he tried to pick with me. In his opinion, he told me in no uncertain terms, I had become an imbecile overnight. There wasn't a thing I could do right. We started arguing about everything. Finally, I threatened to end our association. I wasn't going to continue being verbally abused."

"And that's what the police are using as a motive—your threat to leave him."

"But I think...I'm sure now that there must be something in that safe-deposit box that set this whole thing off. Last night, when I called Hal at his office, I mentioned the box...and later, when that man pulled the knife, he grabbed the list out of my hand first."

"Is that what you were doing there?"

She looked down at an invisible spot on the blanket. He saw fresh tears stand in her eyes. Owen reached over and brushed them away himself before raising her chin.

"What were you going to ask Hal?"

"Most of the things in those boxes had been in Avery's possession since the death of her first husband. I thought Hal might be able, somehow, to help me sort out the list."

"How many things were in there?"

"Between the jewelry, coins, stamps, documents, and various negotiable stocks and bonds, in excess of five hundred items."

"And who else had access to that box?"

"No one but me." She took another tissue and wiped her face. "Avery had laid out exactly how she wanted everything to be handled. I was directed to move all the contents of the boxes in several banks in town to one box, with me serving as executor. Neither Hal or Judge Arnold were allowed to remove anything until the rest of the proceedings were completed."

"And were the rest of—"

"No. I was killed."

"How much money is involved here?" Owen asked. "What do you estimate the net worth of the estate to be?"

"Roughly, I'd say an amount in excess of eight hundred million, including her European holdings and accounts. Avery was from a lot of money, then she married money...and later, with Judge Arnold...well, he was pretty comfortable on his own, so it just continued to build and build."

"I'd say the biggest motive for your murder lies right there with that will."

She shook her head. "But I wasn't inheriting anything."

"Hal was, though, wasn't he?" He frowned as another possibility struck him. "What if the two attacks were unrelated? We're assuming that the attack tonight was directed at you, as well. But what if *Hal* was the intended victim and not you? Would the Judge control all of the estate with Hal out of the way?"

"That wouldn't make sense, either," she protested. "Avery was leaving most of her estate to the Judge, anyway. Hal's inheritance had a lot of strings attached. No, I can't imagine Judge Arnold planning anyone's murder—mine or Hal's—and certainly not from inside a prison."

Owen watched Sarah draw her knees again to her chest. She planted her chin on top. She looked more alert now than she had all night.

"My time has run out. I can't stay here any longer."

"Of course you can." The response spilled out of him without a moment's hesitation, surprising them both. "Look, it's three in the morning. You have to get back into that bed and try to get some more sleep. In the morning, we'll have a better chance of thinking straight."

"I don't think I can go to sleep."

"Try." He helped her to her feet. "I'll be right here if you need me."

The look of gratitude in her gaze touched Owen inside. She glanced down at the sofa and at the pillow on one end. She peeled the blanket from her shoulders and handed to him. "You are a very decent man, Owen Dean. I don't think I could ever repay what—"

"You don't have to." His fingers brushed a new tear off her cheek and she blushed.

"I don't know that I've ever been so emotional." Sarah turned to go, and Owen watched every step she took. At the doorway to the bedroom, he asked the question that had been burning in his mind.

"Would you have married him if he'd asked you again?"

She turned around slowly. Her eyes were polished jade in the light from the kitchen.

"No. I could never have married Hal. I had learned to respect him. I was sorry for all that he'd suffered. But I could never have married him." She leaned against the doorjamb. "I'm the product of a loveless marriage myself. I'd never make the mistake of marrying a man I couldn't love."

Chapter 14

The briefing room outside the Public Information office was crawling with reporters. Cameras flashed intermittently in the direction of a small group of officials facing the crowd. At the portable podium, the district attorney kept his jury face on as he answered the flood of questions regarding the murder. Ike Bosler knew the importance of looking dignified, open, and in control for the pictures that went into the papers. And this was especially important with the governor's mansion up for grabs in a couple of years.

"Do you believe there is any connection between Sarah Rand's murder and this one, Mr. Bosler?"

"Too early to tell."

"Have there been any arrests at all?" another reporter called out.

"The Newport Police have a number of leads that they are following up on. The investigation is still in its earliest stages."

"There was a stabbing outside the Civic Center in Providence last month. Could this be the work of a serial murderer?"

"There is no connection between the two incidents."

"Will you be releasing a composite sketch of a suspect?"

Bosler shot the police chief and Dan Archer a quick look. The captain had taken a handkerchief out of his pocket and was wiping the sweat from his forehead. Chief Calvin nodded sharply.

"We should have one by this afternoon," The district attorney responded confidently.

"Should the tourists be warned of danger lurking in these streets?"

Ike Bosler paused, looking pensive for a long moment. He knew from experience that this was the look that said judicious, circumspect, analytical, commanding. The camera shutters whirred.

"I can say, without hesitation, that the Newport Police Department is doing an excellent job of keeping this city safe for both residents and visitors. The crime statistics speak for themselves. Breaking and entering, robbery, larceny, aggravated assault—the crime rate in Newport has been cut in half since Chief Calvin and I sat down to map out an anticrime strategy at the beginning of his tenure here." The D.A. took hold of the podium with both hands and leaned forward for effect. "Newport has averaged less than one homicide per year for the past five years. In every case, there has been a timely arrest when the facts warranted it, and a successful prosecution. I believe our tourists are in good hands, and it is safe to say that this department, under the guidance of Chief Calvin, is well equipped to serve and protect all of our citizens. The streets of Newport are safer than any city of comparable size in America. We could only wish that Providence were doing so well."

Bosler listened to the knowing laugh of the reporters. Everyone in the room knew that the police commissioner in Providence had been making some noises about a run for governor. Might as well nip that in the bud, he thought.

"Mr. Bosler—"

"That's all we have for now, ladies and gentlemen."

Despite the shouts and questions by the reporters, the D.A.'s departure from the press conference was closely followed by that of the chief of police and Captain Archer.

In the corridor leading to the chief's office, Bosler turned on the two policemen.

"I want you two to listen, and listen good. I don't care if Santa Claus stuck that knife into Van Horn. I want a good sketch this afternoon and a suspect we can feed to the press by tomorrow." The D.A.'s face was fierce and menacing. "I want a clean, open-and-shut case, David. And I'm telling you, Archer, if you fuck up, you'll be doing beach patrol on Block Island. Do you understand me?"

"I saw him, Jake." Frankie looked around the crowded diner and lowered his voice into the phone. "I saw him do it."

"Did he see you?"

Frankie took the cigarette out of his mouth. "I was standing right there. He practically ran me down. Of course he saw me."

"All of a sudden, I'm worried about you."

"You wha—I get it. You're saying this shit 'cuz there's a fucking guard standing next to you with his ear up your ass. Yeah…yeah…your mother is doing much better."

"Serious. We're family. If we don't take care of each other, who will?"

"Cut the shit." Frankie took another cigarette out of his pocket and lit it. "I also saw the bitch again. She is alive, all right. Right there on the street when Van Horn got dusted. Jake, just whose fucking body did you drag out of that place, anyway? I'm thinking maybe you forgot to tell me something."

"Think of it this way, we just followed our directions. If the damn doctor wanted us to do something more specific, he should've said so."

"You're speaking in code, goddammit." He frowned into the face of a purple-haired kid who walked up and stood a step away, waiting to use the phone. Frankie held the phone away from his mouth. "Hey, do you fucking mind?"

The kid made a noise with his mouth and backed up a step.

"Look, Jake, I have to go. But something I forgot to tell you." He lowered his voice and turned his back on the kid. "You won't believe who I saw the bitch get in the car with…after the thing."

"Who?"

"Our new, resident movie star. And they seemed to be pretty cozy together, too. Now try to figure that one."

"Watch out for Ma for me, will you?"

"Yadda. Yadda. Sure. But Jake, Ma says go fuck yourself…and that guard, too." He could hear Jake chuckle once as he hung up the phone.

Frankie poked a fat finger into the boy's chest. "And fuck you, too."

Archer sipped his coffee as he watched the technician click in a new chin on the composite 'sketch' being constructed on the computer screen. The restaurant hostess, their most reliable eyewitness so far, pursed her lips and then nodded.

"That's more like her. Her hair was shorter, I think. At least, what I could see under the baseball hat." She glanced up at Archer. "I'm not going to try and tell you your business."

"We appreciate that, miss." The captain took another sip of his coffee as the technician smirked at the screen.

"But I want to make it really clear. She wasn't the one with the knife. She wasn't the one who stabbed him."

"We understand that. But you said she was near enough to have seen the killer, and she left the scene immediately. She could be very useful to the investigation."

"So she could be another...what do you call it? Another eyewitness."

"That's right." Archer nodded. "How about hair color?"

"I'm not sure," she replied. "She was wearing that hat. Her hair was light, I think. Maybe even blonde. I couldn't see much of it. Light colored eyes. I didn't really look. Maybe blue or something. The eyebrows didn't arch as much as you've got there. Yeah, that's better."

"You said she was really young. Maybe fifteen or sixteen." Archer asked a moment later. "What makes you so sure of that?"

The woman shrugged. "She wasn't carrying anything. No wallet or pocket book. She had to borrow a pen from me to jot down something on a piece of paper."

"Did you see what it was that she wrote down?"

The hostess shook her head. "Maybe some phone number or something? Every store in town is hiring these days. We can't keep any kitchen help ourselves. Maybe she saw a help-wanted number. Actually, she looked like someone who would be looking for their first job. She never really looked straight at you."

"Aha."

"How does this look?"

"Smaller nose. No." She shook her head at the technician. "Yeah. She had a pretty nose. Straight. And a small chin. Delicate."

"You said she disappeared after the incident." Archer prompted again.

"I'd say a long neck, thin from what I could see, anyway." She looked from the monitor back to Archer. "Somebody might have picked her up. There were a lot of cars on Bellevue. But there was too much going on for me to be sure."

The captain pushed his reading glasses onto his nose and flipped open his notebook.

"Normal lips. No, that's too puffy. Yeah, that's about right with the mouth. She wasn't wearing any make-up or lipstick. She had a way of bending her head, the tip of the hat covered most of the face. No earrings."

"No earrings. Why do you believe someone picked her up?"

"I said *might* have," she corrected him. "I saw a car door open in front of the restaurant, and someone got in. It might have been her, but I can't say for sure."

"Which direction was the car headed?"

"North? I'm not good at directions." She shrugged. "Whatever direction takes you toward Memorial Boulevard. The car turned toward First Beach."

"Can you give us a description of the car?"

"Hmm. Black? Blue? Gray? Well it was a dark SUV."

"Can you be more specific?" Archer prompted. "Perhaps a license plate number?"

"Sorry, Captain Archer. There was too much going on for me to focus on those kind of details."

Dan Archer waited until the computer-generated sketch was finished and then took it back to his office. Bob McHugh was standing at his desk within a minute.

"What do you think?"

Archer leafed through a thick file on his desk and pulled out Sarah Rand's driver's license photograph. Putting the sketch next to it, he covered the hat with a piece of paper. "She was there."

McHugh moved the two pictures around a bit and ran a hand up and down his bristly chin. "You want to run it through the computer to make sure?"

"No. I'm sure."

For the first time in all the years Archer had known the burly detective, McHugh actually looked nervous. With good reason.

"We are going to release this to the press, though, aren't we?"

"Yes, we are—but only with the description given by our eyewitness." Archer handed the sketch over. "This should give them something to chase their tails after. Don't forget the age. Fifteen or sixteen."

Scott Rosen's pen never lifted off his legal pad while Judge Arnold and Evan Steele argued possible motives for Hal's stabbing.

"Judge, the whole thing might come down to Hal simply being in a wrong place at the wrong time."

The Judge snorted his disagreement, looked around the small meeting room reserved for inmates and their legal counsel, and then turned his frown on the other man.

"Do you seriously think someone else was supposed to be gutted by that knife?" He turned to Scott next. "Have they done an autopsy yet?"

The lawyer fixed his gaze on his client. "They were supposed to do it this morning. We don't have any preliminary results, yet."

"I talked to the emergency room doctor who saw to Hal," Steele cut in. "His educated guess was that because of the severe cuts and obvious damage to the major organs, the weapon could not have been something as simple as a switchblade. This was done professionally. My own guess would be that the weapon was a double-edged knife, very common in contract murders."

Judge Arnold looked troubled when he turned again to his attorney.

"Don't tell me that they are going to try to pin this thing on me, too."

"You are the only one with an obvious motive, your honor," Scott answered.

"But the Judge had no means…no method." Steele argued.

"You said yourself that this could be a contract murder, Evan," Scott replied. "Your honor, you have been critical of your stepson for as long as you were married to his mother. It is documented that you have been jealous of Sarah's attentions toward him in recent months. It'd be easy to argue that the same person that you allegedly hired to kill and dispose of Sarah Rand was hired for this hit, as well. Even more damning is that Hal's death eliminates the D.A.'s strongest witness against you. With Hal out of the picture, you could very well win your freedom and reap great financial rewards in the bargain. With Hal dead, you stand to gain virtually all of Avery's fortune."

"Whose fucking side are you on, anyway?"

Scott Rosen laid his pen down on his pad and calmly met Judge's angry glare. "You should be thankful, your honor, that I'm on yours."

Her best thinking was always done in the shower.

Sarah savored the piercing sting of the hot water on her scalp and face, and cleared her mind before trying to piece together the part of herself that had come undone these past forty-eight hours. Two people whom she cared for were dead. By staying with Owen, she was exposing him to the same danger.

It had to stop. She had to turn herself in and face the consequences before this man, too, was hurt. Somehow, somewhere in the madness of the past two days, Owen Dean had emerged from the long-buried images of a youthful daydream, only to become a living, breathing human being. What was even wilder, he was a man who matched every expectation she held for a real friend...and more. But then again, Sarah thought, 'friend' could be a pretty loose term. The rest of what was going on between them, she didn't even want to think about. She turned off the water and reached for a towel.

He was on the phone when Sarah stepped out of the bedroom a little later. She felt that same strange prickly warmth spread through her when he looked up, his face brightening as he acknowledged her. He must have showered and shaved while she was still asleep. A cup of coffee sat before him on the desk. He motioned toward the kitchen, and she saw the glass of juice and the cereal bowl he'd left out for her.

Sarah glanced at the drawn shades and the sliding glass door that had been left partially open, giving her glimpse of sunlight and brick and of green grass that she knew led all the way to the seawall. For a moment she had to fight the urge to step out onto the terrace and breathe in the fresh sea air. With a sigh, she instead went to the kitchen and poured herself a cup of coffee, wondering when she would ever have even that small freedom again. She brought the pot in and was refilling Owen's cup as his phone conversation ended.

"Good morning." His greeting was gentle. "You look better this morning."

She had never realized how dark a shade of blue his eyes were until now. "Thanks for last night. I was a mess."

He stood up, and she felt dwarfed by his size, by the air of confidence and potency that he exuded. These were two attitudes she needed to regain. She wondered where she'd lost them. Good lord, she was a wreck, anyway she looked at it.

"You have to have something more to eat than that." He motioned toward the cup of coffee in her hand. "Can I make you some real breakfast?"

"No, thanks. The cereal will be great."

"The phone call was from my production company office in New York," he said while she filled the bowl. "Captain Archer has been busy."

"What do you mean?"

"He'd called them yesterday, making an 'unofficial' inquiry about me."

She sat down on the edge of the chair. "But there is no connection between you and me as far as he could see. Am I missing something?"

"There was my call to the police two nights ago. And then, that same night, you called me from the Van Horn mansion. They must have traced the call."

"Brilliant." Sarah's hand trembled, and she wrapped it around the cup. "I should never have called you from there." She shook her head to clear it. "I did some serious thinking in the shower. I think it's time I turned myself in. I'm putting you at far too great a risk."

"Do you have another copy of that list? The items in Avery's safe-deposit box?"

She was startled by the way he'd changed the subject. "No. I mean not with me. As far as going to the police—"

"Where could we get a copy? Is it on one of your computers at work? Could you somehow download it?"

She watched him pour the milk on her cereal.

"Why are you doing this?" Sarah asked softly.

"Most people like milk on their cereal."

"You know that's not what I mean. Why don't you put me out?"

Owen sat across from her, his expression thoughtful.

"I don't know," he said after a lengthy pause. "I guess I figure, like it or not, I'm already involved. And it'll make everything look a hell of a lot better if we turn ourselves in to the officials with some reasonable amount of evidence in hand, instead of saying, 'Sorry, we were just trying to play cops and robbers, but we didn't do too well.'"

"What do you think is a reasonable amount of evidence?"

"You are the lawyer. You tell me."

His comment bolstered the flicker of confidence she still had left somewhere in her battered psyche.

"Let's think about what we have. Maybe the list is the key. Maybe, with a closer look at it, you and I can see something there that makes a difference."

"It's a good place to start."

"But what about Archer?"

Owen sat back in his chair. "The way I see it, there are two basic scenarios at either end of a whole range of possibilities. At one end, Archer could be innocent of any of this and thinks you're dead. In which case, my connection might just be a distraction. After all, he really just wants to compile as much evidence against the Judge as he can get. And other than getting a search warrant for this apartment—which he probably wouldn't go to the trouble of getting since he's already been in here—he won't find out anything about me that the tabloids haven't printed already."

"And at the other end...he's actively involved in everything?" She played with her cereal when he pushed it at her.

"Right. He's in on the murders, and he knows you're alive. If this is the case, then he has people out there waiting to get you. And if that's true, you won't be safe turning yourself in anyway. You can't make an accusation against him without evidence."

"He might guess that I'm staying with you."

"He wouldn't figure I'm that stupid. Nor you, for that matter. Plus, he practically turned the place inside out when he was here yesterday."

She glanced down at the flakes floating in the bowl.

"Have you always played with your food, or is this a new pastime?"

Sarah found him smiling at her. "Have you always helped damsels in distress, or is this a new pastime?"

He chuckled and covered her hand with his. "I can see you are feeling better. How about me making us some real breakfast? Then we get another copy of that list."

"Are you sure about this, Owen?" She had to ask. "About me staying?"

"Of course I'm sure." He rose to his feet and took the bowl away. "You heard what Archer said. It's an 'unofficial' inquiry. That makes us 'unofficially' involved."

Chapter 15

Is spite of the fact that it was Friday, there was no traffic on New-port Bridge going west toward Jamestown and the mainland. It was half past eleven in the morning, and Andrew Warner turned up the volume on the radio. Shaking his head occasionally, he listened to every word of the newscast on Hal Van Horn's murder. He'd heard the same news, virtually word for word, on the 7:00 a.m. television news this morning. He'd considered waking Tracy and telling her about it before he'd gone off to an early meeting at the college, but he'd decided against it at the last moment.

Andrew picked up his cell phone and glanced at the blank screen. There were no messages waiting. No calls from Owen. And still there was no news anywhere of Sarah Rand being alive.

Andrew desperately hoped Owen knew what he was doing. He'd considered calling him numerous times since yesterday. But every time he'd stopped himself at the last moment.

It wasn't as if Sarah Rand were some kind of flake. He'd first met the young attorney when she'd started her association with Judge Arnold. She'd been bright and charming, a young woman with seemingly unlimited potential. And while some had thought the association was a great opportunity for Sarah, Andrew knew Arnold was the lucky one. And smart. With her looks and intellect and Ivy League degree, Sarah brought a new visibility to the Judge's practice, even at the state level.

Oh yes, Andrew knew that the Judge was well aware of the prize he had lured away from the Boston legal circles. And that was why the news of her murder had been so shocking.

But Sarah wasn't dead.

Andrew took the second gravel road that led up through the woods surrounding their property and parked his car halfway between the road and the north fields.

He only wished the whole situation wasn't so twisted. It would be a dream to have Owen involved with someone like Sarah. Despite all the fame, despite the money and the investments that the young man had managed to accumulate, Andrew knew Owen was not happy. And this troubled him more than anything else.

Today the air was dryer, and much easier on Andrew's lungs, though each passing week was becoming more difficult. He took a large tarp out of his trunk and pushed through the underbrush into the woods. He'd intended to do this yesterday—to go back and cover Sarah's car until she and Owen were ready to take it away. But his argument with Tracy and later his lack of breath had him stranded in his chair for most of the day.

With all the small airports around and so many helicopters going back and forth, the chance of someone spotting the stranded car in the woods was always a possibility.

The sports car was still there when Andrew broke through the bushes. Taking a better look at the shattered side windows, he frowned at what looked like bullet holes in the windshield. The older man shook his head, feeling his chest tighten with worry.

Someone had been trying to kill her. And this someone was out there loose, waiting for another chance.

Andrew spread the tarp over the car. By the time he was done, he found himself completely out of breath. He reached for the pouch at his waist. No pouch. No inhaler.

"Damn," he muttered. He knew where it was. It was sitting right where he'd left it on the kitchen counter. Shaking his head again, he slowly made his way back toward the gravel drive.

Tracy Warner's immediate reaction was to run to the door when she heard the crunch of Andrew's tires on the gravel outside. She couldn't, though. The cold gun barrel pressed against her temple kept her where she was, and she simply covered her mouth with her hands and cried silently. She heard a car door close, and then there was the sound of her husband's coughing.

"Sit," one of the two men ordered, pushing a chair toward her. She saw him move to the window and peer outside.

"Sit," the one with the gun pressed against her head repeated, hurting her arm as he forced her into the chair.

The sound of Andrew's coughing drew her attention. Tracy glanced at the inhaler that he'd left by the coffee pot.

"He...my husband might not be able to make the stairs without it." She pointed at the open pouch. "He needs his inhaler."

"He is coming." The man by the door whispered as he stepped back along the kitchen wall.

Andrew Warner's breathing was more than labored as he pushed the outside door open and stepped in. The college president's jacket was on his arm, his tie already loosened, and the top button of the collar undone. He pulled at the neckline of the shirt as a hoarse cough rose from his chest.

His gaze focused momentarily on the empty beds of his dogs in the mudroom door before he noticed there was anything wrong. He walked into the kitchen. Tracy was sitting and staring wildly at him, while a man held a silver-plated pistol to her head.

"What the hell is this?" he managed to say, as another attack of coughing threatened to shut down his lungs.

"They had badges." Tracy blurted. "I let them in, thinking—"

"Shut up." The man jabbed her in the temple with the gun, and tears ran down her terror-stricken face.

"Just a min—"

"Where did you take her?"

Andrew's heart nearly stopped at the sound of the second man behind him. He half turned, backing against the sink, his intermittent coughs forcing him to choke out his words. "What do you mean by this?"

"They're looking for Sarah Rand." Tracy sobbed. "For God's sake, Andrew, tell them she's dead. Tell them. They won't believe me. They've turned the house upside down."

From where he was standing, Andrew had a clear view of the door leading into the open living room. The furniture had been toppled and thrown about. Shards of broken glass glittered on the floor. The tightness in his chest was getting worst. He could no longer breathe without coughing. The man who'd been behind him suddenly shoved the pouch with the inhaler at him.

Andrew let it drop, and that was when he saw the dogs. He looked up at the killers.

"Let her go." He forced out the words. "She...is totally innocent...of this whole thing. Please...let her go."

"I don't think so, Warner," the man spat out.

"I won't tell you anything until you let my wife..."

"No, Andrew," Tracy gasped, starting to rise from the chair. "I won't let you."

The single shot rang out, and Andrew looked in horror as his wife spun to the floor of the kitchen. Her body jerked and then lay motionless, twisted in the most unnatural way, her blood seeping out of her back and her chest onto the tiles.

Andrew looked at her to an endless moment, and their entire life together seemed to pass before his eyes. The disagreements. The fights. His infidelity. Tracy's continuing forgiveness.

"Christ," he muttered.

He hadn't really loved her. Ever. As hard as she'd tried—as much as she'd deserved better—he'd kept her a prisoner in their marriage, depriving her of the happiness that she might have had with someone else.

Their entire fifty years of marriage had been one long battle. A battle in which Tracy had constantly tried to win his love. A battle in which Andrew had defeated her at every turn.

As Andrew Warner turned to the armed man behind him, he no longer cared about the breaths rattling in his chest. He no longer cared about his wife or his job. He no longer even cared that he'd deprived everyone around him of the peace and happiness that they may have deserved.

He only thought of one thing. He only thought of this one last thing he could do for Owen...his own flesh and blood...and for Becky.

Andrew reached for the barrel of the gun, wrestling for it with all his failing strength until his brain exploded in a brilliant flash of golden light.

Owen grimaced as Sarah took the drugstore bag out of his hand and started emptying the contents out on the kitchen table. Makeup. Hair dye. Cheap, oversized sunglasses.

"Are you sure about this?"

"I can't be a blond anymore. And the hat and sweatshirt look doesn't cut it, either." She read the label on the hair color before picking up the sunglasses and going to the bathroom mirror to look at her reflection. "They were flashing a sketch of me on the five o'clock news. I hope your neighbors in the building weren't watching."

Owen put the bag of groceries on the counter. "I heard two woman talking in the store. About the fifteen…maybe sixteen-year-old girl who might have been a witness to the stabbing."

"If I live through this, I'm giving that hostess a very generous tip for knocking almost twenty years off my age."

Owen watched her come out of the bathroom, the sunglasses in place. "Imagine me in dark brown hair, wearing a scarf and these shades. How would I look?"

"Like Garbo in the seventies?"

She took the glasses off and came toward him. "And remind me to give you a good beating for adding so many years onto my age."

Owen caught her wrist as she tried to punch him in passing. Their gazes locked. The moment hung suspended in time. His hand holding her. The wild beating of her pulse matching the sudden rush of desire in his body.

The sound of the sunglasses slipping out of her hand and falling to the kitchen floor broke the moment. He let go of her, and she immediately leaned down and picked up the shades. Then she turned away.

"I was finally able to download the list. Linda, or someone, must have been in the office today. I tried to call first, just to see if there was an answer. If she was working on the same batch of files, she might know I was accessing them."

She went on talking, but refused to look at him. Owen, however, found his attention riveted to her profile, to skin of her cheeks and the color spreading across them. He couldn't remember ever being as aware of a woman as he was of Sarah. He was certain he had never been so captivated with another person as he was with her.

Unlike the annoying feeling of being reeled in—a feeling that was all too common in his experiences with other women—he felt that with Sarah, *he* was doing the pursuing. And surprisingly enough, he was doing it willingly, gladly. And looking at her now, he realized he was beyond caring about why he was acting this way. What he was doing felt right, and that was all there was to it. Period.

"I want you to look at the list with me." She finally turned to him. "I've gone over it again and again, but nothing stands out. I just can't figure what might be in there that someone would want to kill for."

"Where is the list?"

"On the laptop." She pointed at her computer. "Why don't you go over it and let me make dinner tonight?"

"Had it with my cooking?"

Sarah sent him a smile that started in her eyes. "I'm just trying to give back something in return for all you've done."

"Payback time is coming. Don't you worry about that."

Forty minutes later, they were sitting side by side on the sofa and pouring over the list item by item. But just as Sarah had said before, there was nothing on the list that stood out as unusual. Nothing that would make Judge Arnold want to go back and check the box, in person, twice in one week.

"I assume the safe-deposit boxes were solely Avery's?" Owen asked sometime later, getting to his feet to retrieve the bottle of wine from the dinner table. He topped her glass and refilled his, as well.

"They were." Sarah tucked her feet under her. "But not because she didn't trust him. There were other legalities involved. When Everard Van Horn, Avery's first husband, passed away, everything was left to the wife. Naturally, his will contained all kinds of provisions on how much of the assets would be released to Hal, and when. Because most of the items being in those boxes were left over from Everard's era, Judge Arnold's name and signature was never added to the bank record, except for one. But the items contained in that box are on this list, as well."

"How old was Hal?"

She swirled the wine in the glass, staring at the dark ruby-colored liquid. "He would have been thirty-eight this fall."

"Not old enough to inherit everything that was coming to him?"

Sarah shook her head. "That was the way the Van Horn family operated. Everard and Avery used trusts extensively in their estate planning. Over periods of time, control would have continued to shift to Hal. But based on Avery's last will, he would have been an old man before he ran the whole show."

Owen sat back down on the sofa. "Do you think the contents of those boxes were a surprise to Judge Arnold?"

"No, I don't believe so."

"Did Avery check them often? I mean, were they just left there, untouched, for thirty years?"

"She had some new things in them. They went into the box the Judge had access to while Avery was alive. Here, look at this list." She leaned forward and turned on the screen again. "This matched set of jewelry was a gift from the Judge. The marriage certificate. The deed to the building, dated six years ago. Judge Arnold bought that building in anticipation of opening the offices downtown. He had the deed made out in Avery's name." She sat back, her brow furrowed with concentration. "I'd say the boxes were actively used, but certainly not on a daily basis. Of course, the bank records would show that."

"Did you personally make the transfer on the boxes?"

"Of course. One of the officers of the bank was present with me the whole time. We made the list as we went along."

"And when was that?" Owen asked. "Do you remember the exact date?"

"End of June. Beginning of July, maybe." She put the wineglass on the table and opened up her schedules on the computer.

As Owen scanned the dates over her shoulder, it was fascinating to him to see how hard she worked, and how little time she appeared to have to play. His gaze was again drawn to her profile, to her mouth.

"There it is. June 28 and 29. It took two days."

He frowned, forcing himself to think about the safe-deposit boxes.

"Did you give copies of the list to the Judge and to Hal immediately after that?"

"Within a couple of days. Maybe the early part of the week after.

There was other paperwork involved." She gave him a look over her shoulder. "You are getting at something."

"What was Hal's reaction to the list?"

"I don't know. I didn't deliver it personally. He didn't call me with any questions."

"So he didn't want to go and see the box for himself?"

"Not that I know of." Her eyes narrowed. "But Judge Arnold wanted to. As I told you before, we went to the bank twice."

Owen put his wine glass on the table. "Was he rushed when you took him there for the first time?"

"No."

"Were you with him? I mean, standing beside him when he checked through the box?"

She shook her head. "There was no need for it. We already had an inventory, plus I trusted him."

"Then why the second trip?"

She rubbed a spot on her neck and shook her head. "He spent even more time than the first visit. In fact, I was annoyed that day, because he knew that I had to be in court at one o'clock. It really wasn't like him to be so insensitive to other people's schedules."

Owen took Sarah's hand in his own. "Could it be...is it at all possible that in transferring those boxes, something ended up where it shouldn't have?"

"Are you accusing me of stealing?"

"Of course not." He didn't like the look of hurt in her expression. "I am talking about misplacing something. About Judge Arnold realizing that something, that should have been there, had disappeared."

"On the day of the transfers, both the bank officer and I went into that room with no briefcases. There was no way that I could have—or that he could have—taken anything of value without the other one noticing it. Besides, Judge Arnold never questioned me about it. If anything were missing, his first response would be to ask if we'd seen such and such a thing."

"What if he didn't want to bring any attention to this missing item?" Owen pressed. "What if it were something illegal. Something incriminating."

"I…" She opened her mouth to argue, but then closed it.

"This could be the common link between your alleged murder and Judge Arnold's arrest." Owen's fingers pressed her hand. She didn't pull back from the touch. "Before running into you—just going on what I'd read in the papers—I thought your Judge was an incredibly stupid murderer."

Her gaze was fixed on him.

"Shooting you in your apartment and then taking you on his own boat to dispose of the body? And never getting around to cleaning up after himself?" He shook his head. "But what was even more unbelievable was that he had not even thought to arrange an alibi. This didn't sound like a guy who's been on the bench for so many years as the Judge has. It was just so obvious that he was set up, that I couldn't understand why the police didn't see it. In the end, I figured there was more that the newspapers weren't printing."

"But maybe this is the whole point," she said. "Maybe the police were setting him up from the start."

"Maybe…*if* this missing item has anything to do with them." Owen leaned back against the sofa, his fingers still entwined with hers. "I remember hearing the initial reports of the arrest. He wasn't fighting it. He wasn't making any kind of statement about being innocent. He was looking and acting guilty, but I couldn't figure it."

She sat back too, her head leaning back against the cushions, her eyes staring at the ceiling. "I wonder if anything has happened to Ed Brown."

"Who's Ed Brown?"

"The bank officer who was with me during those transfers."

Owen glanced at his watch and came off the sofa. "Most banks are still open at seven on Friday nights. Do you have the bank's number?"

She looked up the number for him, and he called the bank only to get as far as the receptionist. No, Ed Brown wasn't available. Mr. Brown was on a medical leave. Would he like to speak to the bank manager? Yes? Hold, please.

Owen's introduction was smooth. The manager knew him instantly. Owen was interested in having the bank handle some of his money. Ed's name had been given to him by a friend.

The manager was delighted by the movie star interest, and within five minutes of dialing the phone, Owen knew all about the unfortunate circumstances that had been dogging Ed Brown for these past three weeks.

As soon as Owen hung up the phone, Sarah was in his face. "Please, don't tell me he's dead."

"No, he's not dead," he said right away. "But as it happens, on August 1—interestingly enough, the day before your disappearance—Ed Brown was in a very serious car accident on his way to work. As bad luck would have it, on the same day his house was broken into and burglarized, with a lot of damage to his personal property."

"Where is he now?"

"Still in Newport Hospital. He was only moved out of intensive care two days ago. Between the broken bones and the head trauma, it could be at least a couple of months before he returns to work. Or at least, that's what my new best friend, Jessica-the-bank-manager, thinks."

"So there was something in that box." Sarah turned to stare at the computer.

"A letter. An envelope. It could be something small, unnoticeable. Did you two have anything—pads of paper, a file folder—anything with you?"

"Yes, we did." She glanced back at him. "A yellow legal pad the first day. Paper and a couple of manila folders the next day. There might have been a couple of folders the first day, too. I really can't remember."

"Think back, Sarah. Where was the folder? Where were the boxes? Did the two come in contact at any time? Is it possible that anything, even a piece of paper, could have gotten transferred to the wrong pile?"

She sat on the edge of the sofa, her face buried in her hands for a long time.

"Come on," Owen said encouragingly. "We're getting close here. Start with the first day."

Chapter 16

The state road near the entrance to the Warner home was crawling with local and state police cars, ambulances, uniformed officers, and other officials. Two of the Providence television stations had their vans set up beside the road, their transmission antennae fully extended, jutting forty feet upward into the night sky.

Even after flashing their badges, Bob McHugh and Dan Archer were forced to stop at the beginning of the long gravel drive while the local uniform radioed ahead. Finally getting the go-ahead, the officer waved them through. Within a quarter of a mile up the winding road, the Newport detectives were flagged down at a spot where a half-dozen unmarked cars lined the shoulder.

A few uniformed officers had already opened a pathway into the woods, and flashlights could be seen bobbing and weaving through the trees. A Wickford detective approached Archer and McHugh as they got out of the car. Introductions were short.

"Before you go up to the house, you need to see this," the Wickford man said.

"I hear it's not a pretty sight up there," Archer replied as McHugh tossed him a flashlight.

"A package delivery guy found them. He went to the back door, where he usually goes, and found it open. It was impossible not to see the mess," the detective told them, leading the way to the edge of the woods. "A professional job, from the looks of things. No fingerprints. No sign of forced entry. No witnesses. Not a thing left behind, as far as we can tell. The house was trashed, but so far we have no idea what might have been taken. We were figuring armed robbery by pros until we found something else on the property."

Archer pushed at the branches of the undergrowth, following closely behind.

The Wickford detective flashed his light ahead toward a group of officials securing a site straight ahead. "A direct tie-in to the mess you've got going on across the bridge. We've got Sarah Rand's car."

Archer heard McHugh curse under his breath behind him. The Wickford man broke out of the undergrowth and into a small grassy opening. Archer moved past him and took in the scene. Yellow police tape already marked the perimeter of the site. Two uniforms were setting up floodlights and a couple of cameras were lighting up the area with sporadic flashes. A large tarp that must have been covering the vehicle had been pulled back and laid out for the fingerprint crew. A photographer was taking close-up shots of the windshield.

"The vehicle hasn't been here too long." The local detective pointed his flashlight at the natural debris around the tires. "We figure it was driven in here during the storm Wednesday night at the earliest. Thursday morning latest. Nothing in the trunk or the backseat. We haven't dusted for fingerprints yet, but there are no obvious bloodstains, either."

Archer walked methodically around the car, peering in and then pointing the beam of the flashlight on the mark of the tire threads in the dirt. He took a few steps back, turned and studied the path.

"We've traced the tires back to the main road." The local detective offered. "From the windshield breakage, it looks like someone was shooting at the car from behind. We haven't found the spot yet, but it can't be too far. Would've been a bit difficult driving in the rain with the windshield like that. The driver must have pulled off the main road and tried to ditch the car in the woods."

"Footprints?" Archer asked.

"We've made casts of a few so far. A lot of people have been around this thing. Dogs, too."

"Have someone trace those." McHugh pointed his light at two sets of tracks by a muddy embankment beyond the tape. "See if they lead back to the house."

Archer nodded to the Wickford man.

McHugh walked back to them. "Nobody got any tire tracks on that drive, either, did they? You muttonheads ruined them before anybody even gave it a second thought, I'll bet."

The annoyance was obvious in the local detective's shout as he barked an order at one of the uniforms.

"As a matter of fact, smart guy, there was a high-toned shindig at the Warner house Wednesday night, the night of the storm. The tire tracks of everybody of any importance in the whole fucking state can be found on that drive." He turned his attention back to Archer. "This sure as hell throws your 'Bang, bang, Judge Arnold did it' theory to the fish. If you want my gut reaction—"

"As a matter of fact, I don't. We're not paid to think with our gut." Archer started back toward the road. "Now give me a tour of this freak show."

Sarah dropped the pen on the desk and reached back to rub her aching shoulder. "I think this is all of them—all the cases I was working on the week of June 28. But if I *did* take something by mistake, it could have been buried in *any* of these files."

She heard him approach and then felt Owen's strong hands on her shoulders. He leaned over her, rubbing her stiff shoulders as he read the list.

Allowing, enjoying, wanting such casual contact with him still surprised Sarah a little, but there was a reassuring feeling that came with his touch. A familiar, comfortable nonchalance in the way in which he gently kneaded the knots out of her aching muscles. A pleasant warmth spread through her.

"Where would these files be?"

"At the downtown office. I would bet that Linda had them all filed away before the August break."

His spice scent, the brush of his shirt against her hair, the feel of his fingers—Sarah bit her lip in an effort to keep from melting onto the desk.

"Could we somehow get in there?"

"I have a key," she whispered. "There are night custodians who clean all the offices in the building. Tomorrow is Saturday. We can try to get in early in the morning."

"That's a date."

His fingers went to work on her neck, and Sarah fought down the sigh of contentment rising in her throat. To keep her head clear, she reached for the stack of letters she'd noticed before on his desk.

"Did you know most of these letters are from the same person?"

"Really?" There was no note of interest in his voice.

"Someone named Jake Gantley at the Rhode Island ACI."

His fingers were massaging her scalp, but he stopped and leaned over her again to take a look.

"Since we started this TV show, prison letters follow me wherever I go. Sometimes hundreds a week. Most of them go to the network or the production company offices."

"Do you ever read the ones that come to you?"

"Never. When I think of it, I pass them on to one of my assistants. I think they have a form answer they send."

"These are addressed to Newport—to this address. Isn't it strange that this guy knows where you live?"

"Sometimes it happens. One person tells another person, and then that person tells somebody else." His voice was gentle, as soothing as his touch. "I don't let it bother me."

"A couple of these have been opened." Sarah pulled the open letters out and put them on top. "I thought you never read them?"

"Well, I had to show off my letter opener to Archer yesterday morning."

"Oh yes. Through the closet door, I heard you tell him about Mel's sword. *Braveheart*, huh?" She smiled, holding one of the letters up. "May I? I've never read a fan letter."

He chuckled. "Be my guest."

Sarah leaned back against the chair, and her head accidentally resting against his hard stomach. She shivered as his hands traveled up and down her arms. She couldn't remember her body ever being so charged with sexual tension as it was now. She opened the envelope and took out the letter. Forcing herself to focus on the juvenile-looking script and disregarded the spelling errors, she read aloud:

"Dear Owen Dean,
Just in case you have not had a chance to read my previous letters, my name is Jake Gantley. I am forty-two years old and presently incarcerated at the

Rhode Island Adult Correctional Institution. Known to all around here as ACI. I am serving a sentence for nine years now give or take some.

I am a huge fan of you for years and having started following your latest television production, the idea came to me that someone with my depth of experiense in criminal life..."

The words withered on Sarah's lips as she felt his hand move from her shoulder down to the front of her blouse. The brush of his fingers was feathery-soft, but her body's reaction was immediate and intense.

...experiense in criminal...

Sarah tried to focus on the words again, but he reached over and took the letter out of her hands, dropping it on the desk. She allowed herself to be pulled to her feet and turned in his arms.

"What are you doing?" she managed to whisper as his lips brushed against her brow, the side of her face.

"I'm trying to release some of the tension in your body."

"But I—"

His mouth brushed against her lips, and Sarah lit up with the heat he'd unleashed in her. Before she could stop herself, she found she was threading her fingers into his hair and kissing him with a passion that was nearly blinding in its power.

His arms were bands of steel around her, molding every contour of her body to his.

"Sarah!" he whispered hoarsely against her mouth. "I want you. I want you *now.*"

A wild surge of emotions ripped through her. Desire was battering down old barriers of propriety, protective walls of common sense. A flicker of a thought struck her—she was putting him in danger by becoming more involved than they already were. But that thought was fleeting, as she felt herself being swept away into a world in which she had little experience. A world of longing for another human being. A world where the sometimes faltering dynamic of emotional connection suddenly sprang to life and accelerated—tangling, churning, spinning, weaving—propelled onward and outward by the pure kinetic energy of physical desire.

Sarah found herself lifted onto the edge of the desk.

"Owen," she whispered as his mouth blazed a trail from her lips to her neck. "I...I don't think...we should—"

"Then tell me to stop."

The feel of his mouth moving down the front of her shirt, pressing the fabric against her flesh, made Sarah gasp, clutch at his shoulders and bring his mouth back to hers. She kissed him back—again and again—until the very air around them became charged with their heat. His hands were beneath her shirt. The clasp of her bra came undone. His palms were pressing her aching breasts.

She saw him through a haze of desire. He was even more stunningly handsome than she'd always thought. But now he wasn't up there on some stage or movie screen with some other woman. He was here with *her*, pressed against her with such a jumbled mix of tenderness and desire. No, this moment belonged to them...to just the two of them.

Emboldened, she kissed him again. Her fingers reached for him, touching the muscles on his back and chest before pinching open the buttons of his shirt and pressing her lips against his skin.

"You're killing me," he whispered, digging his fingers into her hair and dragging her mouth roughly to his.

The sound of the phone on the desk startled them both, and he let out a frustrated groan.

"No way," he growled. Sarah smiled as he took her hand, pulling her off desk and starting toward the bedroom.

She cast a parting glance at the clock on his desk. "Wait. Maybe it's something important. It's eleven-thirty at night."

"It's the damn West Coast people. The machine will pick it up."

In the bedroom, Sarah suddenly felt the panic wash through her as Owen sat on the edge of the large bed and pulled her toward him. His blue eyes caressed and devoured her with a single sweeping glance.

"Where were we?"

"I...I don't usually do this." She had to force out the words before she forgot her own name.

"I know. I saw your appointment calendar."

"No...I mean, I don't get involved...this soon after just..."

The look in his eyes was tender. "I know that, Sarah. I don't think that what we—"

She could hear the beep of the answering machine.

"Mr. Dean, this is Carol Doyle, the academic dean of Rosecliff College." The woman's grave voice came through loud and clear. "I'm sorry to call you so late in the evening. But I have...I have some terrible news. It has to do with Andrew. He...well... he..."

As the caller's voice broke down, Owen picked up the phone beside the bed. "Hello, Carol. This is Owen. What's happened?"

Instantly, Sarah felt those same icy claws clutch at her insides. She knew the feeling now. It was becoming a part of her everyday existence. She sat down on the edge of the bed for fear of crumbling to the floor.

Owen's face became hard, but she glimpsed anguish behind the mask. He wasn't saying a word, only listening to what was being said.

When he sat down himself, Sarah knew. Her car. She had left her car on Warner's property. She closed her eyes and prayed, knowing that it was too late.

"Are you there now?"

Owen's question drew her gaze. In the dim light of the bedroom, she saw the tear that slipped down his cheek.

Two thoughts struck her at once. She wanted to go to him, to console him. But at the same time, common sense told her that she should simply walk out of this apartment, clear out of his life. For all his efforts to help her, she had just brought him pain and suffering. Perhaps even worse to his friends. Perhaps he would be next.

"Thank you for calling, Carol."

Sarah watched his hand shake as he hung up the phone. He sat in silence, lost in thought, one hand vacantly rubbing the day's growth of beard along his jaw.

She finally forced herself to her feet, moving to him. He didn't even seem to see her when she sat down next to him and took his hand. One tear, and then another, coursed down his clenched cheek. He was working hard at accepting the news and controlling his pain.

"Something has happened to him, hasn't it? Someone has been hurt again... because of me."

"Don't." He whispered the word low and hard, turning to her as he said it and pulling her into his embrace. She held him, letting her own tears soak his shirt as he rested his face against her hair. "This is *not* your fault. Blaming yourself will not help anything."

"They killed him, didn't they." It was not a question. "They found my car...and then they killed him."

His voice was cold, his words clipped. "These are ruthless people. They kill in cold blood."

"Oh, my God. I should never have dragged you into the middle of this."

Sarah sobbed quietly, and they said nothing for a long moment. Owen broke the silence.

"Long before you came into our lives, Andrew Warner was dying...one painful inch at a time. His suffering is over now. And this may sound warped, but I know he would have preferred to die *any* way other than the way he had ahead of him... suffocating in a hospital bed while his body shut down one piece at a time." Owen stopped for a moment, gathering himself. "For a long time, I've insulated myself from life. I don't know if it was fate or karma or luck that brought us together, but I'm glad it happened. Andrew is gone...he's gone...and I feel...pain and hurt and loss. But I feel something else, too. Something I know he wanted for me. He wanted me here because he wanted me to remember what it is...to be human."

Sarah didn't know for how long they stayed wrapped in each other's arms. He told her everything that the college dean had said. Tracy, surprisingly enough, was still alive, but she was in surgery. Her chance of pulling through was very slight. He told her what the police had told the dean about what had happened—about robbery being the most likely motive behind the killing—but Owen and Sarah knew the truth.

"We need to go ahead just as we planned," he told her finally. "Carol is at the hospital now. I'd like to stop by there and see her first. When I get back, we'll go and check out the files at your office."

"I can go while you're at the hospital."

"No," he objected. "I want you right here, with the doors locked and with the curtains closed, until I get back. Please, Sarah. Do this for me."

She didn't argue. She wasn't about to call for a taxi again. The last time had been too close a call, and now everyone in Newport was looking for a sixteen-year-old who looked just like her.

It was after one in the morning when Owen went back into the living room to make some calls. Sarah used the time to hide in the bathroom and change the color of her hair.

Standing before the mirror, she tried to not think of what had happened. She tried not to blame herself for all these deaths. But it was impossible to ignore the fact that people around her were dying. It felt like a hot poker piercing her chest to think that it might happen again. That it might happen to Owen.

Owen. Why was he at the edge of every thought?

What was happening to her? She was not a woman to grow so attached, so quickly. She was not a woman to trust a man so instinctively or so completely. True, she trusted the Judge, but that trust was based on years of working with the man, of seeing him with Avery.

Sarah stared at her reflection in the mirror. The ability to trust was not her strong suit. It never had been. But that was only natural, she thought. She had been the product of a marriage that never should have happened. Her father, handsome and flirtatious, had come over from Ireland for a summer to visit with friends. In a corner store, not far from Boston's South Station, he'd met a young and innocent clerk and swept her off her feet. Then she became pregnant by him. *Trust me.*

Before the summer heat had given way to autumn's breezes, the two were married, as John Rand faced his responsibility. He'd ended up taking a job and staying in America for as long as he could. But what Sarah remembered most of her parents' marriage were the arguments and the hurt, the accusations and the mistrust. So many nights, before crying herself to sleep, she had wished, prayed…begged silently for them to get along. To love each other. To love her.

But that had never happened. One day, John Rand had packed a suitcase and returned to his homeland, while Sarah had been left behind to fend for herself against a shattered woman's bitterness and pain.

The next time she saw her father had been on her high school graduation day. Sarah had been the valedictorian of her class, but he'd taken her aside after the ceremony to tell her that he was finally divorcing her mother. He was thinking of marrying again.

She had seen him again when Sarah's mother had died. He'd flown over to attend the funeral. It was the least he could do, he'd said. Sarah remembered thinking that truer words had never been spoken.

The third time she had seen John Rand after he left had been two weeks ago at his own wake. She had stood there silently, staring down at the lifeless body, hardly knowing what to feel…or even how to feel. What do you do when a lifetime of hurt has been piling up on your heart, layer upon layer, until an almost impenetrable barrier of scar tissue has formed around it? Sarah knew very well what Owen had been talking about.

Sarah checked her watch and jumped into the shower to wash off the hair dye.

Years ago, when she'd broken up her engagement with Hal, he'd told her it wasn't *him* who was unable to commit. He'd told her it was she who was incapable of maintaining a healthy relationship with anyone. He'd accused her of not trusting him or anyone else and, as a result, failing to invest any part of her emotional self in the relationship.

She had not even tried to defend herself against his words. Life had taught her to trust a person only once…if at all. Hal had used up his chance.

Stepping out of the shower, Sarah wiped the steam off the glass and looked again at her reflection in the mirror. The dark auburn hair was a shocking contrast against her pale skin, but other than that, she didn't think she looked very different.

Owen was waiting for her when she finally came out of the bathroom. He looked extremely tired, but she didn't miss the once-over look of her face and hair and the bathrobe that she was wearing. His bathrobe.

"You look great. But I like your natural hair color better."

"How do you know that I'm a natural blonde?"

He raised one eyebrow. Sarah's face colored as she remembered how he had put her in the shower and later dressed her for bed.

"I called the hospital. Tracy is out of surgery and has been moved to the ICU. I think it'd be best if I go there now."

She nodded and glanced at the clock on his bureau; it was half past two in the morning. "Be careful."

He hesitated a moment, and then pulled her into his arms and just held her.

She wanted to ask him about Andrew Warner again—about his relationship with the man—but she couldn't open up a wound that he was trying so hard to keep closed.

"Get some sleep," he said. "When I get back, we can go and check out those files in your office."

She had dozed fitfully for a while, finally getting up and roaming around the apartment. The morning was still a long way off, and there was no sign of Owen returning.

First News at 5 was just coming on the air when she switched on the television, and she sat up straight as images of her car flashed on the screen. Pictures of Andrew and Tracy appeared behind the newscaster, with an icon depicting the chalked outline of a murder victim superimposed. A picture of Hal. A picture of herself. A picture of the Judge. A live report from the country home of the Warners'. Sarah stared at the news reporter standing outside the police-tape barrier with her car in the background.

Suddenly feeling sick to her stomach, she hit the remote when they switched back to the newsroom. It was too much to bear watching.

Sarah sat quietly, hardly breathing, her eyes squeezed shut. There was no sound except for the gently buffeting sound of the breeze off the ocean and the ticking of the clock. She got up and went to

Owen's desk, picking up the *Braveheart* letter opener lying beside the pile of prison letters. Taking a handful of the letters, she went back to the sofa and sat down.

"Okay, Jake Gantley." Maybe reading an account of someone else's twisted life would take her mind off her own for a while.

The letters were a proposition for Owen to use a memoir of Gantley's own life, a record that the career criminal had been jotting down over the years. Jake's life of crime had started at age eight with an arson charge, and it had gradually grown into more serious activities ever since. Of course, there were no specifics, each letter contained only tantalizing hints aimed at getting a potential buyer interested in the material that he was selling.

Sarah read each one, following the sequence of the dates that they'd arrived at Owen's address. All were pretty much the same, with a variety of attitudes expressed, from casual curiosity about Owen's lack of interest to outright anger. But when she opened the last letter, a folded picture fell out onto her lap. Picking it up, Sarah unfolded it, for a moment staring uncomprehendingly at the photo.

And then, a pain ripped through her with such power that it tore the very breath from her lungs.

Chapter 17

If it was true that rooms have a "personality," Owen thought, then a hospital waiting room was a blank, a void—cold, impassive, unaffected by either time or human suffering. Afternoon faded to dusk, evening merged into night, dawn gave way to daylight, but the space defined by walls of beige or gray or muted greens remains unchanged. Furnished everywhere with vinyl seats of infinite color variations or fabrics designed to last an eon, the room's indifferent reception extended without exception to all the vagrant sufferers who temporarily inhabit it. Some huddled together in a corner like refugees for warmth and support. Some sat alone.

They came. They waited. They left. And time meant nothing.

This waiting room was no different, Owen considered wondering whether the day outside these walls was about to break clear. The only windows to the room opened onto the nurses' station. The only light came from the long fluorescent lights set into the textured white drop ceiling.

The doctors had told him that there would be no change in Tracy's condition tonight. Nor tomorrow, either. Perhaps not for a week, or two weeks…or more. It was incredible, they said, that she was still alive. But to what extent her injuries would affect her recovery and her future—that is, if she should ever regain consciousness—was something that still had to be determined.

Owen had sent Carol Doyle home soon after arriving. Before she left, however, the dean told him that they had contacted Tracy's older sister in Boston, and she was on her way.

Sitting alone, Owen ran through the situation over and over again. He knew Tracy Warner would be mad as hell to know that the only person keeping vigil for her was Owen Dean. But he didn't give a damn what she might think. He was tired of this game that the three of them had played for most of his life. Andrew was dead. The war was over. The dead and the casualties were all that were left.

Now he just wanted her healthy again, before he walked away forever.

Owen got up, stretched and moved to the entrance to the waiting room, staring down at the gleaming tiles of the corridor, hurting inside. Behind the nurses' station, he could see the ICU, with its beds and portable screens, its monitors and life-sustaining machines. There were two other patients besides Tracy, and for a moment he watched a nurse in blue scrubs navigating about the unit.

He'd come to Newport to say goodbye to Andrew. But he'd never thought how much it would hurt when the time finally came. Andrew had gone in a way neither of them could ever have expected. The violence of it sickened Owen. And he'd never even had a chance to say the things he wanted to say. He'd never even had the chance to say goodbye.

He took his cell phone out of his pocket and dialed his home number again. Just as when he'd called the last time, a half hour ago, his own answering message was followed by a beep. "It's me...could you please pick up?"

He waited, hoping for Sarah to hear him—to answer the phone. But there was no response. She could be sleeping, just as he'd suggested. God knows, she must be exhausted. Owen tried to comfort himself with the thought. Hell, she could be in the shower again. She liked long showers, he could tell that already.

But none of this made him feel any easier about leaving Sarah alone in his apartment. He glanced at his watch again. Five-forty-two.

If they hadn't already, the police would surely find Sarah's car on the Warner property. Owen considered whether Andrew would have said anything to his killers about seeing Sarah and Owen together. He turned back to the room, staring at nothing. No, he was certain that Andrew would never have said a word, no matter what.

No matter what...

He heard the ping of the elevator and the click of the high heels coming down the hall. Turning, Owen recognized the older woman as he watched her stop and speak briefly to a nurse on duty behind the counter. With a nod, the woman went to the large, plate-glass window of the ICU and looked for a long time at Tracy and the equipment set up around her.

The last time he'd met Joanne, Tracy's sister, he'd just finished high school. Andrew had forced him to come to some family picnic that Owen had known he wasn't welcome at. He'd only stayed for half an hour. Other than Andrew, Joanne had been the only person who'd been hospitable, never mind civil. No, she'd been downright friendly, and he'd never forgotten her smile.

He guessed the older woman was pushing eighty now, but despite the tragedy, she still had the same welcoming smile when she turned and saw him watching her.

"Owen." That's all she could say, before the tears started. "Thank you for being here."

He went to her, offering what comfort he could, and led her back to the waiting area.

But even as he sat with Joanne, his mind focused again on Sarah. Anxiety was beginning to eat at him, and he began to imagine the worst, all the while cursing himself for leaving her alone.

The first pinks of dawn were beginning to streak the eastern sky when the Porsche pulled into the parking lot of the Port of Entry Motel. Weaving around two potholes the size of Delaware, the driver made her way around to the back, parking next to a stinking green Dumpster. Glancing up at the line of second-floor rooms, she stared for a moment at the light coming through a tear high in the drape in 213.

She flipped on the overhead light above the driver's mirror and put on fresh lipstick. The sky was growing lighter with tick of her Rolex. She switched off the light and glanced impatiently up at 213 again.

Shit, she thought, it was gonna be hot today. She could feel the frigging humidity already.

A newspaper delivery truck pulled up at the corner of the back lot and stopped, leaving the engine running. In a second, a heavyset man stepped out of the door and dumped a bundled stack of newspapers by the corner of the building.

She didn't spare the guy a second look, but after he had roared out of the parking lot, she considered getting out and taking one of the papers. Who knew how long she'd be waiting here?

But when she saw the door to room 213 open, her mind was made up. She shut off the engine, grabbed her cell phone and purse and got out.

"This babe was real good." Her client chucked her good-humoredly on the chin as he reached the bottom of the stairs. "In fact, I wouldn't mind if you were to bring this one around again tomorrow night. Yeah, as a matter of fact, I want you to bring her. I'll bring a new buddy of mine. We'll have a little party."

"I haven't seen her yet." Her eyes flickered away. "But I'll probably have to take her shopping. Which means I'll have to charge you the same as for a new one."

She tried not to show anything as a flash of temper hardened the younger man's face. "Bullshit, Cherie."

"She's going to cost me..."

Before she could defend herself, the man's fingers were gripping her windpipe. With her feet barely touching the ground, she found herself driven backward until her back banged against the railing of the stairs.

"You'll bring her around for free, you greedy bitch. After all the money I throw your way." His face was an inch from hers. The smell of scotch was potent. She couldn't breathe. "After all the fucking damage you did to my other car this week, this is how you show your appreciation?"

She reached up with both hands and tugged at his grip until it loosened a little.

"I'm sorry," she whispered. "Okay, I get it. I'll have her here and ready for you. Just...just leave me a message what time you want her."

He let go of Cherie's throat and patted her cheek. "Now, that's more like it. Still my number-one woman. Where are my car keys?"

She couldn't stop her hands from shaking when she reached inside the purse to get the keys.

"You didn't screw around too much with it, did you?"

"No."

"No smashed headlights this time? No getting chased by the cops?"

"Look, I've said a thousand times, I'm sorry about the other night. But I couldn't let them catch me with the girl in the car." She gave him the pathetic look that he always bought. "It won't happen again. If you want, I'll go back to calling cabs again."

"Nah." He flashed her a handsome smile. "One of these days, Cherie, you'll have limos dropping off and picking up these babes."

She caught the motel room key that he flipped at her. She waited by the stairs, until he'd sped out of the lot. Pressing her hand to her throat, she stayed there a few more minutes to compose herself before going up.

Cherie slipped the key into the lock and went in, quickly closing the door and latching it behind her. Every light inside the dingy motel room was lit, including those in the bathroom. On the battered television set, a black-and-white version of *King Kong* was playing. She'd seen this movie a million times. It was the part where he was fighting with the snake on the cliff. Cherie always hated that part. She turned off the set.

Doing a quick survey of the room as she pulled on plastic gloves, she saw the girl lying curled up in a ball at the head of the bed, a sheet pulled up to cover herself. Cherie went right to work. She didn't want to spend all day here.

"Hey, you are really *something*, baby. Real fine!" She reached inside her purse, took out a folded plastic garbage bag and shook it loose. "In fact, you did so good that we are doing serious shopping today, you and me."

She picked the nearly empty bottle of Scotch off the floor and dropped it into her own garbage bag, then dumped a half-eaten package of chips in, as well.

"What do you say we buy those leather boots you were eying yesterday? You sure earned them, baby. You sure did." Cherie picked up two used condoms by the foot of the bed and put them in her garbage bag, too. Grabbing the open box of them by the bed, she counted what was left. Two more missing.

She walked to the bathroom and checked the trash can. Finding none there, she closed the drain in the tub and turned on the water, walking back into the room.

"I'm running a bath for you, baby. That'll make everything feel good."

When she pulled the sheet off the girl, young knees were drawn up in defense. But Cherie would have none of it. She took the girl's chin and moved her face from side to side, ignoring the dried tears. No bruises. Good enough.

"He treated you okay, didn't he, baby?"

She peeled the girl's hands off large firm breasts and frowned at the blackening marks left from his fingers. At the redness between the breasts.

"Well, that man is a sucker for you greenhorns with big tits. No changing him." She ignored the spatters of blood on the sheets. "But I'll take care of you, baby. We'll take care of each other. That's what friends do."

The teenage girl whimpered a little, but allowed Cherie to roll her toward the edge of the bed. The condoms were all she was looking for. She found both of them, under the girl.

The sharp knock on the door stopped Cherie in her tracks. She glanced at the naked girl folded over her own legs and rocking on the edge of the bed. She gave a quick look in the direction of the bathroom where she could hear the water running in the bath.

There was another knock. She threw the top sheet over the girl's shoulders and went to peek out from the closed curtains.

A scruffy-looking guy was standing with his hand on the door, ready to knock again. In the lot below, she could see the roof light of a taxi.

"Shit." She silently cursed her client. How quick did he think she was?

She opened the door a crack. "Look, I don't need a cab, now. Why don't you come back—?"

The door slammed open in her face. Instantly the scruffy man was shoving her face into the rug. Out of nowhere, cops were piling into the room. A female cop moved past her to the girl on the bed.

"Shit," she muttered again as handcuffs were snapped on. She could hear some goon reading her rights.

So much for frigging limos.

There were so few units in his building that Owen was already familiar with the cars that usually parked in the lot. So the appearance of the blue sedan parked there drew his attention. He frowned, getting out of his own car, but saw no one else as he walked toward the front entry of the converted mansion. No suspicious characters lurking in the bushes or in the great hall of the building. No one anywhere, in fact. Of course, early Saturday morning was not a time when his neighbors were generally bustling about.

Sliding his key into the lock of his door, he realized he was bone-weary. As an actor, he knew very well the demands of working long and strange hours. But the constant anxiety of the past few days was now wearing on him. He couldn't let himself get sloppy. Not now. A mistake could mean another death. His own. Or Sarah's. For an insane moment the worries that had been eating away at him about leaving her alone flooded him with caution. Forcing himself to focus, he pushed the door open.

The first things he saw as he walked in and closed the door behind him were the two suitcases and the laptop lined up beside the wall. The next thing he saw was Sarah, dressed in a dark green suit sitting on his sofa. She lowered some newspapers that she was reading onto her lap and watched him walk in. She looked very professional—like the lawyer that she way, on her way to court or a meeting with a client.

She was definitely on her way out.

The new hair color didn't do much to make her look different from the dozens of photographs that had appeared in every newspaper on the East Coast over the past two weeks. But it was the tough, no-nonsense expression on her face that reminded Owen more pointedly of those headshots. Something had gone wrong since he'd left her few short hours ago.

"What's this all about?" He pointed to the suitcases by the door before dropping his keys on an end table.

She folded the newspapers neatly and put them on the coffee

table before rising to her feet. "Now that you're home, if you don't mind I'd like to use your phone to call for a cab."

Owen's eyes narrowed as he watched the coldness chisel itself on the perfect planes of her face. He could see how this transformation would be a key to her survival in the tough profession she'd chosen.

"You don't need a cab. I'm taking you. But aren't you a little overdressed for a quick stop at the office?"

She didn't smile. Instead, she went around the sofa and reached for the phone on his desk. "Thanks. But a taxi will do."

A couple of long strides and he was at her side. He took the phone out of her hand and put it back on its cradle. "What's going on?"

She tried to reach for the phone again, but he held it out of her reach.

"What's going on, Sarah?" he repeated more sharply.

"Fine!" She turned away, ignoring his question. "I only stayed because I thought I owed you that courtesy. But if you won't let me use your phone, I'll just walk."

"Like hell you will." He growled, taking hold of her elbow. "Why won't you come out and say what the problem is?"

Her eyes were spitting fire when she spun around. Her tone, however, was tightly controlled. "Believe me, it was only because of your decency over the past couple of days, because of Andrew Warner, that I—"

"Cut the bullshit, Sarah! Talk to me."

"Unlike you, I don't like scenes." She glared at him.

"Well, you aren't going anywhere until you tell me why you're acting like this."

"The hell I'm not!" Sarah pushed him, trying to get around the barrier he made.

Owen took a hold of her arm and turned her around until she faced him again. "What has happened to you?"

"I am the same person I've always been. Let go of my arm."

"I will." He leaned toward her until their faces were a couple of inches apart. "When you tell me why you're suddenly shutting me out."

The temper blazing in her face heated Owen's own blood. But his train of thought started running in a different direction. Uncontrollably, his hands tightened on her arm, and his gaze fell on her lips.

"Don't you dare look at me like that after what I found out about you tonight." Her tone—and the look of disgust on her face—had the effect of a hard slap.

"What are you talking about?"

She didn't answer, simply turning her face.

"What the hell kind of a lawyer are you?" he snapped. "How the hell am I supposed to defend myself when you won't even give me a clue of what I've done wrong?"

"You want to know what you've done wrong?" She jerked her arm free and marched toward his desk. "Do you really want to know?"

"Of course, I do." He followed.

"This." She jabbed an envelope into his chest. "How can you defend yourself against this?"

Blocking her path, he tore the open envelope and took out a letter. Something else in the envelope fell to the ground, but he ignored it. She was quick to lean down and pick it up, slapping it into his hand. "This, damn it. Not the letter. *This!*"

Owen glanced down at the photograph for a moment and then looked up.

"This is what has you so royally pissed off?" He laughed mirthlessly. "Well, I'm sorry to tell you this, honey, but I'm a fucking actor."

"Brilliant choice of words, I'd say."

"I mean I act. I'm not having sex with that woman. But there are more than a few shots like this from movies I did eons ago still floating around. Acting…do you understand the word?"

"Yes, I understand the word."

"Then why would a frigging photo from a scene that never even made it into a movie get you so riled up? A photo sent in the mail by some two-bit criminal?"

"You don't get it, do you?" Sarah snapped the picture out of his hand and pointed at the naked woman in it. "Do you know who this is?"

He gave it a cursory glance. "Of course I do. Tori Douglas. Psycho woman. She had a bit part in this movie that, by the way, was made over ten years ago. She's a working actress, but I only know that because for the past couple of years, she's been following me around. Harassing me. Showing up on sets of the show and being generally a pain in the ass. She is obsessed. Lately, she's even gone out of her way to show up and be disruptive whenever I'm doing an appearance. Just at the beginning of this summer, my lawyers had to threaten her with a restraining order if she didn't stop stalking me. What else you want me to tell you about her? I could probably tell you her goddam social security number if you give me a minute."

She took a step back, bumping against the desk.

"Come on, Sarah. Talk to me."

Sudden tears stood in her eyes, and she tried to turn her face away. Owen frowned and took her chin gently in his hand, and looking into her face.

"What is this all about?"

"Didn't you pick up a wallet in my car? You handed it to me."

He thought back. "Yeah...so?"

"But you looked inside of it, didn't you?"

"No, I didn't. Andrew showed up then. But actually, I was thinking more about the damage to the car, the broken glass, how lucky you were to be alive."

Tears ran down her face, and in an instant he had his arms around her. She first tried to push him back, but not very hard. So he held her, and a moment later her arms slipped around him, a sob catching in her throat.

"Tori...Tori Douglas was my friend from California. The one who stayed in my apartment. I thought you knew, but decided to not tell me anything. I trusted you and I thought...I thought you were lying to me like everyone else."

"No," Owen whispered.

She raised her face, and he was kissing her mouth, her eyes. Kissing the tears from her cheeks. Her words had penetrated deeply. When had anyone ever cared for him so much to be hurt like this?

When had he ever cared for anyone so much in return? He drew away, frowning fiercely.

"I never made the connection that this was Tori Douglas. I never put the two together. How could I?"

When Sarah looked up into his face, he only wanted to soothe the hunted look that he saw there.

"Let's not do this ever again," he whispered. "I'm no expert, but when a person trusts another person, don't they give each other a chance to explain?"

"Yes." She closed her eyes, brushing her hot forehead against his lips. "I feel as if the rest of the world is out there, and then it's only the two of us, here, inside. I was so hurt, scared, more than hurt as I felt these things here inside of me. Things about you that I can't explain. Hal used to call me the ice queen because he thought that I don't feel. That I can't love. I don't get angry or retaliate, as if I don't have emotions."

Sarah pulled back until she was looking into his face.

"But you make me feel all those things. I've never been so angry, so destroyed as I was when I saw that photograph of you and Tori. It was like something one might see in a movie or read in a book. My claws were coming out. I had fangs. I wanted to take out Tori's eyes...but she was dead."

"So I was the next victim?" He pushed her arms higher around his neck, molding their bodies together.

"It was ridiculous. I have no claim on you, which made me even angrier. I had no right to feel the way I was."

He cut her words short with another kiss.

They were both breathless when he broke it off. "If we didn't have to get you in and out of that office before things get busy downtown, I'd carry you into that bedroom and give you the opportunity to establish whatever claim you want."

"I'm sick...sick...sick," she said with a broken laugh. "Everyone is dying out there and all that's running through my mind is..." A blush was already spreading into her cheeks again.

"What?" He moved his hand inside the jacket, feeling the curves of her body through the blouse. She closed her eyes and leaned into his touch.

"I can't wait until we make love."

Owen kissed her again. This time she drew back, pressing her fingers against his lips.

"It's getting very late, and I should change into something inconspicuous."

"I can help you change."

"No chance." She gave him a smile that went straight to his heart, setting his body on fire at the same time. "But I'll be needing a lot of help after we get back."

Chapter 18

The blinds to the spacious second-story offices of Arnold and Rand law offices were tightly drawn. Scott Rosen had no difficulty seeing, though. Wood-panel doors had been slid back along a wall, revealing a line of steel file cabinets. He sat on a high stool, scanning the contents of files he'd pulled from an open drawer.

The grandfather clock in the corner—a hundred-fifty-year-old Bristol piece with revolving moons—chimed seven times. He checked his own watch to double-check the time. Lucy liked to sleep a little later on weekend mornings, but he wanted to get home and have breakfast ready for her when she got up.

He was well aware that he'd been an ornery bastard lately. But Lucy, despite being almost nine months pregnant, still put up with his shit. He was an undeserving of her understanding, and one of these days he'd make it up to her. One of these days.

But right now, he had to find what he was looking for.

He slipped the file on his lap back into the drawer, exactly where he'd taken it from. He glanced at the next name on his list, moved his chair down two cabinets, found the drawer, and pulled out another file.

As he opened it, the top letter in the folder caught the lawyer's attention immediately.

"What are you doing here?"

Scott leapt up, banging his knee as he whirled to face the intruder. Even before he spotted the figure by the door, he recognized the voice.

"You scared the hell out of me. I didn't hear you come in at all."

Evan Steele strode into the room and glanced from the file on Scott's lap to the open drawer.

"What are you doing?" he asked again.

Scott's eyes narrowed. "What does it look like? I'm working on my client's case, of course." He closed the folder on his lap. "And what brings you out on an early Saturday morning?"

"You set off the security alarm when you came in." He sat on the edge of the desk. "My dispatcher gave me a call."

"But I shut it down when I came in. Judge Arnold gave me the code."

"We had to install a second system." Evan Steele's sharp eyes studied everything on the desk, including Scott's list. "Standard procedure because of his incarceration."

"I never heard anything about that." Scott casually put the folder in his hand on top of the list. "A silent alarm going straight to your security dispatcher."

"Well, we don't want to have anyone get away, do we?"

Steele rose to his feet and walked around the large office, checking inside the other two private offices and the conference room that served as the law library. Scott watched Steele disappear for a moment as the Naval Intelligence officer went to check the small kitchenette and the washroom.

"I think I'll just take some of these home and work on them there," he said so the other man could hear. He laid his briefcase on the desk and opened it.

"Unless you want your head handed to you," Steele said, coming back into the room and pointing at a box of blue dividers on the office manager's desk. "I suggest you leave a card for Linda with the names of any files you're taking. She's been dealing with too many cops and people from the D.A.'s office these days. The lady is a bit irritated with people messing up her system."

Scott quickly pulled a dozen files, both relevant and irrelevant, out of the cabinet drawers. He scribbled the info they contained on a blue divider for each, slipping them in where the files had been. "I guess these should take me through the weekend. I'll bring them back Monday morning."

Scott joined the other man by the main entrance to the offices. He watched the security specialist type in the codes that Scott had used coming in. Once outside the office, he stopped while Steele opened a locked box on the corridor wall. Whatever the code was, Evan Steele made sure he didn't see it.

"How do I return these on Monday?"

"Give me a call first. I'll meet you here."

Scott waited while the other man closed and locked the box. "Does anyone else, other than you, have these new security codes?"

"No."

"The cleaning crew?"

"We let them in."

"How about Linda? Doesn't she need the code?"

"The office is officially closed until after Labor Day, though what will happen now pretty much rests in your hands, Counselor. Anyway, Linda gives me a call if she has to go in for anything, and I meet her here. Stairs or elevator?"

"Stairs." The two men started down together.

Listening on the stair landing a half floor above the law offices, Sarah tugged on Owen's arm. Together they quietly descended the stairs. A moment later, they heard Steele and Rosen go out the front door of the building.

"I'd say we have five minutes." Ignoring the new box in the corridor, she used her key to open the door. Quickly, she shut off the original security system. "I was here when Steele installed this system. There is a two minute delay and the call goes to his automated system. There's a call back before the signal goes out to the police. I'm hoping that we'll have at least that long before his office calls Steele. So unless he's shut off his cell phone or has stopped to have coffee around the corner with Scott Rosen—either of which is highly unlikely—we'll have approximately five minutes."

Owen followed close behind as she crossed to her office. "What happens if there is no delay on this one?"

Sarah wasn't listening. He watched her scramble through the file cabinets in her own office and then the one by the office manager's desk in the outer office. He stayed close to her and took the folders she handed him.

"I can't believe this," she said a short time later, after pulling a pair of blue dividers out of a drawer. "He took two of my files."

"The Judge's lawyer?"

She shot a look at the door before staring at the card in her hand again and nodding. "Monday…Rosen's bringing it back on Monday."

"What we're looking for might be right here," Owen reminded her. He glanced at his watch. "I think we are pushing the four-minute mark."

She closed the file cabinets and they headed for the door. Quickly, she reactivated the original security box. They were out of there in an instant.

"We can go out the fire exit in the back. It takes us into the alley."

"Who else has that security code?" Owen asked as they went out.

"Everyone," she replied. "Linda. The two part time clerks. The cleaning crew."

They had parked his car in the nearly empty church parking lot, a block up the hill from the law office. Sarah, with a bag over her shoulder, was wearing the oversized sunglasses, khaki shorts, and a sleeveless tank top. She looked like any other early rising tourist in search of an open shop. Owen's well-known face, though, drew gazes as they walked up to the car.

"You're the one who needs the disguise," Sarah teased him, once they were safely inside the Range Rover.

"Yeah? Well, I refuse to be a blond, or wear shades that ugly." He glanced over at her as he pulled out of the lot. She had pushed the glasses onto the top of her head and was already going through the folders she'd taken from the office. Rather than the paperwork on her lap, Owen's gaze was drawn to her profile, to her lips, and then moved downward, taking in the rise and fall of her breasts beneath the tank top. He forced his attention back on his driving.

"I heard that," she muttered, without looking up. "And you'd better keep your eyes on the road."

He laughed and took her hand, kissing it. As a precautionary measure, Owen took back streets all the way to Ocean Drive.

"There's nothing here," she announced a few minutes later.

"Are you sure?"

"I went through them pretty fast, but I didn't see anything that doesn't belong there." She closed a folder and stared straight ahead, her brow furrowed with concentration. "It figures that Rosen should pick the same two files I was looking for."

"Were those the only two he had out?"

"No. I saw at least a half dozen cards in there."

"How well do you know this guy?" Owen gave her a sideways glance.

"Young, a go-getter. Very hungry and smart. He is one of the toughest attorneys in state. Maybe the best. He is driven to win and he's married to his job. Famous for being very involved in his cases, start to finish."

"Do you know him well enough to stop at his place for lunch?"

"Very funny. And I don't know him well enough to burgle his house, either." She leaned her head back. "I know he doesn't live on the island. But even if he did, I would be more afraid of going inside his house, right now, than I would be robbing a bank. He wouldn't think twice about handing me over to Archer, even if he knew they'd shoot me between the eyes on the way to the station. He just wants his client out."

"What happens if he finds what you're looking for?"

"I can only hope that he won't recognize it." Sarah shook her head. "I don't really know why he took those files, to begin with."

"We'll look through these folders again when we get back to my place." Owen placed his hand on her knee and gave a gentle squeeze. "And if we don't find anything...well, Monday is only two days away."

One of Owen's neighbors was pulling out as they turned into the chateau's long drive. Sarah immediately put on her sunglasses, and he returned the friendly wave.

"Never mind involving you in my life of crime, I'm also ruining your reputation by staying here."

"What reputation is that?" Owen asked, noticing the blue sedan in the lot again.

"Well, something must be wrong if you're spending the weekend with some old hag who wears ugly glasses."

He turned off the engine and smiled at her. "Ruin me."

She held the files against her chest and looked back at him, her green eyes deadly serious as she studied every aspect of his face. "Is this real?"

He took her hand. "Come inside with me, and I'll show you how real it is."

Instead of going through the terrace, they went in through the great hall. After stopping by his mailbox, they walked toward his apartment. Owen tucked the new mail under his arm and put the key into the lock. He could feel the heat rising between them. It was electric. The brush of an arm. The way her back arched at the touch of his hand. He opened the door.

The place was just as they'd left it. He locked the door and leaned against it. She walked in, dropped the files and her bag on the coffee table and then turned to him.

The mail dropped to the floor, but Owen didn't see it. All he saw was Sarah. All he felt was how much he wanted her.

She took a step. He took two...and then his mouth was fused with hers, his hands molding her body against his. It was madness, this urgent need in both of them. It was like nothing he'd ever experienced before.

"Sarah..."

Her mouth, soft, desiring, invited him in. Both of them seemed to be starved for a touch that could only be soothed by the other. They were reckless, wanton in their physical desire, and yet somehow aware that this was the first time for two aching souls.

She tugged his shirt free of his shorts. Her hands swept over his back, his belly, they reached for his belt.

"I'm afraid, Owen, afraid of the way I feel about you, about how much I want you." Her fingers slid downward, touched him in places where he'd been praying for her to touch him. "But I don't want you to see me like...like Tori."

"There is no chance of that." He dragged her mouth up for another kiss. "Christ, Sarah! I want you."

She raised her hands into his hair and kissed him deeply.

"I want to touch you," he whispered hoarsely. "I want to make love to you."

His lips brushed over her face, and down over the soft lines of her throat. He lifted her and she wrapped her legs around his waist.

In the dim light of the room, her eyes flashed a wild shade of green. He carried her into the bedroom, and they fell onto the bed. Streaks of morning sun slipped through the closed shades, dancing around them.

He drew back for a moment, peeling off his shirt. When he looked down at her, a tightness gripped his chest. "Have you ever had a feeling that you wanted to stop time, to preserve a moment, carry it into eternity?"

"I have. I feel that way now."

Owen choked down the knot that was rising in his throat. His mouth was deliberate and slow when he lowered himself again. He wanted to savor every taste, every touch, every sigh. She belonged to him at this moment, but the thought of ever being without her rankled deeply. He forced down such thoughts.

A moment later, their clothing cast aside, they joined together. With naked limbs entwined, they made love as neither had ever made love before. Even the wild moment of release was something new, different...almost holy.

Their past, their futures, their joy, and their grief were all a part of this moment. As she clung to him, as he clung to her, their spirits rose to a place entirely new. To a place that was theirs alone. A place built on dreams. A place built on trust.

A place to be preserved, if only in the eternity of this moment.

Chapter 19

The Fifth Ward. Blue-collar chic. Thirty blocks of the old harbor town. Crowded. Bristling with life. Thirty blocks of stores and warehouses and clapboard houses leaning hard against one another, huddled together against a century wind and sleet and rain. Thirty blocks of narrow, winding streets and alleys tumbling westward from Bellevue to a working waterfront that had boasted at one time the toughest whores on the East Coast.

Once the domain of Cork and Dublin-born servants to the gilded "cottages" of Astors and Vanderbilts and Dukes, the Fifth Ward and the Irish who lived there had resisted and then grudgingly given way to the incursions of Italians, Portuguese and finally to the yuppies of every flavor who had moved in over the past couple of decades and reclaimed the neighborhood.

But through it all the Irish never moved out. Kelly's Place. The Irish-American Club. Flanagan's Pub. The Finian Bar. The faces at the bars still stood in not-so-silent testament to the tenacity of a people who have always hated to give up something that was theirs, even when no one else wanted it.

The Fifth Ward.

Parked behind Frankie's black Mercedes, the driver of the dark sedan drained the last of the coffee from the paper cup and watched his partner come out of the dead-end alley. Frankie had been living in the same house in that alley that O'Neals had been living in for three generations before him.

The partner crossed the Thames Street and got into the car.

"Well?" the driver asked.

"He is sleeping."

"For how long?"

"How does forever sound?"

The driver started the engine. "How about the knife?"

"Tucked into a kitchen drawer...under some towels."

They pulled out onto the street. "Did you clean up after your-self?"

"You know I always do." The other man answered as he polished the lenses of his shades on his pants.

"Don't get too cocky. Not after the screw-up the other night."

"Forget about it."

"Fuck 'forget about it'. The boss was pissed as hell. You had your directions and you fucked up. We were supposed to just wait until they made contact and then let Frankie take care of her. But no, you had to jump in, kill the wrong guy and let her get away. And you say 'forget about it.'"

"I told you, I saw the paper in her hand."

"Big fucking deal! That paper meant bupkus."

"But none of us were sure, were we?"

"Yeah…now it's *we*."

"I'd shut the fuck up if I were you, considering the fact that you shot the wrong broad in the face to start with—"

"How the fuck was I supposed to know that?" the driver snapped back. "You were the one who knew her and didn't say squat when we went through the place. But don't try to change the subject. You fucked up then and you fucked up the other night."

The passenger threw a menacing look at the driver. "You would have done the same thing. If she showed the paper to the other guy, and it ended up being the real McCoy, we would've had to get rid of him anyway. This way, they find the knife in O'Neal's house, and he takes the rap."

The man in the passenger seat returned the wave of a traffic cop as they went through an intersection.

"I still say you screwed up. Frankie saw you do it."

"But he won't be doing any more talking now, will he?"

What if he'd already done all his talking, the driver thought angrily as he drove north toward the deserted boatyard in Portsmouth. Making mistakes was frowned on in their business.

But what was unforgivable was letting the people who'd made the mistakes live to make more. He cast a sidelong look at his partner…his former partner.

Unforgivable. And he had a reputation to protect.

Sarah smiled. Even in his sleep, Owen kept a protective arm around her waist and one leg draped over her hip. Her body was still humming from the love they'd made, and her mind...well, that was humming, too.

Sex had never been a high point in Sarah's relationships with other men. Not that she'd had all that many lovers. But the very few who had been persistent enough to reach that particular level of intimacy with her had clearly been disappointed after the fact.

Hal had been one of those. She had discovered another woman in his bed the very same week that she'd made love with him. But his disloyalty had been as much her doing as his, she'd realized after they'd talked the whole thing out. He'd sought her forgiveness—thrown himself on the mercy of the court—and she'd tried to be understanding. At first, anyway. What a fool she'd been.

Nonetheless, Sarah didn't need anybody telling her that she was cold and unresponsive. That she had no experience in ways of alluring a man.

Still, Sarah had not been able to make Hal want only her in the time they were together. She wondered now if she had ever really cared enough to try. That was why it had been so easy to end it, once she'd made up her mind.

She stretched her body and felt Owen stir next to her.

In the past, after such intimacy, all she ever wanted to do was to leave the bed, to get out and walk away from the situation, putting it out of her mind. For Sarah, it had always felt as if what she'd experienced wasn't fulfilling enough to invest any more of herself in it. She must be doing something wrong, she'd told herself.

But this time...everything had been different.

There was nowhere in the world she preferred to be than here, in this bed with this man, for so long as she could stay.

Owen's hand moved up from her waist and his fingers brushed against one breast. Sarah found her entire body come alive again as his leg moved along her hip and his scratchy face nuzzled against her throat. She shivered.

"Ticklish, hmm?" he growled, moving on top of her. "How long did I sleep?"

She turned her head to look at the clock on the table beside the bed. He took advantage of her movement, his mouth roaming her breasts.

"Two hours…" she managed to say. "Not enough, after Lord knows how many nights of getting none."

"That was plenty." His hand moved downward over her belly, making her ache where his mouth was headed.

"You…you must be hungry. We didn't have any breakfast."

"Starved." He gave her a devilish grin. "But I'm about to take care of that right now."

She was wearing one of his longer T-shirts when they finally went to the kitchen for some food. Owen had pulled on a pair of boxers. While he took what he called "real breakfast" fixings out of the fridge, Sarah went to get the bag and the folders she'd dropped on the coffee table. Seeing Owen's mail scattered on the floor by the front door, she went to pick it up.

"Another fan letter by your prisoner friend."

Sarah froze as she saw the additional line of script beneath the address.

"I never read the letter that he sent with that picture." Owen said from the kitchen. "I can't help but wonder, why he sent that particular one. There's no reason that he could know about her."

Sarah looked up from the letter in her hand. Her voice was hoarse, even to her own ears. "He said you had something in common. That you both were intimately familiar with…Tori." She felt gooseflesh rise on her arms as she walked into the kitchen and held the letter out to Owen. He was just getting ready to break some eggs into a frying pan. "But I think you should open this."

He saw the name on the envelope. "'*Hal*' What the hell is this joker doing now?"

Sarah watched Owen tear open the envelope and pull out the single sheet, obviously torn from a notebook. She looked over his shoulder at the five lines scrawled on the page:

I know who killed Hal.
I know you were there.
I know you like fucking dead babes, but she sure don't look dead to me.
Come and see me.
Your fan—Jake Gantley

The dual arrests of Cherie Lake and William Hamilton, also known by the nickname Billy the Kid, brought a sigh of relief to David Calvin, the Newport police chief. The three officers and the two detectives working for Archer on the case over the past year crowded the Chief's office on Saturday morning.

"We had a two-headed monster here, and we wanted to make sure we cut off both heads at once." One of the detectives, a young brunette Calvin had promoted himself, continued her summary of the raid. "Cherie Lake was the recruitment department for Billy. She would check out the girls at the high school—in the stands at sporting events, at the local skating joints, the neighborhood pizza hang-outs, at the beach. She would do her homework, finding out who was having trouble with family, who came from broken homes, who had money troubles. She wanted to know who was interested in getting high but couldn't afford it. She always seemed to zero in on the girls hungry for attention. At any time since we started watching her, we figure she was keeping tabs on least a dozen of them at a time."

The detective paused at seeing Dan Archer walk into the room, cup of coffee in hand. The captain nodded and leaned against a wall.

"Keep going, Sal," the Chief ordered.

"Cherie sure had a bag of tricks. She would take her time reeling them in. She would run this 'big sister, little sister' rap on them. She wasn't going to drag them down to Billy the first night and have him jump them. She was feeling the kid out first and gaining her trust, then she made her move."

The detective who had posed as a cab driver during the raid continued. "Now if she hinted at what she wanted and the girl balked, then she'd back off and come back with it again after a couple of months. Working with the Massachusetts state police, we've been following her from Fall River to New Bedford and back. There were plenty of fish in the pond."

"Corruption of minors. Child prostitution. Interstate trafficking. Conspiracy." The Chief had a hard time not rubbing his hands together with satisfaction. "How far back do her connections go with the Hamilton boy?"

Sally glanced at Archer and continued. "As far as we can tell, two years. They must have been hanging in the same bars. With little money to pay for her expensive habits, it was a connection made in heaven for her. She was a waitress in town before, but she hasn't worked anywhere since two years ago...the first summer that Hamilton started hanging out in Newport."

"Have you checked the town where he goes to school—New Haven, wasn't it?—for anything similar?"

"That's in the works," the other detective put in.

"You do have him nailed this time, don't you?"

"We do." Sally looked again at Archer. "Cherie was also the clean-up crew. But last night, we got in before she could get rid of anything."

Calvin frowned. "But not before the girl was assaulted."

There was an uncomfortable silence. Archer spoke up. "They both gave our people the slip. We caught up with them when Hamilton was on his way out of the motel lot."

The Chief nodded. "Will the girl talk to us?"

Sally jumped in. "She will. Her mother is here, and the girl has already given us a statement. She is willing to testify exactly what he did to her...what he said to her. She is not too happy with Cherie, and she knows Cherie was hitting on a couple of her friends. With this one willing, I think we might find a few girls to come forward now. We have him, Chief."

David Calvin congratulated them, and they all began filing out of his office. He turned to Archer.

"Sarah Rand wasn't too far off the mark, six months ago."

"No, she wasn't," Archer admitted, crumpling the empty coffee cup and tossing it into his superior's trash can.

"Too bad she's not around for us to make a public apology...to her and her client."

"Yeah." Archer headed out of the office. "Too bad."

"This might just be a set up," Sarah cautioned as the Range Rover left the highway. The prison loomed on the north side of the interstate. "He could simply be making this whole thing up."

"I have a very legit reason for talking to this guy. I'm a TV producer. We are constantly looking for fresh material for our shows. Jake Gantley has been corresponding with our writers for a while. It's only natural for me to meet with this guy in person." Owen placed his hand on her knee, trying to comfort her. "Even the warden bought my story."

"Well, I don't." She frowned, looking straight ahead. "Why is it that all these prison officials are so friendly to you? Here, you call in and an hour later you can meet with the guy. Something is not right."

"That's the entertainment business for you." He brought her hand to his lips—a tender gesture that pleased her more than he knew. "People usually like us or hate us. They are agreeable or totally ornery. Now, if I was calling the local police station and wanted a tour of their offices, you can bet I'd be standing in line for weeks."

Sarah knew why, too, having seen some episodes of Owen's shows. Very realistic and not very flattering to the people running the police departments depicted.

"What are you going to do when you get there? He'll know he's rattled your cage, and that's why you're here."

"I am just going in to listen. If he really knows who killed Hal, which means he knows who was trying to kill you…" He gave her a glance. "That's worth whatever price he puts on the information."

"I wish I could come inside with you."

"No chance of that, love," he said tenderly. "I'll park the car in the most public lot I can find near the prison. I want you to sit behind the wheel. Lock the doors. Don't think twice about driving away if you feel threatened at all."

Sarah nodded. She had wanted to come along, not because of

any fear of being left alone in his apartment. She was terrified of something happening to Owen. He pulled into a commuter lot across from the gate leading into the ACI.

"Do you have something to read?"

She backhanded him on his leg. "Who proclaimed you the adult here?"

He leaned over and took her mouth in a lingering kiss. "Much better. Temper and passion in one irresistible adult."

Sarah was still flustered as she watched him cross the parking lot. Vanity had never been a strong suit with her. But Owen's words had touched a tender spot in her heart.

And that was exactly why she was so scared, Sarah thought, as she watched him disappear from her view. Everything about him—from the way he'd treated her the first moment they'd met to their unleashed passion this morning—affected her more than she'd ever thought possible.

Sarah learned as a child that life wasn't fair. 'Happily ever after' was the stuff of fairy tales. People rarely spoke the truth, and people were gunning for her, pure and simple. That was why she was waiting for the other shoe to drop, for the ticking bomb to explode this perverse fantasy that seemed so much like happiness. But the thought of pushing Owen away from her, out of harm's way...

Sarah stared at his broad back disappear through the prison gate, and slid over behind the wheel.

Chapter 20

Owen figured he'd met them all in his time.

As a kid on the streets of Philadelphia, he'd seen them. Hell, been one of them. At boarding school, he'd seen them, too. A higher class of punks, to be sure, but punks nonetheless. More money just meant more expensive vices.

So many of them had the same things in common. Each one thought he was the center of the universe. Each one thought he was above the rules and standards and laws that kept mere mortals from enjoying the pleasures that were 'rightfully' theirs.

Some of those punks were dead, now. Some were sitting in board rooms of Fortune 500 companies. Some were, no doubt, in prison.

Sarah had thought she needed to warn him about the convict on their drive to the prison. She had given him a summary of what she'd read in his letters—of the inmate's early start in a life of crime and his continuous involvement, despite his years of incarceration. Owen had listened, but figured he knew this guy like a book.

But after meeting Jake Gantley in person, he knew he'd been wrong.

Owen had no reason to believe or disbelieve the man's story of his criminal activities. But he hadn't been prepared for the strength of Jake's personality. This was no punk. This was a dangerous man.

Despite the austere environment in the visitor's room, the inmate had greeted Owen from across the divider like a host welcoming an honored guest to a dinner party. Prison clothes notwithstanding, the man looked clean, trim, and polished. His manners were refined, almost cultured at first glance. His manner of speaking was cool, intelligent, and articulate as he explained to Owen some of the problems with crime stories and the motivational problems of current TV characters—including Owen's own character, John McKee.

Owen had tried to remain pleasant and casual, listening to what was being said without showing any hint of impatience. He didn't want to reveal the main reason for this visit. But the hour he'd requested was running short, and Jake had yet to bring up the topic.

"I have done some script-writing myself," the inmate said casually. "With so much time on my hands here, I've completed three correspondence courses on writing in this past year, alone."

"That's great." Owen tried to maintain his level of interest under the watchful gaze of the guard standing just out of earshot near the door.

"In my letters, I mentioned something about the transcripts I've been putting together." Jake's gray eyes squinted, obviously measuring Owen's response. "Of course, before I can share any of what I have to offer, an agreement must be reached, and perhaps a contract drawn up."

"Sure, why don't you send a proposal to my production office. If it's something that might interest our team of writers, the lawyers will contact you."

Owen's pro forma answer had the desired affect. Jake's otherwise smooth expression faltered for a moment.

"I'm well aware of the secret handshakes and family connections that are the foundations of deal-making in your business, Mr. Dean. It's not much different in my line…my *former* line of work. But my writing won't be sitting on any slush pile."

"Then I'm sorry, I can't help you." Owen leaned forward, looking Jake straight in the eye.

"You gave me the impression that you were interested in my material," Jake said calmly.

"I'm sorry to disappoint you. But I have yet to hear anything that grabs me."

Gray eyes focused again. "You saw the picture I sent you."

"From an old movie clip. Even the tabloids won't be interested in an edited clip that's been floating around the internet for a couple of years."

"I met Tori recently," Jake replied.

"Good for you." Owen glanced at his watch.

The voice turned low. "She was in Sarah Rand's apartment."

"The name doesn't ring a bell."

"Then I guess you won't be interested in knowing what I was doing there. Or who hired me to pay her a visit. Or how I ended up ditching the wrong corpse and letting your new girlfriend continue to walk around without a scratch...for now, anyway."

Owen sat back in the metal chair, his face businesslike. "Didn't one of your letters say you've been in prison for a while?"

"Never heard of our state's enlightened furlough program?" Jake flashed him a wide smile. "Most of us can't sit back and wait for the right producer to come around and pay us a million bucks for our work. A man has to make a living."

"Is this the script you're selling?"

"It's a package deal."

"What if I said I'm only interested in this part of the package?" Owen replied.

The two men's gazes collided. The heavy silence was broken by the sound of a heavy metal door banging shut somewhere in the distance.

"If you don't want to deal, Jake, I can walk out right now."

Gantley eyed him with a look devoid of expression, but Owen had seen that look before. If they were on the street right now, Jake would cut his heart out with a spoon.

"Last chance. Are you selling?"

"I might be...for the right price."

Owen had him, now. It was a small victory, but a telling one.

"I'm not interested in any fiction," he said flatly. "I have an office full of writers who can come up with stories."

"This is not fiction. And..." Jake's gaze dropped to the bottom of the glass separator. When he looked up again, he was back in control. "I believe if you knew that there was more than one disgruntled character chasing after your girlfriend, you wouldn't be so blasé." The inmate stared at him. "Do I have your attention, Mr. Dean?"

"Back it up with facts," Owen pressed. "You can be inventing this whole thing based on what you've been reading in the papers."

Jake threw a glance in the direction of the guard. "I was contracted to do a job by a certain individual. When I got there, someone else had beaten me to it. Someone else who was not very bright," he added as an afterthought. "This someone hadn't done his homework. This same someone dusted the wrong lady."

"And how do you know it was the wrong lady?"

"I'm a professional. Details are my life." Jake flashed him a confident smile. "Those fancy earrings that your girlfriend always wears were the first clue. Actually, they should have been a dead giveaway to the dope horning in on my turf. On top of that, there was that music. You don't have to be an Einstein to know someone with your girl's sense of style wouldn't be into Pearl Jam. And then, there was the airline ticket-stub in the pocket of Tori's tight little jeans. She had a nice ass, but her real assets were her—"

"Drop it." Owen spoke impatiently. "Go on."

Jake flashed him another smile. "The place was a wreck, like the genius was looking for something, but then half-decided to make it look like a robbery."

"What did you do?"

"I was hired for a two-step job. You might say, it was a 'dust and vacuum' job. Now, if someone else had decided to take care of the first half for me, who was I to complain?"

Jake glanced toward the guard again.

"Time was running short, if you get my meaning. I wanted to get paid." He shrugged. "I did what any other professional would do in a situation like that. I went around and took the luggage tags off the bag upstairs and mixed in her stuff with your girlfriend's. Then I did whatever else I could think of in the little time I had left. Hey, the first guy had helped me out by knocking off a girl. Now I was returning the favor by messing up the place so that—at least, up front—the cops would think Sarah Rand was the one who'd gotten snuffed."

"Were you the one who dragged her to Judge Arnold's boat?"

"Only parts of her—blood, hair, stuff from the rug. I have plenty of time to read all those crime and detection books. I know what those guys look for and how they collect their evidence. I told you I'm a pro. It's my job to stay up on things. In fact, one of these days, I should write a book about it, myself."

"Where is her body now?"

"You don't want to know." Jake shook his head with a look of feigned distaste.

"Who contracted you to do the job?"

"Now you are getting to the good stuff."

"Well?" Owen asked impatiently.

"Let's start with small stuff and then build up." Jake now wore the demeanor of one business partner talking to another. "I want you to call this cousin of mine, when you get back to Newport. His name is Frankie O'Neal. He is my collection agency. A good guy. Very decent. A little overweight, but I'm working on that. Trying to improve his image, his self-esteem."

Owen wrote down the address and phone number on a piece of paper.

"If we're going to deal, you're going to have to pay. Twenty grand is a fair price for the small stuff, and that'll keep me supplied with pencils and pens."

"I'm not asking you to kill anyone, Jake. You're only giving me a name."

Gantley shook his head. "You know, I hate talking money. On the other hand, if you take me up on my proposal and look at my writing, just to see if you could use some of my stories, then I'll give you a break. But as it stands now, my hands are tied. I have mouths to feed, you know. Well, not really, but it sounds good."

"When do I get the rest of it?"

Jake glanced around. "Tomorrow. That is, if you send some money Frankie's way by then. And no checks."

"How do I know you're not full of shit?"

"You're a smart guy, Owen." The inmate smiled again. "Okay. I'll give you something for free. I read in the paper today that there is a memorial service tomorrow at noon for the millionaire golden boy, Hal Van Horn. Listen good. The one who took out the contract on your girlfriend will be there."

"Half of Newport will be there."

"Look really close. You know the immediate circle of family and friends. You can't miss him."

Owen got up to go, but Jake stopped him.

"I'll tell you something else. By now, the cops know she is alive." He gave Owen a long nod. "If their labs are anywhere near as good as I figure, they already know that the blood they found in the apartment and the boat might match, but they don't belong to Sarah Rand."

"Thanks for the warning."

He was still on hold.

Trapping the cell phone between his shoulder and his ear, Scott Rosen looked at his watch. He frowned and shifted his weight, then stopped.

The attorney stared through the large windows that separated the four newborn infants from the germs and scum that constituted life outside the hospital nursery. An attendant wearing scrubs pushed a fifth glass crib into the room. The new addition—an eight pound, seven ounce baby girl—was wheeled toward the nursery window.

"It should only be another couple of minutes, Mr. Rosen." The voice on the phone was polite.

"Thank you."

Scott looked from the nametag on the glass crib to the wrinkled red face of his daughter. His hand touched the glass. She made an angry face, and the pacifier fell from her pursed lips.

He'd returned home this morning only to find a hurried note from Lucy. It was short and to the point. Her water had broken while he'd been gone. Not wanting to disturb him or his work, she'd simply asked one of their neighbors to take her to the hospital.

By the time he'd gotten to the delivery room, Lucy had already given birth.

Scott's first instinct was that he should be angry at her for not calling him. That thought had fallen by the wayside pretty quickly. After all, who he was kidding? He had been an insensitive jerk throughout her entire pregnancy. Shit, throughout their entire marriage, for that matter. But she had continued to put up with him.

Still, something had changed today, and Scott knew it.

Labor and childbirth had lasted almost three hours. She had gone through it all by herself, without any drugs. When he finally saw her, she looked tired but very proud.

Watching Lucy try to breastfeed their daughter early this afternoon, Scott had seen the new independence. It was as if something powerful had awakened within her.

It had been the two of them—the mother and baby. An experience shared by just them. And then there had been Scott. Looking on. An outsider who didn't even know how to hold his daughter. Something in her look told him that Lucy now realized she could do without him.

Judge Arnold's gruff voice came over the phone. "What do you want Scott?"

"I'm a father." The words tumbled out unexpectedly. What a stupid thing to say. "Sorry, your honor. That's not why I called you."

"Congratulations. How is Lucy?"

"Fine. She is doing just great. Thanks." He was surprised at the sudden warmth in the Judge's voice. "The reason for my call, however, is that I just heard from Senator Rutherford's office. They're very upset that you are refusing to go to Hal's memorial service tomorrow. You understand that the senator had to make a special request for you to be allowed to attend, even with a police escort. As your lawyer, sir, I was surprised—"

"Boy or girl?"

"Your Honor..." Scott walked away from the nursery glass. "I'm your lawyer and not your press secretary, but this—"

"Boy or girl?"

"What? A girl."

"What are you calling her?"

"We haven't really talked about it." He glanced at the nursery window and saw his daughter wailing. The attendant came over and picked her up.

"Well, instead of talking on the phone, Scott, you should be sitting at Lucy's side. Holding her hand. Picking names. What kind of flowers did you have delivered to her room?"

"Flowers? I…I haven't got that far, yet."

"Damn it, Scott!" the Judge snapped at the other end. "Do you understand the meaning of *priorities*? Avery and I never had any children, but by God, she never had to go short of flowers or gifts. Women need that kind of attention from their men. It gives them some incentive to keep us around."

Scott suddenly realized he was foundering. He wasn't accustomed to losing control of discussions with his clients. He definitely wasn't accustomed to being reminded how incompetent he was in the area of marriage.

"Judge, about Hal's memorial service tomorrow. I believe the media will have a field day at your expense if you were not to attend."

"Good," the older man growled. "Let them. You're my lawyer. You make my excuses. But more important, be sure to bring some pictures of your Baby X when you come to see me on Monday. And in the meantime, pass on my congratulations to Lucy. She is quite a girl, Scott."

"But Your Hon—"

Scott heard the phone in his hand go dead, and he knew he'd lost the battle.

Slipping the phone back into his pocket, he looked at his daughter. The attendant was carrying her into another room, and his thoughts returned to one of the files in his briefcase. The one he'd been reading just before Evan Steele had interrupted him.

It was all related. The Judge's open hostility toward his stepson…even now, after his death. Hal's damning testimony to the police and the D.A. about a relationship between Judge Arnold and Sarah Rand. The report Scott had discovered in the files this morning that surely affected Avery's will.

An attendant carrying a large bouquet of flowers came out of a patient's room. It took a moment before what he was looking at sank in.

"Shit," he exclaimed under his breath, heading for the elevator.

He was in the hospital flower shop by the reception desk on the main floor, waiting for his order of two dozen roses to be wrapped when he saw the other man enter the shop. Seeing celebrities around town had never impressed Scott. In fact, he didn't know who most of these people were. He hardly watched any television that wasn't news related, anymore. He didn't go to the movies. Or plays. He was lucky to find time to read a novel, now and then. As Lucy was quick to say about him, he was 'culturally challenged.'

Owen Dean, though, was a face and a name he was quite familiar with. Of the few movies that he'd seen over the years, Dean's had been the ones. He'd read about the success of his television show in the papers, though he'd never seen it. But he'd been very impressed when he'd read that the actor and movie producer was spending a semester teaching at a local college.

The celebrity glanced at the flowers being wrapped and placed an order. As he turned to go, he nodded at Scott before taking a second, closer look at him.

"Excuse me, but aren't you Scott Rosen?"

The lawyer was flattered and baffled at the same time. "Yes, I am."

"I'm Owen Dean." Strong, confident handshake. "I've been reading so much about the Rand murder lately that I couldn't pass up saying hello."

"Thank you," Scott replied, still a bit flustered. "But I'm a little stunned that you recognized me. I mean…I know you. I've been a fan for years, but…"

"Newspapers." Owen smiled. "I'm always interested in the guys behind the scenes. The ones who do all the work. One of the papers ran your picture, though I get the feeling you prefer to work out of the limelight."

"To some extent, that's true. It's the work I love."

"I thought so. That's my latest goal in life. To step into the background a little more."

"So you can do all the work?"

He laughed. "And enjoy it, too. There is nothing fun about being in the spotlight all the time. No privacy. No time for the important things. You know what I mean."

Scott nodded as the two of them walked out of the shop.

"This whole thing, this Arnold-Rand case, must be putting a lot of pressure on you." They stopped by the elevators. "Do you have a defense team, or are you doing it all alone?"

"We're consulting with the best guys in the business—Dershowitz, Miller, Bergman—but we're still in the preliminary stages. Once we get a little more into it, we'll put together a complete defense team."

The elevator opened, and the two men stepped back to allow an elderly couple to exit before they got in. Each of them pressed the button for their floor, but Owen held the elevator as a rather frazzled-looking woman rushed across the lobby, calling for them to hold the door.

"And how is it going, so far?" the celebrity asked as they started up. "I mean, just your opinion, from a defense perspective."

"Fine." Scott waited until the other passenger got off before giving his honest answer. "Confidentially, so far I feel like I'm more in the middle of a conspiracy movie than a murder case. It's difficult to explain."

The door opened onto the maternity floor.

"It was a pleasure meeting you, Mr. Dean." He extended a hand.

"The pleasure was all mine." Owen offered. "Best of luck with the case."

Chapter 21

The sharp spray of water stung Sarah's face and scalp. With her eyes closed, she welcomed the warm needles pricking her skin as she tried to sort out the jumble of plans forming in her mind.

It was already Sunday morning, and she had to think of something to wear to the memorial service without being recognized as herself. A tall order.

But more than what she was going to wear and how she could disguise her looks, the information Owen had brought out of his meeting with Jake Gantley yesterday was preying on Sarah's mind. There had been two people who'd wanted her dead.

One hired killer thought he had succeeded, and the second hit man had proceeded to finish the job according to his client's directions...if Jake Gantley was to be believed.

The one who'd actually killed Tori had been looking for something that they'd obviously not found. The second killer's objective had been to set up Judge Arnold. That had been a success.

And if they both found out that she was alive, then the attack on the road on her first night back from Ireland, and then the second attempt in the Van Horn mansion followed logically.

What it came down to was the same thing. Both people wanted her dead—but for different reasons.

Sarah shivered at the thought of how unimportant her life was to these people. And not just her life. Andrew and Tracy Warner's. Tori's. Hal's. How insignificant life could be.

She took a deep breath, horrified to think that the person who'd contracted Jake was someone that she must know. A friend of the Van Horn family...someone in the immediate circle. She knew all of them, had met them, socialized with them—thought of herself as being accepted by them. What a fool she'd been.

The sound of the shower door opening startled her...and then

Owen stepped in. She shivered at the touch of Owen's hand running down her wet back. She saw him reach around her for the soap and in a moment was lathering her slippery skin. She leaned her forehead against the tiles and felt his body press near.

"I was getting worried that you weren't going to leave me any hot water."

She turned in his arms and smiled as her gaze traveled down his wet and naked body. "I think a *cold* shower is all you need."

"I'll show you what I need."

"Tomorrow could be the big day," Owen said later pensively. "Scott Rosen will be returning those files to the office, and you'll find whatever it is that's at the bottom of all this."

"And by tomorrow, I might finally get hold of Frankie O'Neal. Then we can get Jake to give us a name."

He'd refused to tell her how much money Jake wanted for the information. He would only tell her that it was a bargain. Sarah was indebted in more ways than she could ever repay for all that Owen was doing. If she survived this ordeal, she would see that the payback was extensive.

"It's pretty clear that the motivation for each attack was different. The name that our friend Jake gives us will only lead to the one who wanted to frame the Judge. The other—"

"No matter what, we'll have something significant to take with us to the authorities," he said. "I've already talked to my lawyer in New York about it. He'll arrange for the right people to meet us at the right time."

Sarah looked at him for a moment and then nodded. She'd seen him make a number of phone calls over the past few days. Some of the more recent calls had gone out to the hospital, checking on Tracy's condition. Others, she'd assumed were business-related, and she hadn't paid close attention. She was not unhappy to know that someone besides the two of them knew what was going on. After all, she and Owen could be murdered at any moment.

Sarah decided on a black, short-sleeved dress that she'd purchased in Dublin for her father's funeral. She dried her hair in a new style of bangs on her forehead and put on the large sunglasses.

She couldn't tell much difference herself, but Owen assured her that so long as she remained in the background and held a handkerchief to her face to hide her 'grief,' she would probably go undiscovered. No one was expecting her there.

They weren't planning to attend the entire service, anyway. Sarah's only goal was to poke her head in long enough to get a peek at the people in the front rows and see anything that might jog her memory.

Owen insisted that they might be able to accomplish the same thing from the safety of the street, simply watching the people go in.

She was more willing to take a risk.

He wanted to play it safe and wait for Jake to reveal a name to them.

She *had* to go for herself and, in a way, for Hal. Despite the differences they might have had, there had been good days between them, too. There had been friendship—understanding of late—even sacrifice. Looking into the mirror, Sarah felt the familiar old guilt stabbing her in the heart. Hal had physically stepped into the path of that knife for her.

"I still think it's a mistake to go."

Owen's arm around her shoulders brought Sarah back to the present. She turned in his arm and took comfort in his embrace. The moments of happiness she was sharing with Owen were so undeserved.

"I have to…"

She pulled back and wiped at the tears that she didn't even know had escaped. She didn't want to grieve for Hal in front of him. Owen had put up with enough of her emotional displays. She looked up and down at the dark gray suit, white shirt and the conservative tie.

"This won't do."

"What do you mean?"

"I can't be hanging around you out there…not when you're looking so dashing."

"Keep talking like that, honey, and we're not going anywhere."

She laughed as his arms wrapped around her. "For all the gossip

I've read about you over the years, nothing ever mentioned what a flirt you are."

"That's because I am not a flirt. Besides, this is not flirting. This is honest, straight-from-the-loins lust."

They both laughed and then held each other for a long moment.

"None of this seems real." Sarah said. "You…and me. You wouldn't believe what a crush I had on you when I was younger."

"Does this mean you—"

The sound of the phone interrupted his question, and Owen went to answer it. She knew right away that Captain Archer was on the other end.

"Yes….Frankie O'Neal….Yes."

She sat down on the edge of a chair, and Owen looked at her. "Found dead when?"

Owen ran a hand over his face as if trying to wake himself up. Sarah was too numb even to try to identify how she felt.

"Yes, Captain. That's right. I did leave him a message. No, wait! I left him two messages, one last night and one this morning."

Sarah stared at Owen as he began pacing. She had heard him leaving the vague messages herself. Now the man was dead, and Owen's voice was the one on his answering machine.

"No, I really don't know the man, but I visited his cousin, an inmate named Jake Gantley, yesterday at the ACI. Of course…call the Warden directly. Right. It was Gantley's recommendation that I call Mr. O'Neal."

While Owen listened to whatever it was that Archer was asking or saying, Sarah wondered if this was it. Well, if Owen decided that enough was enough and revealed everything to Archer, she wouldn't blame him at all. In fact, she was almost resigned to it.

"Jake Gantley has been communicating with our production company for a while. He has been trying to sell us some stories. Yes, that was why I went to see him. We might be interested in developing some of his work for one of the upcoming seasons." Owen glanced at Sarah across the room and then walked over and laid a hand on her shoulder. "Gantley instructed me that all the negotiations regarding the writing should be done through his cousin Frankie O'Neal. Right. That's why I called him."

Owen paused again for something else that was being said.

"Really...that's too bad. So he must have been dead before I even talked to his cousin."

Sarah pressed his hand against her shoulder.

"The letters? Of course...I'll call my production company on Monday and have them forward them to you immediately."

There was another pause. "Yes, I'll be in town for a while. Of course. Call me if you think of anything else."

Sarah felt Owen's grip tighten.

"Yes, I heard about the tragedy from Dr. Doyle. Yeah, the dean at Rosecliff. She called me. Yes, I've been to the hospital a couple of times already. This morning when I called, everything was still the same. Thank you, Captain....Yes, Andrew was a good friend."

When Owen hung up, Sarah continued to hold on to his hand.

"We need help." she whispered. "I'll call Evan Steele. He is a jack-of-all-trades. Security expert. Background checks. Investigations. He's got to be helping Scott with the Judge's defense. He'll be able to get me in and out of our offices."

"He'll turn you right in."

She shook her head. "Not if I tell him that I'm turning myself in tomorrow. I'll explain things to him. I've known him, and he's worked for me and for the Judge, for as long as I've been in Newport. We worked well together in the past. I know he trusts me."

"And what would that accomplish," Owen asked. "Talking to Steele?"

"I'll get him to let me into the office tomorrow morning. With no clock ticking, I can check through the office thoroughly. Hopefully, Rosen will have returned the files by then. I can go through Linda's files. I didn't think of it before, but what if she hadn't filed everything away, yet." She felt a knot rise into her throat. "We can't let someone else die, Owen."

"This death could be totally unrelated." Owen pulled Sarah to her feet. "And it sounds like the cops have a history with this guy. In fact, I wouldn't say that Archer made this sound like a high-priority investigation. Of course, he's got a pretty full plate these days."

Sarah shook her head. "I can't risk it anymore. Please, Owen, let's not fight over this. I want this thing over and done with. And other than what Jake Gantley knows, whatever I might have displaced from those safe-deposit boxes is my only clue. I've got to spend some time in that office."

She could see in his face the battle that was being fought inside his head. Finally, he nodded.

"Okay. Then do you still want to go to that memorial service?"

"Absolutely. Steele is probably there, anyway."

"Call him afterwards, Sarah. You can't make any assumptions what his reaction will be when he sees you alive."

She agreed. The next twenty-four hours were all that she was giving herself to solve these killings.

Playing it smart, more so than playing it safe, was the name of the game now.

For nearly an hour, Jake Gantley sat without moving on the top bunk. His legs hung over the edge. His back was ramrod straight. Eyes, intense and unblinking, burned the paint off the concrete wall four and a half feet away. Every muscle in his body appeared to be fixed in stone. His hands were fisted in his lap.

His cell mate, Amir, leaned against the stainless steel sink, never looking directly at Jake, but keeping him in his peripheral vision. He'd heard in the yard about Frankie's *adios* a good half hour before the warden had called Jake in to break the news. Word traveled fast inside the house, and Amir was feeling very lucky he'd heard before Jake did. There was no telling what a guy as dangerous as his cell mate might do. Now he could keep an eye on him.

There were a lot of people on the inside who'd had dealings with Frankie for one thing or another. He was a decent bookie, fairly honest. Frankie even had enough connections that you could generally count on a job or two through him when you needed it. The fat boy had paid his dues with the family in Providence, too—before things started falling apart up there—so the current management now let him operate pretty much free of charge.

And no one fucked with him for one reason...Jake Gantley.

Now, killing Frankie made no sense. The word in the yard was that he was shot in his bed. One cat said he heard it was a family hit out of Providence. Another who was connected there said it must have been the Westies from New York. That made more sense—Amir had heard there was a job that went bad last year, and Frankie'd been fingered to take the blame.

Well, whoever did it, they might as well just kiss their asses good-bye. Amir could see that much in Jake's face.

Amir ran a hand over his shaved head. He'd been ready for his cell mate to freak out when he got back from talking to the warden. He hazarded a quick look at Jake. Still deadly quiet. There was killing in the eyes. Amir didn't care to be anywhere near the man, though there wasn't much to be done about it. It wasn't that he was scared. It was just that he knew when Jake finally exploded, it'd be blood he was after. And he'd come to like Jake's wise-ass, mouthy attitude too much. He sure as hell didn't want to kill him.

One of the guards came by the barred door, and Amir watched as Jake jumped down from the bunk to go and talk to him. He knew the man and Jake were running a deal.

Strange, Amir thought, that Jake did nothing to hide what he was telling the guard. No whispering. No nothing. Not cool. He looked past them. He could see the two brothers directly across watching. Definitely, not cool.

"Call this number for me. Tell the guy who answers to come and see me this afternoon. Tell him I'll have his scoop for him. Tell him, never mind the favor I asked for yesterday. Tell him, it has to be this afternoon. Get it?"

"How about if nobody answers?"

"Leave a message. Call back again if you have to. Don't you know how to act like a fucking secretary?"

"Hey, easy does it, Jake. What's his name?"

"Owen Dean," Jake answered.

Amir could see how impressed the guard looked. "You know him?"

"Jump on this, and I'll get him to autograph a picture for your wife. Now get moving, I need to get this show on the road."

Chapter 22

A big neon sign. With a great big fat neon arrow pointing down at her and huge block letters reading "Look at me!"

Might as well, Sarah thought. She'd already realized that standing beside Owen in public was certainly no way to avoid attention. With his six feet two inches of muscle and a face that most Americans knew better than their own next-door neighbor's, Owen Dean turned heads wherever he went. And because he was such a celebrity, whoever walked with him or stood beside him drew people's attention, as well. Well, this was the kind of scrutiny that Sarah couldn't afford right now.

On the other hand, if she were to stay away from him, the attention he attracted would certainly allow her to move more freely.

The memorial service was to be held at Trinity Church, an old colonial building of white clapboard, distinguished by its Wren-inspired steeple, and the fact that George Washington had once or twice attended services there. The church, sitting at the top of a large green, looked out over the harbor and the trendy shops and restaurants of Bannister's Wharf. Spring Street, which ran directly behind the church, was relatively empty. Only a few tourists and interested onlookers hovered on the cobbled sidewalks, watching the well-dressed coterie of Newport's elite entering the church. A news van was parked in a nearby loading zone.

Owen had been dead set against Sarah going inside the church, but she'd won that battle, as well. Now, however, she felt her stomach knotting up at the thought of entering. Several large groups converged on the entrance at once, just as she and Owen, walking on opposite sides of Spring Street, came up to the church. Mingling with the small crowd, Sarah kept her handkerchief to her face, looked no one in the eye, and entered the church.

Owen hung back a little, pretending to look for a moment over the fence at the epitaph on one of the headstones in the historic churchyard, all the while watching Sarah enter ahead of him. Inside, she skirted a crowd in the vestibule. He followed a group into the church.

Owen wasn't about to engage anyone in conversation, but if anyone pressed him, he had a good line ready as to why he was attending. He would just say that he knew Hal Van Horn was a close family friend of the Warners—as he was himself. With Tracy still unconscious in the hospital, Owen felt it was incumbent upon him to represent the Warners and pay their respects. And no, he wasn't planning on using the bizarre murders plaguing the seaside town for his TV series.

Sarah was standing with dozens of people packed under the gallery. Every gated pew was filled, and the galleries above were jammed to capacity. Owen stood one pillar to her right. Far enough to draw attention away and yet close enough to get to her if there was a need.

Leaving her large sunglasses on was not an issue, as many were doing the same thing to hide tears shed for Hal. Sarah fit right in with the hundreds of mourners filling the hall.

In the front of the church, beside the white pulpit that rose a good six feet above the tops of the pews, a stand of flowers had been erected around a large portrait of a youthful Hal standing behind his mother.

Waiting for the service to start, Sarah stared at the portrait for a moment, and then turned her attention to two women talking quietly behind her.

"I'm surprised how quickly they arranged all this," one woman commented.

"I heard they don't know when the medical examiner is going to release his body."

"It's amazing what's going around. I heard that the stabbing had to do with a drug sale that went bad."

"I heard that the attack was an arranged suicide put together by Hal himself. You know he's been terribly depressed since Sarah's death."

"Genevieve told me—you won't believe this—Hal and Sarah Rand had a son before she came to Newport five years ago, and she'd put the kid up for adoption. She said Judge Arnold was not aware of this until recently. He became so upset with the news—that Sarah would deprive his wife of the joy of being a grandmother—that he had to kill her for Avery's sake. Can you believe anyone would tell a story like that?"

"You'll never guess who's watching us. Owen Dean."

"Where?"

The service started. An organist played a beautiful eighteenth-century piece that Sarah thought Hal had probably never heard in his life. A clergyman she didn't recognize then spoke at length about death and eternity. A soloist delivered a moving rendition of the requisite "Amazing Grace." Finally, Senator Rutherford mounted the pulpit and began to tell stories from Hal's childhood and adolescence. Suddenly, Sarah was stunned as he began to relate a conversation he'd had with Hal a week ago.

"Many of you might know or might have heard how greatly Hal suffered after Sarah Rand's murder not so long ago. Well, what you have heard is true. I remember his last words to me very clearly. 'Gordon,' he said, 'Sarah and I had found a rare thing in this world. Friendship. Affection. Devotion. Love. I worshipped Sarah, and Sarah...for some reason...worshipped me. No two people out there have ever been better suited for each other than Sarah and I. Gordon,' he said, 'the future was ours to conquer. Happiness was ours for the taking. Out of respect for my mother's memory, we had decided to keep it quiet for a while. But we both knew. Our time should have been now. We were going to tie the knot.'"

Sarah glanced at Owen. A hardness had crept into his face as he looked up at the senator. Suddenly, she wished she could speak out, tell the truth within the walls of this church, tell everyone that this was far more than a ridiculous exaggeration of what she and Hal had been to each other. It was a lie. But how could she? She wanted to move to Owen's side and touch his hand. She wanted to be sure that he wasn't believing any of this.

"'We were soul mates, Gordon,' Hal told me not a mile from this spot. 'What we shared was close to divine. What I lost can *never* be replaced in this lifetime.'"

Rutherford paused to control his quavering voice and quite a few handkerchiefs made their way to onlooker's faces.

Sorrow, however, was not what was infusing Sarah's spirit at this moment. The senator's misrepresentation of the truth appalled her, disgusted her. It was a lie, and she couldn't believe that Hal would ever have said such things. Nonetheless, rather than demonstrating what had been good about Hal, this maudlin mush only served to highlight for her all his flaws.

She had reconciled her past with him. She had no desire to dredge up the futility of their relationship. It was behind her now. But these fallacious words—no matter how well meaning the senator was in speaking them—were hurting her more than she'd ever thought possible.

And then it struck her. Slowly, at first, the thought emerged, gradually blocking out the eulogy and filling her with repugnance. She'd never really been Hal's type, but she fit a need for Hal. It just came down to image. She fit just the right image for his family, but mostly for the benefit of the Judge, who exerted great influence over Hal's mother.

Unlike the legion of other women that Judge Arnold had always found lacking, one way or another, Sarah had immediately been welcomed by the family. She was a self-made woman on the way up. An underdog who was about to succeed. Hardworking. Smart. A good lawyer. Fairly attractive, but never flashy. She could see it now quite clearly. At some point Hal had gone out in search of the perfect vehicle for his move into responsible living, and Sarah had been it.

She thought back to their first meeting. It had been arranged by one of Hal's friends. It was no accident that he'd been in a certain restaurant on a certain night. Sarah had been an unconscious pawn in his schemes from day one.

"Love outlasts death and the ravages of time." Rutherford's words echoed in the church. "These were my words to Hal that day. Having suffered for so many years ago as Hal was suffering that day, I shared with him the comfort that has kept me going. 'Someday you and Sarah will meet again,' I told Hal that night, 'as, someday, Julia and I will rejoice in joining together again…for eternity.'"

Once more, the senator paused to gather strength and collect his voice.

"Those two lovers are now together again."

Many heads bowed. Sarah dabbed at her eyes as a photographer snapped a shot of a woman openly weeping near her.

"But I never considered for an instant how soon Hal would be taken. Well…" Gordon Rutherford gazed up into the choir loft at the rear of the church. "'Good night, sweet prince, and flights of angels sing thee to thy rest.'"

From the green outside, the low melodic wail of a solitary bag-pipe could be heard. Very effective, Sarah thought, focusing her attention on the people sitting in the first pews.

The senator was joining Scott Rosen in the pew where Judge Arnold would have been placed if he had attended. In the next closed pew, Sarah looked over a number of Hal's friends and em-ployees. Looking the most upset by the ordeal was Gwen Turner, his secretary. Gwen would have walked to the ends of the earth for her employer. She would have swallowed fire or walked across hot coals if Hal had asked her to.

Across from them, Evan Steele sat beside Linda, the Judge's of-fice manager. Sarah considered that for a moment. When it came to the ongoing war between Judge Arnold and Hal, people gener-ally had to take sides. Though Sarah had been reasonably success-ful, it was almost impossible for anyone involved with the family to remain neutral. Evan Steele had always been in Judge Arnold's corner. There was no doubt where the man's loyalties lay.

With them, she noted the familiar face of Fran Bingham, a girl-friend of Hal's as recently as a month ago. The woman's face was a mask, and Sarah couldn't help but wonder how Fran felt about all this talk of Hal's eternal love for someone else.

She was not surprised to see Captain Archer standing in the crowd under the far gallery. The detective's pale, tired face showed no emotion regarding the proceedings whatsoever. He might have been watching grass grow, for all he was showing.

She edged behind a pillar and looked again at those sitting near-est the front. There was a story behind most of them. Any of these people might have had a grudge or two against Hal. But none of them, Sarah believed, had ever had a reason for wanting her dead. Neither could she imagine any of them wanting to set up Judge Arnold for the murder. She frowned and glanced over in time to see Owen backing out the open church door. His nod was almost imperceptible, but Sarah knew he'd have the car where they'd agreed to meet.

As another of the Van Horn's family friends climbed the podium to recite a poem, Sarah started working her way along the side wall toward the door.

She couldn't take this anymore. And it was stupid to stand there and allow all her negative thoughts about Hal to take her down. The air in the place had become suffocating. It felt as if a great weight had somehow rolled onto her back. A sea of people stood in the way, but Sarah pushed through.

Of course, what confused everything in her mind was Hal Van Horn stepping in front of her on Thursday night, sacrificing his own life to save hers.

Was he a hero or a coward? Was she a realist or an ungrateful monster?

She was almost to the door.

Someone was watching her. Sarah felt it as surely as if a hand had been laid on her shoulder. Quickly, she glanced around. The poem-reading friend was just finishing and the organ overhead came to life. Mostly, all she saw were people's backs.

Everyone's attention seemed to be focused on the front of the church. But she still felt the weight of someone's watchful gaze. Accidentally, she bumped into an elderly couple standing away from the wall.

Mumbling her apologies, she pressed on. When someone touched her elbow, she veered immediately to the left, around a heavyset man in a suit. Panic seized her at the feeling of someone still on her heels. She tried to push past the people blocking her path, but wherever she turned there were more of them.

She felt someone grab for her arm again, and she tugged hard to get herself loose, shoving past a young man who had just stepped into the open doorway.

Her low heels slipped on the first stone step, and she practically went headlong onto the sidewalk outside the church. She regained her footing, and turned around to look back at the church. Only the backs of people inside the door were visible. No one was watching her. No one was following her.

More people were strolling in the bright sunshine along the street. Sarah looked at the church again. Nothing. Only the sound of the organ. She started down Spring Street.

She was losing it. The entire thing had been a product of her imagination.

Owen was to meet her two streets away. She tucked the handkerchief she'd been carrying in her purse and fell in behind two gay men sauntering along hand in hand.

"Miss Rand."

The sound of her name whispered in her ear was as terrifying as the metallic object she felt pressed into her back. Her heart hammering in her chest, Sarah winced at the viselike grip he had on her upper arm.

"Nice and easy, Miss Rand."

There was something about the voice that struck a familiar cord.

"Eyes straight ahead," he growled, jabbing the pistol into her kidneys for emphasis. "Keep walking."

She could feel the jacket or something that he had draped over his gun hand bumping against her. She felt her legs becoming rubbery. No one was looking at them as if anything were wrong.

"You…you have the wrong person." She finally managed to get out the words.

"I don't think so, Miss Rand."

She guessed he was fairly tall. From the grip he had on her, she knew he was very strong. Everything she'd ever heard and learned about attacks on women flashed into her head. They were in a public place. Even though he was holding a gun, she knew she had to fight him here to have any chance of surviving.

"Now, we are going to walk nice and easy across the street and get into my car."

She planted her feet.

"Act stupid and I'll kill you here, Miss Rand. We don't mind public scenes. Remember your boyfriend?"

Sarah's gaze flickered toward a blue sedan just pulling out of a parking space up the street. Her abductor gave her a harder shove, and she started across the street.

They were half way across when she saw the blue sedan unexpectedly speed up, heading right at them. She planted her feet again, refusing to be pushed.

Sarah sensed her attacker's surprise at the onrushing car and her reaction. As the pressure of the gun against her back disappeared and his grip relaxed, she tore her arm away, kicking him as hard as she could in the shin before diving toward the sidewalk.

Behind her back, she heard the dull sound of the car striking his body and then the screeching of brakes. She turned in time to see a large gray-suited body land on the road, roll over once, and then lie still. The gun, still in his hand, lay on the pavement half hidden by the trench coat over his arm.

Everything stood still for a moment.

"Oh, my God!" came a cry from the opposite sidewalk.

And then Sarah was running.

Chapter 23

Thick and smoky brown, the layers of oblivion lay heavy on her eyes. Slowly, painfully, she forced her way up through the layers. Sometimes she thought she would never break through them. Sometimes she saw no purpose in it anyway. But on she went, clawing and pushing.

Her throat was dry and scratched and incredibly sore. Despite whatever it was that she felt pressing tightly against her ears, the loud metallic buzz and the rhythmic pounding of machinery continuously filled her head. Something was stuck in her nose and a heavy weight on her chest wouldn't let Tracy Warner take a breath at her own pace.

She couldn't open her eyes. She couldn't move her mouth. She tried to move her fingers, but she didn't know where they were.

The blankets of brown smoke again began to pile on her, and she felt herself sinking again.

Before she drifted off, she remembered seeing Andrew walking into their kitchen. The gunman was holding his weapon to her head. She remembered seeing her husband's expression. In spite of all that was happening, in spite of all that was about to happen, his eyes had never moved from the sight of his two dogs.

When Owen saw Sarah running up the street, he knew something was wrong. He immediately started the car and pulled it into the intersection. She had no sooner climbed in before Owen was on his way.

The sunglasses were thrown to the floor. She immediately had her head buried on her knees. He could hear her irregular gasps for breath. It was difficult to keep his eyes on the road, but Owen turned up a side street as the sound of sirens erupted behind them.

"What happened?"

"Did anybody see me get into the car?" she asked.

"No."

"Please, make sure nobody is following us. Please!"

He glanced in the driver's mirrors. "No one. What happened?"

The sound of sirens could be heard coming from all directions. Rather than heading back onto Ocean Drive, Owen made a detour out toward the beaches.

She lifted her head. Her face was raw, and her fingers were ice-cold as Owen reached over and placed his hand on top of hers.

"A man, a gunman, came up behind me outside of the church. He knew who I was. He wanted me to go with him. But when we were crossing the road, this car...a dark blue car came at us. Somehow I got away and...the man was hit." Sarah hid her face in her hands. "There is no getting away. Not anymore. You said...you can ask your lawyer to arrange for something, for me to hand myself over to the right authorities. We've got to do it. I can't take this anymore. If they recognized me like this, they...they could be waiting for us at your apartment."

He glanced again in the side mirror.

"Did you see the man's face? The gunman?"

"No. I couldn't. But I don't think I knew him. He was really large like a football player, and his voice...wait!" Her face snapped in his direction. "It was the cop who stopped me on my way back from the airport. I'm sure of it. He was the one. My God...everybody is connected. We could be so close."

She took hold of his hand, gripping it tightly. "I'll call Steele. I'll have him let me in the office tomorrow morning. Could we somehow have someone meet us there or pick us up after?"

"I'll try," he said reassuringly. "But what happened after the car hit the gunman?"

"I don't know. I ran away."

"Did you see the driver? Do you remember anything about the car?"

She shook her head. "Blue. Dark blue. That's all I remember. But he was aiming at us. I saw him speed up."

The car wound along the country lanes, and soon they were back to the more easterly of the two main roads heading north on the island. She could see sailboats on the blue waters of the Sakonnet

River, beyond the sloping fields.

Owen reached for his cell phone and dialed a number. Speaking to someone named Susan on the other end, a woman Sarah assumed must be one of his assistants, he gave her a number of directions. Before hanging up, he asked some questions about a house near Little Compton, a quaint village on the far side of the Sakonnet. When he was finished, he turned to her.

"Can you make do with what you have with you until tomorrow afternoon?"

"Yes," she replied, watching him dial another number.

She was glad to know that at least one of them could stay cool in the face of all this chaos. His confidence helped restore in her some of the courage that, like blood from an unstaunched wound, had been oozing out of her for days now.

"There's a message from Jake Gantley," he told her, tossing the cell phone onto the console. "He must have heard about his cousin's hit. He is willing to talk if I get there this afternoon."

"I think you should go," Sarah whispered. "I'll come with you."

"If these people have guessed a connection between us, there is no point in checking into any hotels tonight. We'd be less safe there than at my apartment. That's why I asked Susan to arrange for us to stay at her in-law's house south of Little Compton. Nobody can connect us with the place. Susan says they're away sailing around Nantucket this week."

"Will we be able to get into the cottage?"

"She gave me the security code to their garage. Says there's always a key under a flowerpot by the back door. We'll get in." He gave her a quick glance. "Do you want to come with me to the ACI, or would you prefer that I take you to the house first?"

"With you," she answered instantly. "Things are moving too fast, Owen. Once we get there, I'll sit behind the wheel, make sure no one sees me…"

"Good." Her hand was fluttering nervously in her lap, and he caught it in his own. "Because I really don't want to let you out of my sight."

She smiled. "Do you mind if I use your cell phone?"

The noise and the commotion in the street were a marked contrast to the serenity that had reigned inside the church.

Dan Archer strode along the cobblestone sidewalk and watched the activity with a frown on his face. The street had been blocked off, which struck him as a good thing, since it seemed like every police car, ambulance, and a fire-rescue truck on the island had already arrived at the scene. The TV crew was loving it, and even a few 'mourners' from the church had followed them out onto the street to catch the action.

With Evan Steele on his heels, Archer pushed through the crowd around the blue sedan still sitting in the middle of the street. One of the uniformed officers trying to push back the gawkers immediately hailed the captain.

"Glad you're here, sir."

"What happened? Did somebody get hit with a car?"

The uniform nodded. "Strange one. The EMT's are still working on the guy who was hit, but it's a waste of time. Jack and Stan arrived on the scene first. They said he was already a goner."

Archer looked over at the blue sedan. In the black-and-white, two officers were talking to a man they'd put in the back seat. No doubt, the driver of the vehicle. "What the hell was he doing?"

"This is where it gets really weird, sir." The uniform nodded toward the body lying on the street and the group of people working on him. "The victim had a 9mm on him. I don't mean *on* him. The guy had it in his hand—and the safety was off."

"What?"

"Looks like he was ready to shoot someone. And that's exactly what the guy in the car says. Before we put him in the squad car, I heard him say he was coming down the street, and all of the sudden he sees this guy, the victim, pulling out a gun. With all the people around, he gets nervous or something. Instead of hitting the brakes, his foot goes on the gas pedal, and *boom*—the guy with the gun goes into orbit. There is a lot of damage to the front of the car. I wonder if insurance covers that."

"Any witnesses?" Archer asked.

"Tons. And so far, everyone saw the same thing. Ed talked to this old lady—" he pointed to another police car. "—who is over there in my car. She thought the guy with the gun was walking behind a young woman. In fact, *her* story is that she thinks he was forcing this woman to go somewhere…that is, before the blue car changed the odds a little."

The patrolman looked up the street. "She thinks the woman came out of that church door behind you, and the gunman showed up behind her. Now, Stan has the statements and all that…"

"Okay." Archer pushed past the uniform, going to where the body of the gunman was lying.

Evan Steele began to follow the captain, but the ringing of his cell phone made him stop and reach for it.

"Evan." The voice was as familiar to him as his own. "Please don't say or do anything to bring any attention to yourself or this call. Please, Evan!"

"Who is this?" He stepped away from the patrolman, pressing the phone closer to his ear.

"This is Sarah…Sarah Rand. I need you to listen to what I have to say."

Owen gave her a reassuring look, and she closed her eyes, concentrating on the call. Sarah could hear the sounds of sirens coming through the phone.

"Can I talk to you? Is this a good time?"

"Go on." Evan Steele's voice was clear and businesslike, and she knew he was moving away from the source of the background noise.

She gave Owen a nod. "I don't know what the heck is going on, but I came back from Ireland to find myself supposedly murdered."

"That's right. Go on."

"I don't want to talk too much now, but there are people out there who know I'm alive and are trying to kill me. That's why I haven't talked to the police or come forward yet. Are you in front of the church?"

"Near it."

"The guy who was hit by the car was one of them."

His voice dropped low. "You were here?"

"Yes." She rubbed her temple. "Listen, I know you're probably wondering how I could let the Judge remain in prison while I'm walking around free. Well, I'm going to the authorities tomorrow. Everything will be sorted out by then. But for now, I need your help. I need to get...well, something that will blow open this situation. It'll reveal what these killing are about. Can you help me?"

"What do you need?"

"I have to get into the downtown offices tomorrow morning. I have a feeling that something was mistakenly taken out of Avery's safe-deposit box somehow. I've come to believe it's a letter or an envelope. Whatever is happening has to do with that letter, or envelope, or whatever it is that was misplaced. Would you let me in?"

"But you don't know what it is?"

"No. But I have a strong suspicion that once I get into the files, I will be able to put my hands on it." She tried to put as much enthusiasm as she could into her words. "This will solve everything, Evan. Help me get in."

There was another lengthy pause. The sound of voices and traffic in the distance.

"Where are you staying?"

"Somewhere safe, but don't worry about that. I can get to the building. I still have my key to the outside door. Could you meet me...say, on the stairs?"

"Wait. I have to check something."

Sarah could tell that he hadn't bothered to cover the mouthpiece, as she heard him talking to Scott Rosen, who must have approached him. After a minute, he came back on the line.

"Make it ten," he said quietly. "The Judge's lawyer will be stopping by at nine to drop some files off. I'll need time to get rid of him, but then the office is yours."

"Thanks, Evan," she said, giving a thumbs-up to Owen. "We'll clear this whole mess up."

"We'll all be happy to see that. Please be careful." A pause at the other end. "And I want you to know that hearing from you is just too good to be true."

Archer had to hold the phone away from his head to save an eardrum and looked at his wife across the kitchen table. To say that David Calvin was upset was like saying there was a dollar or two floating around Newport.

"I don't know what the fuck you've been up to, Dan, but if you think for a minute I'm going to let this blow up in our faces like another Von Bulow fiasco…"

"I can explain everything, Chief."

"You bet your skinny ass you'll explain." Calvin shouted. "Who the hell do you think you are not disclosing those reports to the D.A.'s office? Don't you know Rosen will sue our fucking asses from here to West Jabroo? Does the term *false imprisonment* mean anything to you? Jesus F. Christ…the newspapers will hang us!"

Archer could almost hear Calvin tearing the hair out of his head.

"A crime was committed, Chief. The blood samples in Judge Arnold's boat matched the samples taken from Rand's apartment. We had probable cause for bringing him in."

"But you fucking knew that none of it was Rand's blood."

"We only got that report last week."

"And the fingerprints at the house?"

"Last week, too. Everything we know, everything that led me to believe she was still alive, is less than five days old."

"It takes less than five days to go to the fucking moon, for chrissakes! Why in God's name have you been sitting on these reports? I'm telling you right now, Archer, I'll yank your badge and mount your ugly head on my wall if you don't have a—"

"Because there was a leak, Chief." Silence.

"What?"

"We have a canary in the department. For what we're doing, I needed to buy some time."

"Keep going."

Archer quickly explained what he knew of the case and his suspicions and finally the involvement in the case by another law enforcement agency—the same agency that had contacted David Calvin half an hour earlier, notifying him in strictest confidence of the operation planned for tomorrow.

Calvin's voice had grown sulky by the time Archer was finished. "And why the hell couldn't you tell me any of this on Friday? Do you know how stupid I looked when I got the call just now? The whole fucking lot of them knew what was going on in my department, and I'm just sitting here with my thumb up my ass. My own fucking people."

"Not people, sir," Archer asserted. "Just me. McHugh had only seen one of the reports, and he thought I was already sharing it with you. I am the only one in the department guilty of withholding information, sir."

The tired detective pulled the phone again away from his ear as the Chief gave him another blast of obscenities. When Calvin finally ran out of breath, Archer answered the rest of his superior's questions.

"When those vultures start picking at the bones," Chief Calvin told him. It's going to be your carcass out there. When the media finally gets wind of this, it's going to be you standing out there. And I'll be at the far end of the dais, Archer. Do you understand me?"

"Aha."

"What?"

"Yes, sir."

"When Ike Bosler decides to skin somebody alive, I'm handing *you* over, Dan. Do you get that?"

"Yes, sir."

The sound of the phone slamming down on the other end was a clear hint that the conversation was over. He glanced over at his wife, who was just putting his cold dinner into the microwave.

Archer mimicked his boss's voice. "And when the department is getting glowing praise for solving the murder of the century...I'll be sure to give you full credit, Dan."

Chapter 24

"I'm telling you straight. It was Hal Van Horn who took out the contract on Sarah's Rand's life."

Even hearing it again, Owen still had difficulty comprehending Jake Gantley's words.

He hadn't believed everything that had been said in that memorial service today. Rutherford was making most of that stuff up, and Owen knew it. Still, he'd felt there had to be some truth in the senator's words. After all, there were a lot of people there who were pretty open about their grief. Before the service he'd heard someone say there'd been no memorial service held for Sarah after *her* murder. So in a way, he'd decided, today had been a chance for Newport to say goodbye to both of them—to both Sarah *and* Hal.

But now this!

"Hal was the man," Jake repeated yet again.

"Are you sure about that?" Owen had to ask. "I mean, you didn't deal directly with him. Could it be that Frankie made a mistake?"

"No mistake. It was him," the inmate asserted, his face darkening. "Now, you know that I won't admit any of this if you go running to the cops. But why the hell should you? Van Horn is a stiff."

Jake Gantley's face was hard when he threw a sidelong glance at the guard standing at the far end of the visitor's Room.

"I can even point you in the right direction where you can get some proof for your girlfriend, if she needs it."

"Give it to me."

"Okay. To come up with part of the payment, Hal wanted to do a legit draw on his trust fund. So Frankie takes him to meet with a jeweler friend we know in Warwick. Hal walks away with a five-dollar glass diamond handsomely displayed in a thirty-dollar setting. He was supposedly giving this ring as an engagement ring to his girlfriend. The ring comes with papers saying it's worth fifty grand. Hal pays the fifty grand out of his trust, and Frankie walks away with the money and his instructions for the hit. Very simple."

"What were his exact instructions?"

"The same as what I told you before. Step one—I'm to dust her and bag the body for disposal."

Owen could see in the inmate's gray eyes the total lack of interest in the human life he was discussing. Just business. Interesting that Frankie's life represented something else to Jake, Owen mused.

"As it works out, the first step is done for me, and the second step turns out to be a piece of cake, too. Anyone with a half a brain can walk down onto the docks in Newport and get onto any one of those boats. With Hal's help, Frankie just made sure that we got onto the Judge's boat at the right time—after the old guy was back from his regular Wednesday cruise and before the cleaning guys from the yacht club went on board to shine up the bells and whistles."

Christ. Owen felt the hackles on his neck rising. The double-crossing son of a bitch. Based on everything that he'd learned today, he could see killing Hal Van Horn himself. And to think that Sarah felt such guilt over what had happened to the creep.

"My guess is your girlfriend can probably think of a few million reasons my client hated her so much. But I'll tell you that the ax Hal had to grind with the Judge was all about the old lady's will." Jake gave him a sarcastic smile. "These spoiled rich boys are far more brutal than mild-mannered poor boys like me, I can tell you."

"Is that so?"

"Absolutely." Jake leaned back in his chair. "We've got one over in the intake center right now, I hear. This Billy Hamilton that got busted down in Newport the other night...another rich boy. Last night's *Journal* had the whole story. You should look at it."

"I saw the headline." Owen had left Sarah poring over the newspaper. She'd zeroed right in on the story.

"An Ivy League pretty boy who gets off on raping underage Portuguese girls." Jake smirked at him. "I know some of the cons in here can't wait to bend Billy-boy over a steam pipe. We'll just see how good Mr. Prep takes it up the ass."

"Let's just stick to Van Horn. I do want to know if that diamond ring deal was the last time your cousin communicated with Hal."

Jake's face grew hard again. "No. Frankie was always the nervous type. He had high blood pressure. High cholesterol. He smoked. If you told him something was bad for his health, he automatically reached for it. I always told him he had a self-esteem problem. Anyway, I figured he didn't need any more stress in his life, so I didn't say nothing about the girl not being Sarah. I figured, we were paid and the arrows for the hit all pointed to the Judge, no matter who the babe was. Case closed."

"When did Hal call to complain?"

"Last Wednesday afternoon. Your girl had left him a message on his machine from the airport." Jake frowned. "Apparently, Van Horn is out on Block Island, calls into his message machine, and pretty much shits in his pants. Anyway, he calls Frankie at O'Malley's Pub from the Block and chews his ass for not doing the job right and tells him he has to finish it. Now, my cousin was a good guy, but he was never what you would call a genius...and Van Horn shook him up a tad. And even though Frankie could talk tough, he was no stand-up guy. Anyway, Hal tells him she's headed for the Judge's place and also tells him where he can get a key. Then Frankie just goes and hides in the house until she gets there."

Owen was grateful for Frankie's lack of expertise in the killing department.

"He didn't want to mess around with guns and blood and all other shit like that. And he was also afraid of Sarah knowing some self-defense shit and beating the crap out of him, so he thinks, piece of cake, I'll just turn on the gas and lock her in the kitchen." Gantley rubbed an impatient hand over his face. "Well, that didn't work, though the poor dope probably could've blown himself up and half the neighborhood for good measure. End result, Frankie's the one who gets sapped by your girl."

"And was this the last time Hal contacted your cousin?"

Jake shook his head grimly. "Hal calls him and tells him that your girl is going to be in front of La Forge by the tennis place to meet up with him. He wants Frankie to trail them into the alley behind that grocery store down the street, then he can whack her. So instead of telling Hal to fuck himself, my simpleton cousin goes for it. But when he is standing waiting for Van Horn to connect with her, he sees this other guy pull a knife. Now, according to Frankie, there's some shoving and then Van Horn gets between the guy and the girl. Frankie didn't think Hal ever saw the knife at all. But bang...the asshole takes it right between the ribs."

All Owen remembered of the scene was thinking how quickly he could get Sarah out of there.

"Now Frankie is actually relieved to see Van Horn dead, since that's the end of the job. But he also knows how I've been trying to become a big-time writer and all that, so when he sees the girl getting into your car, he makes tracks and calls me a little later."

The two men stared at each other for a long moment through the glass.

"Why are you telling me all this."

"Simple. Because Frankie recognized the guy who dusted Van Horn. The sad thing is that the scumbag recognized Frankie, too. Get it? The guy who killed Van Horn—the guy who was really trying to kill Sarah Rand—is also the guy who killed Frankie."

"Who was he?"

"One of Newport's finest."

The hospital visitor's lot, baking in the late afternoon sun, contained only a smattering of cars. Scott Rosen parked his green BMW under a tree in the corner of the lot and was sweating before he made it to the main entrance.

He frowned in the direction of the gift-and-flower shop by the front door. Closed on Sundays. His hands felt empty as hell as he headed toward the elevator. At the last minute, he veered toward the reception desk, identified himself and asked for Tracy Warner's room number. Mrs. Warner was still in the intensive care unit, but the receptionist gave him the floor number.

Scott didn't want to admit that he was dragging his feet...that he was putting off the inevitable. He refused to admit that he wasn't quite ready to go and face his wife and his new daughter.

His new daughter. Shit, he thought. What kind of a man was he, anyway?

A man with a job to do, he rationalized. Sarah Rand's car was found on the Warner property. That fact linked his case in some way to the attack on Andrew and Tracy Warner. To represent Judge Arnold to the best of his ability—something he'd sworn to do—he had some responsibility in checking on this woman. He would just make one quick stop at the ICU.

The fact that he'd seen Owen Dean having flowers sent up to Tracy Warner the day before had nothing to do with anything, even though catching up with the actor some time in the future was something Scott would enjoy.

The corridor on the floor where Mrs. Warner was staying was a reflection of the empty parking lot, though infinitely cooler. On the counter of the unattended nurse's station, he saw a large bouquet. No doubt the flowers he'd seen Owen choose and send up yesterday. Beyond the glass windows, in the unit itself, a number of attendants were moving briskly to and from one of the beds. He realized he couldn't tell who was a doctor and who was a nurse. Screens had been drawn around two of the other beds.

Frowning, he turned away and looked into the waiting room. A solitary older woman sat reading a newspaper.

Pleasant gray eyes lifted in greeting.

"I'm sorry, I didn't mean to intrude."

"By no means. Come in, Mr. Rosen."

Scott glanced around him, extremely flustered by the recognition. "I…Have we met before?"

"No, we haven't yet had the pleasure." She stood up with excruciating slowness. "Heavens, these old bones."

He moved toward her and the woman extended a cool, smooth hand in greeting. "I am Joanne Emerson, Tracy Warner's sister. Your wife and I met this afternoon."

Scott felt himself reddening. He shook her hand in greeting.

"This is a very distressing floor, especially for someone of my age. Nothing to cheer one up. I wanted to give away the flowers friends have been sending my sister. They can't have them in the unit, and there is no place to put them all out here." Joanne pointed to a single bouquet on a corner table. "I love the maternity ward. I went down there earlier, and your wife was taking a walk in the corridor, so that's how we met."

Lucy was already on her feet? Scott tried to keep the shocked look off his face.

"That's...that's great!"

"You don't know how lucky you are that your wife's doctor is letting her to stay the two nights here. Because of HMOs, you know, these days they act like having babies is no more traumatic than going to the dentist. In and out. In and out. You *do* have someone to give her a hand when she gets home tomorrow, don't you?"

She was coming home *tomorrow*? Another wave of embarrassment hit him.

"Of course," he lied, wondering if that kind of help was something he could arrange through the hospital.

"I'm not surprised." Joanne continued on without a pause. "Your Lucy is a lovely young woman. She is also very proud of you. That is a very nice picture of you that she carries in her wallet. That's how I recognized you—she showed it to me. We got to talking about all sort of things. She even told me that you're quite involved with this Rand murder case. I have been following the whole thing through the newspapers in Boston. The poor dear. Sarah Rand was from Boston's South End, you know. She also went to Harvard. As you can imagine, she is a favorite topic for the media at home."

Joanne went on talking about the coverage of the case and about Sarah's life as it had been revealed in the papers, and Scott tried to appear attentive. All the while, however, his mind was stuck on the woman's words about Lucy being proud of him. He couldn't even imagine her pulling a picture of him out of her wallet to show a stranger. Shit, he didn't even know she carried a picture of him in her wallet.

Proud of him? For some time now, he'd been afraid—and was still afraid—of Lucy waking up and realizing what a failure he was as a husband.

He glanced at his watch. "If you'll excuse me. I think I'd better head down there myself."

"Wonderful!" Joanne ushered him toward the elevator. "Tell Lucy I might stop by to see her and the baby tomorrow morning before she leaves."

"I will." He turned to go, but at the last minute turned. "I forgot to ask. How is your sister?"

"The doctors tell me they're seeing some encouraging signs this afternoon, whatever than means." She lowered her voice. "If you ask my nonmedical opinion, my sister is not going to come around until she can unload fifty years' worth of crap, if you'll excuse the term. I mean no disrespect to the dead. But it's amazing how some women need to be hit hard over the head with a bat before they realize what an ass they've chosen to spend their lives with."

As the elevator descended to the maternity floor, Scott decided on the perfect gift he could buy Lucy to preserve their marriage. A hard hat.

The problem with that, though, was that he didn't even know what size hat she wore.

Chapter 25

Hal had taken out the contract on her life. Hal.

Sarah wasn't surprised, somehow.

The information Owen brought out of the prison made her feel wounded, lied to, betrayed, angry. But after having had a chance to sort out her thoughts during the memorial service earlier today, she could no longer feel surprise at the news.

"Four years ago, he courted me to help strengthen his battle against his family, but things didn't work out the way he'd planned. He must have felt deserted in seeing me go over to Avery's and the Judge's side." Sarah leaned her head against the side window and thought of the events of recent months as they sped along the highway toward Providence. Blurred lines of blue and green and pink houses along the highway blended with the grimy brick red and black of deserted shops and factories.

"But that is hardly reason enough to have someone killed." Owen's hand reached for hers.

"I guess it was for Hal. Everyone had a purpose for him. My purpose for existing was to get Judge Arnold off his back. Avery's purpose was to set right the will left by Hal's father and make sure he received all that was his by birthright. We both failed to act as he expected us to act."

She swallowed hard. "You know, I should have guessed how angry he was at the time of the reading his mother's will. He shut down on me. Wouldn't tell me how he felt about anything. I even advised him that it was within his rights to challenge the will. Although I was executor to the estate, I was well aware of how ill she'd been in the last months of her life and how influential her husband had been during that time. It was no secret that Hal and Judge Arnold never saw eye-to-eye on anything at all."

"He didn't contest it, did he?"

"No." She shook her head. "Foolishly, I assumed his decision was made out of respect for his mother. He seemed to be doing well enough with his company, so I thought he was happy to let things stand as they were."

"What were the stipulations of the will, anyway?"

"Hal would continue to get a yearly allowance, which was relatively small compared to the size of the estate. This was consistent with the trust that had been set up by Everard Van Horn. Outside of that, he could draw lump sums on the principal, but not without all types of trustees' approvals and signatures. The level of approval depended on the amount he wanted to draw."

"I assume Judge Arnold was one of those trustees."

"Of course."

Sarah stared straight ahead. Unexpectedly, a fierce anger bubbled to the surface.

"I was *so* naïve. I can't believe I let myself get caught in the middle of all this. *Both* of those men tried to use me for their own purposes. I was a loyal partner to the Judge, worshipping the ground he walked on. I did as he advised, and learned, and saw my own practice begin to flourish. And that was just fine, so long as I didn't try to exert my own independence in anything that the Judge already made up his mind on." She laughed bitterly. "And Hal...I tried to remain a friend to him. But from his perspective I was a horrible human being all the way around. I was his mother's lawyer, and the office partner of his worst enemy. I knew about the stipulations of the will and did not warn him about it. And I was the ice queen."

"Don't." He immediately pulled the car onto the shoulder of the highway and turned to her. "You can't blame yourself for a family that was clearly dysfunctional long before you ever arrived on the scene."

He cupped her chin, looking into her eyes. "You should be proud of how you have acted. You've been walking a tightrope with balance and integrity. You used great judgment. And in the end, you didn't let either of them manipulate you."

He kissed her with such tenderness that Sarah felt the warmth wash down through her, wrapping itself around her heart. When he pulled back, her eyes saw only him.

"What scares me now is what we still don't know. We can't forget what Gantley said about arriving at your apartment and finding that someone else had done the job." His gaze lingered on her face a moment longer. "Frankie recognized the guy who knifed Hal. Jake Gantley says the recognition went both ways, and that's why his cousin was murdered."

His face was all business again as he pulled back on the highway

"Did he have a name or a description? Anything we can go by?"

"Uh, yes he did. The killer's name is Paul Yeats. From what Gantley says, he was a—"

"Newport cop until six months ago." She finished the sentence for him.

Owen's head snapped in her direction.

"Remember what I told you about the run-in I had with the Newport Police? About the fifteen-year-old and the cops who had intimidated the girl?"

"I remember."

"Well, the younger cop—the one who was forced to resign—that was Paul Yeats." She leaned down and gathered the newspapers she had folded at her feet. She opened it up to the front page and headlines. "This is the same case. They just cracked it. William Hamilton was the creep who'd raped my client. And this woman, Cherie Lake, was the one who'd arranged it back then, too. This has been going on for a while, and there were a number of underage girls who'd been lured in and used."

Sarah leafed through the pages again until she found the section she was looking for. "They even mention my name and the lawsuit against the department last spring. But here…they also mention the two officers involved. The older one is in Florida and refused to make a statement to the reporter who contacted him. The other one, Paul Yeats, still lives on the island but couldn't be reached."

"That's why Jake mentioned the article."

"What do you mean?" She dropped the paper on her lap. "Is Yeats trying to kill me because of that lawsuit?"

"What else do you know about Yeats?"

"He had military background. I believe he was a marine MP. No wife or kids. He'd moved in the area after getting out of the service. A real man's man. Uncomfortable…in fact, I'd say hostile toward women. An Ollie North type when it came to following orders, though not as bright. Not surprisingly, he was well-liked by other men in the department, though the female officers didn't have much to say on his behalf."

"Following orders," Owen repeated. "An ex-cop, possibly with good connections to area police departments, perhaps even with access to police cars. Also an ex-marine having expertise with close combat."

"He wasn't the one, who stuck a gun in my back this morning."

"You said there were two officers who stopped you on the road last Wednesday night."

"That's true. He could have been the other one." She watched Owen maneuver the car through the S-curve in Providence before heading south along the eastern side of the Narragansett Bay. "But these two are only peons, aren't they?"

"Damned ruthless peons, but peons nonetheless. They had to be operating on orders from someone else."

Sarah wiped her sweating palms on her dress. "Is everything all set for tomorrow?"

"I think so. We just have to hope that Rosen keeps his promise."

All but two of the cribs in the nursery were gone. Scott saw the blue caps and name cards on the sleeping babies and guessed his daughter was in with Lucy.

The smell of dinner was already wafting out of some of the rooms when he turned toward his wife's private one. Sounds of conversation mixed with a laugh here and there and a baby's soft cry seemed such a natural part of this section of the hospital, so different from the stillness of the ICU three floors above.

By the door of Lucy's room, Scott saw the untouched tray of food on a rolling table. He took another step in and frowned at the empty bed. His heart suddenly sank at the thought that she'd already checked out of the hospital without even telling him.

A soft cooing from a portable crib made of see-through plastic drew his attention at the same time that he heard a toilet flush. In a moment, the bathroom door opened. Standing motionless in the door, he enjoyed the eternity of thirty seconds of watching his wife before she noticed him.

She looked good. No, she looked beautiful, he corrected, admiring the warm smile she gave the infant as she leaned over to pick her up.

"I'm right here, sweetheart. Such a face..." She froze with the baby in her arms as her gaze lit on him. "Scott."

"Is this a bad time?"

"Of course not."

For the lack of something better to do, he shoved his hands into his pockets and leaned against the doorjamb. A stupid half smile edged onto his face as he watched the baby's mouth continue to move in her direction.

"I...I think she is hungry."

"She is *always* hungry." Lucy laid the infant against her shoulder, supporting the fragile head and neck with her hand. "I think I ordered steak and potatoes for dinner. If you pull the cover off that food and cut up the meat real small, we can feed her some dinner."

He straightened up from the door, pulling his hands out of his pocket. "You're not serious."

Her laughter was a kind music that he had been missing in his life for too long. His spirit lifted, his mind cleared somewhat.

"Now that's more like it." The dimples that used to drive him crazy now appeared. "You know, you've been acting like a real jerk the past couple of days. Come over here."

He did exactly as she told him. They sat on the small sofa side by side. He watched her breast-feed the eager infant, and then she taught him how to hold the baby.

Sitting there with his daughter in his arms, he realized he'd never held a baby in his life. She smelled like milk and bath powder. Holding her made him think of dreams and innocence. He pushed the knit cap away and rubbed his cheek on her soft wisps of hair. The perfect little fingers moved. He stared in awe at the fingernails. Even they were so perfect.

"So you two are coming home tomorrow?"

"Hopefully, early in the morning." She kissed him over the

baby's head. "Now, I can call a—"

"No. I'll be here," he said, meaning it. "Lucy, I need you to give me a chance. I promise to be a good father...and a much better husband."

"Don't be silly!" She shook her head, though her expression was thoughtful as she turned her face away. They had never discussed it, had never openly said the words, but they'd both known for a while that he'd been standing on a ledge. As he stared at her profile, he knew that this was Lucy through and through, pouring it all inward and acting as if nothing was ever wrong.

When she turned her attention back to him, Scott saw her gaze go from the sleeping face of her daughter to his pleading eyes.

"We'll be here waiting for you."

Chapter 26

The small cottage sat on a grassy knoll overlooking a sparkling deepwater inlet south of the village. Sarah looked at it, thinking that she was dreaming. Wrinkled roses of red and white and pink, bent by the sea winds, bloomed on small knolls of sand and stone. No trees grew tall or straight here. None was strong enough to withstand the battering of the Atlantic winter storms unscathed, and gnarled scrub pines rose out of hollows like defiant squatters.

In the east, the pale azure of the sky was in full retreat from the deepening blues. Seabirds wheeled above in the distance, and she could hear in her mind their plaintive cries. The calm water of the inlet beyond the cottage was a dark, unnamable shade of blue and green. Every line, every color was incredibly sharp in the brilliant light of the setting sun, and as she turned her gaze, she saw that the western sky itself had become a divine palette of golds and reds, blues and purples.

Sarah could see no other houses nearby as the car traveled down the dirt road that led to the cottage. The rolling hills and the low, thick growth of brambles obscured the prying eyes of neighbors, yet still offered a clear view of the peaceful countryside that spread southward to the sea.

The cottage itself was an old-fashioned Cape Cod building of one-and-half solid stories, with natural shingles that had been stained and weathered to a handsome gray. On one side of the house, trellised red roses climbed up and onto the roof. White windows with green shutters and flower boxes sported bright red geraniums in full bloom. Beyond it, a brick path led down to a boat dock. The effect nearly took Sarah's breath away.

She got out as Owen opened the garage. On their drive over, they had stopped to buy whatever toiletries they would need and enough food to take them through the night. He parked the car in the empty garage and closed the door. Sarah helped him carry the bags. The key was under the flowerpot by the door, just as Susan, his assistant, had promised.

"So *beautiful*." she whispered, switching on the light just inside the kitchen doorway.

Despite the rustic look of the outside, the interior of the cottage was a very airy and comfortable open space that combined kitchen, family and living room. A set of stairs by the front door led upstairs. The patina of the wainscot and wide-planked pine floors lent a warmth to the place, and it smelled of wood fire and cinnamon and fresh salt air. As she dropped the bags on the kitchen table, it occurred to her that the mix of new and old furniture served to make it a real home, rather than some magazine spread.

"I always dreamed of living in a place like this."

She moved to the window above the sink, looking out over a stretch of land and the inlet in the quickly fading light.

"A garden." She smiled, planting her hands on the counter and leaning farther forward to get a better view. "I would have put my garden there, too. And yes, I'd have a shed for gardening tools just there. And I'd get a golden retriever puppy that'd chase after the birds and be wet from swimming every day and smell—"

"And you'd need a van…"

His voice was a warm whisper in her ear. Sarah's breath hitched in her chest as she felt his warmth close around her. His hands rubbed the fabric of her dress against her skin. She felt his teeth scrape over the sensitive skin beneath her ear.

"You'd need a van to take a wet dog around."

One hand cupped her breast, the other slid down her stomach, and lower. She leaned her head back against him as his teeth nibbled her earlobe.

His voice was a husky growl. "How about a couple of kids to go with the van?"

She leaned to one side and turned her head to look into his face, only to find the sultry look of sincerity and desire there irresistible. Instead of an answer, she dug her fingers in his thick hair and kissed him deeply.

Although they'd already made love numerous times, the force of his passion at this moment was unmatched by anything she'd experienced before, leaving her breathless before its power.

Afterward, their clothes lying in piles around their feet, Sarah saw her naked reflection in the kitchen window. Gripped by a kind of wonder, she watched as his hands cupped and caressed her, bringing her body instantly to life yet again. It was as if he could not get enough of her, bury himself deeply enough in her, hold her tightly enough to him. As he made love to her a second time, she watched the two of them rising together on undulating waves of passion.

And in that reflection, she saw something else. On her face she saw the unmistakable presence of joy and hope and trust...obliterating in an instant the loneliness of a lifetime.

By the time the fire engines had made their way into the compound, the long row of storage units was a blazing inferno, lighting the black sky with flames and smoke and gases from the melting metal buildings. The fences around the compound hampered the entry of the larger trucks, and the narrow lanes between the rows of units quickly became clogged with vehicles and hoses and falling ash. With unexpected violence, unit by unit exploded in a series of fierce blasts, sending firefighters scurrying for cover as molten cinders rained from the summer sky.

After five hours of intense effort, the fire was brought under control. Getting the nod from the fire captain, the arson investigator opened the back of his van and led his Labrador retriever onto the property.

Specially trained to isolate a variety of volatile substances, even the smallest amounts of fuels and solvents that might be used to accelerate a fire, the dog circled the rows of storage units her nose skimming over the ground. In less than fifteen minutes, the dog and its trainer had covered the outer perimeter of the disaster area, and began to focus on the section where the blaze seemed to have done the greatest damage.

Pawing and scratching an area before a large file storage unit that belonged to a local law firm—a unit that had been reduced to a blackened hole of steaming metal and paper ash—the four-legged specialist gave the investigators a starting point for taking samples.

It would be hours before subsequent lab analyses could confirm that traces of flammable liquids were indeed present in the crevices of concrete before the storage facilities of the law offices of Charles Hamlin Arnold and Sarah Rand. Dan Archer, however, didn't need to wait for the reports to know what had happened.

What he wanted to know—what no Lab bitch would tell him— was *why* someone had torched the Judge's old files.

Gordon Rutherford held the snifter of brandy up to the light, appreciating the play of light through the amber liquid.

"I know both of these men have been long time friends and contributors to your campaigns, Senator, but an eight-point drop in the polls could have a snowball effect when you'll want to be looking your strongest. We don't want anything to affect the support of party's national committee regarding your potential place on the next presidential ticket."

Rutherford took a sip of his drink as Edward North, his young chief of staff, drew a file stuffed with newspaper clippings out of his open briefcase.

"We made the initial decision that there was not much we could do about the Judge Arnold association. It was unavoidable that every damn article would mention that the two of you had started your law careers together." Edward spread specific clippings on the table. "But here, the damn liberals have changed their tactics. Now every report and news article pertaining to the Arnold case contains a direct attack on you and what you stand for. They are attacking your principles, Senator, never mind your specific stand against gun control. Look at these…"

"Law and Order…Double Standards For the Rich." Edward held the clipping up. "They claim you are always quick to give a press conference whenever any type of crime is committed in the state, but that you've kept quiet with regard to Judge Arnold."

"'*Loser* the Latest Label for Rutherford.'" Edward picked up another piece. "They've dug up the names of everyone you have had even casual social interaction with and listed something that is potentially objectionable about every one of them."

"And now with this Hamilton case. Look at these editorials…

'Meet the Senator's Pals.' Again hinting at your involvement with unsavory, though wealthy, friends. 'Billy the Kid: Like Father, Like Son.' Innuendo that similar charges may have been filed against William Hamilton, Sr., thirty years ago, only to have been dropped and then expunged from the record."

The chief of staff held the last article up for him to see.

"'Dining Out: Murderers and Rapists at Rutherford Soirée.'" Edward's customary composure was beginning to slip, and he ran a hand through his hair and pulled at his collar.

The senator studied him. "What do you want me to do?"

"Make a statement. Disassociate yourself from them. Call them what they are. Show them for their true colors. Be more judicious in your choice of friends."

The senator stared for a long moment at the open folder on the table and took another sip of his drink. "No one is perfect, Edward."

"That's not true, Senator. Your reputation is impeccable."

"That's your job to say so." Gleaming white teeth flashed in the tan face. "But all of us—and that includes you and me—have little skeletons that we hide in our closets. For instance, how long do you think we can keep the fact that you're gay under wraps?"

"Being gay is not a crime, Senator," Edward objected, immediately growing red as a beet.

"Very true. But it certainly would be a liability to a conservative, unmarried politician who has every intention of one day being President of the United States."

"Senator, I don't think—"

Rutherford snapped his fingers, silencing him. "Even if our system of law were not built on the fundamental belief that we are innocent until proven guilty, maybe I believe having consensual sex with young…yes, even supposedly underage women is no worse than two male adults committing sodomy and other unnatural sex acts."

The senator sat back and smiled at the sight of the color rising in Edward's neck. The young man began stuffing the clippings back into the folder.

"You see, Edward? Sometimes this tough old warhorse can be

almost liberal in his positions." The senator leaned forward. "You'll learn soon enough that this far from an election, polls don't mean a thing to me. Judge Arnold and I do indeed go way back, and there is no way in hell I'd walk away from him, just because he's landed in a pile of shit. If we get a little of it on us, so be it. *Loyalty* will be the spin we put on what we do now. And as far as the Hamilton situation…hell, they've already arrested the little twerp. I never personally liked the boy, anyway, so they can cut his dick off, as far as I'm concerned. But William Sr. and his companies have consistently been our single largest source of campaign contributions over the years. There is no way I'm going to cut my ties with that family."

The locks on the briefcase closed with a loud snap.

"Do we understand each other, Edward?"

"Yes we do, Senator." With a curt nod, Edward North strode out of the room.

Feeling a bit awkward about sleeping together in a stranger's bed, they instead lay entwined in each other's arms on the sofa. Through the open windows the summer sea breeze washed over them.

Sarah had just finished telling him about her childhood, and about her parents, and about how awkward she'd felt attending John Rand's funeral.

"But even stranger than the feelings I'd had at the funeral was the way I felt on the flight back from Ireland." She planted her chin on Owen's chest. "I was totally, totally alone. I suppose, technically, I still had an uncle and two aunts across the Atlantic, and a few cousins on my mother's side whom I've never met. But all these people were even greater strangers to me than my father had been."

The breeze suddenly felt cooler on her skin, and Sarah reached for the afghan behind them. Owen shifted his weight, tucking Sarah's body between himself and the sofa and covering the two of them with the blanket.

"It's an odd feeling having no one to call—nobody to send a card to at Christmas, or to have Thanksgiving dinner with. Of course, it's not as if I ever did any of those things with my father, but it was nice to know that someday, if one of us wanted to, there might be a chance of it happening." She rubbed her earlobe. "You know those earrings I always wear, the star-shaped ones? They belonged to his mother, and he gave them to *my* mother when I was born."

"I suppose those kinds of connections are important."

She shrugged a shoulder. "Maybe. But you know, I never really acknowledged him. Not with the people I knew. It's ironic to think that I was supposedly murdered three weeks ago, and no one in this town even had a clue that I might have a father still living. There was no one they should notify. Well, I…I guess we severed that parent-child connection too many years ago."

Sarah looked up sadly into his dark blue eyes. "Sorry to inflict such a sappy life story on you."

He leaned over and brushed his lips over her cheeks, her eyes, her lips.

"We are a pair." He smiled, twirling a strand of her short hair around his finger. "When I was very, very young, I dreamed of having a house with a yard, and a dog, and parents who were around. As I got a little older, having a roof over my head, and food in my belly, and a mother who was conscious became my greatest wish. And then, not long after that, I would have done without the food and roof part if I could have had my mother someplace safe, someplace where she wasn't getting beat up regularly…someplace where she wouldn't need to do drugs."

Every nerve in Sarah's body cried out for her to try to sooth his pain. But she waited, giving him a chance to pour out what she guessed had been tucked away for years.

"I've come to accept all of that. I don't have nightmares about those days anymore. I'm not even embarrassed every time some rookie reporter decides to dig into Owen Dean's checkered past." He shrugged. "That's life. We can't control the hand that is dealt to us early on. But I've tried my damnedest to control what I've done with that hand ever since."

Sarah watched him for a long time stare at the white ceiling.

"She never told me who my father was. At the beginning, I was too young to know the difference or ask. Later on, our lives became too messed up to matter." His hand slid up and down her arm, warming her. "You had a name for John Rand. Even though your parents were estranged, he was still your father. I only knew a kind of tough, strange guy named Andrew Warner. I've never known what the hell his connection was, just that he showed up one day out of the blue and acted like he wanted to take care of us."

Sarah felt the tension coil inside of him.

"My mother was really sick. I don't know if it was the boozing, or the drugs, or the rough handling of her men, but I was street-smart enough to know that Andrew wasn't coming around to get anything from her." He laid his hand across his brow. "That scared the shit out of me at the time. I'd seen stuff like this on the street. We were living in a third-floor dump on Bainbridge in Philly. Some of these mothers…a lot of them messed up like my own, put their own kids out to start whoring for money. A lot of times, these guys that would come into the neighborhood would have money, like Andrew.

"But, the thing was…she'd never done anything like this before. In fact, anytime she brought somebody back to the one room we had, I'd grab a blanket and go up and sleep on the roof until she came after me. But I knew already that people change, even mothers. I also knew my mother was getting too desperate to care about anything."

Sarah's hold on him tightened. She found herself holding her breath as he talked.

"I got hold of a knife and started carrying it. Anytime Andrew came around, I'd stay away. He would bring us food, but I wouldn't touch it. I'd see him giving my mother money, but I would get sick to my stomach thinking I knew what it was for. I stopped sleeping, even, figuring this jerk was going to come collect what he was paying for one night when I wasn't paying attention. The friendlier he was, the more hostile and scarce I became. But it didn't matter, he still continued to come around."

He rubbed his eyes tiredly. "About six months after he started coming around, he took my mother to a hospital where they told me they were going to keep her for at least a couple of weeks, maybe more. Andrew wanted me to go and live wherever the hell it was that he lived then, while my mother was in detox." Owen gave a bitter laugh. "He was lucky he didn't get that knife in the gut that day. Instead, I just ran away. Of course, I didn't really run away. I hung around streets of Philadelphia. I didn't even stray too far from the neighborhood. These were the faces that I knew. And Andrew couldn't find me."

"My mother finally came back from the hospital, and I was waiting for her. But two days later, I saw the needle on the bathroom sink, and I knew it was only a matter of time before she'd be gone for good."

"Did you ask her then who Andrew was?" Sarah asked.

"Yeah…well, in so many confrontational and childish words, I guess I did." He shrugged. "But other than the fact that he was an old friend of hers, she wouldn't say a thing more about him. And then I came home one day and she was sitting dead in a corner of the bathroom, the needle still in her arm."

Owen drew a deep breath and stopped for a moment. She knew he was seeing that horrible place, that horrible day.

"What happened after she passed away?"

"I was going to take off again, but I was still a kid. I'd only turned ten that summer. I didn't want to live on the streets. I knew what happened to kids there, and it was no different than the worst I could get from Andrew. So when Andrew told me that he'd taken care of things and I should go with him, I took my knife and I went with him."

He looked down at her and touched her cropped hair.

"I was wrong about him—about what he wanted. He took me to his house, but that was quite a scene. His wife didn't want me there, period. And she wasn't shy about saying so. Andrew was furious, but he let her have her way for some reason. I was in and out of there the same afternoon. It was one of the longest days of my life.'

"He found me a boarding school. A prep school in Connecticut, filled to the rafters with white rich kids. That was another disaster, considering I was a street kid with a wise mouth with nothing behind me and nothing ahead of me. I was trouble from the get-go. I won't bore you with the details, but somehow I finished there and even went off to college."

"But you didn't stay in college, did you?"

"That's where the tabloids pick up Owen Dean's life," he answered. "No, I didn't. I don't know if it was pride or independence or hormones or what. Who knows? But I wasn't even through my first semester when I realized that I couldn't let Andrew take care of me anymore. He'd been very decent. Always paying my tuition. Continually getting me out of all kinds of trouble that should have gotten me expelled. At least once a month, he had come to see me. We'd go out to eat and talk of nothing during the entire meal. I just couldn't understand it. I couldn't understand him."

He looked into her face. "The rest of it is an open book. Moving to L.A. Getting lucky doing small roles, first in commercials, then low-budget films. Acting was something that seemed to come naturally for me. Some of Andrew's principles stuck, I suppose. While I was scrambling around for parts, I started at UCLA and over a ten-year period actually ended up with a couple of degrees. And then the career took off and life went on."

She touched the cleft of his chin, the hollow of his throat. "Did you see much of Andrew and his wife after that?"

He laughed mirthlessly.

"Tracy hated my guts. I'd sensed it as a kid. I knew it as an adult. So I resented the fact that Andrew continued to drag her with him to L.A. at least once a year. He'd come up with any stupid reason to come, just so we could stay in touch. So yes, I did see them occasionally." A dark flush crept up his neck. "He was the only person I had in this world. As cold and strange and unexplainable that it was, he was my only connection with the past. And the fact remained that I owed him. I owed him a lot."

Sarah's hand rested on his chest.

"And this is what really makes me angry about the whole thing." He turned to look at her. "There were times in the past when I thought maybe…maybe Andrew is my father. Why else would he hang around all these years? I'd tell myself…just accept him for what he is and stop analyzing things. But you know…he'd use figurative bullshit all the time. *You are a son to me, Owen,* or…*I want to be like a father to you.*"

The words caught in his chest, and he covered his eyes.

"My pride wouldn't let me ask him. If it was true, I wanted *him* to tell me. I wanted him to tell me about my mother. About who she was before becoming so wasted. For all I know, my mother could have been born in an alley with a needle already in her arm. But then again, the late sixties and the seventies were tough on a lot of people."

Tears slid down Sarah's face.

"Andrew had lung cancer. He would have been lucky to live till Christmas. He asked me to come to Newport, and I thought we would finally settle the past."

"I am sorry, Owen. If it weren't for me, my car…on their property, they would be…"

"Don't!" he cupped her face. His fierce gaze met hers. "I lost a friend sooner than I'd hoped, but Andrew was already refusing treatments. He was going to die even before the time the doctors were giving him."

"But you also lost the answers to your past because of what happened to him."

"But look at what I've gained."

Her lips trembled when they touched his. As he wrapped his arms around her body, she pressed herself against him until they became one.

"But I'm so scared, Owen. I don't even dare to dream."

"Listen, we both know about being scared. I have an idea, though, that some dreams can only happen one day at a time."

Chapter 27

The lawyer waited for Evan Steele's answering machine prompt to sound, then started his message.

"Hello, Evan. Scott Rosen calling. It's seven in the morning. If you're in the shower, hopefully you'll get this message before heading downtown. We'd planned to meet at the Judge's office at nine, but I'm going to pick up my wife at the hospital before I go down there. So, we can swing by the office after I pick up Lucy, just to drop off the files. We might run a little late. It might be closer to ten. On the other hand, if you want to call me on my cell phone, I can swing by now...on my way over to the hospital. Well, whatever works for you." He paused for a second and then added an afterthought. "Just don't forget to shut off those security alarms before I get there."

The clerk at the gift shop came back on the line. "You were correct, Mr. Dean. Mrs. Rosen is being dismissed early this morning. It would better if you have us send the flowers to their residence. Do you have the address?"

"Yes, hold on a minute." Owen thumbed through the phonebook, but the only address and phone number he could find was the attorney's office. He gave the woman on the phone the address, anyway.

"And will that be all?"

"I'd like an identical arrangement sent to Mrs. Warner—same floor as my order two days ago."

"You know that they won't allow any arrangements to be delivered to the ICU."

"Deliver it to the attention of Mrs. Joanne Emerson. She's Mrs. Warner's sister."

The clerk quoted him the total cost of the two bouquets. "Anything else?"

"That's it."

"I'm a big fan of yours, Mr. Dean." The girl started rattling off all the movies she'd seen him in, but Owen's attention had turned to Sarah, coming down the stairs. Dressed in the same black dress as yesterday, with the tips of her short hair drying out at all different angles around her pale face, she looked pretty damn good for a dead woman. He watched her gaze wander around the room, taking in every corner, every window and every detail before finally coming to rest on the sofa, where the two of them had spent most of the night, talking and making love and talking again.

Before last night, he'd never opened his heart to another human being the way he had to Sarah. He'd never known what it was to want somebody for eternity. For eternity, he thought.

"Is somebody on that phone?" Sarah mouthed the question.

He turned his attention back to the phone and found the young woman still talking. "I'm sorry, but I have to go now. Thanks for all your help."

"What is this about?" She looked down at the open phone book on the countertop.

"I just sent Rosen's wife two dozen roses to his office."

A curious eyebrow went up.

"I forgot to tell you I met him at the gift shop in the hospital on Saturday. I asked around and found out his wife had delivered a baby that morning."

A wry smile tugged at her lips. "What are you trying to do? Charm him, hoping he won't sue after he finds out we've intentionally been keeping his client in jail?"

He winked at her. "Actually, I was hoping to get invited over for dinner, so I can rob his house." He closed the phone book and put it away. "Are you ready to go?"

"It's only ten past seven. Aren't we a little early?"

"Not for what I have planned."

"What are you up to?" She planted her feet as Owen wrapped an arm around her waist, ushering her toward the kitchen.

"Nothing. Really. I just thought we could stop at the hospital first. I wanted to run in and see if Tracy's condition has changed at all. Then we can stop at some fast-food place where I can buy you a high-fat, high-calorie breakfast—you're way too thin. And then we can scope out the office downtown before you go in."

She looked convinced. "I straightened up the bathroom upstairs, but give me ten minutes here to—"

"Forget it." He placed a kiss on her lips and started her toward the door again. "We'll call Susan from the car and have her send in a professional cleaning crew."

"Hey, we didn't make *that* much of a mess," she complained. "When this whole thing is over, I'm going to send a note and a gift to Susan and her family." She cast another wistful look at the place before they walked out. "This was a very...special place."

Evan Steele was waiting at the top of the stairs for the office manager as she made her way breathlessly up. Seeing the rolling suitcase in the woman's hand, he descended the few remaining steps and took it from her.

"Still refuse to take the elevator, Linda?"

"I've told you, walking those stairs is my only exercise, Evan."

He hefted the suitcase. "What you got in this, a dead body?"

"Don't joke around like that." The middle-aged woman stood on the landing and tried to catch her breath. "This was a whole bunch of Sarah's files that I'd taken home to sort out before we closed for the summer vacation. Some vacation."

Steele rolled the suitcase out of Linda's way, and the two entered the suite of offices.

"Thanks for meeting me so early," she said, putting her purse under her desk. "I've had five phone calls from clients last night and two this morning, all of them asking to have certain files sent over to their new attorneys. I think that fire has everyone really shaken up. Not that anyone needs to worry. There was nothing even close to current in storage there. Did you go over?"

Steele moved the suitcase next to Linda's desk and laid it on the ground. "Yes, I did. In fact, I've been beating a path from the storage facility to the police station and back again. Good thing you called me on my cell phone, or you wouldn't have gotten hold of me." He ran a hand over his face. "It's been a long night. I'm looking forward to a hot shower and a shave."

"You don't have to stay here, you know," the office manager called over her shoulder as she went toward the kitchen. Evan heard the sound of water running and the rattle of the coffee can. "I'll be here when you get back. I may spend all day here, in fact. There is an awful lot I need to catch up on."

Steele glanced at his watch. 7:35. His gaze was drawn to the suitcase of Sarah's files that Linda had brought in.

"I know the truth about why you're hanging around here." The office manager smiled at him as she walked back into the office.

Steele stared at her. "Is that right?"

"You've been missing my coffee. That's why you're not racing out of here."

"How did you guess?" He gave her a half smile, then walked to the closed blinds at the window overlooking the street. He glanced through the slit in the blinds at the already bustling Monday morning traffic. "Actually, Scott Rosen is coming around about nine to bring back some files he borrowed on Friday. I had him leave a card for everything he took."

"I'm glad that I was able to train *somebody* right in this office." He watched her kneel before the suitcase and open it. She pulled a stack of folders and placed them on her desk. "Bless her soul, Sarah used to be real good at staying organized. Doing the filing for her was real pleasure. She kept everything sorted by date and client and file number. Poor thing."

Linda slid open the doors concealing the wall of file cabinets. "I don't know what the heck happened to these folders, though. They were a mess. It took me forever to go through them. It looked like a tornado hit them."

She gave Evan a glance over her shoulder. "You know, I have a feeling this was not Sarah's work."

"What do you mean?"

She focused on where she was putting a specific folder in the cabinet before continuing. "On August 1, I know Judge Arnold spent all day here. When I came around at noon to take some more of these files home with me, I found him at Sarah's desk, going through her things. Now, I don't know what he was looking for, but he acted very guilty when I asked him if there was anything I could help him with. I think this mess was his work."

"Have you mentioned any of this to the D.A.'s people?"

"Evan Steele." She gave him a scolding frown over her shoulder. "You know better than to ask me what I've said and haven't said to Ike Bosler. Ah, I can smell that coffee already."

Evan watched Linda march toward the kitchenette, and he glanced again at his watch before checking the street.

There wasn't much time left. He had to get rid of Linda, somehow, before Sarah arrived at the office. She'd specifically said she wanted to keep the whole thing quiet until she came in and found whatever she was looking for.

He couldn't agree with her more.

They had been sitting idly in the hospital visitor's lot for ten minutes, at least. Sarah watched Owen reach for his cup of coffee and drain what was left in it. All the while, his gaze never wavered from the one-way entrance into the lot.

"What are we waiting for?" She whispered her question.

"Why are you whispering?"

"To get your attention." Sarah saw him smile. She was anxious about everything that lay ahead of them today. But at the same time, she knew this was it. The end of the road. She was moving out into the open, come what may.

But they still had to get down to the office. It was still early, though, she told herself, and she knew Owen wasn't going to let her take any unnecessary risks.

Sarah drew a deep breath. God, she hoped so desperately that they would find whatever it was that was missing. Without it, explaining her actions to the officials would be a nightmare that she wasn't looking forward to. With no proof, it was very possible charges could be filed against her for obstruction. She didn't even want to think about the possibility of them trying to charge her with Tori's murder.

And then, of course, there was always the happy prospect of getting murdered herself.

"Okay, you have my attention. Now, stop that look."

"What look?"

"Your 'the sky is going to fall on us at any minute' look."

"Oh, that look." Sarah hazarded another glance at him. "Isn't it?"

"That's what you got me for, love. I'm just here to try to hold it up until you can get out from under. Just call me Atlas."

She tried to swallow the tennis ball that suddenly formed in her throat. "If you say one more nice thing like that to me, I may just cry, you know."

"Really?" His gaze shifted to her, but as his hand touched her cheek, something in his peripheral vision snapped his head around.

"Bingo! Here he is."

"Who?" Sarah followed the direction of Owen's gaze and saw the dark green BMW pulling into the visitor's lot.

"Put your glasses on. Get out of the car and walk up toward the corner. Stay away from where he is parking. Quick, Sarah!"

Walking as casually as she could between the rows of cars, she kept an eye on the BMW. Before she could reach the edge of the lot, the lawyer pulled into a spot near her.

Sarah felt the panic prickle along her spine. If Rosen even glanced her way, he might recognize her. Before she could change direction, she saw the lawyer climb from behind the wheel.

But his attention was not on her. She watched Rosen pulling something out of the backseat. A baby's car seat.

"Scott. Scott Rosen."

Owen's shout confused Sarah even more. She stopped between two cars, pretending to be looking for something in her purse. The hood of Owen's car was up.

"Glad I ran into someone I know. I was just checking on Tracy, and I come back to find the battery on my car is dead. I have to be downtown in ten minutes for an important meeting, otherwise I would call in for service, but I'm running so late..."

Sarah continued out toward the street. She went all the way to the corner before turning around. Looking back at the parked cars, she was shocked to see Owen getting into Rosen's BMW as the rangy lawyer hurried toward the hospital entrance, carrying the car seat under one arm.

Immediately, she hurried back to Owen's car. Before she got there, the BMW had been parked in front of the Range Rover. The hoods of both cars were raised and Owen was pulling some cables out the back of his own car.

"What are you doing?" she called quietly, coming up to the car.

"Playing with wires." He waved the jump-start cables in her direction. "Rosen's briefcase is on the backseat. While I try to ruin these two cars in under five minutes, why don't you check inside the case and see if any of your files are in there."

"What if he locks his briefcase?" she complained, diving into the backseat. Pulling the thing onto her lap, her fears were immediately confirmed.

"Hurry, Sarah! He is coming back down with his wife and baby in a couple of minutes, and I'm supposed to have the keys back at the receptionist's desk in the lobby by the time they come down."

She looked more closely at the combination lock and found the last of the three dials caught between two numbers. She adjusted it to one number. When that failed, she clicked it the dial back to the next digit.

The locks snapped open.

"A car is coming." Owen called.

Sarah's heart raced, her fingers flying as she leafed through the layers of files and papers in the man's briefcase.

Two more cars pulled into the lot.

"Christ, it's a party." Owen added before getting behind his own wheel and starting his car.

"I have them." Just as she began pulling her own files out of the lawyer's suitcase, the one below them caught her attention. It was also from their own office, and it had Hal's name on it. Glancing quickly inside, she saw a letter addressed to Judge Arnold. The letterhead was from a private investigation firm out of Providence. She took that file, as well, and shut the briefcase again, adjusting the last lock digit to where it had been before. Moving out of Rosen's car and into the Range Rover, she saw Owen pick up the wires that he'd pretended to use, and throw them into the backseat.

"I'll be right back. Lock the doors."

Every inch of her body hummed with the excitement. She locked the doors as he'd told her and watched him drive Rosen's car to an empty spot. A second later, Owen was jogging across the lot to the hospital with the keys in his hand.

Her fingers itched to open the files. But her heart was drumming wildly she couldn't tear her eyes off the door he'd disappeared into.

The sound of sirens swiveled her attention toward the road. An emergency rescue vehicle and a police car rounded the building and headed for the emergency entrance. Sarah's gaze snapped back to the visitor's entrance.

"Please, Owen. Please…"

The sight of him stepping out of the building, unharmed and alone, filled her with unexpected joy. She bit her lip, trying to contain her excitement as he hurried to the car.

"Well? Anything?"

Instead of an answer, she threw her arms around his neck and kissed his flushed face before pulling back.

"Thank you."

"For what?"

"For coming back." Her emotions were getting the better part of her. She quickly opened up the top file on her lap. "Sorry, I haven't looked at them yet."

He took a hold of her chin and lifted her face. She saw the tenderness in his gaze.

"We'll have lots of time later. Now get to work."

"Yes, sir," she quipped, focusing her attention on the paperwork in her lap. Owen started the engine, then headed for the lot exit.

"You do know that Rosen will figure out you've taken the files before the morning is over," she said as they drove down the street. "I don't think he's going to take too kindly to people going through his briefcase."

"Yeah. Maybe I should call that flower shop back and have the card on the flowers addressed to Scott Rosen and not to his wife."

"Go ahead and joke," she said seriously, "but Rosen is known as a man who goes for the throat."

Chapter 28

Compared to the steady string of stories about homicides, stabbings and forced teenage prostitution that had lately been gracing the pages of the local newspapers, the Sunday night fire at the Newport storage facility didn't stir much interest among the prisoners at the state's Adult Correctional Institution. Judge Charles Hamlin Arnold, though, had a personal stake in this latest disaster.

He'd first heard the report during dinner. Afterward, listening to the radio, he'd heard an interview with a couple of the firefighters. They had been pretty impressed with the intensity of the fire and the accompanying explosions. Sitting alone in his cell, the Judge considered what he might have lost in the fire. The firefighter's comments had told him to fear the worst.

The tape had surely been destroyed.

The noose around his neck was getting tighter. Time was running short.

The preliminary hearing on the murder case was scheduled to take place in two days. But at this point, having the case ordered to go to trial was the least of the Judge's problems. In fact, if he didn't start doing something about it right now, he wouldn't live long enough to stand trial. He'd be killed within these walls.

A couple of inmates at the Intake Service Center had come suspiciously close to him this morning. Another, sitting at the next table during breakfast, had never taken his eyes off him. Scum.

From his bench on the other side of the walls and barbed wire, Judge Arnold had watched the failings of the penal system for too many years. He was well aware of the power structures that were allowed to exist inside these places. Murders and drug-dealing and racketeering and money laundering were as common in here as they were on the outside. More common.

And so were contract hits.

The Judge wondered if there were a way he could find out if

there was a price on his head already. He could make a better deal. Pay more. Make the pot more lucrative in exchange for a little protection from the same people.

But then again, maybe not. As a former Judge, he'd put more than a few of these dirtbags in here. It was always said that in Rhode Island, all it took was a dime for the phone call to have somebody erased.

Walking to the stainless sink and turning on the water to wash his hands and face, Arnold thought of the more ambitious plan that had been forming in his head for the past few days. Hell, what did he have to lose?

Calling the guard, he asked him to call Ike Bosler's office for him. He wanted a private meeting with the district attorney, and he wanted it this morning.

Steele drained his third cup of coffee before walking to the window, drawing the blinds, and staring impatiently at the parking lot across the street.

"It's no big deal if he doesn't bring the stuff back today, Evan." Linda chirped from her position by the file cabinets. "I have plenty here to keep me busy."

"I thought Rosen would be punctual, at least."

"Give the guy a break. He had a baby on Saturday morning. His wife is probably coming home today." There was laughter in her voice. "I know he doesn't seem like the affectionate type, but his kind usually falls the hardest."

The blinds fell with a distinct snap.

The woman turned to him with surprise. "You look just too tired. Why don't you go home and get a couple of hours sleep."

He shook his head. "I need you to run an errand for me this morning. It's actually for the office. I was going to ask Rosen to do it, but since he is not coming…"

Linda cast a mournful glance at the stacks of files she'd organized at her desk. "Is it something that needs to be done? I mean, this is the only day this week that I was planning to be here, and I have these things to get to…and with so many phone calls and everyone looking for this and that…"

"Yes, it needs to be done now." His tone was sharper than it should have been and he immediately got her attention.

She dropped the files in her hands unceremoniously on the desk and stood up. "All right. What is it?"

"I need you to carry some information to the police station for me. The stuff has—"

The ring of his cell phone brought Steele up short, and he answered it immediately.

"Hi Evan. It's Sarah."

"Hold on a minute." He took his empty coffee mug and, ignoring Linda's curious looks, headed toward the kitchenette. Once there, he turned on the water for some background noise. "Are you on your way?"

"I think I found what I was looking for."

"Where? What is it?" His voice rose. He walked to a corner of the kitchen, the running water totally forgotten.

"I'll call you back when I know more."

"Where are you, Sarah?"

"I'll call you back."

He could hear traffic in the background. "Are you going to the police?"

"Yes. Not the local police. But I'm handing myself in today."

"Sarah—"

"I have to go, Evan. I'll promise to call you as soon as I can."

"Sarah—"

The phone disconnected at the other end.

"What did you say?"

Steele turned abruptly and found Linda standing in the doorway to the kitchen. The woman's face was pale.

"Who were you talking to, Evan?"

He considered his options for a long moment before making up his mind. Resigned to the inevitable, he tucked the cell phone back into his pocket and met the office manager's gaze.

"I was talking to Sarah," he said, moving toward her. "Yes. She's alive."

☙ ❧

"You still have to explain to me why we had to go through all that, when we could have just walked into my offices later and found the same thing."

Owen shrugged. "Call it actor's intuition, or better yet, call it actor's training. It's all about understanding character. If I were Rosen and my wife were coming home with a baby, there's no way would I bother returning those files today. And aren't you glad we did?"

Sarah put the phone down and picked up the envelope again. She turned it over, studying the sealed edge.

"Are you sure this is it?" Owen asked, trying to maneuver the car through the traffic and, at the same time, keep an eye on her.

"It has to be." She turned the letter over again. "Hotel stationary. Fairly old. Look how it has yellowed along the edges."

"Maybe it's Rosen's. He could have stuffed it in there by mistake."

"He could have," she admitted. "But this is Judge Arnold's handwriting on the front. *Philadelphia, September 10, 1982, 1 of 2.*"

"Rosen is the Judge's lawyer."

She looked down at the open file on her lap. She picked up the legal pad where the envelope had been hidden. "I was using this pad of paper when I was moving the items from Avery's safe-deposit boxes. Here are some of the notes I took that day." She turned the pad in her hands. "I must have laid it down and the envelope somehow slipped in between the pages."

"Open it." He gave her an encouraging nod. "It's the only way to find out."

"If this is evidence of some crime, we could be charged with tampering and obstruction and Lord knows what else. Archer's forensic people would flip." She stared ahead for a second. "But of course, this could just be a hotel receipt, and we'd look like real fools handing it over."

He pulled the car into the empty parking lot of a church. He locked the doors, but left the car running.

"Open it, Sarah."

Her hand shook and her heart raced as she opened the sealed

flap. Inside, there was a single folded piece of stationary and she pulled it out. This paper, too, was discolored a little from what she assumed was age. She opened the note. The same hotel's elegant letterhead and two lines of script in Judge Arnold's handwriting were the only thing on the page.

Sarah read aloud the first line, which was nothing but a series of numbers. The second line, though, caused her brow to furrow.

"Strawberry Mansion Bridge?"

"That's a bridge in Philadelphia." Owen said. "It goes over the Schuylkill River in Fairmount Park. Do you know what the first line of numbers means?"

She stared at the numbers for a moment before it hit her.

"Yes," she said excitedly. "It's a specific location in our dead files."

She glanced at the back of the envelope again and the inscription '1 of 2'.

"I wonder if that's where '2 of 2' is."

"Where do you keep the dead files?"

"In a storage facility here in Newport. We can start there. I have the code to get into the outside fenced-in area, and I have the key to the unit itself."

They were out of the lot as soon as she gave him directions to the facility.

"But why all the secrecy?" she murmured to herself. "And what's the significance of the date? September 10, 1982."

"Was Arnold a Judge by then?"

She thought back. "No. He had just gone out on his own around then. Arnold and Rutherford were law partners for a few years, until Rutherford won his seat in the Senate." She shook her head. "No, in September of 1982, they would still have been part-ners...although Gordon must have already won the primary by then. Yes, that was the year that Rutherford won his first election. November of 1982."

She stared at the letter in her hand again.

"The rest of the answer to this must be in this part two. And whatever it is, it's probably been sitting in those dead files for as long as this envelope sat in that safe-deposit box."

"Christ."

Sarah's head lifted and she looked past the fenced perimeter at the storage facility. Or what was left of it.

"Looks like they beat us to it again." Owen snapped.

Scott pulled into the last available spot in the parking lot. He left the car and the air conditioner running. He turned to Lucy. "It won't take me more than five minutes."

"We'll be here." She turned and leaned into the back seat to look at the baby, secure in the infant car carrier.

Though Lucy had told him that his daughter was not very sensitive to noise, Scott was quiet as a mouse as he took his briefcase out of the back seat. With a smile at his wife, he hurried across the street toward the office building.

He had a key for the outside door. From there, he took the steps three at a time to the second floor. He tapped once on the doors to the offices. Waiting for Steele to open up, Scott balanced the briefcase on one knee and reached inside of it for the files. The stack that greeted him seemed much thinner, but before he could inspect it more closely, the door opened and he looked up to see the pallid face of the office manager staring out at him. Red-rimmed eyes and splotches on her cheeks made it obvious that the woman had been crying.

"What's wrong, Linda?"

At his question, fresh tears burst forth again, surprising him. "It's...I can't believe it. I don't like people pulling my leg, but if it's true...I just don't know."

She made no sense, and Scott followed her inside.

"What's going on?" He demanded, dropping his briefcase on a chair.

"This call." She wiped at her eyes. "It could have been a crank call...but..."

Scott found himself losing his patience. "Who called?"

"Sarah." The woman turned to him. "Sarah Rand called. She called Evan Steele, told him that she is alive."

Scott felt every muscle in his body go rigid. "Where is Steele?"

"He just left. A minute ahead of you. He was going home to

shower and change. He said he had to decide if this was a crank call or if it was real. He's coming back soon, he said." She balled up the tissue. "I think we should call the police right now. Let them do what they need to do. They can trace the call, or whatever."

Linda continued to talk, but Scott had already started pacing the room, his mind racing with what could be the ruin of everything. He stopped abruptly before the office manager.

"I don't want a word of this to get out."

Her mouth opened to argue, but she snapped it shut as she saw the anger blazing in his eyes.

"Do you hear me, Linda?" he repeated more threateningly. "I'll take care of the police. But for right now, not one damn word about this can get out."

Chapter 29

They were at least six hours away from Philadelphia, but as far as Sarah was concerned, they might as well have been six hundred hours away. After all, it would take her at least that long to understand everything that was going on.

Owen's phone rang again. And again, she had very little success in comprehending the one-way conversation. Sarah felt her fuse begin to burn shorter.

Back in Newport, after seeing the burned-out storage facility, Owen had insisted that there was no way she was handing herself in to the authorities in this town. He had no faith, he said grimly, in their ability to keep her safe.

They were going to Philadelphia.

As soon as they'd started on the road, she'd heard him call someone named Stu Ramsay, whom she gathered was his lawyer in New York. And immediately following that, he'd called an Agent Hinckey. FBI, she assumed, though she had no idea where he was located. From what she'd been able to hear at her end, this conversation wasn't the first time the two of them had spoken about Sarah's case. In fact, the tone of the conversation had sounded more as if Owen was just keeping Hinckey up to date.

Listening to this conversation had confused the heck out of her. She'd never guessed how much Owen had involved the outside authorities in her situation.

As they rode through Connecticut, Owen explained to Sarah that after Hal's stabbing, it was clearly demonstrable that there was indeed a conspiracy to kill her. That night, Owen had called his lawyer, who in turn had contacted the Bureau. Agent Hinckey had been the investigator already assigned to the case, based on suspicions they had that linked Sarah's 'murder' to two other murders dating some years back. Hinckey had been in touch with Owen since that first day.

She didn't know if she should be angry with him for not revealing any of it, or if she should be happy that he had enough sense to take those precautionary steps.

Well, whatever she was feeling, Sarah would no longer tolerate being left out of the loop.

Another glance in the side mirror bothered her. The same blue sedan had been following them for quite a while.

"We're going directly to Fairmont Park," Owen said as he ended the call. "Most likely, they'll meet us when we hit Kelly Drive in Philly."

"Somebody is following us." She glanced again in the mirror.

"Good! I was wondering when he was going to get here."

"A friend of yours?"

"Not really." He gave her a half smile, obviously conscious of her darkening mood. "At least we haven't met personally. But I was told he is with the FBI, as well. Out of their regional office. He's also the guy who ran down your would-be killer yesterday after Hal's memorial service."

"Really." She stared back at the car, feeling better. "Where's the dent from the accident?"

"They must have given him another company car."

"How come he doesn't have the guy's head mounted on the hood?"

"I…" He cleared his throat. "Maybe there was a line at the taxidermist."

Sarah suppressed a smile. Though she felt nothing for the dead killer, she didn't want to look happy. She wanted to tell Owen that she was angry at not being trusted with her own life.

"He's been staking out my place and keeping an eye on you since Friday."

She restrained the urge to say something sharp about why he'd felt the need to take her to that lovely cottage last night. But then again, she thought…

"After the attempt on your life yesterday, I wasn't sure how long it would take him to get clear of the Newport authorities. I wasn't about to risk putting you in any more danger than necessary. That's why we went out to the place in Little Compton."

Brilliant, she thought. Now he was starting to read her mind. Why had she let him get this close? Surely, after she was in the hands of the authorities, this would be the end of it. The end of them.

Five days was not enough time for someone of Owen's celebrity to form a serious attachment to someone like her. They lived different life styles. They had different needs. Different goals in life.

She wasn't going to be another Tori in his life—obsessed and too blind to see she was not wanted.

It hurt to think of ending this almost before it began. But there seemed to be no options.

"Hinckey is going to call back in a few moments. He didn't say much about it just now, but it seems that while we were speaking on the phone, he was getting other information coming to him about the Strawberry Mansion Bridge."

It would certainly help with the explanations she'd be making if something substantial did come out of this discovery, Sarah thought. She was fully prepared to take whatever should come as a result of her decision not to go to the police immediately. And if they didn't believe her, so be it. She knew no matter what happened, there would probably be charges. Obstructing a murder investigation. Tampering with evidence. Leaving the scene of a crime.

The phone rang again disrupting Sarah's train of thought. From Owen's greeting, she knew the caller was Agent Hinckey again.

"That makes it much simpler."

His blue gaze turned in her direction, and her treacherous stomach fluttered at the feelings he wrought in her. When he hung up the phone, his hand reached for hers.

"They are starting to dig."

"Dig where?"

"At a spot beneath the bridge."

"But from the way you described it, the bridge must be a huge structure. How do they know where to start? Or what to look for?"

"Judge Arnold has decided to make a deal." Owen said. "He told them exactly where to dig."

"And did he say what to look for?"

He nodded, turning his attention back to the road.

"A woman's body."

Ike Bosler nodded to the group of men before him as he put down the phone. "They're starting right away."

They were too many people stuffed in the small conference room at the state's Intake Service Center. At the moment, no one seemed to mind.

Judge Arnold accepted a cigarette from Dan Archer and let the police detective hold a light for him. He took a deep drag and sat back in the chair, crossing his legs.

"Okay, Ike," the Judge said. "What's next?"

"We'll go through with our part of the deal. You'll get the complete immunity you've requested." Bosler frowned as he looked over a pad of paper containing his assistant's scribbled notes. "In addition to what you've already given us—where we will find the body, et cetera—we'll need all the other details, as well. Dates, names, places, other clients who were involved. Whatever information you have regarding the second incident. And then this last one. We'll only get one chance at this, so we—meaning both sides—need to put everything on the table."

"We all have the same goal, sir," Archer added, speaking to the Judge. "The more comprehensive a report we put together now, the sooner we'll have him."

The Judge glanced over at the unreadable expression on Scott Rosen's face. The attorney leaned forward and spoke confidentially to him. "Are you sure about this, Your Honor? You're sure you want to do it this way?"

The older man took a long drag from the cigarette. The tic in his neck was jumping uncontrollably. He finally gave a thoughtful nod to his lawyer.

"Yes I do, Scott. Too many people have died. I want to strike back now, before he gets me. And I also want to get even. I want to kick that son of a bitch's ass for what he did to Sarah. She mattered to me in a way I'd be hesitant to try to explain to this crowd." He waved his cigarette in the direction of the others in the room. "But there was no reason for that bastard to kill her like that."

"Judge, are you telling me the district attorney's office has not informed you of the latest findings regarding Sarah Rand?"

The Judge stared in confusion at his lawyer for a moment before turning angrily to Ike Bosler. "They haven't told me dick. What's going on, Counselor?"

Rosen also looked at Bosler, who showed nothing of the discomfort he must have been feeling.

"We are done talking, Ike. No more statements. No deal." He rose abruptly to his feet. "Time to clear this room."

"Now, just a minute." The district attorney was on his feet in a flash. "Listen to me, Scott. There is no reason to act rashly."

"No reason, Ike?" Rosen towered over the other man. "You don't bother to tell my client that Sarah Rand is alive…and you call that no reason?"

The Judge's weight sank back against the chair, and his cigarette dropped to the floor. The room fell dead silent. His hand shaking, he reached up and rubbed his neck.

"She's not dead…she…" He leaned forward and buried his face in his hands. Arnold's eyes were red when he finally looked into the lawyer's face. "They didn't tell me a goddamn thing."

"No reason?" Rosen repeated his accusation, and pandemonium broke out in the room.

"We really haven't had much time to talk now, have we?" Bosler said, silencing the other voices.

"You had plenty of time to coerce some key information out of him before I even got here, Ike."

"Hey, the Judge asked for this meeting. Your client voluntarily surrendered the location of—"

"What are you trying to do? Pin a twenty-year-old homicide on him and let the real killer walk again?" He picked up his briefcase off the metal table. "You call this putting everything on the table? Mr. District Attorney. Well, when I'm done with you and these clowns, you can kiss that governor's mansion—"

"Stop right there, Rosen." Bosler retorted. "Damn it, we were running short on time. We have no intention of failing to follow through with our part of the deal."

The D.A. looked at Archer and McHugh.

"Besides, with the Newport Police leaking information to every paper and TV station between here and Boston, I just assumed every goddamn person on the East Coast knew Sarah Rand was alive."

"Hold on a fucking minute," McHugh put in, looking like a bomb about to go off.

"Shut up, Bob," Archer said quietly before turning to Scott. "We did find our leak. We suspended one very sorry dispatcher this morning. But as far as no one notifying the Judge directly, blame it on me. So many people knew she was alive. I mean...*you* knew. We just assumed...wrongfully assumed, maybe that the Judge had already been told. But we're playing it straight. We'll give you everything we have, now. Isn't that right, Mr. Bosler?"

The district attorney gave a curt nod. Archer gestured for Rosen to sit. The lawyer glared at the detective.

"Let's listen, Scott," the Judge said gruffly.

With a fierce frown at the D.A., Rosen settled into his chair. "We're listening."

"Thank you. I won't repeat what I'm sure everyone knows. But you have to understand, much of this is still just theory." Archer ran a hand through his thinning hair. "We know there were at least two killers tied into all the recent events. We believe both of them were contracted by the suspect to commit all the murders. This includes the murder of someone—still unidentified—in Sarah Rand's apartment and the removal of the body. Also, we believe the same two were responsible for the stabbing death of the Judge's stepson, Hal Van Horn, the shooting of Andrew Warner and his wife, and also the murder of a local low-life named Frankie O'Neal. This last murder was committed because Frankie had been an eyewitness to Hal's stabbing. They even planted the murder weapon in his house."

"Unfortunately, one of the two hired killers was a former Newport police officer, kicked off the force six months back," Bosler put in. "Through his connections on the force, he was able to access information that he and his partner used in the killings."

"Both killers are dead. The ex-cop's body was found last night in a Portsmouth boatyard. The second man was killed yesterday in

Newport. He was hit by a car driven by an FBI agent who wisely did not identify himself at the scene as a law enforcement officer." Archer glanced at the Judge before meeting Rosen eye-to-eye. "That's pretty much it. Everything new, anyway. Now I say we just move forward—starting now."

Surprisingly, Archer's explanations calmed the room. Scott Rosen turned to look at his client, who'd never moved from the chair. His gray eyes were pensive as they watched the scene unfold before him.

"What do you say, Your Honor?" Rosen asked.

The man's gaze focused on the lawyer's face. "So Sarah is really alive."

Scott nodded.

"As we speak," the D.A. offered, "Attorney Rand is being escorted to FBI agents, where she'll remain under police protection until we all decide on the next step."

As the Judge fell silent again, the tension in the room mounted. Bosler watched him, but he was not alone in his concern that Judge Arnold might change his mind.

Dan Archer kept an eye on the D.A. They both knew they needed the Judge to catch the bigger fish. And Rosen was right; without him, Ike Bosler could kiss the governor's mansion good-bye.

Archer shifted his weight from one leg to the other. Actually, they all had a lot riding on this. And there was a lot more at stake now than just the stinking case sitting on his desk. For him, at least.

He'd known years ago that women like Julia Rutherford didn't just run off.

He'd known her when she'd been Julia Byrne. Of course, no one had ever expected her to stay put in Newport. She was too good for the Fifth Ward. Beautiful and smart, she'd always known where she was going.

And she'd known how to get there. It was no secret in the neighborhood. An apartment on Bellevue, a couple of society parties, and pretty soon she was running with the right crowd. And as soon as she hooked Rutherford, nobody seemed to recall where she'd come from, either. When the political nod had come, she'd been ready for that, too. She was going to take the ride right to the top.

But then, when Gordon Rutherford was looking like a shoe-in as the next U.S. Senator from Rhode Island, she runs off with some other guy? Never to be seen again? No way. Not Julia Byrne.

Archer had known it then. He knew it now. Julia Byrne would never have thrown everything away practically on the eve of seeing her husband becoming a U.S. Senator. No way.

"I can testify until my teeth fall out." Judge Arnold's words drew Archer's attention. "But after the fire at the storage facility last night, we don't have a lick of proof that supports anything I say. Nothing that links him directly. It's my word against his."

"We can fix that." Bosler replied. "We've got the plan to nail him this time. But there is one question that we need answered first. Did the suspect have any knowledge of what exactly was contained in the letter that Attorney Rand holds now?"

Arnold chose his words carefully before answering. "He knew I was holding for safekeeping two pieces of evidence or documentation that, together, tied him to the original crime. To insure that he wouldn't be tempted to eliminate me, I let him know long ago that one of those pieces was a taped telephone message from him in which he admits, in rather panicky tones, his direct responsibility. He also knew the second item was a letter from me. But as far as what information the letter contained, he has no idea." Arnold rubbed his neck. "The tape was really the only worthwhile thing I had on him. But that was destroyed, along with everything else in the fire last night."

"You're assuming Attorney Rand didn't remove it beforehand." Archer put in thoughtfully. "I believe we want, at this point, everyone to think she had the means and opportunity to take possession of that tape."

Chapter 30

They never made it to Fairmount Park. Just before crossing the state line from Connecticut into New York, two more unmarked cars joined their caravan and their route was redirected to Justice Department offices in Manhattan.

Arriving at their destination, Owen found himself being nudged into a separate channel while Sarah was whisked away for questioning by lawyers who'd just come in from Washington.

Owen's lawyer, Stu Ramsay, arrived on the scene. There was never a question that this was only a fact-finding session, since these same people had been aware of every step he and Sarah had taken over the past few days.

Almost every step, Owen corrected himself, thinking of the cottage.

Hours dragged by, but he still wasn't allowed a chance to speak to Sarah. And as the afternoon edged toward evening, he was still waiting.

Earlier in the afternoon, and on Owen's direction, Stu Ramsay had tried to inject himself into the middle of Sarah's questioning, but he had been instructed that Attorney Rand was fully cognizant of her rights, and that she was in no need of additional counsel.

Sometime later in the afternoon, one of the investigators approached Owen, telling him that he was free to leave. The agent wanted him to know that it was critical that nothing of what had taken place should be discussed for some time. For the purposes of the investigation, no one should know that Owen Dean had ever met Sarah Rand. Just two strangers. No connections. No association. Thank you, Mr. Dean. Don't let the door hit you on your way out.

But Owen wasn't ready to go.

A little after eight o'clock, Stu came back from a discussion with the Justice Department official who had taken charge of the operation. They had yet to see Sarah reappear from the conference room door that she'd passed through hours earlier.

"She's fine, Owen," the lawyer assured him. "And I've been talking with Hinckey on the phone. He's on his way here from Philadelphia. He guarantees that they are not investigating her. They understand she was the victim. They're after bigger game."

"I'm not going anywhere without her, Stu." Owen said as he poured himself another cup of coffee. "You go on. But I'm waiting here until they let her out."

"All right. I'll give it one more shot."

Ramsay was his lawyer because he *always* got his way. And Owen knew it was only because of Stu's tenacity that half an hour later, a female investigator came over with him. Owen was led through two sets of doors before coming to a windowless square of a room where Sarah was waiting for him.

She looked pale and weary. But as he entered, he saw the life return. He didn't wait for the door to close behind him before taking her in his arms. She wrapped her arms tightly around him and buried her face against his chest. They stood like that for a long time.

"I'm taking you home," he whispered in her ear. His hands caressed her hair, her back, trying, by touching her, to soothe the ache that had been dogging him through the endless hours of waiting.

"I can't. They have big plans for me."

"What kind of plans?"

"I'm going back to Newport tonight. They've organized a big show for tomorrow morning where Sarah Rand supposedly steps out into the public eye and tells the world she's alive."

"Why? To put you in the spotlight for some lunatic to take aim at?"

She shook her head. "They know what they're are doing. We've gone over it again and again. I'm going to help them catch the guy behind it all."

"They're using you as bait." he said. "I can't fucking believe it. As if you haven't had enough people trying to stab you, or shoot you, or kidnap you. How many lives do they think you have?"

"I can't hide forever. I need to get this over with and get on with my life." She paused. He felt a sadness weighing her down. Her green eyes were shadowed with something akin to loss when they looked up to meet his. "As it stands now, I'm a target anyway. And I'll continue to be until this is over. I have to cooperate."

There were things that she wasn't telling him. He could feel the tension in every inch of her body. His hands moved along her arms. She was cold.

"Let me come with you. Be part of it."

"I can't." She shook her head. "As far as anyone is concerned, there's no record of 'us' that exists in the public eye. It's better this way. Fewer complications. No hard feelings. We split right here. Right now. It's better, Owen."

"No."

Her words hurt him. She couldn't seriously expect him to just walk away from everything that was happening between them. She couldn't seriously expect him to simply forget the energy that sparked to life when they touched each other.

Frowning, he came to a decision. He had to trust her now to do what she felt had to be done. But he wasn't about to let her go. That battle was not finished. Right now, she was exhausted and harassed and frightened, and he would put aside what he wanted. That was a battle for another day.

He watched Sarah move away from him, putting as much distance as she could between them. She was shutting him out.

"What's the running time for this show?"

She looked over her shoulder at him, a perplexed look on her face.

"They're unveiling you before the press tomorrow. What's next? When is this whole thing a wrap?"

"I can't talk about it. The less anyone knows, the better. The safer it'll be for everyone."

"Cut the shit, Sarah."

She glared at him. "Soon. It'll be over soon. That's all I can tell you."

"Then I'll be waiting."

"Waiting for what?" She folded her arms across her chest.

"For you, damn it!" he said with more heat than anger. He took a step toward her. "I'm going back to Newport, too, and I'm going to wait until this whole thing is finished. And when it is, we are going to pick up where we left off."

"No. We're not. It's over, Owen. We've never met. We've never talked. We've never become…intimate. Please. Let's just keep things simple."

"I hate simple." He took another step toward her. "I don't care what kind of bullshit they want to feed the media, but you and I will continue to be a *we* until we can have a rational talk, without the weight of the world on your shoulders. Hey, when that happens, if you can convince me that you don't care for me at all, then you can kick the door in my face."

"I don't care for you," she blurted out the words, but they echoed hollowly in the empty room.

"You're a terrible liar, Sarah." He turned to go, but stopped by the door. "And I'll tell you what else, I don't care what gets fed to the press or what everyone in America is led to believe. Here is my plan. I'm going to sit on your front steps until you get tired of tripping over me. And I'm going to keep running into you until people think I'm your personal assistant. And I'm going to work my ass off at being incredibly nice to you. And that's only the start."

He strode out of the room without waiting for her response. Outside, he ran into a new face coming down the hall. Owen answered the man's smile with a glower as he read the name badge dangling from his lapel.

"Mr. Dean, I'm so glad I arrived in time to meet you."

"Listen to me, Hinckey." Owen ignored the FBI agent's extended hand and instead met him eye to eye. "I don't know what the fuck you guys are planning to put her through tomorrow or over the next few days. But I'll tell you something, if you let anything happen to her…"

"We won't, Mr. Dean," the agent said, the smile gone from his face. "We have everything mapped out to the smallest detail. Attorney Rand will be perfectly safe. You have to trust us."

"That's the problem, Hinckey. When it comes to Sarah Rand's life, I can't afford to trust anybody."

Anyone watching might have assumed the dozen or so men and women working with shovels and brushes belonged to one of the local colleges or universities. The vans holding the equipment had no insignia on the sides; and only one bored looking policeman sat in his car, discreetly parked some distance from the footing of the bridge. To any casual passerby, it looked like an archeological dig, perhaps arranged as part of a summer course or workshop.

Everyone knew how important it was to keep a low profile on the digging that had started on the southern foot of the Strawberry Mansion Bridge. The involvement of media at this stage of the investigation equated to throwing all the evidence into the Schuylkill and watching it sink for good. Timing was everything, and those in charge knew that regardless of their find, there could be no statements made until final approval was received from the center of the operation, which had now moved to Newport, Rhode Island.

It took the group less than four hours to locate and dig the grave. The directions had been specific. In a shallow grave, they found the remains of the skeleton. After examining the jawbone, the pelvis, the skull, and forehead, the forensic anthropologists on hand were able to identify the remains as female. Once back in their labs, there would be no need for forensic facial reconstruction or for other estimates regarding the person's height, weight, racial group, or occupation. Thanks to the statement given by Judge Charles Hamlin Arnold, they had their answer.

A dental record comparison was made, however. There was no question now. The bones belonged to Julia Rutherford, who had last been seen on September 10, 1982, at the Philadelphia hotel where her husband was giving a luncheon speech.

Late Monday night, the discovery of the skeleton and its identity remained a secret while they waited for further testing. By Tuesday morning, they knew for certain the cause of death, as well. The victim had sustained repeated blows to the head, evidenced by marks on the skull, sufficient to cause internal cerebral hemorrhaging.

In layman's terms, Julia Rutherford had been beaten to death.

The press conference began promptly at 11:00 a.m. on Tuesday morning on the steps of the old courthouse. A bulleted fact sheet was handed around, but the details were sketchy. Sarah Rand, the Newport attorney who had been missing since August 2, had contacted the local police department that morning. Judge Arnold had been released from custody and would not be available for questions.

Sarah stood on the steps, facing the mob of reporters and thinking she probably would have received more compassion from a pack of hungry wolfs. The lights the TV news crews had set up were blinding her. Questions were fired at her so fast that she couldn't tell who was asking them.

Three others were standing with her. Beside her stood Ike Bosler, the District Attorney, and Scott Rosen stood on the far end. Chief Calvin stood to Sarah's right, occasionally taking hold of her elbow and looking like a bounty hunter who'd just bagged a huge prize.

A general statement had been read by the D.A. As far as his office was concerned, a homicide had occurred in Miss Rand's apartment in her absence, but Judge Arnold was no longer considered to be a suspect. The traces of blood in the Judge's boat had obviously been planted by a third party. The case was very much open and under investigation, and any information the public might have…et cetera…et cetera…

"Can you give us the name of the victim?" One of the reporters shouted at the chief of police.

"I'm sorry, but we are not releasing any more information regarding the victim until the immediate family has been notified."

"Has Attorney Rand told you where she buried the body?"

Sarah frowned at the question, but the D.A. jumped in quickly.

"Miss Rand is *not* a suspect in this case. I repeat, *not* a suspect. But to answer the other part of that question—we still have not recovered the body."

An anchor woman from a Providence TV station shouted a question at Sarah. "You still haven't told us where you've been, Ms. Rand. Why have you taken so long to come forward?"

Similar queries echoing that one.

Sarah felt the men on either side of her edge backwards. Summoning all of her courage, Sarah stepped up to the microphones. Speaking truthfully, she told of having gone to Ireland for her father's funeral and how, upon her return, she had been totally unaware of the events taking place in Newport.

"And when did you get back?"

"This past weekend."

Camera shutters were clicking a mile a minute, and a current of excitement shot through the reporters. Sarah took a deep breath.

The anchorwoman again. "I repeat my question. Why did you wait so long to come forward?"

"Where have you been hiding?"

Sarah raised a hand to silence the crowd. "I...I stayed with some friends for a couple of days. I was in New York. They had no idea what was going on here. I only drove back this morning."

"Your car. How is it the police found your car on the late Andrew Warner's property?"

"Did you know the Warners?"

"How did your car get shot up?"

"I knew them casually," she answered. "I feel very bad about the death of Andrew Warner, and I'm praying for his wife's recovery. I suppose we can only assume that someone must had stolen my car from the airport parking lot, but that question would be better directed to Chief Calvin."

"When did you have your hair done?"

She unconsciously reached up to push back the strand of hair that had fallen across her forehead. "When I was in Ireland."

"Was there a problem with being a blonde?" A few chuckles in the crowd.

"No, I just needed a change."

"Have you heard about Hal Van Horn's murder?" Silence.

"Yes." She swallowed once. "Yes. I heard about Hal."

There was no hesitation in her answers. Dressed in a power suit of black, Sarah Rand looked very much the sharp attorney that she was rumored to be.

Edward North heard one of the reporters ask about Hal, and the cameras moved in tight on her face. For the first time, there was just the hint of a pause...and then the vulnerability showed in her eyes.

"Did you see that?" Edward asked of no one in particular. News of the Judge's release had reached the senator's office immediately. Several staffers sat huddled around the television screen in the library of Senator Rutherford's office.

"She's upset. What's wrong with that?"

"No." Edward shook his head. "She faked it. This is all an act."

"You are way too cynical. The poor woman. She's been through hell this morning."

"She faked it." Edward pointed at the screen again for emphasis. He turned and saw Senator Rutherford leaning against the door-jamb. His tanned face was glued to the television set like the rest of them. "What do *you* think, Senator?"

"She's good. Damn good. She's the kind I want in my corner." He left the library. Edward followed and caught up to him in Ruth-erford's office.

"I owe you an apology," the younger man said when the two of them were alone. "You were correct about maintaining a position in support of Judge Arnold. I think you should give a news con-ference, as well. Loyalty, good judgment, fairness to the unjustly accused. It all will work very well for the advertising."

"Fuck the campaign," Rutherford snapped as he sat behind his desk. "If we don't take care of a couple of things right now, we're going to have bigger problems to worry about than losing a few votes."

For a long moment, Edward North stared in surprise at the sen-ator, then closed the door of the office.

"Just tell me what you want me to do, Senator."

Chapter 31

Sarah was free to stay in any hotel in town, but she had chosen to come back here, to this place she'd once called home.

She might as well have been in Tibet for all the feeling of familiarity that greeted her.

For the longest time, Sarah stood with her back pressed against the front door, her gaze taking in every telltale sign of the horrible crime that had been committed inside her home. A large section of the rug in the entry hall had been removed, the subflooring still showed where Tori's blood had seeped through and dried. There were dark speckles staining the wall, as well. The antique mirror sat propped on the floor against the wall near the stairs. Shattered shards of silvered glass lay on the floor around it.

Sarah had called Tori's mother this morning from the courthouse. Mrs. Douglas had been notified by the Newport Police of her daughter's murder only an hour before, so Sarah's call had dovetailed into the grieving that had already begun. It had been a difficult and draining conversation for both of them. There were many questions that couldn't be answered. At the same time, Mrs. Douglas had not allowed Sarah to take the blame, and this had been a genuine relief. She'd wanted Sarah to come out and visit her sometime. And with that promise, she had hung up.

She pushed herself to walk beyond the entrance. The entire living area was a mess. Books had been haphazardly pulled from the shelves. Some of the photographs on the desk were missing. Some of the frames were broken and the photos torn as they were pulled out. The answering machine was missing, as well.

The place smelled faintly of chicken that had gone bad, left too long in a refrigerator drawer. She knew that it was the smell of death. The death of the young woman who'd died in her place.

Anguish, raw and hard, tore at her…and the tears began to fall.

Sarah dropped her bag on a chair and rushed to the large doors overlooking the Atlantic Ocean. She yanked the draperies aside, feeling them tear from the rod. She didn't care. She had to get out. She couldn't breathe. The glass door banged back against the door stop.

By the time she stepped onto the terrace, Sarah was gasping for air. The sea breeze, salty and cool, felt comforting on her skin. As soon as she opened her eyes, she saw the yellow police tape by the terrace stairs. Another vivid reminder that a life had been irrevocably wasted inside.

She believed what Owen had told her about Tori's persistence bordering on obsession. She believed what he'd told her about the picture sent to him by Jake Gantley.

Tori loved control. She loved the feeling of ownership. In all their years of friendship, Sarah had seen men break and run as soon as they'd felt the grip of the young woman's possessiveness. Tori also didn't accept rejection very well, Sarah knew, so Owen's disinterest would only have motivated her more.

Owen.

Sarah leaned over the stone wall of the terrace and looked out at the sparkling surface of the ocean. She wiped the tears from her face. She couldn't allow herself to think of him now. And she hadn't the time for mourning, either.

Not for the dead. Not for the living. Certainly not for love.

There was too much that still lay ahead of her.

The sound of the phone ringing inside the open door startled her. Her first thought was to let the answering machine pick up. But after a couple more rings, she remembered that the police had taken the damn thing. She walked back and picked up the handset.

"Don't you know how dangerous it is for you to be standing in the open like that?"

She carried the cordless out onto the terrace, this time looking around until she spotted him sitting on the rocks a few hundred yards down the Cliff Walk. The lone figure was holding a cell phone to his ear.

"I'm perfectly safe, Owen." She spoke calmly, gently, trying not to indicate in any way how much this call meant to her. "They have me under their protection."

"If you're talking about the two bozos they have dozing off in that car on the street, I don't call that protection."

"Rutherford's hired killers are out of commission. Archer and company don't believe the senator is any threat to me."

"Bullshit."

She watched him stand up on the rocks. The tide was coming in, and she could see the swells rise and fall around him. Even from this distant her pulse jumped and her heart soared with feeling for him. She turned her back and walked to the other end of the terrace, yanking the yellow police tape down.

"I...I have to get my things out of your place."

"I'll bring them over."

"I don't think that's such a good idea." She balled up the tape and went inside.

"Then you can come over and pick them up yourself."

"I..." She tried unsuccessfully to blot his image from her mind. "I don't think that's a good idea, either. How about if I send a cab over? If you wouldn't mind sending them back—"

"Forget it. I've decided to hold everything hostage."

She found herself smiling.

"So when is the big day?" he asked.

"I don't know. Maybe tonight or tomorrow. They're calling me about it. Which reminds me, I should get off the phone."

"I'll let you go," he said after a long pause. "I miss you."

Sarah heard him disconnect before she had a chance to answer. She walked to the terrace and looked out where she'd seen him standing, but all that remained were rocks and the rolling sea. She leaned against the door with the sea air around her, daring herself for a moment to dream.

A moment was all she had until the ringing of the phone again reminded her of what lay ahead.

Agent Hinckey was sitting in the passenger seat of the Range Rover when Owen got back to his car.

"Make yourself right at home," Owen muttered under his breath as he got in. "No sense locking anything in this neighborhood."

"How about rolling down the windows? I'm cooking in here."

Owen shook his head, but turned the key and opened the windows. Fresh salt air immediately swept through the car.

Hinckey loosened his tie. "How is she doing?"

He ignored the question and instead let his temper show. "Your guys are not doing a damn bit of good sitting where they are. Anyone can stroll up the Cliff Walk and get inside her place without the slightest trouble."

"We offered to have someone inside with her, but she refused. Don't worry, we're watching the terrace door, too." Hinckey waited until a trio of elderly birdwatchers hiked past the car. "We're also having Rutherford watched. He even looks this way, and we pull her out."

Owen wished the words would ease his fears, but they didn't.

"The reason I'm here…" The agent waited until he had Owen's attention. "After talking to Sarah and Judge Arnold, we're still having a hard time tying up all the loose ends of this thing."

"You haven't arrested the big guy yet. What do you expect?"

"Somehow I doubt he's going to be tremendously helpful in providing detail." Hinckey shook his head. "And with the two hit men dead, we've been left with a lot more guesswork than I'm comfortable with."

He faced Owen, who settled back into his seat.

"Sarah told us she took a certain letter by mistake from a safe-deposit box. Arnold tells us that he put that letter in there a long time ago to protect himself against Rutherford. Now, the Judge was upset when he realized the envelope is gone, but he didn't come right out and ask Sarah what she did with this envelope.'

"Okay, now Rutherford knows the Judge is holding something that incriminates him. But then Avery Van Horn dies, the safe-deposit boxes get shuffled, and Rutherford somehow learns that the evidence incriminating him in his wife's murder is missing. That's question number one, but let me push on.'

"So Rutherford hires his own thugs to go and take care of the two people who had access to the safe-deposit boxes, and I'm guessing with specific instructions to bring back whatever it was that the Judge was holding. Ed Brown, the bank officer, is almost killed and his place is ransacked. And this other woman, Tori

Douglas, who is staying at Sarah's, gets shot in the face. They check the condo, but find nothing."

Hinckey watched the cars on the road for a while.

"Now this is where things really get shaky for me. Why the hell would those two killers take Sarah's body to the Judge's boat and leave all that stuff for us to find? And what made these guys tap Hal Van Horn's phone?"

"Hal's phone was tapped?"

"Yes, it was. That's how they could intercept her in Wickford on her way back from the airport. Now going back to Hal, why the hell did he lie to Archer about not checking his messages? We've talked to his secretary, and she thinks that he was checking his phone messages since Sarah's alleged murder."

"Maybe he had something to worry about."

"Damn right, he did. We've traced a number of phone calls that he made to Frankie O'Neal in the month prior to his stabbing. One of them took place the night of Sarah's arrival. Another one occurred moments before he went out to meet her on the night that he was stabbed." The agent's eyes were eagle sharp when they turned on Owen. "From pictures, Sarah has already identified Frankie as the man who made the other attempt on her life in the Van Horn mansion. So what the hell was the connection between Hal and Frankie and Rutherford? Where they all connected? Or were there two different parties closing in on her?"

Hinckey stopped and waited.

"I'm an actor." Owen eyed the agent. "Do you want my professional opinion?"

"No. I want to know what the hell Jake Gantley told you when you visited him at the ACI this past weekend."

"Work stuff." Owen shook his head. "Sorry Hinckey. Can't help you there."

"Don't get cute with me, Dean. We know Jake and Frankie were somehow both in this. We know Jake was on a furlough the afternoon that Tori's murder took place. We can tie him into it with our eyes closed."

"I'm sure you can. And that's why you're talking to the wrong guy. Jake is a deal maker. Why don't you talk to him?"

"You know, I can have you arrested for withholding evidence."

"It won't wash. I'm a producer. I hold interviews with dozens of Jake Gantley types every year. They're all essentially liars, but my interest is in finding material for my show. I don't have the resources or the interest to separate the truth from the fiction in what these people tell me. And I've made it company policy not to run to you guys every time we hear a weird story." He shrugged. "These people have plenty of time on their hands to think up some pretty wild stories. As far as I am concerned, they could all be feeding me piles of shit. So long as it doesn't smell too bad, I'll buy it."

At seeing the frustration on the other man's face, Owen gentled his tone. "You guys have your methods. But I'll give you a piece of advice regarding Gantley. He has an incredible ego. Treat him like he's John Dillinger, and you'll get your answers cheap."

Chapter 32

On Wednesday morning, the sun was already hot when Sarah took a cab from her condo to the Bellevue Avenue mansion of Senator Rutherford. It was a short ride, but her mind was racing.

She'd had a call from Judge Arnold on Tuesday night advising her of the time and place of the meeting. The two of them hadn't said much on the phone. Despite their four years of working closely together, these past five days had created a chasm that she knew would never be bridged.

Sarah still had the extra file that she'd taken out of Rosen's briefcase in her possession. The contents of the file were a life story of Hal from his early years in high school and college up to the present. The file contained dozens of investigative reports, all done with a focus on Hal's lifestyle, on his vices, and on his friends.

And all of it had been conducted on behalf of the Judge.

Hal was far from being a saint, and Sarah had always known it. But these reports made him look far worse than she had ever imagined. Summaries of his gambling, drinking, drugs, and spending habits. Photocopies showing astronomical credit card debt. More graphic and much more damning were the photos of Hal's sexual dalliances. There were at least a dozen pictures of him with various young women, sometimes with more than one, often in compromising positions, and sometimes in very public places. It was the picture of a self-indulgent spendthrift, a confirmed hedonist. It was the picture of a life out of control. It was a depiction that Avery would have found appalling, to say the least.

None of this was crushing for Sarah. From the beginning of her relationship with him, she'd known that Hal was very much a product of his wealthy upbringing. So there were no real surprises there. And interestingly enough, she realized that even after seeing all those photographs, she had not come close to feeling the way she had when she'd discovered that picture of Owen and Tori together.

The dates on the reports went way back, but what had bothered Sarah the most was the fact that Avery had been copied on everything that was injurious to Hal's image. One could easily argue that Judge Arnold had been making certain for a long time—from the time Hal was in prep school—that Avery should see her son as lacking the character and the responsibility needed to handle the demands of such a huge inheritance.

The most recent letter in the file was the most incriminating of them all. In this, the investigator notified the Judge that, as requested, a fresh set of the older prints had been mailed to Avery on a specified date. Sarah remembered the date; it was two months prior to Avery's death—the very time when she'd insisted on changing her will yet again.

Sarah couldn't understand any of these people. She'd lost the respect she once held for Judge Arnold. She disliked Hal for giving in and becoming what his stepfather expected him to be. And she felt sorry for Avery, a woman who had allowed herself to be manipulated for all of her life.

The cab came to a stop before the iron gate of the mansion, and Sarah paid the fare and got out. She was ready to go and get this thing done with. She was ready to get on with her life.

As always, the grounds of the estate were meticulously groomed. The short walk up the drive gave Sarah a chance to clear her mind of everything but what she was here to do. After ringing the front entrance bell, she was surprised to see Edward North answer the door. She had met Rutherford's young chief of staff a few times. Most recently, they'd exchanged a few friendly words at Avery's funeral. But she hadn't expected him to be letting her in.

"Am I early?"

"Not at all. Please come in."

Sarah followed the younger man through the large foyer and a maze of elegantly furnished rooms and hallways. Though she tried not to let her nerves get the better of her, there was clearly no one else around. How easy it would be for these people to get rid of her right here. They arrived at a closed set of double doors.

"Please make yourself comfortable in the library. The senator will be right down, and Judge Arnold called to say he is on his way."

Sarah went inside and the door closed behind her. Two large glass windows on either side of a pair of French doors looked out over an extensive terraced lawn. Small, formal gardens graced each level with flowers and greenery. Beyond the lawns, a fence separated the estate from the Cliff Walk. From there, it was a sheer drop to the sea. There would be no way out of here.

Though it was cool in the mansion, she was sweating. She unbuttoned the jacket of her white silk suit and, in an effort to calm her nerves, looked at the impressive collection of books covering the walls. The smell of freshly brewed coffee wafted from a hot plate stationed on a side table under one of the windows. A silver tray of pastries sat beside a number of delicate gold-rimmed cups.

She studied the symmetrical arrangement of two leather chairs around a small leather sofa near the fireplace. Her attention was drawn to a large mahogany desk across the room.

Reaching inside her shoulder bag, Sarah touched the single tape for assurance.

She didn't have to wait much longer. Voices could be heard coming down the hallway. The door opened, and Judge Arnold and Senator Rutherford entered the room together.

"Sarah!" The senator's greeting was welcoming, as if nothing at all was wrong in the world. The Judge, on the other hand, only nodded vaguely in her direction before walking toward the coffee pot.

"I was just asking the Judge here about this mystery meeting you've requested for this morning." He led her to a leather chair. "He tells me he doesn't know anything about it, except that you had to talk to both of us at the same time and that it was quite urgent."

"It is," she announced. "But I need both of you to be a part of this discussion, for there is no sense in belaboring the issue."

Her barb was directed at Judge Arnold, who continued to stand with his back to them.

"Charles? Are you planning to join us?" Rutherford called to him.

Scowling, the Judge sat. Taking a deep breath, Sarah looked from one man to the other.

"As you both know, I came across a certain document while I was transferring some of Avery's belongings to a new safe-deposit box. Now, the action of taking possession of the document occurred by accident and with no malice intended. And as you also now know, I left for Ireland having no idea of the chaos that remained behind."

"Before you get too far into this," Rutherford interrupted, "I don't know what document you're talking about. This is all very new to me."

"You can play dumb, if you want to, Senator, but it serves no purpose here." She met him eye-to-eye. "You can hear my proposition regarding what I want in exchange for a certain incriminating letter and tape, or I can hand these pieces of evidence over to the police. I am certain they'll be more than a little excited to learn what they contain."

"Well, your intention of blackmailing us is clear enough, Ms. Rand, but I don't believe I am the originator of these documents." He gentled his tone. "Certainly you don't expect me to bargain for something, when I have no clue what it is. So if you would be kind enough to tell me what it is exactly that you have."

She nodded. "I have in my possession a letter written in Judge Arnold's hand. In the text of this document, there are three references made. The first one pointed me to a dead-file location at our office's storage facility, where I was able to retrieve a tape of a conversation made eighteen years ago. In this tape, you, Senator Rutherford, make a plea to your then-partner to come and help you...as you have just accidentally killed your wife in the hotel room you were staying at in Philadelphia. The second item in the letter is the location of where the Judge indicates that the two of you buried your wife afterward. Strawberry Mansion Bridge. Do I need to continue?"

"That's all a lie." Rutherford turned sharply to Arnold. "Julia ran away. There were witnesses who saw her leave the hotel and get into a cab."

"I did mention that there are three items listed on the letter, didn't I?" Sarah interrupted. "The third note made by Judge Arnold is in reference to a junior attorney named Andrea Beck, a woman with similar coloring to your wife. Ms. Beck was, by the way, also attending that conference in Philadelphia that same weekend. As the Judge indicates in the letter, Ms. Beck willingly put on your wife's clothes, answered to your wife's name, and essentially aided and abetted you in staging a scene where a number of hotel employees could testify later that your wife left the hotel the next morning under her own volition, without you."

Sarah could see the senator's complexion begin to pale beneath his tan.

"Unfortunately," she continued, "Andrea Beck was killed during a burglary in her apartment three months after your wife's disappearance."

Rutherford walked to his desk and took the seat there. His hands were steepled before him.

"Go on." he said quietly.

Sarah tried to contain her own anxiety. "I spent the last few days making phone calls and reading some archived newspapers issues about Andrea Beck's case…which, by the way, is still open. What I found most interesting was the similarity in the method in which we were both murdered." She stared at Rutherford. "Shot in the face. Did you use the same people to do the job, Senator? Or is that simply a mandatory requirement for an array of contracted hit men?"

"Why did you have Andrea killed, Gordon?" The Judge's voice was a low, accusing growl. "She believed you when you said the whole thing was an accident. She wasn't going to tell a soul about it."

"Shut up, Charles." Rutherford snapped. He turned his glare on Sarah.

"Nice try, Ms. Rand, but you don't have a thing on me." He stood up. "And it would have been wise, young lady, to check your facts before you dragged your little ass in here. Those storage files were burned to ashes this past weekend. There is no way you could get anything out of there."

She smiled. "You are quite wrong, Senator. Not about the fire Sunday, which I know you paid to have set. Fortunately, I took the tape on Thursday… the same day that one of your paid henchmen mistakenly stabbed Hal instead of me."

"I still say you are bluffing." He pressed a button on his desk. "I had nothing to do with my wife's disappearance."

Sarah reached for her briefcase and took out a tape, holding it in the palm of her hand so that both men could see it.

"Then I guess you won't be wanting this?"

At that moment, a tap on the library door was followed by the entrance of Edward North. "Did you need something, Senator?"

"Yes." Sarah saw Rutherford open a drawer in his desk and pull out a pen and a pad of paper. "Come and sit here and take some notes. Miss Rand was just getting ready to explain to us the terms of her blackmail."

Startled, North nonetheless walked in and went to sit in the chair Rutherford vacated. The senator joined Arnold and Sarah. "May I examine this tape?"

Her fingers closed around the tape. "Although this is a duplicate, I would prefer that you not listen to it. At least, not until we've discussed the terms of our deal."

"You greedy little parasite, you won't get a dime from me. Do you hear me? I had nothing to do with my wife's disappearance. And I say there is nothing on that tape. As far as that letter goes, Arnold wrote it to incriminate me. Perhaps *he* killed my wife and Andrea Beck."

"As you wish," Sarah said as she dropped the tape in her bag and rose to her feet. "I would advise both of you gentlemen to contact your lawyers. I'm turning these over to the authorities this morning. And Senator, I think your political career is about to come to a crashing—"

By the time she saw North advancing with the gun in his hand, it was too late.

A single shot rang out, and Sarah Rand fell back on the chair, her blood already staining the white silk suit.

Chapter 33

"What are you doing?" Paying no attention to the gun that was now pointed at him, Judge Arnold leaped to his feet to check on Sarah. "Call an ambulance—right away. There must still be time."

His hands covered with her blood, the Judge looked back over his shoulder and found neither of the men moving.

"Call for help, damn you!"

He crossed quickly to desk and reached for the phone himself, but Rutherford tore it out of his hands. As he turned, the senator yanked him by the collar and pushed him roughly into a chair. Stunned, he stared up into the barrel of the pistol North was holding nervously. Rutherford actually frisked him.

"You know I don't carry a g—" A light went on. "You think I'm wired?"

Rutherford nodded to Edward North, and the younger man tucked the gun into his pocket before moving to check on Sarah.

"She's clean," North said a minute later. "No wires that I can see."

The senator looked at her. "Is she alive?"

"I think...barely."

"Get the tape out of her bag. Check it out."

"You won't get away with this," the Judge barked at his old partner. "There is no way you can push this one under the rug."

"You'd be amazed what I can get away with these days."

Arnold shook his head in disbelief. "How could I have been so stupid? I actually believed you that day. You told me it was an accident and I believed you."

"With her big mouth and her ambitions, Julia *was* an accident waiting to happen. She was good for that connection with the blue-collar crowd, so I had to put up with her. My mistake was in doing it myself. She asked for it, you know. Threatening me...asking all those questions about my contribution list, always wanting more. That day in Philadelphia, she went too far." Rutherford's face was hard and bitter. "She asked for it, and she got it."

"And what about Andrea? She worshipped the ground you walked on. She would never in a thousand years—"

"One of the plagues of my existence—" He glanced over at Sarah. "—is to be surrounded by ambitious women. It would have been just a matter of time before Andrea tried to dig her nails into me, too. She was high risk. She had to go."

Rutherford walked to his desk and picked up the phone, dialing a number. On the other side of the room, North pulled a cassette player out of a side drawer and inserted the tape he'd taken out of Sarah's handbag. Listening through an ear piece, he pressed a button on the machine, never taking his eyes off the Judge and the senator.

Rutherford spoke into the phone. "We're finished at this end...Yes, as we planned. Of course." The senator looked at Sarah. "Listen, it's the Judge's regular boating day, and I think he can't wait to get back out on the water after his time behind bars. Yes, she's going with him. Sort of a 'kiss and make up' excursion, except that they aren't coming back. Understand?"

"*I* don't understand you." Arnold tried to push himself to his feet.

"Good." Rutherford, still holding the phone to his ear, pushed the Judge back into the chair. "They need to be picked up here. Of course I want you to do it yourself. Yes, just step on it. We'll be here."

"Is this worth it, Gordon? Is it worth killing so many people, worth the price of this monstrous chain of corruption, just for a Senate seat?"

Rutherford's face broadened into a smile as he looked at his old partner. "Don't make me laugh. There is no difference between us, Charles. You and I are the same."

"Bull."

"Say what you want. We've just set different goals for ourselves." He stood over the Judge. "My goal is within sight. The presidency is only an election or two away. You, on the other hand, just think of the way you've always controlled Avery. And why? You couldn't wait to get your grubby claws on her money. On Hal's money. And I think you loved running his life, making him beg."

"There's a limit to how far I will go to get what I want."

"Recognizing that you have a limit means recognizing that you're a loser, Charles." Rutherford moved toward North and the tape cassette. "I have no intention of living my life like it's some kind of slow death."

He cast a half glance at Sarah, and the blood that was staining his chair. He came to a sudden stop, scrutinizing the figure of the woman in the chair. He saw her body twitch once from the wound. Her hand was lying against the spot where the blood flow was now slowing.

"Edward."

The other man lowered the ear piece.

"Anything?"

"Not yet."

"Then come and finish this first." Rutherford moved behind the chair and grabbed a fistful of Sarah's hair in one hand. "Finish this."

He pulled her hair until her head lay against the back of the chair. His eyes narrowed as he noticed the color rising in her skin. He felt for the pulse on her throat.

"What the hell…?"

Sarah opened her eyes and stared up at him. "Bastard."

Two dozen police officers, FBI agents, and Justice Department officials burst into the room. Swarming in from the terraced lawns and through the house, they surrounded the senator in an instant, forcing him against the wall. Before he could even open his mouth to voice a complaint, an agent was cuffing his hands behind his back and reading him his rights.

Across the room, Edward North and the Judge were talking to Agent Hinckey and watching the proceedings. Dan Archer helped Sarah to her feet, but she could only stare at Gordon Rutherford with a look of disgust.

As the officers prepared to take the senator out of the library, the Judge approached him, ignoring his old friend's glare.

"I guess recognizing a limit can have its advantages."

The entire estate was crawling with police cars and rescue squads. There were people everywhere, and Sarah couldn't wait to get away.

The agents who had come to her condo this morning to help her with the body suit had told her that there would be additional help inside the mansion. Until it actually happened, though, Sarah hadn't guessed that Edward North would be that help.

The cool she'd maintained throughout the ordeal was suddenly gone. She could feel intense weariness, and she only wanted to escape.

A medic checked Sarah before she was even allowed out of the library. In the entrance foyer of the mansion, a female police officer loaned her a blue jacket with NPD in large yellow letters across the back and a matching cap. Grateful for them, Sarah went to the bathroom and changed out of the blood-stained jacket and shirt, removing the apparatus that had produced the effect of the bloody gunshot wound. Her pants were soiled with the fake blood, too, but she was too tired to worry about perfection.

Outside of the bathroom, Archer was waiting for her. The detective's greeting was uncharacteristically enthusiastic, though she wouldn't call the look on his face a smile exactly. She could understand. This was probably the biggest collar of his life, and he was obviously thankful for her help. She thought for a moment that he was going to hug her.

"Well, you've certainly had a brilliant week, I'd say." She handed him the apparatus. "First, Billy Hamilton and now this."

He nodded, and his face resumed its customary lack of expression.

"Ms. Rand, I'd appreciate it very much if you could come down to the station sometime today. We have about a mountain of paperwork that we need to complete."

"Sure." The two of them walked toward the front door. "I just need to get home and change, then I'll be there."

"Thanks again," he told her by the door. "And I guess this is as good a time as any to apologize for whatever…ahh, difficulties…you and I might have had in the past."

She knew he was talking about the Hamilton case. "Apology accepted. Congratulations on that arrest."

"We never let up on our efforts to get the son of a—well, you know."

She nodded, but as she turned to go, the detective stopped her.

"Please give my regards to Mr. Dean." Archer actually smiled. "Off the record and just for your information, I knew you were there in his apartment when I went through it last Thursday morning."

"You did?"

"You were in the closet. That was the only place I didn't check."

"And what makes you so certain that I was there at all?"

"Your appointment book was lying open on the end table. For the two weeks prior, I'd been eating, sleeping, breathing and reading everything that pertained to Sarah Rand. Recognizing your handwriting was nothing."

"Just like the detective in…" She paused. "What was that movie? *Laura*?"

Archer colored. "Ha. Except in the movie, the handsome detective gets the girl in the end, not the movie star." He cleared his throat. "I didn't say that. One word of this to my wife and you'll find me floating in the harbor."

Sarah was actually smiling by the time she got outdoors and made her way past the line of official vehicles choking the drive.

A police officer let her through the barricade they'd set up to hold back the curious onlookers and the media. Pulling her hat down over her eyes, Sarah pushed past them. A half block down Bellevue, a car slowed down in the street.

"Need a ride, Sarah?"

"I sure do."

Stepping out from between two parked cars, she climbed in without thinking twice.

Owen watched Sarah get into the charcoal-gray Lincoln two cars in front of him and instead of parking his car on the street as he'd originally intended, pulled immediately back into the traffic, trailing the other car.

Following his instincts, he reached for the phone and dialed Newport police. Quickly, he introduced himself and asked to be connected with Captain Archer, explaining that it was urgent.

Yesterday, Owen had sat down with Agent Hinckey and Archer, this time hitting it off much better with the police captain than he had in their earlier meetings. Archer had had one of his people contact Owen this morning to tell him that the operation was completed, and that he could come and pick up Sarah.

A moment later, Archer came on line.

"Have you arrested all your suspects? Are there any loose cannons out there?"

"My boss thinks I'm the only loose cannon around here. Where are you? I thought you were coming for Ms. Rand."

"I was, but it seems someone else beat me to it." Owen ran a yellow light to keep up with the Lincoln, still two cars ahead of him. "Do you have everyone? Are all the heads accounted for?"

"We just traced the last call that Rutherford made. We've identified the last suspect we need to pick up."

"With all due respect for your procedures, would you tell me if your suspect drives a late-model, charcoal-gray Lincoln...I can't give you the license plate from here."

There was a second's pause on the line.

"Yes, he does. What's going on? Are you following him?"

"I am. And he has Sarah with him."

She felt as if she was babbling on, but she couldn't seem to help herself.

In just a few minutes, she had not only thanked him profusely for the ride and for his help, but also had given him a quick rundown of the events this morning. Everything would be on all major news stations before the day was half over, anyway, she'd decided.

"From the way I understand it, the Justice Department has had Senator Rutherford under investigation for some time, for campaign fraud and for possible connections to some organized-crime families. Now, murder was—"

Sarah stopped midsentence as the Lincoln made the wrong turn off Bellevue.

"If it's out of your way to drop me at my apartment, I can just get out here and take a cab for the rest of the way. Or I could walk. It's really not that far from here."

"No, it's not out of my way at all." Evan Steele replied, making another turn and heading in the opposite direction of her condo.

Sarah felt a sudden chill settle in the pit of her stomach. "Do you have to make a stop anywhere first?"

"No."

She glanced out the window as the car picked up speed on the narrow road. "You *do* remember where I live?"

"Of course."

"Then why are you heading this way?"

He gave her a glance. "What's wrong? You don't like the scenic route?"

She saw something in the eyes—and she knew. The truth poured on her like ice water.

"What were you doing in front of Rutherford's house, Evan?"

"Just driving by." His eyes never left the road. The car ran a yellow light and turned onto America's Cup Avenue, heading north.

Sarah tried to jog her memory regarding what she knew about the man. She couldn't come up with much. He'd been in the service at one point or another in his life, and she always thought of him as a security expert who had started his own company years ago. But as far as the person behind the face, she knew nothing.

Downtown, the traffic was bad, but Steele maneuvered through it. By the Visitor's Center, three lines of cars suddenly came to a halt, but he swerved up onto a sidewalk, cutting around the stopped cars.

"If you wouldn't mind letting me out at the next corner, I have some errands that I need to run in town."

The next corner was history before she could even finish the sentence.

The car took a sharp left at the end of the street, and Sarah clutched at the door handle to keep herself steady.

"It was you Rutherford called, wasn't it?"

There was no answer.

"You were going to take the Judge and me to his boat." Again, only silence.

"You're going to kill me anyway, aren't you? Then, damn it, at least give me an answer."

He sped onto the ramp for Newport Bridge.

"It figures Rutherford would pick someone like you to do his dirty work for him. Someone smart. Someone who has all kinds of connections with mercenaries. With people who'll do anything for money. He had you hire those two killers. You made all the arrangements. Well, guess what? You're the one who will show up on the books as the responsible party for all these murders. He'll walk away scot-free, and you'll spend the rest of your life in jail."

Steele frowned as he was forced to slow the car on the bridge. Traffic ahead was moving at a crawl.

"He has already been arrested, you know. Evan, this is your chance to turn yourself in. You could make a deal with the D.A. Ike Bosler wants to nail Rutherford so badly that he'd agree to anything. You can help him put the senator behind bars."

The line of cars came to a complete stop at the top of the bridge. There were no cars coming in the opposite direction, either. Steele veered the car to the left so he could see the reason for the hold up. From his scowl, it was obvious that he couldn't see much.

"What are you going to do to me?" she pressed.

His continuing silence was beginning to play on her nerves.

"I mean, if you're going to kill me, why don't you just shoot me in the head or throw me off the bridge right here. Let's just be done with it. I'm no use to you." Sarah reached quickly for the door handle, but his fingers closed around her throat, and he pushed her back against the seat. His thumb pressed against her windpipe, and Sarah felt her head about to explode.

"I've had it with all your talking. Now, sit there and listen. You got into my car. Bad mistake. Don't worry, you're going to get what's coming to you—but when I'm ready."

She clawed at his grip, and he eased up only enough for her to let out a gasp.

"After all the trouble you've caused me, I'd have no problem breaking your neck right here and dumping your body on the road on my way north. Or maybe you can behave yourself, and I'll let you live a day or two before I decide a good way to turn you into some cash." His grip tightened again around her windpipe. "Which is it, Sarah? Will you shut up or not?"

She felt her lungs burning. Her fingers tried to push his hand away. She tried to nod her head.

He eased his hold again. "What'll it be, Sarah?"

She nodded.

When he pulled his hand away, she reached up to touch her neck. Her throat felt bruised and raw. She could barely force the air in and out. It took a few long moments before she could take a decent breath.

Sarah saw him unlock and push the driver's door open. He stood with one foot on the ground, peering at the traffic jam ahead of him. Her own door remained locked.

She didn't know how she gathered the strength, but she swung her legs up and delivered a solid kick with both feet to his hip, almost knocking him down. Steele took two or three steps sideways to regain his balance, and that was all the time Sarah needed to scramble out the open door.

He dived after her, but Sarah leapt out of his reach, landing on the hood of the car behind them. Rolling to the other side, she hammered desperately on the window asking for help. The young woman behind the wheel slammed down the lock on her door and shrank back. Sarah glanced over her shoulder and saw Evan Steele standing a foot away.

"One more step and I'll blow your brains out right here." His hand was inside his jacket.

At that instant Sarah realized that there was not much difference dying now or later.

As she turned, he grabbed at her, but Sarah tore out of his grip, running as fast as her legs would take her along the line of cars that was forming.

Sarah hadn't gone ten steps when his rough grip on her arm yanked her back. With one frenzied motion, she turned around and kicked him on the shin, wrenching her arm free.

She ran. Everything around her was a jumble of madness. Sky and road and the bay all blended together in one confused scramble.

She recognized the black car after she was already past it. As she turned, she saw Owen swing the door open hard, driving Evan Steele sharply into the center of the road.

Sarah dragged herself back along the Range Rover, trying to catch her breath as the two men struggled on the concrete highway.

"Help him!" she screamed, pushing herself away from the car and toward the fight.

Steele was armed, she remembered, panic washing through her. The sound of sirens from both sides of the bridge and the beating roar of a helicopter descending upon them, muted her cries.

Suddenly, Owen fell back against the hood of the car, and for one insane moment, Sarah looked on a scene of absolute clarity. As if the moment had been frozen in time. Steele lifted his gun, pointing it at him.

There was no hesitation in her action as she threw herself between the two men. Steele fired.

Turning, she saw the blood on the hood of the car just as the police cars came screeching in around them.

"*Owen!*" She ran to him, her heart in her throat, unable to tear her eyes away from the blood pumping from his shoulder.

He pushed himself away from the hood and reached for her as she came near.

"My God! Please, Owen...please don't die...let me see!"

Sarah knew she was hysterical, but she couldn't help herself. Her arms wrapped around him. He tried to straighten up, but she felt him putting his weight on her for support.

His voice was strained. "Are you okay? Did he hurt you?"

"No! My God...Owen...please!"

She pulled his bloody hand away from the wound. The front of his shirt and his sleeve were already soaked and red.

An ambulance came to a stop right behind them. It seemed to be mere seconds before medics were sitting Owen against the car and checking his shoulder. She stood and looked at the activity behind her. Already handcuffed, Evan Steele was being pushed into the back seat of a police cruiser.

Sarah turned around and found the medics laying Owen down on a stretcher. In a minute, they were wheeling him toward the back of the ambulance.

"Come with me?"

Tears were coursing down her face, but she didn't care. She could only see his outstretched hand.

"Mad senators and armed mercenaries couldn't keep me away."

Chapter 34

It was well past dark when Scott Rosen pulled into the long driveway of their home. As he drew near the house, his heart sank as he noted the darkness in every window. It was just the ghost of a structure against an empty landscape. Even the lights on either side of the front door—lights that Lucy always left on when he was late—were dark.

Instead of pulling the car into the garage, Scott parked in the driveway and sat for a moment staring at the expensive home that he'd once thought would fill the void that his long hours of work had created in their marriage. He'd been stupid enough to think that the right car, and the right house, in the right neighborhood would be enough. Later on, when they'd talked about having children, he had never considered what might be required of him in raising them. In fact, it had occurred to him that it might be another positive thing in filling Lucy's life, easing the pressure on him a little more. Guilt gnawed at him now for even thinking it.

Well, having this baby had been a feat Lucy had accomplished successfully and without him. Scott knew, with her usual courage and independence, his wife would quite capably raise their daughter without him, if need be.

But Scott wanted desperately to be part of this.

He'd had the best of intentions on Monday of making everything right. But all hell had broken loose. And here he was, two days later, and all he had seen of his wife and daughter had been glimpses of them sleeping, during the few short hours that he'd come home each night to catch some rest before getting back out there.

This morning, before he'd left the house at dawn, Lucy had come down with the baby. Without mincing words, she had told him that she was thinking of taking their daughter and going away to her sister's house in Connecticut for a while.

Scott knew this was the first step—the first step in the dissolution of a marriage.

He took his briefcase and dragged his tired frame out of his car and headed toward the house. He wanted to fight this. He desperately wanted to win back his family. But he didn't know how much of a chance his wife would give him after the way he had neglected her over the course of their marriage.

Instead of going in through the garage, he used his key and walked in through the front door. The house inside was as dark and empty as it looked from outside. He didn't even bother to turn on any lights. Instead, he loosened his tie and tossed it with his jacket and briefcase on a chair. He went straight to the phone.

He was dialing Lucy's sister in Connecticut when the sound of voices in the background stopped him. For a crazy moment, thoughts of contract killers and Evan Steele raced through his mind. But before rage and panic could translate into action, the sounds registered in his brain as coming from the television in the den.

It was too much to hope for, but Scott forced himself to dream. Turning on lights as he went, he made his way through the house.

He stopped at the sight of his sleeping wife on the leather sofa, the baby nestled on her shoulder. The light from the television cast a soft glow on Lucy's face. A love, so long ignored, stirred and beat strongly in his chest. The baby moved, and Scott saw Lucy's eyes open. Immediately, she spotted him.

"You're back."

"You didn't go."

Scott knelt beside her and embraced her. How do you pour the affection of a lifetime into a single embrace? You can't, he thought, trying anyway.

"I've been watching the news all day. I can't believe it. The senator...and then the helicopter shots of the bridge and the shooting. I was so afraid you were there."

"I'm so sorry, honey...for all of this. For leaving you alone and—"

"Don't." She touched his lips with her hands. "I was so insecure during this last month of my pregnancy. I thought you were…maybe…that there was another woman."

He'd never expected this. "Lucy, I've been guilty of many things, but cheating on you has never crossed my mind."

"I know." She blushed. "I was so messed up that I actually started checking on you. Checking the numbers of people who were calling you here, calling your office to make sure you were there. I think my hormones were at it, full force."

"No. It was me. I know I've been acting differently with this case. I had accepted the case. I was committed to it. But at the same time, I was torn by the layers of lies that kept surfacing." She turned her feet on the sofa, and Scott sat next to her. "I've never been more confused about a case than I was with this one."

"Why?"

"Because the Judge wasn't telling the truth to me, and I knew it. He was hiding something, hiding many things. Nothing jived. He would tell me there were no problems between Sarah and him, but ten other people would tell me they'd been fighting. And as I started spending more time with him, I realized that the respect I had for him for so long had been misplaced. He was innocent of the crime he'd been accused of, but in many ways, he was responsible for much of what happened."

"What do you mean?"

"I didn't have all the answers until today. But tomorrow morning there will be a statement made by the D.A.'s office about the complex situation surrounding these homicides. There were two people trying to engineer Sarah Rand's murder. Senator Rutherford *and* Hal Van Horn."

"But I thought Van Horn loved Sarah."

"He had become so screwed up and bitter since his mother's death that he decided murder was the way to get what he believed was his and get revenge at the same time. The Judge had been on him for a long time, and Hal finally got tired of it." Scott's fingers caressed the soft fuzz of hair on the baby's head. "Thirty years of pressure can do it to anybody, I suppose."

"But what about Rutherford?" Lucy asked. "The news said the senator was being held for a number of murders—including his wife's murder eighteen years ago."

"Though it's doubtful, that first one may have been accidental. The others were murder."

Lucy winced as she tried to move the baby on her shoulder.

"My arm is asleep."

Scott took the baby. He stared down at the sleeping face of the angel in his arms, and a knot the size of a fist formed in his throat.

"How was the Judge involved?"

"At the time when Julia Rutherford was killed, her husband was on the cusp of making it big. He was on his way to the Senate, and the big time. He panicked and called his partner and friend, Charles Arnold, for help."

"If it was an accident, they could have called the police and been honest about it."

"I know. In the statement that the Judge gave Ike Bosler on Monday, he claimed that this was *his* recommendation to Rutherford when he received that phone call in the middle of night. Interestingly enough, an answering machine had initially answered the call, but then the Judge had picked up the phone upstairs. The entire conversation was taped."

"And Arnold drove to Philadelphia that night?"

Scott nodded. "He says by the time he got there, Rutherford had gotten himself together. He'd even sought the help of Andrea Beck, a young lawyer who worked for him and Arnold. Anyway, the Judge's story is that the other two overrode his advice, and he ended up being the third person in a conspiracy to hide the accident—except he had his suspicions that it may have been a murder instead."

"He could have turned Rutherford in. He had the tape."

"I don't know what stopped him. Maybe it was a 'good old boy' thing, or maybe Rutherford had something against him that would affect his standing with Avery. I don't know. But he claims he didn't realize the extent of his mistake until Andrea Beck was killed. He immediately suspected Rutherford. Then, to save himself—in case Rutherford had other ideas—he told the senator that he had a tape and a letter explaining everything. And he also told him these things were tucked safely away where, if anything were to happen to him, they would be turned over to the police."

"So Rutherford backed off."

"For eighteen years."

Scott went on and explained how Sarah mistakenly taken the letter, how it had ended up in his own briefcase without his awareness and about how Owen Dean and Sarah had gotten the letter back.

"But how did Rutherford know that the letter was missing?"

"After his wife's death, the Judge told Evan Steele that there was a certain important letter missing—without divulging its contents—and asked for his help in locating it. Steele had been paid by Rutherford for years to keep a close eye on his old partner. Steele passed on the information to the senator, who used the occasion of Avery's death to question the Judge about the safety of those documents. Everything pointed to Sarah Rand. That started a chain of actions in which Steele hired people to find the letter and kill her at the same time."

"But what about Andrew Warner's murder? The news said that was connected."

"We don't know that yet. Dan Archer thinks Steele's men tracked Sarah's car to the Warner property, and thought they were hiding her. If Mrs. Warner survives, maybe we'll find out for sure."

"Why did they have to go through all that at the senator's mansion today? Wasn't the tape incriminating enough?"

"It would have been, if they had it. The problem was that Sarah called Steele on Sunday evening, telling him that she had misplaced a letter and she needed to get to the office. Then Steele put two and two together and figured the letter might not have a tape in it. He guessed that the tape might have been with the old files in the storage facility. So he torched the place." His fingers caressed the baby's soft hair. "This was the same night I got a call from the D.A.'s office. They were already sweating what I would do about the mishandling of this case. They told me that Sarah was alive, and that the feds were planning a sting operation where everything would get cleared up. Because of the delicacy of the operation, they asked me not to reveal the info to anyone, no matter what their level of involvement with the case."

Lucy turned on the light beside the sofa. "And to think all these people seemed so normal to me. I must be a horrible judge of character."

"No. You're not." He reached out and stroked her cheek. "They fooled everybody."

"Now what's going to happen to the Judge?"

Scott shook his head. "Nothing. He made a deal with the D.A., and he is home free."

He looked down at his daughter's face as she began to make little noises of complaint.

"What is going to happen to us?" he asked quietly before lifting his face and looking at his wife.

She touched the cleft in his chin. "Nothing, so long as you make a deal with your wife and daughter never to shut us out again. Never to forget us. Never…"

He leaned over and kissed her mouth. "Whatever your conditions…I'll sign."

Chapter 35

Owen was dressed and ready to go when he heard a soft knock on the partially open door. A second later, Sarah peered inside the hospital room.

"May I come in?"

"You'd better." He couldn't help himself from smiling at the change in her. She was wearing the antique earrings that had once been her signature accessory. Her hair was back to her own natural color again. The jade-green suit matched the color of her eyes, serving to bring out the brilliance of them. "Wait a minute, do I know you?"

Before she could answer, he had taken her hand and was pulling her toward him. She wrapped her arms around his waist, giving plenty of room for the sling holding his arm in place.

"I thought I was escorting a sickly creature out of here today. Wounded, weak, someone who needed to be taken out in a wheel-chair."

"You're back to being a blonde. The Sarah I got to know was a brunette. Are you sure I know you?" he asked again, drawing her closer.

She kissed him deeply.

"Well, do you?" she asked, pulling back.

"I'm not sure. Want to run that by me again?"

She laughed and was about to kiss him again when a knock on the door made her leap out of his embrace. He smiled and held on to her arm.

Joanne Emerson poked her head in the door. Tracy Warner's older sister had come to visit Owen a couple of times during his stay at the hospital, and he had made a point of introducing her to Sarah the day before.

"I heard you're on your way out."

"That's right. How is Tracy?"

"She is awake."

Owen was speechless for a minute. As recently as last night, she'd still been in a coma.

"I told her you were here. She wants to see you."

Her second comment stunned him more, for Owen knew that Tracy, on her best day, never had any desire to see him. He looked at Sarah.

"I'll wait here."

Although the bullet wound in his shoulder had nothing to do with his legs, an attendant escorted him to Tracy's room. Before going in, he was warned that she'd been awake for only brief intervals this morning, and that he shouldn't be surprised if she drifted off in the middle of his visit.

Owen entered with all the apprehension that he'd had as a young boy meeting the woman for the first time. Unlike that time, however, when he'd been suffering from his mother's death and from fears about his future, this time a different kind of concern was gnawing at him.

He wanted to let go of the past. He wanted to let go of the hard feelings. He wanted to forget whatever had been. Whatever should have been. He held no grudge against anyone, and he wanted no one holding any grudge against him. A tall order, considering the history the two of them shared.

Monitors and IVs still crowded the wall by her head. Tracy's eyes were closed. Her age was more pronounced than he'd ever noticed before. He walked next to the bed and, on an impulse, placed his good hand on top of hers. Her skin was cold. She appeared to be sleeping.

Just as Owen thought there was little chance of her awakening now, he felt the slightest movement of her fingers beneath his. He wrapped his hand tighter around hers.

"Tracy?"

The eyes were slow to open. When they did, he wasn't really sure that she was focusing on him.

"Tracy. It's me…Owen." He felt the muscles in the fingers tense, and he cursed himself for coming up. She had enough to deal with, right now. "I'm sorry. I misunderstood. I'll go away."

He paused before letting go of her hand. "Before I do…I just want you to know that I am sorry for what happened to Andrew. I'm sorry for what you're going through now. I'm…well, I'm also sorry for all the heartache that having me around caused you in your marriage."

"I don't know what Andrew was about. I don't know what he wanted from me. And I don't know why he went to such lengths to make life miserable for you, knowing how you felt about me. I want you to know that even before…before all this, I was sick and tired of the game that he was continuing to play. To him, everything was your fault or my fault, never his own doing. In a way, I think he wanted you and me to continue holding the other one responsible, hating each other, so he would never have to face up to his own mistakes. His own failings."

The unfocused eyes continued to stare at the ceiling.

"There is a lot that I don't know or understand about him, but I want you to know that I've given up worrying about it. I'm going away and I'm staying away. So you never have to worry about having me around."

His hand squeezed Tracy's once before letting go. "Now, go to sleep and get well."

He was almost to the door when he heard her voice.

"Owen."

He didn't know if he'd imagined it or not. He turned to the bed. Her eyes were still open, but this time they focused on him as he drew near.

"I'm here, Tracy."

Sarah held on to his hand and didn't say a word as the nurse pushed Owen's wheelchair to the front entrance of the hospital. She had seen his eyes. She'd watched him pull on the sunglasses in the corridor. She had felt his need just to hold on to her hand.

Outside, a black stretch limo was waiting for them at the door. She had offered before to drive, but Owen had insisted.

Once they were inside and the car had left the hospital, Sarah saw him remove the glasses and reach for her.

"Tracy wants to see me again. She told me…told me that Andrew was my father."

She wrapped her arms around him and made no effort to stop her tears.

He told her exactly the few words that Tracy had said to him. She listened as he poured out his emotions through the words. And she smiled and cried with him as he tried to make peace at least with the memory of the man who had fathered him.

They rode in silence for a long time before Sarah looked out the windows and realized that they were not going to his apartment as she'd been told.

"Where are we?"

She had her answer as the cottage came into view, the sparkling waters of the inlet visible beyond.

"What…what are we doing here?" She turned to Owen and found his blue eyes watching her and nothing else.

"Susan tells me her in-laws want to sell this place."

"And are you…interested in buying it?"

"Only if you give me the right answer."

"What's the question?"

"There's the question of a dog…a van…a couple of kids…marriage."

"Owen…" Sarah felt her heart racing in her chest. All the dreams of her life were tied up in this one moment—tied up with a tangle of insecurities. "I…you and I…have different lives. I have to find a new job, maybe open an office of my own. I belong here. You are used to the fast lane. You can't be happy in my life, and I can't live in yours."

She turned her face away.

"I want to tell you something. I have made a point of pushing my presence steadily behind the camera rather than in front of it. And that's because fame might be great when you are twenty-five, but when you get to my age, it suffocates you. I want to enjoy a life without the glitter and emptiness that goes with that glitter."

Sarah looked back at him.

"But more than anything else, I want to be with you. I want to get up every morning and see your smiling face on my pillow. I want to go to bed every night and have you in my arms. It's you, Sarah. I want you." He took hold of her hand and looked into her eyes. "But if you tell me you don't feel anything for me, I'll go away."

"You didn't last time."

"You weren't playing fair last time."

"I love you, Owen, but that doesn't mean that everything will just work out because—"

He silenced her with a kiss. When he pulled back, she was robbed of her complaints.

"I want you to know something else. I have trusted you from the moment you got into my car on that wild and rainy night. Now, I want you to trust me…once…in marriage. In building a life here. Forever."

She looked at the cottage. She looked back at the man she loved. She saw in his eyes the promise and felt the bonding of two souls.

"I trust you, Owen. Now *and* forever."

Author's Note

We could not close this novel without thanking, first of all, the many readers of our May McGoldrick novels. To those kind readers who have followed us on this exciting journey into the world of suspense in the contemporary world. Thank you for giving us this opportunity. Thank you for your goodwill. Thank you for your loyalty. Thank you for reading this far.

In addition to our readers, we also like to thank Greg O'Sullivan, of Verizon Telephone, Miriam O'Sullivan of the Thomas Travel Agency, David Gale of the Souderton (Pennsylvania) Police Department, the wonderful librarians of the Samuel Pierce Branch of the Bucks County Free Library, and the Rhode Island Department of Corrections for their incredible patience in answering our many questions.

Lastly, we'd like to thank our boys for their love and patience and for letting us put every holiday on hold until we finished this book.

Thank you for taking time to read *Trust Me Once*. If you enjoyed it, please consider telling your friends or posting a short review. Word of mouth is an author's best friend and much appreciated.

Also, you can visit with Sarah and Owen again in our next Jan Coffey suspense, *Twice Burned*.

As always, we love to hear from our readers. Write to us at:

JanCoffey@JanCoffey.com

Nikoo & Jim McGoldrick
www.Jan Coffey.com

Complete Book List as of

Novellas

Thanksgiving in Connecticut
Mercy

Writing as May McGoldrick

Made In Heaven
Ghost of the Thames

Scottish Dream Trilogy
Dreams of Destiny
Captured Dreams
Borrowed Dreams

Secret Vows Series
The Rebel
The Promise

Tess and the Highlander

Highland Treasure Trilogy
The Firebrand
The Enchantress
The Dreamer

Flame

The Intended

Macpherson Trilogy
Beauty of the Mist
Heart of Gold
Angel of Skye

The Thistle and the Rose

Writing as Nicole Cody & May McGoldrick

Arsenic and Old Armor (originally Love and Mayhem)

Writing as Jan Coffey

Road Kill
Aquarian (YA Novel)
Blind Eye
The Puppet Master
The Janus Effect
Cross Wired
Silent Waters
Five in a Row
Tropical Kiss (YA Novel)
Fourth Victim
Triple Threat
Twice Burned
Trust Me Once

Relationship Books

Scribbling Women and the Real-Life Romance Heroes
Who Love Them

39230769R00181

Made in the USA
Lexington, KY
12 February 2015